Kurt W. Treptow, Editor
CLASSICS OF ROMANIAN LITERATURE
Volume II

MIRCEA ELIADE

# MYSTIC STORIES

THE SACRED
AND THE PROFANE

TRANSLATED BY ANA CARTIANU

EAST EUROPEAN MONOGRAPHS, BOULDER
In cooperation with EDITURA MINERVA, BUCHAREST
DISTRIBUTED BY COLUMBIA UNIVERSITY PRESS,
NEW YORK

1992

EAST EUROPEAN MONOGRAPHS, NO. CCCXXX


ISBN 973-21-0271-3 0-88033-227-1
Library of Congress Catalog Card Number 91-72637

Printed in Romania
(Tipografia Bucureştii Noi)

Mircea Eliade (Chicago, 1968)

# CONTENTS

Introduction by Kurt W. Treptow . . . . . . . . . VII

I. Miss Christina (Domnişoara Christina) . . . . . . 1

II. Doctor Honigberger's Secret (Secretul doctorului Honigberger) . . . . . . . . . . . . . . . 135

III. The Gypsies (La ţigănci) . . . . . . . . . . . 181

IV. Rejuvenation by Lightning (Tinereţe fără bătrîneţe) . 218

Note on the pronunciation of Romanian Words . . . 303

# INTRODUCTION

This book is the second volume in the series, *Classics of Romanian Literature*. It is a collection of literary works by one of the leading figures of culture and science from Romania, Mircea Eliade. I first encountered the work of Mircea Eliade as a student of history when I read an English translation of his book, *De Zalmoxis à Ghenghis Khan (Zalmoxis, the Vanishing God*, Chicago, 1972). I found his work on the history of religions to be both informative and stimulating. It led me to investigate the historical sources concerning the ancient God of the Geto-Dacians, the forefathers of the modern Romanians ; the result of this research was my first published article, "A Study in Geto-Dacian Religion : The Cult of Zalmoxis." I became well acquainted with Eliade's scientific work and admired his scholarship, but it was only later that I discovered him as a writer of fiction.

Mircea Eliade was born in Bucharest, Romania in 1907. He graduated from the University of Bucharest in 1928 with a degree in philosophy, after which he went to India, where he studied at the University of Calcutta until 1932 His soujourn in India proved to have a decisive impact on his later career. Its influence is apparent in both his scholarly work on the history of religions, and in some of the literary selections contained in this volume, in particular *Doctor Honigberger's Secret* (1940) which is centered on the Hindu belief in Nirvana. After returning to Romania, Eliade received his doctorate and taught at the University of Bucharest where he wrote some of his finest literary works, including the novelette contained in this volume, *Miss Christina* (1936), which is a fantastic story about the undead, *strigoi* in Romanian. In 1939, Eliade entered the diplomatic service, working in England and Portugal during World War II. Following the war and the communist takeover of Romania, he taught in Paris at the École des Hautes Études. He never returned to his native land. Later, he came to the United States to take a post as a professor of the history of religions at the University of Chicago. Among his prodigious works written during his permanent exile from his homeland are the other two stories contained in this volume, *The Gypsies* (1959) and *Rejuvenation by Lightning* (1976). These stories, like all of Eliade's literary works, were originally written in Romanian. Eliade explained the reason for this in an interview : "From time to time, I feel the need to seek out my roots, the land of my birth. In exile, the native land is the language, is a dream. And it is then that I wrote my novels." Eliade's scholarship on the history of religions earned him international acclaim. Among his most important scholarly works are, *Traité d'histoire des réligions* (1949), *Le Mythe de l'eternel Retour* (1949), *Images et Symboles* (1952), *Le Sacré et le Profane* (1956), *De Zalmoxis à Ghenghis Khan* (1970), and *Histoire des croyances et des idées religieuses* in three volumes (1976—1983). He died in Chicago in 1986.

While Eliade's academic work is world renowned, his literary work is less known. The reason for this is that most of it was written in his native language, Romanian. The present volume is an attempt to make some of the finest literary work of this great scholar available to the English-speaking world. Those who are familiar with Eliade's scientific work will readily recognize its influence on his literary creations. There are two general themes that unite the four stories comprising this book. First, each of them deals with different aspects of the supernatural, thus giving this volume its title, *Mystic Stories: the Sacred and the Profane*. The other common element in these stories is that each is set in Eliade's native land, Romania. His personal vision of the country he knew before the second World War is evident in his literary works.

The translator of these stories, Ana Cartianu, has dedicated many years of her life to making Romanian culture known in the English-speaking world. She has long been recognized as the pre-eminent translator of prose into English in Romania and has a vast list of publications, having translated works by the leading figures of Romanian literature.

This series represents an important step in cultural cooperation and exchange between Romanian and American institutions. Many people helped make this project possible. In addition to the translator, Ana Cartianu, I would like to thank Sorin Pârvu and Adriana Cişmaş for their help with this project.

KURT W. TREPTOW
Iaşi, Romania
February, 1991

Mr. Nazarie rose abruptly leaning against the wall. Egor and Sanda came up to him smiling uneasily. "You mustn't mind Simina's jokes," Egor said, "she's a freakish child. And it is actually, her greatest joy to sit by her mother at mealtime, even when guests are present."

"She's only nine," Sanda put in.

Ms. Moscu had been looking on with a smile as if asking to be excused for not joining in the discussion. She could well imagine the interest of such a discussion — scholarly, instructive — but she was too tired to follow the argument. Mrs. Moscu hadn't heard a word, of course. The sounds had slipped by her ears, no response, no imprint.

Egor led Mr. Nazarie to the end of the table, pointing to a seat by Sanda's side. "What a strange, unaccountable weariness," the painter thought, looking once more at Mrs. Moscu's face.

"Thank you indeed," the professor mumbled, sitting down. "I realize I have hurt a child. An angelic child, too."

He turned and gave Simina the warmest of looks. Mr. Nazarie was a man young enough, under forty, and the look he gave Simina was trying to show an afffection, both protective and ingratiating. His clean nondescript face of a scholar had become excessively bright. He was smiling at Simina, a broad, open-mouthed smile. Simina held his eye with ironic, biting firmness. She looked deep into his eyes a few seconds, then picked up her napkin to conceal a very faint smile, and slowly turned to her mother.

"You've come for the diggings, of course," Egor suddenly asked.

The professor was still self-conscious, so he was even more grateful to Egor for an opportunity to speak about his profession which he passionately loved.

"So I have, dear sir," he briskly answered, drawing in a breath of air. "As I was telling our hostess, we have taken up again the diggings at Bălănoaia this summer. A name possibly not suggestive of much, yet the protohistoric research station of Bălănoaia is of some importance to Romanians. A famous *lébes* was found there, a large Ionian dish wherein, as you know, they used to serve the meat at festive meals."

The memory of this *lébes* that he had minutely examined represented an invigorating image for Mr. Nazarie. With gusto

# MISS CHRISTINA

## I

Before entering the dining room Sanda took hold of his arm, detaining him. It was the first familiar gesture she made during the first three days they had spent together at Z.

"You know, there's one more guest, a professor."

Egor looked into her eyes, in the semi-obscurity of the room. They were dancing. "Maybe she's leading me on," he thought, drawing near and trying to put his arm round her waist. But the girl tore herself away, took a few steps and opened the door of the dining room. Egor controlled himself and stood in the doorway. The same lamp was on, with its white, blinding wire-sieve ; too strong a light, artificial, harsh. Mrs. Moscu's smile was now more wan. (A smile that Egor had learnt to guess before even seeing her face.)

"This is Mr. Egor Paşchievici," Mrs. Moscu solemnly announced, pointing with a firm arm to the door. "He has a foreign sounding name," she added, "but he is a true Romanian. He is a painter, his staying with us is an honour."

Egor bowed, trying to say a few flattering words. With increased emotion, Mrs. Moscu directed her arm to the newcomer. She rarely had an opportunity of making ample, solemn introductions.

"Mr. Nazarie, university professor, a glory of Romanian science," she continued.

With firm steps Egor went up to the professor and shook his hand.

"I am just an insignificant assistant lecturer, dear lady," Mr. Nazarie mumbled, trying to hold her attention another moment. "So very insignificant."

But Mrs. Moscu had dropped into her chair, exhausted. The professor was standing by her, his sentence unfinished. He dare not turn to the others, afraid he might look ridiculous or offended. For a few seconds he was uncertain as to what do. Then he made up his mind and took the chair on Mrs. Moscu's left.

"This chair is occupied," Simina said in a low voice. "I always have my meals by mother's side."

and some melancholy he evoked the feasts of those days, not grotesque barbarian meals.

"Because, as I was telling our hostess, the whole flat country of the Lower Danube, more particularly north of Giurgiu, formerly knew a flourishing Greek-Thracian-Scythian civilization, in the 5th century B.C."

Talking had instilled courage into him. He looked again, insistently, at Mrs. Moscu, but only met the same wan smile, the same absent face.

"Bălănoaia, mama," Sanda tried to draw her attention, almost shouting across the table, "the professor is engaged in archeological research at Bălănoaia."

In hearing his name Mr. Nazarie became again self-conscious when suddenly finding himself the object of general attention. He tried to protect himself with his hand, to excuse the loud voice Sanda had had in calling to her mother. Mrs. Moscu seemed to wake from a numb sleepy state. But it had been a real awakening ; for a few seconds she recaptured the freshness of face, the dignity of her pure smooth brow.

"Bălănoaia," she said, "that's where an ancestor of ours had his lands."

"Aunt Christina, too," Simina quickly added.

"She too," Mrs. Moscu briskly confirmed.

Sanda frowned at her younger sister. But Simina quietly and meekly looked down into her plate. In the strong light of that lamp, her dark curls lost their strong shine like old silver. "Yet what a serene brow, what doll-like cheeks !" Egor wondered. He couldn't take his eyes off her face. The features had a precocious perfection, a stunning beauty. Egor felt that Mr. Nazarie was also contemplating her with equal enchantment.

"We're not very talkative today when left alone," Sanda said, addressing herself mostly to Egor.

The painter understood the meaning of that voice trying to tempt him, to lead him on. He tore himself out of the torpor he felt in considering Simina, and was about to begin telling a swaggering anecdote that he was always successfully producing in family circles. "We are not talkative because we are intelligent : like my friend Jean..." Egor would have said, but Mr. Nazarie took the lead : "You're sure to have lots of guests all summer long, here in the country."

He spoke for a few minutes without taking a breath as if he were afraid to stop, afraid that the silence would have the better of him. He spoke about the diggings, about the poverty of the archeological museum, about the beauty of the Danubian lowlands. Egor was furtively giving Mrs. Moscu an occasional glance. She was listening as if entranced, but the painter could well see that she didn't hear a word. Sanda availed herself of a pause in Mr. Nazarie's speech and said in a loud voice :

"Mama, the meat is getting cold."

"The interesting things the professor is telling us !" Mrs. Moscu said in a low voice. She then began to eat with her usual appetite, her head slightly inclined over her plate, never looking at any of the others.

As a matter of fact she was the only one who was eating. The others had hardly touched the meat. Mr. Nazarie, though hungry after his journey, had not succeeded in eating more than half his helping. The meat had a sickening smell.

With the short gesture of a mistress, she called the housemaid who was quietly waiting by the door.

"I told you never to buy ram's meat," she said with suppressed anger.

"I couldn't find any fowl, ma'am," the woman pleaded, "what we had, they killed yesterday and the day before. Those that were not killed, died. There was one more goose, but I found it dead this morning."

"Why didn't you buy some in the village ?" Sanda asked still more angry.

"No one would sell," the housemaid promptly answered. "They would not or had none," she added with implied meaning.

Sanda blushed and bade the woman to clear the table. Mrs. Moscu had finished the meat.

"What wonderful things the professor told us about Bălănoaia !" she began in a sing-song voice, "so many idols underground, so many golden jewels."

The professor hesitated.

"The golden ones are seldom found," he interrupted. "They were rare in those times. These were rural civilizations, only villages. The gold was usually to be found in the Greek ports."

"There was gold too, jewels of ancient gold in those days," Mrs. Moscu continued.

"Aunt Christina had some, too," Simina said in a whisper.

"How do you know ?" Sanda asked, chiding. "Why don't yon keep quiet ?"

"Mother told me," Simina said pertly, "as well as nanny."

"Nanny should not fill your head with fairy tales," Sanda replied severely, you're growing up, you can't go on believing tales and nonsense."

Sanda considered her sister with the slightest smile, both scornful and indifferent. She then looked at Egor, gravely searching his face ; she seemed to be wondering if he, too, believed the same thing, if he, too, could be so naïve.

The conversation was lagging again. Mr. Nazarie turned to Egor.

"The wonderful idea you had to return to these Danubian lowlands," he said. "I don't think anyone has yet tried to paint such places. They seem desperate at first sight, bare and empty, badly sun-scorched ; then do you realize their astonishing fertility, their charm."

He spoke sincerely, enthusiastically. Egor considered him, astounded. To begin with, he had taken him for a piteous scholar, sullen and shy, but Mr. Nazarie's hands moved with consummate grace ; and the words he spoke had a personal vigour, a strange freshness. He seemed to utter them differently, with depth and fullness.

"Mr. Paşchievici is a great artist, but very lazy too," Sanda spoke, "He's been three days with us and has never opened his painter's palette."

"I could interpret your amiable remark in several ways," Egor said courteously, "I might think for instance, that you are impatient to see me at work, in order to hope for my speedier leave-taking."

Sanda smiled back encouragingly. Egor understood exactly all those shades of joking grace and whimsicality betraying impatience, temptation, appeal. "Sanda is, anyway, most wonderful," he thought, although he could by no means understand her behavior during the last few days. How different from the flighty Bucharest girl who was leading him on with such courage and who had given him such a hearty handshake when he accepted to come to Z. for a whole month.

"Maybe she's afraid of something, she's afraid of the guests," Egor told himself the first evening.

"The truth is that I don't feel up to anything just now," he went on, turning to Mr. Nazarie. "Not up to painting anyway. It's the beginning of autumn and it feels more like high summer, maybe that's what makes me so tired."

"I could find a better excuse, should he ask me," Sanda said with a laugh. "We've had three somewhat noisy days, too many friends, that's what it is. Tomorrow and after he'll be able to work, when we are left by ourselves."

Egor began to play with his knife. He had to grasp something cold and hard, to squeeze, to relieve his nervousness.

"You won't even feel my presence," Mr. Nazarie added, "you'll only see me here with you."

He made a swift comprehensive gesture around the table. Mrs. Moscu thanked him, looking absent.

"It is a great honor to have you with us," she began, her voice suddenly much firmer and more sonorous. "You are an asset to Romanian science."

"She's sure to like these words quite a lot, she keeps repeating them with a kind of fervour." Egor sat with downcast eyes relaxing the pressure on the knife. Secretly, Sanda was watching his gestures. "God knows what he thinks of mother," she thought, suddenly growing angry.

"Dear lady," Mr. Nazarie spoke quite astounded, "your praise is certainly meant for my teacher, the great Vasile Pârvan. He was indeed a great genius and the pride of the Romanians."

He had been waiting some time for such an occasion : to be able to talk, to say things unconnected with this strange meal, with these hostesses that he could not understand. He spoke with respect and reverence about Pârvan. It was he who taught him the skill of digging. He, a forerunner, had proven that the proud possessions of the Romanian lands lay in their pre-history. The magic of digging, life in the tents, the thrill of every discovered object.

"An iron comb, a nail, a fragment of a pot," Mr. Nazarie went on, "all these humble and neutral things, that a wayfarer would not bother to pick up, these mean more to us than the finest book, and even, possibly, the most beautiful woman."

Smiling, Sanda was trying to catch Egor's eye, expecting an ironic look. But the painter was listening respectfully, sympathetically.

"An iron comb sometimes reveals a whole civilization," Mr. Nazarie added, addressing Mrs. Moscu once more.

Suddenly, he broke off, in the middle of his sentence, as if short of breath. He sat rigid, looking at Mrs. Moscu. He was afraid of closing his eyes. He might have possibly been faced with an even stranger apparition behind his eyelids.

"Shall we have coffee ?!" Sanda asked that minute, rising noisily.

Mr. Nazarie felt cold sweat on his shoulders, on his chest, along his arms. As if he were slowly entering a wet, frozen zone. "I'm very tired," he thought, clutching his hands tight together. He turned to Egor. The latter's gesture seemed hard to understand : he was smiling, two fingers up in the air, as if in a classroom.

"Will you have coffee, Mr. Nazarie ?" Sanda asked.

"Thank you, delighted, delighted," Mr. Nazarie answered.

It was only when he saw the coffee cups on the table that he realized what it was that Sanda had asked and he calmed down. At the same time he looked again at Mrs. Moscu without misgiving. The hostess' lowered brow was leaning upon the right palm of her hand. No one spoke. He saw Simina's face turned to him. She was considering him in wonder, even with suspicion. As if she were trying to unravel a mystery. It was an absorbing, unsatisfying preoccupation, far beyond childhood.

## II

Mr.Nazarie very carefully opened the door. In the corridor he found a petrol lamp burning low. He took it down from a peg in the wall and began walking cautiously, anxious to make no noise. The wooden floor covered with cherry-coloured paint, was creaking, even in carpeted places. "Why on earth did they give us rooms so far apart !" Mr. Nazarie thought, slightly irritated. He was not afraid, but the distance to Egor's room was a long walk. He had to pass by a number of doors, not knowing if there was anyone inside those rooms, or if he was creating a disturbance. On the other hand, if those rooms had actually been vacant the corridor would have acquired a sense of emptiness ; Mr. Nazarie wouldn't even think such a thought.

Egor's room was at the very end of the corridor. He knocked on the door, joyfully.

"I hope I am not intruding," he said, opening the door, "but I am not at all sleepy."

"Neither am I," Egor said, rising from the sofa.

It was a large spacious room with a balcony looking out on the park. The old wooden bed was placed in one corner. A wardrobe, a wash stand, a sofa, a stylish desk, two chairs and a *chaise-longue* formed the rest of the furniture. However, the room was so large that it seemed sparsely furnished. The objects were far apart and you could move at ease.

"It's a pleasure," Egor went on, "I was trying to find a way to relieve insomnia. I didn't bring any books. I thought I would be very busy in the daytime."

His next thought remained unspoken : "I used to think, moreover, that I would spend the evenings with Sanda."

"It's the first night to turn in so early," Egor continued. "I used to stay out late in the park ; there were many guests, young people. But I think they were too much for Mrs. Moscu. Don't you smoke," he asked, offering his open cigarette case to Mr. Nazarie.

"Thank you, no, I don't. But I meant to ask you, all these rooms nearby, aren't they lived in ?"

"I think not," Egor said smiling, "The guests were lodged here ; a whole floor for guests. The rooms downstairs are also empty, I believe. Mrs. Moscu lives in another wing of the house, as do the young ladies."

He was thoughtful. He lit a cigarette and sat on a chair facing the professor. They were both silent.

"A wonderful night !" Mr. Nazarie said after a time looking up to the balcony.

Large contours of trees, as yet indefinite, loomed out of the dark. Egor turned. A wonderful night indeed. But really, to bid goodnight to the guests at half past nine and retire at the same time as your mother, like a good little girl...

"If you keep quite still for a while," Mr. Nazarie spoke, breathing in slowly, without hurry, "you can feel the Danube... I can."

"It must be quite a distance, though," Egor said.

"Some thirty kilometers. Maybe less. But it's the same night, you can feel it immediately."

Mr. Nazarie rose and went to the balcony. No, there won't be a moon for a few days, he realized as soon as he faced the dark.

"It's the same air, too," he added, slowly turning up his face and inhaling the air, open-mouthed. "You never lived near the Danube, it seems. Or else, you seldom happen to miss this scent. I can feel the Danube even in the Bărăgan plain."

Egor laughed.

"Isn't it a bit too much to say that you feel it in the Bărăgan plain ?!"

"No, it isn't," Mr. Nazarie explained. "Because it isn't the smell of water, it's not a humid air. It's rather a stagnant smell, much like the smell of clay and of thistles."

"That's vague enough," Egor put in smiling.

"Yet, you're soon aware of it wherever you may be," Mr. Nazarie went on. "You sometimes feel as if whole forests must have been rotting very far away, that the wind should waft such a scent, both complex and elementary. Formerly there were forests nearby. There was the Teleorman."

"This park, too, seems to be quite old," Egor said stretching his arm over the railings.

Mr. Nazarie gave him a gentle look, unable to conceal a smile of contempt.

"Everything you see here is under a hundred years old. Acacia. A poor man's tree. You can barely see an elm tree here and there."

He began eagerly discoursing about forests and trees.

"Don't be surprised," he suddenly said interrupting his flow of words and laying his hand on Egor's shoulder, "I had to pick up all this from people, out of books, from scholars, as it happened. For the diggings, of course ; I had to know how far the Scythians, the Getae, and whoever the others could have settled."

"Not many traces around here," Egor said, trying to divert the discussion into pre-history.

"There may be," Mr. Nazarie unassumingly said. "There must have been roads, even villages on the forests' borders, especially close to the valleys. Anyway, wooded lands where trees grew for hundreds of years on end are bewitched. That's a fact."

He ceased and began again inhaling the air, his whole body gently stooping over the railings into the night.

"What joy every time I feel the Danube, even in such places as this," he went on in a lower voice. "It's a different spell, a welcome magic, nothing frightening about it. People living around large water streams are both wiser and braver ; adventures took place here also, not only on the seashores. But the forest, you see, is terrifying, maddening."

Egor laughed. He took a step inside the room. The lamp-light was again full on his face.

"Hard to understand," Mr. Nazarie went on. "The forest is frightening even for you, an enlightened young man with no superstitions. It's a terror that no one is free from. Too much vegetation, too much identity between old trees and men, human bodies especially."

"You mustn't think that fear drove me away from the window," Egor said. "I came away because I wanted to light a cigarette. I'il join you again."

"Not necessary. I believe you. You cannot be afraid by a mere acacia plantation," Mr. Nazarie said, coming back into the room and sitting down on the sofa. "Yet what I told you is perfectly true. If it hadn't been for the Danube, the people in these surroundings would have gone mad. The people of some two or three thousand years ago, of course."

Egor was considering him in wonder. "The professor's more and more interesting," he thought, "in two more hours he'll recite poems with dead men's skulls."

"I was forgetting to ask you," Mr. Nazarie began anew. "Have you known our hostess some time ?"

"I've only known Miss Sanda, not very long either, some two years. We have some friends in common. Mrs. Moscu I've only met when I came here, a few days ago."

"She seems to be very tired," Mr. Nazarie said.

Egor shook his head. The seriousness of the professor was amusing, as if imparting a secret, an observation that he alone was making. "Saying it to me who has been trying to memorize her smile for so many days."

"I landed here by chance, so to speak," added Mr. Nazarie. "I was invited here by the police commissioner who seems to be an old family friend. But I'm beginning to feel uncomfortable ; aren't we in the way ? I'm under the impression that Mrs. Moscu is quite unwell."

Egor spoke as if he were apologizing. He, too, had been unwilling to stay on, realizing from the first that the hostess was tired out. The other guests, however, did not seem at all impressed by Mrs. Moscu's weakness. Maybe they had known her longer and had gotten used to it. Or, possibly, the ailment is not so serious. Sometimes, particularly in the mornings, Mrs. Moscu eagerly followed every discussion.

"Her strength seems to go with the sun," Egor added somewhat solemnly after a short interval. "She's worn out in the evenings ; occasionally sinking into a kind of lethargy, all the more strange since she preserves the same smile, the same mask."

Mr. Nazarie could clearly see her wide open, cold, intelligent eyes ; he could also see the smile brightening her face which was so misleading. "No, the painter is wrong in speaking about Mrs. Moscu's mask. It is no mask, it is a face alive, concentrating, even very attentive. The smile, anyway, renders her present, as if her whole being were listening enchanted by the words you speak. At first, such attention is almost intimidating, making you blush. But you soon realize that she hasn't been listening, that maybe she hasn't even heard your words. She has been permanently watching your gestures, seen your lips moving and she knows when to interrupt."

"It's quite extraordinary !" Mr. Nazarie went on following his train of thought. "She knows when to interrupt, when to put in a word, to make you aware of her, so that her silence should not upset you."

Egor was listening with still greater wonder than in the beginning. He was not yet prepared to consider him intelligent or sensitive. "He's got an artist's virtues," he thought, "yet he's so shy, so awkward."

"Aren't we rather exaggerating ?" he said, rising and pacing the room. "Maybe it's just chronic exhaustion, if there is such a term."

"There is not," Mr. Nazarie said, unwillingly putting some irony into his words. "Chronic exhaustion would actually mean a deferred death."

He disliked these last words and, in his turn, rose from the sofa trying to walk the room. He felt the same stupid, cold sweat on his back. He frowned on the sofa as if trying to test its unassuming reality, its physical indifference. He frowned on it, furious with himself and with the childlike suggestions of his nerves.

"No doubt," Egor spoke from the other end of the room, "we are exaggerating, we're too sensitive. Just look how children behave with her, the little girl especially."

He stopped by the door as if listening. A servant trying the doors to see that they are locked or looking for something along the corridor. A careful light step, the more irritating since you anticipate it instead of hearing it. Suddenly, a very light creaking of the floor boards ; then waiting and not hearing anything for a few moments, long moments. The servant walks holding her breath, on tiptoes, lest she should trouble your sleep. "Idiotic peasants," Egor thought, highly annoyed that the noise had subsided, "it is better to step firmly so you'd hear it all the time."

"I thought someone was walking along the corridor," Egor said, beginning to pace the room again. "Tomorrow I'll put up a notice on my door : 'No tiptoeing, please walk firmly in the corridor.' Otherwise it gets on your nerves : as if you were expecting burglars. True that burglars wouldn't get here quite so easily," he added with a laugh, "but nevertheless it gets on one's nerves."

Mr. Nazarie had gone to the balcony. He was again leaning out into the dark.

"The nights are warm here," Egor said. "We could have sat in the park rather than shut inside."

He noticed that the professor gave no answer and slowly withdrew into the room. "He's thinking, philosophizing about the Danube," he said to himself suddenly joyful. "Yet, as a matter of fact, his assertions are not illogical in a way : a river, a large water course, with wide hospitable shores." That minute he realized how splendid the Danube was, how sure of itself, how virile. He wished he were far away, on the deck of a yacht slowly sailing up the river, lying on a lounge chair, listening to the radio, or in the midst of young people. You soon grow bored without the young, without noise around. Life, presence, or else... Nervous, he turned his head. He thought he was not alone in the room, that someone was insistently watching him. He had distinctly felt the sharp drilling of a look behind him and such sensations always got on his nerves. And yet he was alone. The professor remained outside. "Somewhat rude of him," Egor thought.

"Maybe he's not feeling well and I should speak to him or help him." He took a few steps towards the balcony. Mr. Nazarie met him with a bright look.

"You'll forgive me for staying outside," he said. "I was dizzy. I'm beginning to think I'm tired indeed. These places do not agree with me."

"Maybe they don't agree with me either," said Egor laughing, "but no matter. What really matters is the fact that I can't offer you anything except a drink. I hope you won't refuse a cognac."

"In other circumstances I would have refused. But tonight I must find something to act against the coffee that I absent-mindedly drank. If I don't sleep tonight I shall be no good tomorrow."

Egor opened his travel bag, produced a freshly opened bottle, and took two large water glasses from the wardrobe. He carefully poured a thimbleful into them.

"I hope this is good for sleeping," Mr. Nazarie said, finishing his drink in one gulp.

He then buried his face in his hands and began rubbing it as if it had been squashed. "He drank it as if it were plum brandy," Egor thought. He began sipping his own cognac with utmost delight. The alcohol had established a different atmosphere in the room : friendly, boyish, exciting. He no longer felt any strange gaze. He had settled comfortably in his chair and was smelling the unseen vapour from the glass. A well-known odor reminding him of many bright relaxing moments spent with friends, or certain women. "A welcome thing, alcohol," he thought.

"May I have a cigarette as well," the professor asked at that moment. He was still red in the face and choking. "I may have better luck."

He actually smoked with some success. Egor refilled the glasses. He was in much better spirits, ready for a chat. "If only Sanda were here, if she'd have the least bit of imagination... It would have been so pleasant sitting and chatting on a night like this, with an amusing companion like the professor, a bottle of cognac at hand. After all, that's why you go into the country ; to talk long into the night, to listen to each other talk. No one will listen in Bucharest."

"Drink this one slowly, professor," Egor joked.

He was bent on talk, on confessions.

"I meant to ask and I forgot : how do you manage those archeological finds ?" he said.

"Quite simply," the professor began, "very simply."

But he ceased as if strangled. For a moment they gazed deep into each other's eyes, each trying to understand if the other had felt the same thing, the same rising terror. Then they seized the cognac glasses at the same time and drank them in one gulp. The professor no longer buried his face in his hands. On the contrary, the alcohol had done him good this time. However, he dared not question Egor ; he could tell by his look that he had had the same painful impression, the same disgusting terror. To feel someone approaching, ready to listen to you, someone you cannot see, but whose presence you feel in the throbbing of your own blood, and in the glint of your neighbor's eyes...

They both tried to talk about different things. Egor was rapidly searching for a subject, a pretext. Something far away from this room, from this hour. For a few seconds he couldn't think of anything. He was frozen, but he wasn't afraid. He then felt something quite unlike anything he had experienced before. Unspeakable nausea mixed up with terror. Just a few seconds. It sufficed to grip the glass and swallow a shot of cognac and everything fell into place.

"Have you ever been to Marseille ?" he asked abruptly, seizing the bottle and refilling the glasses.

"I have, some time ago, soon after the war," the professor promptly answered. "Things must have changed since then."

"There is a bar, close to the Savoy hotel," Egor glibly continued, "it's called *L'Etoile Marine*. I remember perfectly, that's what they call it. They have a custom that if you like cognac, you should begin to sing."

"That's an excellent idea !" the professor said. "But I have no singing voice to speak of."

Egor considered him contemptuously : "He's afraid to sing, he's ashamed." He raised the glass to his nostrils and breathed in firmly. He swallowed a mouthful, then tilted his head back a little and began in a drawling voice :

*Les vieilles de notre pays*
*Ne sont pas des vieilles moroses,*
*Elles portent des bonnets roses...*

## III

Mr. Nazarie heard the banging on the door and decided to wake up at last. He'd been fighting sleep for the last half hour. He would open his eyes, feel the fresh morning air, the bright light in the room, then fall asleep again. A light broken sleep, all the more refreshing. As if prolonging a state of bliss that would be difficult to recapture. The more stubborn his resistance, the more soothing his sinking into sleep. One more second, just one more. As though in the depths of sleep an ever-conscious certainty were persisting, the certainty that he would soon wake from that blissful floating state and be fully projected into the outer light. The knocking on the door actually woke him up.

"Good morning, sir."

A woman, fairly old, came in with a cup of milk.

"It's late, isn't it, I believe it's very late," said Mr. Nazarie.

The woman smiled, never looking into his eyes.

Mr. Nazarie rubbed his brow. He had a slight headache and a bitter taste in his mouth. He was suddenly sorry for staying in bed so late. The bliss he had regretfully left behind now seemed altogether disgusting. He was also feeling tired, sad, hopeless, for no reason at all. Yet, he always felt this way after first waking up in a strange room. A wide, unaccountable inner void ; the vanity of vanities. But he remembered the glasses of cognac he had drunk the previous night and he grew angrier with himself. "Just to drink for no reason at all, waste your time with a dawdler..."

"Do you want hot water, sir ?" the woman asked.

"No, by no means hot water," Mr. Nazarie felt like punishing himself. He would take pleasure in washing with cold water.

The woman closed the door and Mr. Nazarie jumped out of bed quickly. The dizziness and his slight headache persisted. He filled the basin with cold water and began to wash. Last night's events were coming to light, one by one. He felt like laughing. What stupid hallucinations, what senseless fear ! Enough to look around and see this light, this autumn chill, this hot milk fuming fresh and gentle, enough to realize the worthlessness of all imaginings. "I didn't even learn how to smoke," Mr. Nazarie ironically thought, while dressing. He then sat at the table and drank the whole cup of milk never touching the butter or jam. He broke a bit of toast and finished dressing while crunching away. "Last night's meal was nothing to speak of," he remembered, "Had I not poisoned myself with cognac, I should now have been as hungry as a wolf. The meal was nothing to speak of and they all noticed it. The meat had a smell of sheep, the vegetables underboiled. The saving dish was corn mush with cheese and cream." He smiled at himself in the mirror. "I forgot to shave. Maybe that's why she asked about hot water. Too late now. I'll shave just as well with cold water."

Quietly, without hurry, he took his razor out of his travel bag and began to lather with a shaving stick. A slow sad melody gently filtered through his memory. Vague, the song drifted a few seconds, fretting, vanishing, recovering :

Les vieilles de notre pays...

"That's what Egor was singing last night," he joyfully remembered. He also remembered the cause that had set the painter singing. "He too had felt the same thing," Mr. Nazarie thought smiling. He could easily smile now, last night's scene seemed far away and ridiculous. He went on lathering in still higher spirits. "And yet I felt as if someone were listening. I remember distinctly. During the meal, too... it was then somewhat more serious, it was, in fact, very serious." But there was so much light in the room, such certitude in those white walls, in the bit of clear sky that he saw in the mirror, in the smell of soap that he felt all over his face.

Mr. Nazarie carefully fixed his razor blade. He enjoyed every gesture, every object that he touched. He began to shave carefully, looking into the mirror, pursing his lips, trying to do it properly, so that his lips, too sharply rounded, should not impair the symmetry of his face.

*

Mr. Nazarie spent the morning walking aimlessly in the fields. His thoughts were by no means bent on pre-history. As a matter of fact he had no hope of lucky finds in these vast, monotonous plains. North of the manorial house on the way to the village the knolls began, but Mr. Nazarie had intentionally gone in the opposite direction. This way was so pleasant just before the autumn ploughing began. There was no cloud, no shadow anywhere, yet the sun was not tiring ;

unknown birds were flying high up in the sky, you could hear the grasshoppers and crickets chirping. A vast peace, full of life. A man's step became part of that musical body of sounds which together formed the peace and loneliness of the fields. "The glorius Wallachian plain," Mr. Nazarie thought. "Two or three more weeks and it's the end of my vacation. Bucharest, student examinations, the study ; if we could only do good work at Bălănoaia."

He was back at the manor a few minutes before meal time. He met Simina walking by herself in the park.

"Good morning, young lady," he cordially said.

"Good morning, professor," the little girl answered smiling. "Have you had a good night's rest ? Mother shall ask the same question, but I wanted to be the first to ask."

Her smile imperceptibly changed into a short, still chuckle. The professor could hardly take his eyes off her face, a face of matchless beauty. She was like a doll ; a beauty so perfect that it seemed artificial. Her teeth were too white, her hair too black, her lips too red.

"I slept wonderfully well, young lady," said Mr. Nazarie, approaching her and trying to slip his fingers through her curls.

"She's really a wonderful child." With the palm of his hand above the little girl's head, he was suddenly afraid to caress her. Her smile kept him at bay. Awkwardly, he drew back his hand. Simina was no longer a child. Nine years old, so they told him last night, but how feminine in her walk, what charm in her small, rounded movements.

"You didn't prevent Mr. Egor from working last night, did you ?" Simina trickily asked, slightly knitting her brow.

Mr. Nazarie did not try to conceal his surprise. On the contrary, he was glad of an occasion to praise the child, to seem taken in by her ruse, and thus make friends with her.

"But how do you come to know that I visited Mr. Egor last night ?" he asked.

"I presumed !"

She broke into laughter. The professor stood before her, tall, awkward. Simina soon collected herself.

"It always happens. Whenever two guests meet," she said, "they get together in some room. Mr. Egor's room is the finest. That's where the guests usually come..."

She did not utter her whole thought. She smiled a child-like triumphant smile and took a step towards Mr. Nazarie.

"Yet, I don't think it's right," she whispered, "Mr. Egor has work to do. He ought to be left alone at night."

Saying that last word the smile vanished from her face. She was now stern, cold, commanding. Mr. Nazarie was now less sure of himself.

"True, quite true," he muttered, "it happened once, it won't happen again."

Simina looked him straight in the eyes, insistently, almost impertinently, then without another word she wrenched her whole body away from the professor and made her way into the park.

"Maybe she knows something that I don't," thought Mr. Nazarie. "I wonder if there's a plot laid concerning Egor ? Night meetings in the park, sentimental walks, that's how it usually begins. Simina is doubtless in the know."

Mr. Nazarie went to his room to wash his hands before lunch. "But it's rather stupid to allow a little girl to understand such things," he went on thinking. "Especially such a sensitive child as Simina."

He hurried downstairs, making straight for the dining room. He had heard the gong. He'd been informed of this local habit : five minutes after the sounding of the gong, the meal was served, any number of the guests being present. They were all in the dining room, except Simina.

"Did the professor sleep well ?" Mrs. Moscu asked.

She did not seem quite so tired that morning. She wore a grey dress with a pale pink collar. She did seem younger indeed, refreshed. Her bare arms soared with added grace, tender, in polished, rounded gestures.

"Did you really sleep well ?" Sanda asked in her turn, trying hard to conceal her surprise.

The maid stood by the door, listening. She was looking down, her hands behind her back, as if waiting for an order, but she, too, was listening, equally interested.

"I slept wonderfully well," Mr. Nazarie answered, "I was afraid of a sleepless night to begin with, but Mr. Paşchievici was so nice as..."

He turned to him. Egor was smiling and playing with the bread knife. "Which means he has told everything,"

Mr. Nazarie thought, "he's probably told how we both imbibed alcohol and, possibly, other funny things about me."

"I suppose Mr. Paşchievici has told you," he added.

"There wasn't much to tell," Egor interrupted. Mr. Nazarie only then realized that Egor could not have related last night's incidents in detail. He would have been ashamed of himself. Last night's imaginings certainly looked ridiculous now, but, nevertheless, they shouldn't be made public. He looked him straight in the eyes. Egor did not seem to understand, to remember anything. "He's ashamed," Mr. Nazarie thought, "as I was."

Simina just entered the dining room. She hastily sat in the chair on Mrs. Moscu's right, having previously taken a look round the table.

"Where have you been, young lady ?" Egor asked.

"I went to see if there were any letters."

Sanda put up a smile. She ought to give her a piece of her mind. Not in front of the guests, of course, but one day she should scold her for all these useless lies she was telling.

She looked up somewhat scared. Someone was eating so ravenously that the noise of the munching jaws filled the room. It was as if a sudden unnatural silence had descended on the dining room ; you could only hear the labor of the jaws. It was Mrs. Moscu. Sanda turned pale. Mrs. Moscu quite often forgot herself during meals and ate with a great appetite, but she had never displayed such voracity. No one spoke. They all listened, feeling uncomfortable.

"Mama !" Sanda called.

Mrs. Moscu went on eating, her chin practically touching her breast. Sanda leaned over the table and called a second time ; no effect. "She'll be sick," Sanda thought, terrified. Egor pretended not to notice. Out of the corner of his eye Mr. Nazarie was looking on in terror. Simina alone looked quiet, as if nothing were happening.

She placed her hand lightly on Mrs. Moscu's arm and said:

"I had a dream about aunt Christina last night, mother !"

Surprised, Mrs. Moscu stopped munching.

"You know, I, too, have been dreaming of her constantly during the last few nights. Such strange dreams !"

She placed her knife and fork decently on the edge of her plate and turned to the guests. Having sensed her gesture, Mr. Mazarie was startled. He was afraid of looking into a face which had just awoke from a state of unconsciousness (for that was the only way he could interpret the barbarous way Mrs. Moscu had ben munching a few minutes before). He was genuinely surprised to face a quiet, intelligent demeanor. No doubt, Mrs. Moscu did not remember the painful previous scene, even if by some chance she was conscious of it.

"You may smile, professor," she said, "but I must confess that dreams are my second world."

"By no means, dear lady," was Nazarie's hasty answer.

"Mother means something different by this second world," Sanda intervened, happy that a painful incident had passed easily. "Different, anyway, than the usual meaning of the words."

"I am very interested to know," said Mr. Nazarie, "such things are always fascinating."

Mrs. Moscu approved, fervently nodding assent.

"We shall sometime have a talk about this. Not now, of course."

She turned quickly to Simina, "What was she like in your dream, Simina ?"

"She came to my bed and said : 'You're the only one who loves me, Simina !' She wore her pink dress and carried her tiny umbrella."

"That's the way she always comes," Mrs. Moscu said emotionally.

"She spoke about Sanda," Simina added, 'Sanda is forgetting me. She's now a grown up young lady.' That's what she told me. And I thought she was crying. She took my hand to kiss it."

"That's her way," Mrs. Moscu said, "she wants your hand or your arm to kiss."

They had all been listening in silence. Sanda was smiling, a smile of contempt, looking awry at her little sister. "I ought to make her break this silly habit," she thought. Then she suddenly flared up :

"Why do you tell lies, Simina ? I'm sure you dreamt of no one, much less of aunt Christina."

"I am not lying," Simina said calmly, "that's what she told me. I remember perfectly what she said about you : 'Sanda is forgetting me.' I then looked into her eyes and she seemed to be weeping."

"You're lying," Sanda spoke more loudly, "you didn't dream at all."

"Maybe I didn't dream," she said in a low voice turning to her mother.

Sanda bit her lip. "She's grown impertinent, too, she doesn't mind the guests, either." She then saw Egor, as if for the first time. An ardent overflow of tenderness seized her. A good thing not to be alone, to be next to someone who might love her, might help her.

"How come little Simina should know aunt Christina?" Mr. Nazarie asked in the midst of silence. "I rather think she must have died young."

Mrs. Moscu turned quickly to the professor. Mr. Nazarie had never seen her so vivacious. Emotion, impatience and memories did away with her everpresent smile. Egor was observing her in wonder, with incipient fear; since her eyes were liquid, the eyesight occasionally abnormal and dense, as a magnifying glass.

"No one knew Christina," Mrs. Moscu said with a deep sigh, "neither Sanda nor Simina. Sanda was born during the first year of the war, nine years after Christina's death. But we have a full length portrait of Christina painted by Mirea. The children know her by that portrait."

She ceased abruptly, her head bent. Mr. Nazarie tried to break the silence. It would actually have been painful for them all to turn dumb.

"Did she die young?" he asked.

"She was only twenty," Sanda spoke quickly trying to ward off Mrs. Moscu's reply. "She was seven years older than mother."

Mrs. Moscu did not seem to have heard. She continued, in the same low voice, as if ready to give in to her usual weariness:

"It was she who died instead of me, poor dear. They sent me to Caracal with my brother, she stayed behind on the land. That was in 1907. And they killed her."

"Right here?" Mr. Nazarie asked, fearfully stressing the word.

"She had come here from Bălănoaia," Sanda said. "The property was then very large, you know, before the expropriation... It's so hard to understand however... The peasants loved her..."

Egor began feeling uncomfortable. He had heard the story before and yet not quite the same. Certain details he was now hearing for the first time, others, much more significant, had been left out. He tried to catch Sanda's eye, but only met the same anxious, irridescent look, shifting from Mrs. Moscu to Simina, as if she were afraid of something else being said.

"Let's have coffee on the veranda," Sanda suddenly said, rising.

"It must have been a frightful blow," Mr. Nazarie added to soothe the hostess.

But Mrs. Moscu only gently nodded as if to acknowledge the ordinary thanks that guests utter in rising after a meal.

★

Coffee was served on the veranda. A September afternoon was beginning, as still and clear as glass ; the sky was unbelievably blue and the trees seemed to have grown motionless since the beginning of the world.

"I might try my luck now," Egor thought. As a matter of fact while walking across the dining room he had felt Sanda's hip very near himself. He had then taken her arm in a friendly manner and the girl, trembling, had acquiesced. The emotion, the well-known suspense had been transmitted. The girl's body drew near to his own for a few seconds then drew away abruptly. In that movement of fear Egor envisaged his best hopes, but he had to insist on talking to her. He came up, coffee cup in hand.

"What are you planning to do this afternoon, Miss Sanda ?" he asked.

"I shall beg your permission to accompany you in the park to watch you paint," the girl said with a smile.

Egor began to laugh. He was about to give a flippant answer, but he met Simina's severe face. The little girl was watching him intently, as if trying hard to understand something that was going on without her knowledge.

Mrs. Moscu's voice was then heard : "Mr. Egor, have you seen Christina's portrait ? They tell me it's Mirea's best work."

"If there is any such by Mirea," the painter ironically added.

"Why do you say that before seeing it ?" Sanda nervously asked, "I am sure you'll like it."

Egor did not understand the harshness in her voice. He was standing with his cup of coffee in his hands, between the two sisters.

He couldn't think of any answer. "It was a blunder," he thought. "If you wish to win a well-born lady, you shouldn't be intractable in art. Aesthetic criteria are not always the best."

"Any second rate painter may produce a masterpiece if he can only forget himself for a minute," Mr. Nazarie spoke sententiously.

"Mirea was a very great painter," Mrs. Moscu said, "he was a glory of Romanian art, the country may well be proud of him."

Snubbed, Mr. Nazarie blushed. All the more so as Mrs. Moscu had suddenly, risen and was inviting them all, with a somewhat inefficient wave of the hand, to see the portrait.

Neither Sanda, nor Simina were any calmer. "Whatever concerns Christina is actually sacred to them," Egor thought. "Atfer all it's not a worthless feeling. Loving and sanctifying a dead person, even in the most trivial pictures." He remembered Daphne Adeane. "I shall tell Sanda about her," he thought comforted, "it's a fine thing Sanda is doing ; the love and pride she takes in aunt Christina is splendid." Egor was now mentally absolving little Simina too. "They are noble beings, too sensitive. I'm behaving like a boor."

"It's rather untidy in here," Sanda said as she opened a massive white door. "It is a drawing room that we don't enter too often."

They all felt this. There was a sickly sweet smell and the air was stuffy. It seemed cooler, a melancholy and artificial coolness. Egor looked for his companion. Mr. Nazarie was walking lightly, as if trying to excuse himself in his modesty, trying to make as little noise as possible, to pass unnoticed. Simina was behind him. She came in last. Her face was radiant with solemn emotion which lent a feminine paleness, unnatural in a child's face. "Extraordinarily sensitive these girls are," Egor thought.

"Miss Christina !" Mrs. Moscu announced. "That's what they all called her."

Mr. Nazarie felt terror, like a grip in his breast. Miss Christina was smiling out of Mirea's painting, as if she were looking right at him. She was a very young girl, attired in a full dress, long and slim in the waist, black curls hanging low upon her shoulders.

"What do you think, mister painter ?" Sanda asked.

Egor was standing away from the portrait. He was trying to realize the source of so much melancholy and weariness in his soul while facing this virgin who looked him straight in the eyes, intimately smiling as if she had chosen him out of the whole group, to confess to him alone her endless loneliness. There was much yearning and much sorrow in Miss Christina's eyes. Vainly did she intimately smile and grip her small blue umbrella, slyly raising an eyebrow as if asking him to laugh at her hat, too large and overly decorated, that she naturally couldn't bear to wear, except because it had been mama's wish : "A young lady should not pose unless impeccably dressed, it's not done." Miss Christina was suffering in he immobility. "Would she have guessed that she was to die so soon ?" Egor asked himself.

"So you like it, don't you ?" Sanda asked triumphantly. "Since you don't say anything, I guess it means you like it."

"Such a model required no less than a masterpiece," Egor said quietly.

Miss Christina's eyes glittered more enticingly for a moment. Egor placed his hand on his brow. What a strange smell in this room. Could it have been her own room ? From the corner of his eye he looked at the opposite wall. Mrs. Moscu said it was a drawing room, but there, in the corner, stood a large white curtained bed. He looked up at the picture once more. Miss Christina had surveyed all his movements. Egor could well read the look in her eyes ; she had seen him discover her bed and did not blush, on the contrary, she went on gazing into his eyes, somehow provokingly. "Yes, this is my maiden chamber, and that's my bed, my virginal bed," Miss Christina's eyes seemed to speak to him.

"What is your opinion, professor ?" Sanda asked once more.

Mr. Nazarie was stunned as soon as he set eyes on the portrait. At first, he believed he saw again the apparition of the night before, that vapory face that had approached Mrs. Moscu's shoulders at dinner. Terror had frozen his being. Simina passing by, considering him with surprise and suspicion, woke him out of his fright.

"I think it's extraordinary," Mr. Nazarie said in a hoarse voice.

He was now quiet. An unnatural peace, a slight callousness. There was a queer smell in the room ; not the smell of a corpse, nor of funeral flowers, but a fragrance of youth cut dead, arrested and preserved here between these four walls. Youth long gone. The sun did not seem to have come into this room, nor had time impaired anything. Nothing seemed to have been freshened up or changed since Miss Christina died. This smell was the fragrance of her youth, miraculous remnants of her perfume, of the warmth of her body. Mr. Nazarie now understood all these tiny, strange things. He was actually surprised to understand so promptly and to accept so fast.

"Really, an extraordinary thing," he added looking at the picture again.

But it was not the apparition in the dining room, not the same. A great likeness, Miss Christina was very much like Mrs. Moscu ; she resembled Simina too. But her face could be quietly contemplated. It was only during the first minutes that he was frightened. He then thought that he saw the apparition again. He just thought ; for the other one diffused a desperate terror that was not in the portrait. The weariness, the sadness of the room, came from other worlds and spoke a different language to the soul.

"I should like to try and paint this picture," Egor said, "paint it my way, not make a mere copy."

Sanda came up to him seizing his arm anxiously.

"A good thing mother didn't hear you," she whispered.

Egor had spoken in quite a loud voice, but Mrs. Moscu, in an armchair covered with white cotton, as usual never heard a thing. Mrs. Moscu's eyes were examining the room. Life had another pulse here. Her thoughts always ran differently here, not in this actual space, nor in this present time. Egor had given her a passing look as she seated herself in the armchair and he understood : Mrs. Moscu constantly came back here, to this room, into those former events.

"A good thing she didn't hear you, it would have beeen a shock to her," Sanda said in the same whisper. "She won't let anybody in here. Today was an exception. There's something else, too..."

But Simina was too close. Mr. Nazarie, too, was coming up, maybe to tell them that they ought to retire.

"But aunt Christina would like to have a second portrait painted," Simina said. "How do you know that mother wouldn't like it ?"

"Simina, you know a lot of things," Sanda said meaningfully looking into her eyes.

Then she turned her back and approached Mrs. Moscu. "Mama, we have stayed long enough. We must leave."

"You wouldn't let me stay another minute, would you ?" she begged.

Sanda shook her head severely.

"With Simina," Mrs. Moscu begged again.

"Especially not with her," Sanda said smiling.

She took her arm. Egor and Mr. Nazarie followed. They avoided looking at each other at first, but having reached the veranda they couldn't help it. Egor lit a cigarette, having first offered one to the professor. Mr. Nazarie refused with a smile.

"I don't think it's the same thing, my dear maître," Mr. Nazarie said.

That moment Sanda came up. The former vigor and hardness had left her face. Sanda was now, once more, the capricious and available young lady.

"Are we ready to work, Mr. Egor ?" she asked.

Mr. Nazarie was glad to retire at such a neutral time.

## IV

Egor did not do any work that afternoon. He carried his easel along several paths and settled down in various corners of the park. At last he hid his utensils at the root of an elm tree and began a walk with Sanda.

"It's a pity to work on such a fine day," he said.

Then he asked her how many poems about autumn she knew. He had questioned to tease her, but had to listen to her in wonder, not always with pleasure, reciting one poem after another. He would have liked to come sooner to intimate talk, maybe to confessions even. Thus, Egor was getting ready for love. Autumn above all was simply miraculous, excluding any vulgar move. The poems, however, were fairly numerous. Time was quickly passing. He had to take a step forward. He decided to call her by her christian name.

"What do you think of Nazarie, Sanda ?"

"I think he is a sly one," Sanda answered correctly, as if ignoring Egor's intimate tone. "Have you noticed his quick change of face ? He never looks quite the same man."

Egor laughed. The girl's answer had been delightful indeed. Moreover, he had placed the conversation on more accessible territory. They could laugh, they could joke. Having reached the far end of the path, he pressed her waist. She was still addressing him as "Mr. Eror", possibly to irritate him.

Soon, however, they had to go back. It was tea-time. Simina was waiting for them, pacing about, her eyes on the gravel. Mrs. Moscu was on the veranda, reading a French novel. Mr. Nazarie had excused himself, he would not be back until dinner time. He had set out towards the village to examine certain artifacts.

They had a quiet cup of tea, Sanda and Egor being the only ones to speak. Simina looked thoughtful. She was the first to rise having folded her napkin and collected the crumbs in her plate.

"Where are you going, Simina ?" Sanda asked.

"To Nanny's," the little girl replied without turning.

Sanda's eyes followed her till she disappeared among the trees.

"I don't approve of this friendship," she addressed Mrs. Moscu. "Nanny fills her head with all kinds of fairy tales."

"I've been telling her so, many times," Mrs. Moscu said in defense.

"What does Nanny tell her ?" Egor asked.

"The most absurd tales," Sanda spoke in a weary, irritated tone.

"She's at the age for fairy tales," Egor interrupted, "she's only nine. She's living in fantasy."

Annoyed, Sanda looked at him. She possibly meant to say more, but was content with few words.

"Nanny's fairy tales are a queer kind of fantasy."

★

That very evening Egor got an idea of nanny's queer fairy tales. He had gone for a walk round the park to see the sunset in the plain. He stood leaning against an acacia tree watching the sinking fiery globe, "away and not so far away," he remembered the folk verse with real pleasure. "Only such a line could actually describe a sunset in the plains," Egor thought. And all of nature petrified for a few seconds after the sun's sinking. Then how strangely the silence quickens into life ! If only there were not so many mosquitos," Egor thought, lighting a cigarette as a defense.

In the cool of the evening smelling of dust and weeds, the cigarette was tasteless. He threw it away and slowly made for the house. He entered the park by a side gate. On the left there were large courtyards, outhouses, and vegetable gardens. Egor wondered who was looking after all these domestic matters, who supervised and paid the servants, who sold the crops. Mrs. Moscu's husband had been dead for a few years ; her sister-in-law owned land in a different part of the country. Maybe some superintendent, some inherited bailiff.

Lamps were being lit. "Those are the kitchens and the rooms of the domestics," Egor thought. A whole row of small white rooms with a low veranda. Women were passing, a timid child was looking puzzled at the large country house. A fresh smell of hay, cattle and milk. "It's going to be a wonderful night," Egor thought looking up into the transparent sky.

"Aren't you afraid of the dogs ?"

The voice had come so unexpectedly that Egor stepped back. Simina had appeared by his side. "How on earth did she walk so quietly, what path did she take to show up right behind my back ?"

"What about you ? Aren't you afraid of walking here by yourself ?" Egor asked.

"I've been at Nanny's," Simina quietly answered.

"Ever since you left ?"

"Nanny was busy, I attended her."

"And she told you fairy tales, didn't she ?"

Simina smiled, a crushing smile. She picked a burr stuck to her dress, then smoothed out the pleats. She was very astutely delaying the answer.

"Sanda told you that. But it's true. Nanny tells me a new tale everyday. She knows a lot."

"It must have been a very long one today if you stayed so late," Egor said.

Simina smiled again with the same false shyness. In meeting her eyes Egor experienced the painful feeling of being caught in a trap, that a sharp sly mind was working there in front of him, not a child's mind.

"The tale was a short one," Simina said, "but Nanny had to pay the workers' wages as she always does."

She spoke the last words in a drawling voice, intentionally calling Egor's attention to them. As if knowing his former perplexities and wishing, incidentally, to clarify them. Egor suddenly felt ill at ease. The girl was reading his thoughts without his knowledge. She had stressed certain words with such subtlety, then ceased, looking down.

"A short tale, a very short one," she added.

It was obvious that she expected to be questioned, that she was waiting for Egor to ask her to tell it. He tried to resist the temptation, but he couldn't. Simina was awkwardly silent, biding her time.

"Will you tell it to me ?" Egor said at last.

"It's about a young shepherd who had fallen in love with a dead empress," Simina calmly began.

The words sounded so strange on her childlike lips that Egor shuddered.

"What a repulsive, absurd tale !" he suddenly exclaimed, in a sharp voice, "Sanda is quite right."

Simina was not disturbed by Egor's outburst. She waited for his anger to subside, then she began in the same voice.

"That's the tale. That was the young shepherd's destiny."

"Do you know what a man's destiny is ?" Egor asked.

"That which is preordained, the fate or destiny of a man," Simina promptly answered as if reciting a lesson. "Everyone is born close to a star, with his own good or bad luck. That's what it is..."

"You may be right," Egor said smiling.

"Once upon a time there was a shepherd boy," Simina quickly began, leaving him no time to interrupt her. "When he was born the Weird sisters said to him, 'You shall love a dead empress.' His mother heard this and began to weep.

The other Weird one, for there were three of them, took pity on her sorrow and added, 'And the empress shall love you too !'"

"You insist on telling me the whole story, don't you ?" Egor stopped her.

"It was you who asked me to tell it." She then snubbed him with sullen silence. They stood in the middle of the main drive. Far away you could see the lamps of the domestics' rooms. On the opposite side the manor rose darkly ominous in the pale evening light.

"Don't you know another tale, a nicer one ?" Egor said, just to break the silence. "The one she told you yesterday, for instance, or the day before yesterday."

Simina smiled. She took a deep breath, as if unwilling to look at the large house on their right. Her neck was taut, her head high.

"Yesterday's tale was very long," she said, "and the day before yesterday's was no tale, but a real story about Miss Christina."

Egor jumped and felt frightened. It was not the sudden dark, here among the trees even darker, but Simina seemed to have purposefully stopped here. Her eyes, with dilated pupils, shone, while her head was in a state of unnatural immobility. Egor had been frightened by the tone in which she had spoken the last words. She always knew how to stress certain words, to give them the meaning she intended, to stab them as if with red hot iron upon your heart.

"Why do you call her 'Miss Christina' ?" Egor asked angrily. You used to call her 'aunt,' for she's your aunt of course."

"It was she who asked me to call her 'Miss,' and stop calling her aunt lest she should seem older."

Egor had difficulty controlling himself ; he was furious with this small creature who was lying so shamelessly, with such devilish slyness.

"When did she ask you ? How is it possible for someone who's been dead almost thirty years to ask such a thing ?"

His voice was sharp, his look fierce, yet Simina continued to smile. She took such pleasure in the man's fury, a man so large and strong, against herself who was not yet ten years old.

"She asked me last night, in my dream."

For a moment Egor hesitated, confused. But he wished to sift the matter, to understand what was lurking in the mind of this terrifying child.

"But today in the drawing room I heard you say 'aunt Christina'."

"No, I did not," Simina replied quite calmly, "today I did not say 'aunt Christina'."

Nor did Egor actually remember to have heard her say it. But her firmness and her victorious smile were frightening. He would certainly speak to Sanda, even to Mrs. Moscu. He felt ridiculous, standing in the middle of the alley, in the dark, trying to confound a small girl. He suddenly wished to turn his head to the manor and take the first step back home, since Simina had not moved for several minutes now. Then, suddenly, the little girl threw herself into his arms, quite terrified, screaming. Egor was alarmed at her scream and picked her up. Simina had placed her hands on his cheeks, holding his face close to her own.

"I thought someone was coming that way," she whispered.

She was pointing to the opposite side of the park. She forced Egor to look that way, a long stare, to soothe her.

"There is no one, my child," Egor said confidently. "It was only your imagination. Quite a natural fear, too, if you listen to absurd tales everyday."

He was still carrying her in his arms, fondling her. Strangely enough, her heart did not beat rapidly from fear. Her body, too, was quiet, warm, and cordial. Not one feverish jerk, not one drop of sweat. Her face was serene, composed. Egor suddenly realized that he had been taken in, that Simina had feigned to be frightened and jumped into his arms only to prevent him from turning his head and look at the house. As he realized this, fury combined with terror seized him. Simina instantly felt the change in Egor's muscles, in his pulse.

"Please put me down," she whispered, "I'm all right now."

"Why did you lie, Simina?" Egor asked in anger. "You didn't see anything, at least not over there."

He stretched his arm pointing to the border of the park. But his arm was still shaking and he drew it back quickly. Not fast enough for Simina not to notice. The little girl looked at him smiling, giving no answer.

"Maybe you saw something in the other direction," Egor went on.

He didn't, however, look at the house. He said "the other direction" without turning, without pointing an outstretched arm to the end of the park. He grew angrier as Simina seemed to guess even his most secret fears and doubts.

"Perhaps something you didn't want me to see," Egor added.

He was genuinely frightened. Simina was standing before him, her hands behind her back, biting her lips to stop from laughing. This mockery, however, did not dispel the obscure terror that possessed Egor.

"You may safely turn," Simina said, inviting him with a gesture of her hand to look the other way. "You are a man, you can't be scared... like I was," she added looking down upon the gravel.

She then abruptly proceeded to walk to the house. Egor followed, his teeth clenched, his breath coming quick and hot.

"You know, I shall tell on you, Simina !" he said menacingly.

"I was expecting it, Mr. Egor," she said without looking back. "Please forgive me if, in my panic, I jumped into your arms. Mother won't easily forgive this misbehavior. You're right to tell on me."

Egor grasped her arm and gave her a jerk back to him. The girl acquiesced, putting up no resistance.

"You well know it's a different matter," he murmured coming close and speaking the words solemnly.

But he would have found it difficult to say what the matter was. He only knew one thing : that Simina hadn't been afraid and that she had forced him to look towards the other end of the park so that he shouldn't see something she had seen... But she herself, why had she not been frightened ?

"True, it was silly to be frightened," Simina said.

They were now before the veranda. Egor used to go up to his room to wash his hands before dinner, but tonight he gave up something so complicated. He entered the office adjoining the dining room which the children used to wash their hands. Mr. Nazarie seemed to be waiting for him in the doorway.

"If you're not busy after dinner let's have a short walk," he said coming close. "I want to tell you a few interesting facts that I picked up in the village."

"And I shall tell you an equally interesting thing," Egor added with a smile.

Of course, the terror and anger in the park were now gone as if by magic. He was actually sorry to have lost his temper with the child. "Simina keeps back some serious things," he thought, "I shall have to be very careful." Yet no such wise thoughts calmed him down, but rather the light he had found inside, the presence of people there, healthy and alive.

They sat down to dinner. Egor gave Simina occasional glances. He always met the same innocent eyes, the same carefully concealed firmess. "She believes I won't tell, I won't betray her," Egor thought. He was carefully preparing his surprise. Sanda was sitting by him, looking somewhat tired.

"I haven't been feeling well today," she apologized.

Mr. Nazarie spoke about his observations, about artifacts and the difficulty of digging at random. He no longer had his former verve and enthusiasm. He talked about his activity that day, in order to prevent silence from falling over the room.

"Do you know, Simina told me a fairy tale that Nanny told her today," Egor began.

Sanda blushed red and turned to her sister.

"I found out quite late that Nanny wasn't here this afternoon, that she'd gone shopping to Giurgiu," Sanda said. "Simina, you'll be severely punished."

Egor hardly knew where to look. Mrs. Moscu was gently waking from her usual torpor.

"What about that fairy tale of ours, Miss Simina ?" Egor wickedly asked.

That moment he realized the great delight one can experience in taking vengeance on a child, torturing it when it is at your mercy. However, Simina gave him such a look of contempt that Egor's anger flared up again.

"It's a tale I have long known," Simina politely answered.

"Then why did you lie for no reason ?" Sanda asked.

"Answer, don't be afraid, my child," Mrs. Moscu intervened. "Don't be afraid of punishment. If you've been wrong, speak up bravely."

"I am not afraid of being punished," Simina calmly spoke, "but I cannot answer."

She looked Sanda in the eyes with the same exasperating serenity and firmness. Her sister flared up.

"For the time being you'll go to bed without dessert and leave the table right now. Sofia will see you to your room."

For a moment Simina seemed to lose her self-control. She became pale, pursed her lips, sought Mrs. Moscu's help. But Mrs. Moscu shrugged her shoulders, smiling. So Simina rose producing her contemptuous smile and saying "good night" she kissed Mrs. Moscu's cheek and went to her room.

"I am very sorry for our little lady," Mr. Nazarie said, "She is so good and so small. Maybe she didn't deserve such severe punishment."

"I am sorry, too, for I know how sensitive she is," Sanda said, "but we have to cure her of this habit of pointlessly lying."

Mrs. Moscu nodded in approval. Nevertheless, this scene had been rather trying for she hardly said another word the rest of the meal.

"Now you know the kind of tales she listens to," Sanda said to Egor.

The painter shivered as if in terror. He asked himself, however, if Sanda realized what her sister was doing.

"There is something more serious," Egor said, "I have a feeling that she doesn't simply listen to all these tales. Most of them she makes up herself."

The moment he spoke those words he knew he had committed a blunder. Sanda gave him a stunned, harsh look.

## V

Once alone, Egor and Mr. Nazarie made their way towards the gate. They walked a long time without speaking. Suddenly Mr. Nazarie plucked up his courage.

"Would you really mind if I asked you a very personal question ? For instance if you are really in love with Sanda ?"

Egor hesitated in answering. Not so much surprised by the professor's indiscreet question, but considering the answer he was to give. Frankly speaking, he didn't quite know if he was actually in love with Sanda, as Mr. Nazarie had stressed in his question. He liked the girl. A brief fling, even a love affair, that was what he was joyfully looking for. Sanda was intimately associated with his artistic profession, with his unavowed ambitions. A sincere answer would have been difficult.

"I see you are hesitating," Mr. Nazarie went on. "I wouldn't like to misjudge your silence, to believe you've been hurt by my somewhat brutal question. But if you're not really in love with Miss Moscu, I would advise you to leave this place as soon as possible. I will also leave, perhaps as soon as tomorrow, maybe even before you."

Egor stopped walking to realize better the professor's words.

"Has anything happened, anything serious ?" he asked in an undertone.

"Nothing as yet. But I don't like this house, I don't like it at all. There is a spell on this place. I felt it the very first evening. There's nothing healthy here. Not even this artificial plantation, a park of acacias and elms planted by man's hand."

Egor laughed.

"So far there's nothing serious," he said. "I can even quietly light a cigarette."

Mr. Nazarie looked at him perplexed.

"This very cigarette might make you think twice," he continued. "Have you forgotten last night's painful scene ?"

"I had almost forgotten. Something happened today, however, that reminded me of it. I'll tell you in a minute.

"I can see you are in love and do not intend to leave. I don't blame you. But I'm afraid it will be very difficult, very difficult indeed. Do you, at least, believe in God, do you pray to the Mother of God, do you make the sign of the cross before going to bed ?"

"Never."

"So much the worse. You should learn that much, at least."

"But, after all, what serious things did you find out in the village ?"

"Practically nothing. Yet I feel uneasy in this house and I am never wrong. There's no merit in it, but I'm not wrong. I've been living a long time by myself, close to the earth, that was before I started the diggings. I'm almost very nearly a peasant's son. My father was a sergeant in the army in a village close to Ciulnița. Don't judge me by my bald head and my being a university professor. I do feel these things. I am a bit of a poet too ; I only wrote verse in high school, but I'm still a poet at heart."

Bewildered, Egor was listening to the nervous and incoherent sentences of Mr. Nazarie. The professor was sinking in a sea of words, memories, and emotions, striving in vain to get out of it. At first, his words were firm and reasonable. Imperceptibly, however, incipient delirium accelerated his speech. His voice was somewhat strangled, his breathing faster. "Why should he tell me all these things ? To explain his leaving, to prepare it ?"

"Professor," Egor stopped him calmly, "you're afraid of something."

He stressed the word unconsciously, as he had done, a few hours earlier, while talking to Simina. And as he stressed it, he felt a strange, absurd shiver running down his spine.

"Yes, I am," Mr. Nazarie stuttered, "I admit I'm scared, but this is not the point."

"I'm afraid it is," Egor said to him. "We are both adults and we lose our heads. To begin with, let me tell you that I have no intention of leaving."

He liked the sound of his own voice, hard and firm, in pronouncing the last sentence. Having made up his mind, he felt courage and confidence. He liked hearing himself talk. "After all we're no children."

"I do not know hov much I'm in love with Miss Moscu," he added in the same manly voice, "but I came here to spend a whole month, and I will stay. If only to try the strength of my nerves."

He laughed mirthlessly. The things he had just said were solemn.

"Good for you, young man," Mr. Nazarie excitedly spoke, "however, I don't want you to think that I am so frightened as to be unable to reason. And weighing things properly, I don't advise you to stay. Let me add : nor would I advise myself, for I will stay on, too."

"It would have been awkward if you had suddenly gone, just like that," Egor replied.

"I wouldn't have been the first guest to leave after two days' stay," said Mr. Nazarie, his eyes on the ground. "Sad and strange things I found out in the village, young man."

"Please, stop calling me 'young man,' call me Egor."

"Alright, I'll do that," Mr. Nazarie acquiesced with a smile (it was his first smile that night). "You know," he began, having looked round to make sure that no one was listening, "you know, when it comes to Miss Christina, well... There's something not right about her. This fair young lady was no honor to her family. People tell a good many tales."

"That's the way of peasants," Egor sententiously declared.

"I happen to know them better," Mr. Nazarie went on, 'it's easy to make up a legend with such horrid details. For they are indeed odious details. Could you have imagined that this well born virgin would tell the bailiff to thrash the peasants with a whip in front of her, thrash them blood red? Could you, now? And she would tear off their shirts... and what not... She was actually the bailiff's mistress, the whole village knew this. This man was a beast, of insane, unimaginable cruelty."

Mr. Nazarie ceased. To tell all the things he had heard, what men had whispered into his ear at the pub, or on the way back to the manor, was more than he could do. That thing about the live chickens whose necks the young lady used to wring, was more than he could stand or repeat. Even though he wouldn't believe everything, these were savage details that curdled the blood in his veins.

"Is it possible!" Egor thoughtfully spoke, "judging by her face you couldn't have imagined such a soul. Maybe it's not altogether true. It's thirty years since, people may have forgotten and mixed things up with other legends."

"Possibly, anyway Miss Christina's memory is still alive in the village. Children are afraid of her name to this day. Then her death, her death sets you thinking. For it was not the peasants who killed her, but the bailiff whose mistress she'd been for some years. You may wonder what devil was fretting within her to drive her to debauchery and cruelty at the age of 16-17. The bailiff killed her out of jealousy. The uprisings were on..."

Confused, Mr. Nazarie ceased. He dare not go on with his tale. The young lady's deeds seemed actually devilish, altogether inhuman.

"It won't bear telling?" Egor whispered.

"Oh yes, it will. But it's frightful. People say that the peasants on other lands had come and she summoned them into the bedroom, two by two, to divide her goods. She said that she wanted to give away all her goods, with papers in order, if they only did not kill her. In fact, she would let them all take turns in abusing her. She encouraged them herself. She received them in twos, lying naked on the rug. The bailiff finally came and shot her, but he, too, was killed when the soldiers came ; some of the peasants were shot, others, as you know, were sentenced to the salt mines. Facts did not spread abroad, but the family, relatives, friends heard soon enough."

"Unbelievable," Egor mumbled.

He lit another cigarette. He was nervous, upset.

"Such a woman leaves marks upon a house," Mr. Nazarie continued. "That's why I was feeling oppressed, restless, depressed. Just imagine, they didn't even find her body, to bury it!" Thus he spoke after a pause during which he seemed to have been debating whether to confess this particular detail as well.

"They might have thrown it away, into some abandoned well," Egor said, "or maybe they set fire to it, who knows."

"Maybe," Mr. Nazarie whispered thoughtfully, "though peasants dont generally burn corpses."

He stopped and looked around intently, fearfully. The trees of the park were far behind. The fields open, ploughed here and there, vanishing in sombre distance. There was nowhere a clear streak on the horizon. Just absurd tangled shadows.

"Not the best place to talk about corpses," Egor said.

Mr. Nazarie stuck his hands into his pockets, nervously. He didn't seem to have heard Egor's remark. He was thinking his thoughts or possibly hesitating whether to complete his confessions. He was gulping in air as was his habit, his mouth wide open, his head thrown back. Yet he felt good in the cool night, no trees about, no moon overhead.

"Miss Christina's disappearance is, nevertheless, strange," Mr. Nazarie began, "people say she has become a ghost."

He spoke naturally, no catch in his voice. He was still gazing up at the sky. Egor controlled himself, trying not to smile.

"I hope you're not of the same opinion," he said, a certain amount of irony in his voice.

"I have never had such problems," Mr. Nazarie answered. "I can't say whether I should or should not believe in such a horror... as a matter of fact it's of no consequence."

Egor made haste to help him.

"That's what I think, too," he said.

He realized that he was lying, saying quite the opposite of what he actually meant, yet he felt that at such a time he should believe what Mr. Nazarie believed.

"It is nevertheless true that all these incidents have changed the Moscu house and family," Mr. Nazarie added, "I don't feel at ease there. All that I've told could very well be mere inventions of the villagers, but personally I feel the same thing, something oppressive here."

He put out his arm pointing to the park. That minute he thought he saw so many terrifying things that he started to speak at once faster, more precipitately, breathing deeply.

"It's fear gripping him," Egor realized. He wondered at his own lucidity; standing so close to Mr. Nazarie, to a man who was again a prey to terror, yet watching him with detachment and even analyzing him. He dare not, however, look in the direction of the park. Mr. Nazarie's momentarily extended arm had upset him more than all his frightened words. He may possibly see something there; maybe the same thing that Simina saw. And yet he was still clearheaded; just a very light anxiety was troubling his soul.

"You shouldn't be afraid!" he suddenly said interrupting Mr. Nazarie's outburst. "Don't look that way, the house."

Mr. Nazarie would not or could not obey. He stood staring at the park. He was gazing, his whole being tense, waiting.

"And yet there's something coming from those parts," he said.

Egor turned his head too. The shadow of the park suddenly loomed distant, compact. There was nothing there. You couldn't see anything, just a faint glitter on the left where the domestics' houses were.

"No one is coming," he spoke manfully.

That minute he heard a howl that froze the blood in his veins. The howling of a dog, scared stiff, mad with fear; sounding lugubrious, infernal, the groans could then be heard much nearer. A muffled noise too, as of a hunted beast, hotly breathing. Out of the dark, a big grey dog threw himself at their feet, ears flattened, trembling, and yelping. He sprawled at their feet, fawning, pressing his head against their ankles, licking their hands, sighing. Now and then he would rise from the dust and begin to howl. The same terrified unaccountable howl.

"He's also frightened," Egor said patting him. "He too, poor dog."

But it felt good to have it here at his feet, a warm, living, strong animal. It felt so good, as he was standing in this field open on all sides, yet again closed in, far away, by the misty circle of the horizon.

## VI

That night Egor was dreaming one of his usual dreams, uninteresting and hardly dramatic. Friends of his student days, relatives, pointless voyages, illogical dialogues. This time he seemed to be in a French town, in a room not his own, leaning against the door and listening to the conversation between one of his professors and another young man whom he did not know.

They were talking about a recent exhibition of paintings and about wooden chests.

"I like heavy wooden chests, full of secret, strange, exotic things," the young man began. "I always contemplate them with a thrill, lying closed as they do, in shops or on the docks, enclosing goodness knows what burden of treasure within their wooden planks."

After the first words, Egor understood. The young stranger talking was, in fact, his friend Radu Prajan, long since dead, killed in a stupid street accident. He recognized his voice and his excitement when talking about wooden chests. That was Prajan's way of speaking when alive. He liked oils and dyes, for their strong and complex smell, "technical", "synthetic" smells that suggested boxes, wooden chests, anything that was shipped from afar, from some exotic harbor or some factory. How different he appeared now. Had it not been for his voice and words, Egor couldn't have known him. His hair had grown so long that fluffy locks seemed to cover his shoulders. At every movement of the head they fluttered round his cheeks, almost covering his ears. He was constantly talking to the professor, never noticing Egor. Egor's impatience grew with every uttered word. "He's dead, however, he thought, Prajan has long been dead. Maybe that's why he won't turn to me, won't recognize me. This long hair too, womanlike, he's grown it to avoid being recognized."

Yet that very minute, with an abrupt, frightened movement, Prajan turned to Egor and took a single step toward him.

"Since we were talking about you," he quickly said, "mind what you do, for you are in great danger."

"Yes, I see what you mean," Egor whispered, "I know what you're trying to tell me."

These were Prajan's own eyes now. His face was beginning to resemble his former, real one. Just the hair was too long, unnaturally and disgustingly long for a man.

"I, too, am very careful," Prajan added, shaking his locks. "Here, no one can harm me under this cloak."

Indeed, Prajan was now far away, as if somewhere higher up, for Egor raised his arm without reaching him. He could see him, but felt him to be far away, inaccessible. That very moment he realized that Prajan had been driven away by fear, put to flight seemingly by some invisible power. His professor now stood by Prajan, together with some other unknown persons, they were all frightened by something that was going on under their eyes, something that was possibly going on behind Egor, for he himself could not see anything. He just looked at them bewildered by their terror, by their abrupt flight. All around Egor objects became filmy, losing consistency. Fear was getting hold of him too. He turned his head and found Miss Christina's body by his side. She was smiling, as in Mirea's picture. But her dress was different : a blue dress with fringes and plenty of lace. She wore long black gloves that made her arms look even whiter.

"Away !" Miss Christina ordered, frowning and slowly raising her arm toward Prajan.

Egor felt fearfully dizzy in hearing her voice in his dream. It seemed to come from the outer regions, from another world. Egor tossed as if ready to waken, but Miss Christina grabbed him by the arm and whispered into his ear :

"Quiet, my dear, don't be afraid. You are in your room, in our room, my love."

Indeed the setting had suddenly changed. Miss Christina's orders had chased the shadows, the changed face of Prajan had vanished, the walls of the strange room had melted. Egor looked around, bewildered. He looked for the door he had been leaning against a few minutes earlier. Everything had senselessly disappeared. He was in his room ; surprised, he identified each object. There was a strange light, neither daylight nor lamplight.

"Such a long time to wait," Miss Christina whispered again, "long waiting for a man like you, a man handsome and young."

She had drawn so close that Egor felt a whiff of unbearable violet-scented perfume around him. He tried to take a step back, but Christina took his arm detaining him.

"Don't run away Egor, don't be afraid that I am dead."

But Egor was not afraid of talking to the dead woman. He felt embarrassed by her warm approach, by the violet scent that was too strong, by such feminine breathing. Miss Christina was excited, eager, and impatient ; she breathed deeply like a woman in the presence of a man.

"So handsome, so pale," Christina added.

She leaned over him, so close that there was no room for him to retire. He buried his head in his pillow, that was all he could do. For only now did he realize that he was sleeping in his bed and that Miss Christina was stooping over him, trying to kiss him. Terrified, he waited for the touch of her lips on his mouth, on his cheek. But Christina just inclined her forehead low down over his brow, that was all.

"No, I don't want to," she whispered, "I won't kiss you like that. I am afraid of myself, Egor."

She suddenly drew back a few steps from the bed and gave him a long look. She seemed to be struggling within herself, trying to control a blind, savage urge. She was biting her lips. Egor began to be amazed at himself, lying so quiet by a dead woman. What luck ! it is all happening in a dream, he thought.

"But you must not believe everything that Nazarie told you," Miss Christina went on, approaching the bed again. "It's not true, I haven't done those things that people tell ...out me. I've been no monster, Egor. I don't mind what ...hink, but I don't want you to believe the same absurd

things. It's not true, do you hear me, my darling ?! It's not true."

Her words sounded ever so clear in that room. "What if someone could hear this and believe that I slept with a woman tonight," Egor thought. But the same minute he remembered that it was all in a dream and calmed down, smiling.

"You're so handsome when you smile," Christina said, sitting on the bed.

She lazily pulled off a glove and threw it over Egor's head on the bedside table. The scent of violets was now even stronger. Bad taste to put on so much scent. He suddenly felt a warm hand caressing his cheek. His blood seemed to have drained out of his veins for the sensation of that warm hand, an unnatural, inhuman warmth, was terrifying. Egor felt like yelling with horror, but there was no strength in him, his voice died in his throat.

"Don't be afraid, my love," Christina then whispered. "I shall not hurt you. You I won't hurt. I shall only love you."

She was speaking slowly, distinctly, her voice occasionally very sad. She was regarding him unappeased, hungry. And yet a shade of infinite sadness sometimes descended into her glassy eyes.

"I shall love you as no mortal man has ever been loved," Christina added.

She considered him with a smile, a few seconds. Them her voice became more musical, more rhythmic :

*"My heartstrings ache when every eve*
*You vent your cruel desire ;*
*Your eyes, so gloomy, make me grieve,*
*And scorching is their fire..."*

At the very first sentence Egor felt overcome by an obscure apprehension. Those words he had heard many times. He now remembered quite clearly : Eminescu, *The Evening Star.* Miss Christina had quoted Eminescu before. "Her favorite poet in those days," Egor thought.

"Have no fear, Egor, my love," Miss Christina repeated, getting up. "Whatever may happen, have no fear of me. To you I shall behave differently, differently... Your blood is too precious to me, my darling. From here, from this my world, I shall join you every night ; at first in your sleep, Egor, and then in your arms, my love. Have no fear, Egor, do trust me."

That moment Egor suddenly woke up. He recalled every detail in the dream with extraordinary precision. He was no longer afraid. His whole being was in a state of confusion as if after great effort. What first caught his attention was the strong scent of violets. He rubbed his eyes, smoothed his brow passing his hand over it several times, but the scent was still there, going to his head. He suddenly saw Miss Christina's black glove by his side. "I am not yet awake, I'm still dreaming," he thought in fear, "I must do something to wake up. I'll go mad if I don't." He was nevertheless wondering at the lucidity of hi sthoughts. He waited, firmly hoping to wake up. Yet he could feel his hand on his brow ; he caught himself touching his body. Therefore, he was not asleep, not dreaming. He bit hard into his lower lip. He felt the pain. That moment he wanted to jump out of bed and put the light on. But he saw, two steps away, standing upright and motionless, Miss Christina's well-known figure. The phantom pinned him to his bed. Egor slowly clenched his fists drawing them close to his body. He could feel them. No possible doubt. He was no longer asleep. He was afraid to close his eyes, but, for a few seconds, he looked down, then up at Miss Christina again. She was still there, giving him a glassy stare, smiling, wrapping him in her violet scent. He began to move. "Out Father, who art in heaven, oh Lord !" These words had suddenly sprouted in Egor's mind, words from some long forgotten child's prayer and he kept breathlessly repeating them. Miss Christina stopped and her smile seemed to become sadder and more hopeless. Egor realized she knew he was praying ; she had guessed everything. "She knows I am awake and will not leave..."

Christina took another step. The swish of her silk dress was extremely clear. No shade, no detail was lost in the silence of the room. Miss Christina stepped firmly. A woman's steps, light, yet alive and emotional. When she came up to the bed, Egor again felt her body and was aware of the same sensation of artificial, disgusting warmth. His flesh stiffened with a spasm. Miss Christina constantly looked him straight in the eyes, as if to assure him beyond any doubt of her concrete, living presence ; she then passed by and picked up her glove on the bedside table. Again that bare arm and the scent of violets. Miss Christina went on gazing at him as she elegantly put on her glove. Then with the same feminine, graceful step, she went up to the window. Egor lacked the courage to follow her. He lay, fists tight by his body, rigid, bathed in cold sweat, alone in the dark. For the first time in his life, he felt utterly alone, under a curse. No one and nothing in the other world could reach him, to help, to save him.

For a long time he did not hear anything. He realized that he was trying to deceive himself, for he had been aware of the exact moment when Miss Christina had left the room. He had felt her terrifying presence disappearing from that space. He had felt this in his blood, in his breathing. Still, he had been waiting, lacking the necessary courage to turn his head to the window. The door to the balcony was open. Maybe she was still there, had not left, was just hiding. He knew, however, that fear was senseless, that Miss Christina was no longer in the room, nor on the balcony.

He suddenly made up his mind. He jumped out of bed, and put on his flashlight. Feverishly, he fumbled for matches and lit his oil lamp. The strong light frightened a large moth which began desperately fluttering, knocking against the walls. Egor took the lamp and went out on the balcony. Night was waning. You could feel the dawn somewhere, quite close. There was a cold mist, in the motionless air. No flutter in the trees. No sound anywhere. He was suddenly afraid of his loneliness and shuddered. Only then did he actually realize how cold he was. He turned out the light and entered the room. The stong scent of violets struck him.

The moth went on flinging itself about, striking the walls with muffled sounds, occasionally touching the lamp. Egor lit a cigarette. He smoked eagerly, without a thought. Then stood up again and closed the balcony door. Sleep only came with broad daylight and the last cock-crow of that night.

## VII

The woman was knocking on the door in vain. It was locked and the guest did not wake up to unlock it. "Sound asleep as if he'd been carousing all night," the woman thought with a shy smile. But the milk was getting cold. She looked at the laden tray placed on the nearby table. "Maybe the professor can wake him."

She found Mr. Nazarie dressed, ready to go out. She stood a few seconds in the doorway, somewhat ashamed ; it was awkward to say she was there to ask Mr. Nazarie to wake Egor.

"Are you, by any chance, one of the villagers ?" Mr. Nazarie asked, seeing her shyly waiting.

"I come from Transylvania," the woman said proudly. "But Mr. Egor will not get up. I knocked on the door, he doesn't hear."

"That's the way of artists. They sleep a heavy sleep," Mr. Nazarie said speaking rather to himself. But he was worried. He almost ran to Egor's room and knocked so hard on the door that Egor woke up in a fright.

"It's me," the professor apologized, "it's me, Nazarie." He heard the key turn in the lock. Then he heard Egor's steps hastening to the bed. After a decent interval he entered the room. The woman followed with the breakfast tray.

"It looks as if you were fast asleep," Mr. Nazarie said.

"From now on I shall be very fast asleep in the mornings," Egor said with a smile.

Then he silently watched the woman as she carefully placed the tray on the bedside table. He waited for her to leave, then suddenly asked Nazarie, "Tell me, please, what does the room smell of ?"

"Violets," the professor quietly answered.

He thought that Egor was startled and that his face had suddenly turned pale. He tried to smile.

"So it's true," Egor said.

Mr. Nazarie came closer to the bed.

"It's true," Egor continued, "it was no dream, it was Miss Christina herself."

Taking his time, quite collectedly, he told him what had happened that night. He was even surprised at his exact memory of all the details. He spoke gravely, frequently pausing to swallow. His throat was dry. He was thirsty.

★

Before the midday meal Egor heard that Sanda was ill. She wouldn't be able to join them in the dining room. He asked permission to see her just for a few minutes. On that occasion he would also excuse himself for leaving. It would be easy to tell her that he couldn't possibly stay on, now that Mrs. Moscu and herself were both ailing.

"Whatever has happened ?" he asked, trying to sound unconcerned in entering Sanda's room.

The girl gave him a sad look, struggling to put up a smile that would not come. Her eyes indicated a chair. She was alone and Egor felt a bit uneasy. There was a feminine smell in the room, too personal, too warm. The smell of blood.

"I am not at all well," she murmured. "Last night my head was spinning. I had a headache and now I can't even get up."

She looked him deep in the eyes, with love and terror altogether. Her nostrils trembled. Her temples were very white.

"All my strength is gone," she added, "I am exhausted just speaking."

Alarmed, Egor came up to the bed and took her hand.

"But you must not tire yourself out," he began in a live, optimistic voice, "it's probably a cold and a bad headache that has exhausted you. I was just thinking..."

He meant to say : "I was just thinking that we, your guests, are too much for you and that we ought to leave." But the girl suddenly began to weep, her head hanging low.

"Don't leave me, Egor," she whispered feverishly, "don't leave me alone. You are the only one in this house who can save me."

She was addressing him familiarly for the first time. Egor felt a warm flow of blood throbbing in his cheeks. Excitement, happiness, shame at his cowardice, what was it ?

"Don't be afraid, Sanda," he murmured, bowing over her. "Nothing is going to happen. As long as I am here with you, nothing will happen to you."

"Oh, if I could only tell you..."

That minute Egor was prepared to tell her everything he knew, all that had frightened him. But he heard the sound of steps in the corridor and jumped in the middle of the room. He was nervous, excited. Sanda's words, however, had given him unflinching confidence in himself. He was protecting, defending.

Mrs. Moscu entered the room, as if by chance. She did not seem at all surprised to find Sanda sick, under the bedcovers, and Egor standing there in front of her.

"Aren't you going to get up ?" she asked.

"I won't get up today," Sanda answered, trying to speak calmly and smiling, "I want to have a rest."

"The guests have been to much for her," Egor said joking.

"Not by any means," Mrs. Moscu said, "we are always very happy to entertain distinguished guests. Where is Simina ?" she asked, after a short pause.

Egor and Sanda gave each other a quick look, both blushing as if remembering an evil secret, in spite of themselves.

"I haven't seen her," Sanda said.

"I'll go and find her."

Egor thus found an opportunity to retire and return later when Mrs. Moscu would be gone. He set out with a firm step. The look in his eyes was hard, his brow pensively anxious. He was ashamed of his cowardice. He had been meaning to leave and hadn't even dared to tell Mr. Nazarie. He had even contemplated composing a telegram summoning him back as he had once read in a book, long before. Sanda's voice and words had awakened in him a stubborn fury, to risk, to brave danger, as well as to begin a strange devilish adventure, which attracted him like an unknown poisoned fruit.

He inquired in the dining room. No one had seen Simina. He went down the steps of the veranda and made his way to the back rooms of the domestics. It would be an occasion to see the mysterious Nanny. He met the housemaid and asked her.

"The little lady has gone to the old stables."

She pointed to a far-away, half dilapidated shed. Egor made for it calmly, his hands in his pockets, smoking. He would not allow his meeting with Simina to look like an expedition. "A witch's nest," he thought, the minute he entered the stable. It was an old, long neglected building, the roof broken in places. Almost dark. At the far end he caught sight of Simina, sitting in an antiquated barouche. On seeing him the little girl quickly threw down a duster that she had in her hand and stood up. She was expecting him and Egor saw in her eyes that the contest would not be an easy one.

"Why are you hiding here, Simina ?" he asked, pretending to be cheerful and ready for fun.

"I was playing a game," the little girl answered without moving a hair.

"What a funny game !" Egor said coming up, "in the oldest of carriages and full of dust." He grabbed a lantern, but found no dust. He then understood Simina's movement, the duster she had thrown away on his entering.

"It is a very old coach, but it's clean," he added. "I can see you're fond of it, looking after it, keeping it clean."

"No," Simina defended herself, "I was just playing. And I was mindful to keep myself clean."

"So what were you hiding, why did you throw the duster away ?" Egor quickly asked in order to confuse her.

"I couldn't have shaken your hand with that duster," Simina calmly answered. She stopped a minute, smiling. "I thought you were going to shake hands," she added, coquettishly looking him in the eyes.

Egor blushed. He had blundered already.

"Whose carriage was it ?" he asked.

"Miss Christina's," Simina answered.

They looked hard into each other's eyes. "She knows," Egor realized, "she knows what happened last night."

"Aunt Christina," Egor said as if he hadn't noticed anything. "Poor old woman ! What a dilapidated, antiquated carriage, like the poor old aunt herself. These cushions supported her old bones when she would go out for some air."

He laughed.

"This barouche took her all around her lands," he went on, "and the wind set her shivering and disheveled her white hair... or was it grey ?" he abruptly questioned turning to Simina.

The girl had been listening with a smile of infinite pity and mockery. As Egor turned to her, Simina looked back at him, trying to conceal her smile, as if ashamed of his own shame.

"You know perfectly well that Miss Christina," she said, emphasizing that word, "that Miss Christina never grew old."

"We don't know anything about her, neither you, nor I," Egor somewhat brutally interrupted.

"Why do you say that, Mr. Egor," Simina candidly asked, "since you've seen her."

Her eyes had a devilish glitter and a triumphant smile lit her face. "She's luring me into a trap," Egor thought, "but if she utters one more word, I'll throttle her and threaten to kill her, till she confesses all she knows."

"You've seen her picture," Simina added after a carefully considered pause. "Miss Christina died very young. Younger than Sanda. Younger and lovelier," she continued.

Egor stood perplexed a few seconds. He couldn't think what more to say, how to force Simina to give herself away, that he might ask her.

"You like Sanda, don't you ? Am I right ?" Simina suddenly asked.

"I do like her and I'm going to marry her," Egor said, "and you shall come to Bucharest, as my little sister-in-law and I shall raise you myself ! You'll see how all these phantoms shall vanish from your mind !"

"I can never understand why you grow cross with me," Simina timidly defended herself.

The threat, maybe Egor's loud and manly tone, had tamed her. She looked around as if afraid, as if expecting a helpful sign. She suddenly calmed down and began to smile. She was staring into one corner of the shed. Her eyes were now glossy, a faraway look in them.

"No use staring," Egor said again. "No use waiting. Your aunt has long been dead, food for worms and turned into dust. Do you hear me, Simina ?"

He seized her by the shoulders, almost shouting the words in her ear. He was himself taken aback by the harsh voice, by the words he had just shouted. The little girl was actually shaking. She had turned pale and her lips were tight. But as soon as she broke loose, she was herself again. Again she looked over Egor's shoulder, a fascinated, happy look.

"You've given me such a shake," she complained, her hand on her brow. "I've got a headache now. It's easy work to be strong-handed with children," she spoke in a lower voice, as if to herself.

"I want you to wake up and come down to earth, you little witch," Egor flared up again. "I want these phantoms out of your head, for your own sake, for your own salvation."

"You know very well they are not phantoms," Simina now spoke provokingly. She jumped out of the coach and walked past Egor with absolute dignity.

"Don't hurry, we'll go together," Egor said. "I had come to look for you. Mrs. Moscu asked me to. How was I to know that I would find you dusting a barouche some hundred years old."

"It dates since 1900, from Vienna," Simina calmly said, never turning, walking on across the stable. "1900—1935, thirty five years exactly."

They reached the door. Egor opened it wide letting the little girl walk out before him.

"I was sent to look for you because Sanda is ill," he continued, "did you know that Sanda was ill ?"

He was surprised to see a small vindictive smile.

"Nothing serious," he added quickly, "it's only a headache and she keeps to her bed."

The little girl did not answer. They walked side by side, across the large yard, under the cold autumn sun.

"By the way," Egor said before they reached the house, "I meant to tell you something that may interest you."

He took her arm and stooped low over her, to be able to whisper something in her ear.

"I meant to tell you that if anything happens to Sanda, if... do you get me ?... Then it's the end of you, too. That won't be just between you and me, of course. You may tell, but not to Mrs. Moscu. She, poor Mrs. Moscu, is not to blame."

"I shall tell Sanda, not mother," Simina said bluntly. "I'll tell her I don't understand what you've got against me."

She tried to wrench her arm away. But Egor pressed deeper into her flesh. He felt real joy at thrusting his fingers into her soft, tender, devilish flesh. The girl bit her lips in pain, but no tear softened her cold, metallic eyes. This opposition drove Egor out of his mind.

"I'm going to torture you, Simina, not just kill you quickly," he whizzed between his teeth. "I'll only strangle you when I have plucked out your eyes and wrenched away your teeth, one by one. With a red hot iron shall I torture you. Go on, tell this, you know whom to tell. Let's see if..."

That moment he felt such violent pain in his right arm, that he let the girl go free. The strength had oozed out of his body. His arms hung limp along his hips. And he didn't seem to realize where he was, what world he was in.

He saw Simina shake herself into shape, press the pleats of her frock and rub off the marks of his fingers on her arm. He also saw her smoothing her hair with her hand, set her curls in order, and fasten a hidden hoop that had come undone on the way. Simina did all this without looking at him. She didn't even hurry. As if he had ceased to exist. She made her way to the house with a lithe, quick step, displaying a noble grace. Egor looked at her in amazement until her small figure was lost in the shadow of the veranda.

## VIII

After the midday meal Mr. Nazarie and Egor were invited into Sanda's room. They found her even more exhausted, her eyelids blue. Her arms looked very white, resting limp upon a warm woolen shawl. Sanda smiled and pointed to chairs for them to sit down. But Mrs. Moscu, standing by the bed, a book in her hands, continued reading.

*"Viens donc, ange du mal, dont la voix me convie,*
*Car il est des instants où si je te voyais.*
*Je pourrais pour ton sang t'abandonner ma vie*
*Et mon âme... si j'y croyais !"*

She had read very beautifully the last lines, almost in tears. She closed the book with a sigh.

"What was it ?" Mr. Nazarie asked, perplexed.

"The preface to *Antony*, the undying drama of Alexandre Dumas Père," Mrs. Moscu gravely explained.

"The kind of reading that doesn't at all suit the moment," Egor would have liked to say. "Je pourrais pour ton sang t'abandonner ma vie." It was too cruel an irony, almost savage. And then that sigh of Mrs. Moscu's. Regret ? Resignation ? Helplessness ?

"I've been continually reading to her for half an hour," Mrs. Moscu proudly said. "I like reading aloud, as I used to do. I then used to remember thousands of lines by heart."

She was smiling. Egor looked at her astounded. She was now an almost different person, with strong, firm gestures. She had been standing so long at Sanda's bedside and wasn't yet tired. It seemed as though she had been revived by a miracle ; as if she had acquired Sanda's youthful vigor.

"I used to know some poems of Eminescu," Mrs. Moscu added with zest, "poems by the greatest Romanian poet, Mihail Eminescu."

Egor sought Sanda's eyes. They were feverishly bright, as filled with some restrained fear. The young girl stared at him for a second. Then, as if fearing to give herself away, she murmured :

"Mama, you've been reading long enough. You'll be tired. Do sit down."

Mrs. Moscu did not hear. She took her temples between her hands, searching her memory, trying to put together those famous lines..

"Those famous lines," she said, talking to herself, "the eternal lines..."

Sanda did not give up. A volume of Eminescu's poems was there, on the shelf, side by side with other favorite poets, but she would not see the book in her mother's hands, not for the world. She was afraid of her mother's unnatural passion for certain Eminescu poems. Long ago she had told her that though only a little girl of eight or nine, Christina would recite, on a summer's night, lines from Eminescu. "She's going to remember again, now," Sanda thought in terror.

*"Descend, o sweet Hyperion,*
*Glide down upon a ray,*
*Into my home and thoughts anon*
*And brighten up my way."*

With the very first line Sanda bowed her head, depressed. A heavy weariness suddenly took possession of her whole body. A smouldering whirl was sucking in the blood of her veins. Every minute she was afraid of fainting.

"I am the vesper from on high, and you shall be my bride!" Mrs. Moscu went on triumphantly.

"Whence this sudden physical strength, this radiance of her person, the full, melodious voice?" wondered Mr. Nazarie. Mrs. Moscu seemed to remember one stanza after another with brief hesitations, charming fumblings. "There are stanzas that she leaves out, however," Egor noticed. He was listening dumbfounded, almost impassive, his eyes on Sanda, watching her body twitch under the covering shawl. "I ought to do something," he thought, "I ought to get up, go near and comfort her, whatever her mother may think." Though, judging by the ecstasy in speaking her lines as she gradually recalled them, you could see that Mrs. Moscu neither heard nor saw anyone around her.

*"For I am living, you are dead..."*

Mrs. Moscu's voice suddenly broke, overcome. She was dizzily swaying in the middle of the room where the emotional impact had projected her. Again she put both palms of her hands on her brow. A gesture of annihilation, of despair this time.

"I don't know what's wrong with me," she said, "I feel tired."

Mr. Nazarie helped her to a chair. That liveliness, that full and robust voice of a warm-blooded woman, could it possibly have been an illusion ?

"You see, mama, if you won't listen to me," Sanda whispered very faintly.

Egor had come near the bed. He was now scared by the girl's pallor, by those eyes unnaturally sunken in their sockets, the cold skin revealing, however, a fever smouldering deep down.

"I'll go for a doctor right away," he said frowning. "You're not at all well."

Sanda gave him a grateful smile that she tried to maintain as long as possible. But she wouldn't, not in any case, let him call a doctor. Not now at this unexpected outbreak of ancient occurrences and ailings.

"Don't hurry away from me," Sanda said, "I don't need a doctor. I shall be quite all right in a few hours and tomorrow we'll walk in the park."

That minute Mrs. Moscu got up, again animated by a new fervor.

"I remember now, I remember the most beautiful lines of *Lucifer*.

> *"My heartstrings ache when every eve*
> *You vent your cruel desire,*
> *Your eyes, so gloomy, make me grieve,*
> *And scorching is their fire."*

Sanda took Egor's hand. She was trembling. Frightened, she was staring fixedly into his eyes. "She, too, knows," Egor thought. A second after he wondered at his own firmness and self-control. He was no longer scared ; close to Sanda, her frozen hand buried in his hot clenched fists, he felt all that she knew, all that she saw beyond his shoulders, behind his back. He wouldn't turn around, lest he should break the course of that terrified, paralyzed gaze. Mrs. Moscu had now ceased reciting and her silence added a graver note to the unusual silence in the room. Egor could hear the girl's heart thumping. He could also hear Mr. Nazarie's heavy breathing. He, too, feels something, maybe even sees something. No use keeping anything back from him, from now on.

"Mama !" Sanda suddenly exclaimed with a supreme effort.

Egor guessed what Sanda's desperate words meant. It was her attempt to wrench Mrs. Moscu out of that horrible communication, secret, forbidden, inhuman. "Mother, people are watching !" Sanda's eyes seemed to say. Mrs. Moscu turned to Mr. Nazarie.

"Why did you suddenly stop talking, professor ?" she asked in surprise.

"I haven't talked much today, dear lady," Mr. Nazarie apologized. "I was listening to you recite. I was wondering at your memory."

Mrs. Moscu looked him in the eyes, as if trying to make sure he was not joking.

"A poor memory with a book in your hand," she said wearily, placing *Antony* on top of the other books on the shelves. "Fortunately, I still have quite a number of books. Here, I've brought Sanda books for several days' reading."

She pointed to a whole pile. Mr. Nazarie gave them a look : *Jean Sbogar, René, Ivanhoe, Les fleurs du mal, Là-bas.*

"From Christina's library," she added. "The books she liked best. So did I, of course."

She smiled wearily and went to Sanda's bed.

"And you, why did you cease talking ?" she asked with unintelligible surprise. "Why did you, too, stop ?"

Sanda's eyes reproved her. Mrs. Moscu sat on the bed by her. She took the hand that Egor had given up a few minutes before.

"You're frozen, so cold !" she exclaimed shuddering. "I must give you some tea. As a matter of fact it's time to get up. Sunset is almost here. The mosquitos are coming."

"She's raving," Egor thought, somewhat upset. He looked at Sanda for some advice, a sign in her eyes. He, too, was paralyzed, fascinated by this incipient delirium.

"Maybe we had better be going," Mr. Nazarie's dry voice was then heard.

"Nothing to be afraid of, I am here," Mrs. Moscu encouraged them. "They can't hurt you, they fly overhead, that's all."

"You should have taken quinine," Sanda whispered, "mother speaks of mosquitos. They're very dangerous now at sunset."

"They have actually started coming," Mr. Nazarie's dry voice was heard again. "Strange how they swarm in clouds outside the window ! Can you hear them flying, Egor ?!"

Egor, too, did hear them ; whole dense swarms such as he had never seen before. Where did they come from in such numbers ?

"A sign of drought," Mr. Nazarie spoke again. "I'd better close the window."

But he didn't move. He stood there, in the middle of the room, fascinated, his eyes on the swarming clouds outside.

"No need to," Mrs. Moscu said, "it's not yet sundown. Besides, there's nothing to fear as long as you are with me."

Egor felt a shiver running down his spine. This voice, dry, neutral, that he almost failed to recognize, frightened him. A voice coming out of a dream, out of other spheres.

"You should, nevertheless, take quinine, if only half a pill every day," Sanda murmured, this time under her breath.

Her voice trembled, too. Yet now, at least, she no longer sees anything, no longer feels any presence, Egor realized. He looked at the professor. He was still in the middle of the room, he had not moved. His eyes followed, seemingly, some unseen flight, for his look dwelt far above the swarms. Nor did he, in any way, ward off the mosquitos which, little by little, came into the room. "There is a smell inside here that attracts them. Far too many of them curiously coming straight here. Maybe the same smell that struck me this morning," he recalled, "the smell of blood."

Mrs. Moscu gave them all a warm, protective and intimate look.

"Come on, children," she said, "it's almost sundown, let's make her get up."

Her voice was cheerful, yet inattentive. A voice from afar, from a very strange, cold gladness.

"Get up, Sanda," Mrs. Moscu spoke again, "evening is almost here. You're frozen."

Egor clenched his fists, obstinately driving his nails into his own flesh. "I must keep my wits about me. I mustn't lose my head." He tried to retain Sanda but the girl pushed him away, gently and lovingly ; she got out of bed. She was no longer trembling. She very carefully looked for her slippers.

"Must I go, also, mama ?" she asked, very docile.

"Can't you see ? It's time," Mrs. Moscu said.

Egor caught her in his arms and spoke into her ear :

"Stay here. What do you mean to do ?"

The girl stroked his cheek, sadly.

"It's nothing, Egor," she whispered, "I'm doing this for mother's sake, you know."

That minute Egor felt a sharp pin-point piercing the skin of his wrist. Unconsciously he struck it with the palm of his hand. A mosquito was squashed ; a blot of blood nearby. "A beastly sting," Egor thought.

Looking up, Sanda saw that blood smirch. She ran to Egor and took his hand.

"Hide yourself," she spoke hastily, "go away, mother mustn't see you... She turns sick."

Egor rubbed his hand against his clothes till the blood was completely gone.

"Please, go away, I beg you !" Sanda spoke, "go and take your quinine tablet."

Her imploring voice made him more stubborn. This frenzy, the boundaries of which he did not yet know, all these words, the meaning of which he could not grasp !

"I won't leave unless you tell me where you want to go," Egor said menacingly.

"Have no fear, my love," Sanda said.

Egor shuddered. He now remembered most precisely, in every detail, last night's incidents.

"Aren't you glad that I call you that ?" Sanda again asked, sadly.

Egor looked her in the eyes, trying to pierce through her, to use his will power to master her entirely, to keep her to himself. Yet he felt he was losing hold of her, he felt this warm and enticing life slipping through his fingers.

"It's not you who're saying this, Sanda, this is none of your saying !" Egor exclaimed.

Sanda began to weep quietly. "So, it is true," Egor thought.

Mrs. Moscu had come near ; as if those whispered words, the girl's weeping were nothing to her.

"If you stay on they'll suck you up too," she said, "and it's turned so cold, too. They'll suck you up. So it happened to our hens, geese, cattle.. .Whatever was left of them, what was left."

Egor turned his head and said bluntly :

"I'm very sorry, Mrs. Moscu, but Sanda is to stay here in bed till I summon the doctor."

His voice had been so unusually strong that Mrs. Moscu was perplexed, looking in turns at Egor and at Mr. Nazarie. Obviously, she did not quite understand what they were doing here, by the girl's bed.

"You may be right," Mrs. Moscu spoke after a few seconds. "You're both scientists, you know better than me! But do shut the windows quickly. That's what you must do first, shut all windows."

Egor was still shaking after the brutal courage he'd summoned up to speak. Both his arms were pressing down Sanda's body, trying to keep her in bed. The girl tossed, resisting.

"I've to go at all costs," she was drowsily protesting. "I'm doing it for mother's sake, I told you. There's nothing left in the yard... The fowls, the cattle, the dogs!"

Mr. Nazarie, too, had come near, wringing his hands. The mosquitos swarmed around him. You could hear them, a thick, barbarous, and far-away buzz. An oppressive chant like a fever.

"Do let me go, Egor," Sanda again implored, defeated. "It will be worse if you don't. I shall never get well, I tell you."

Egor began to shiver. Why this sudden cold, good God! He could hear Mr. Nazarie's teeth rattling in his mouth. He saw him standing by, petrified, white to the gills, shaking. He did not fight the mosquitos. Occasionally he shook his head to rout them.

"Shut the window, won't you," Egor commanded.

The professor timidly approached the curtains. He dare not go farther. He, too, was behaving as in an unnatural feverish sleep. Yet he clearly understood what was going on around him! Everything that had happened seemed now transparent; that sickly mutton meat of the first evening, the maid's queer words, the fowls dying... That dog, too, crawling at their feet, his blood-curdling howl, the heavy breathing of an animal hunted by the unseen...

"Why don't you shut that window?" came Egor's commanding voice again.

What unusual, unnatural cold! What a vacuum in this room where the smell of the girl's blood had filled the air a short while ago.

Mr. Nazarie went nearer to the window. He was afraid of looking out. A stupid nervous fear that he could not control. In grasping the window handle his arm shook. For the first instant he thought that a woman was looking at him from without, looking intently, watching every gesture, as if waiting for something to happen, a grave, decisive gesture. Daylight was still lingering outside.

The sky was, nevertheless, paler, more fluid. Here was a different space, a different heaven. Closing his eyes for a second and suddenly opening them again, Mr. Nazarie saw Simina, a few meters away from the window, standing among the flowers, gazing at him. He tried to smile on her. The little girl bowed with infinite grace. Yet the very same second she gave herself away. She had been gazing too high up, much above the window. "She didn't expect to see me," Mr. Nazarie realized. She was waiting for someone else, not here at this window, but elsewhere. Simina quickly understood that she had given herself away. She suddenly blushed, took a few steps towards the house and raised her hands to Mr. Nazarie. But the professor gravely, silently closed the window looking down. The cold in the room seemed even more distressing. He stood a long time by the window, frozen, worn out. He could now hear the mosquitos humming very near him, surrounding him on every side, leaving him a wreck. He began to realize that he was dreaming and was afraid. What if he were never to wake from this unearthly sleep, from this world of fevers ?

## IX

It was nearly ten o'clock in the evening when Egor came back from the station. With difficulty he had succeeded in calling Giurgiu, for a doctor. The doctor of the district, who lived in a neighboring village, inspired no confidence.

The lights in the manor were now burning low. He found Mrs. Moscu, Mr. Nazarie, and Simina waiting for him in the dining room. The table was laid. A prematurely old woman, her hair in a cherry-colored kerchief, was pacing about in the dining room. No one spoke. Pale, Mr. Nazarie was staring into the void, like a prisoner taking his rest.

"We shall have a poor meal tonight, you know," Mrs. Moscu said. "The housemaid went to the village and is not back. She won't come back anymore. It's nanny who's serving tonight."

So this is Nanny, Egor thought. He considered her with increased attention. You couldn't have told her age and what a strange gait, as if she'd tried a lifetime to walk limping and was now trying to walk naturally. She would occasionally knock against the furniture feeling no pain. Her head was almost entirely covered by that kerchief. You could see her nose, broad, crushed, white. You could see her mouth, lint-white, like a frost-bitten wound. Nanny always kept her eyes on the ground.

"Anyway, we shall get corn mush with milk and cheese," Mrs. Moscu added.

They sat down. Mr. Nazarie was impatient and perplexed like someone suddenly woken from sleep.

"And Sanda, how has she been feeling ?" Egor asked.

No one answered. Mrs. Moscu had begun eating and very likely never heard the question. Simina was looking for the salt shaker like a good polite girl. Mr. Nazarie looked quite distracted.

"Has anything happened to her ?" Egor asked after a few long silent seconds.

"No. She was asleep when we left," the professor answered. "At least that's what I am hoping. Or, maybe, she had just fainted."

He suddenly looked up from his plate and gave Egor a serious look.

"It would have been better if you had brought the doctor along, I think," he added.

"He will be here in the morning, by the first train," Egor soothingly said. "We must tell the coachman now to get the coach ready for tomorrow at dawn."

Mrs. Moscu was listening with a puzzled look as if she didn't understand who they were talking about.

"I fear we shall soon have no coachman," she mumbled quite calmly. "The man has been asking for his wages today. Nanny, don't you give him his pay before he brings tomorrow's guests from the station."

"It's just the doctor," Egor said.

"There might be others," Mrs. Moscu hopefully said. "It's the height of the season, September. At this time, in previous years, the house was full of guests. A lot of young people, girls and young men of Sanda's age."

The words she had murmured somewhat wistfully sounded even more hopeless in the lonely room.

"There have been plenty of guests this year too," Egor tried to break the silence.

"They left too soon," Mrs. Moscu, continued, "but someone is sure to come... Maybe some relatives."

Simina smiled. She knew that no relative had come to X for some time.

"It's not the best time for company," Egor said, "Sanda is quite seriously ill."

Mrs. Moscu seemed only just then to remember that her daughter was not dining with them, but lay exhausted in bed. She looked for her round the table and made sure that she was not wrong. Sanda was not there.

"I must go and see her," she said, rising unexpectedly.

Simina kept her seat quite calmly. She seemed to ignore that guests were still present, for she began playing with her knife, cutting the corn mush into very thin slices on her plate.

"Why do you teach her so many ugly fairy tales, Nanny ?" Egor asked turning his head.

The woman stopped in the middle of the room, surprised at this strange voice addressing her unexpectedly, flattered, too, that a young and handsome gentleman should speak to her. For a long time she had only spoken to servants. She never entered the big house while the guests were present.

"I haven't taught her any fairy tales, sir," she spoke boldly, "since I don't know any. The young lady is the one to teach me."

She had a dull voice, as if consisting of several lumps. Egor suddenly remembered a play that had been the rage some fifteen years before, remembered the voice of an old woman in it, a poultry merchant. But nanny's voice was unlike anything. Nor were her eyes, of a putrid blue, always on the ground, staring and wet. A blind woman's eyes, you might have said, had she held her head up, stiffly.

"Our young lady who knows all the books," she added grinning.

"She's now trying to smile," Egor realized with a shudder. Those eyes, too, frightened him, in which you'd have expected different looks, not the sunken, smouldering glint betraying a disgusting womanly lust. Egor felt nanny's starved look unclothing and licking him all over. He suddenly flushed up and turned his head away. Shame and disgust caused him almost to forget the question he had asked. However he remembered about it when hearing Simina laugh. The little girl had propped her neck against the back of the chair and was choking with laughter, displaying all her teeth in the strong light of the lamp.

"She's lying !" she managed to say in between fits of laughter.

This laughter was violently humiliating for the two men. The nanny, too, smiled, behind the chairs. "They're making fun of us," Egor thought. "Simina mostly. She has felt the meaning of nanny's looks. That, too, she knows, that, too, she understands !"

Simina pretended to fight down her fits of laughter, concealing her mouth in her napkin, pinching herself hard. Yet she would constantly steal a look at nanny and burst out again, choking, tearful. At last she got hold of the knife and began cutting with it, in short quick movements, as if trying to do something to take her mind off her laughter and calm down.

"Put down that knife," Mr. Nazarie then spoke, "or your guardian angel will turn its back on you."

He had spoken suddenly, but his voice had been severe and grave as if long pondered. All at once, Simina lost her mirth. She drew in her shoulders as if feeling cold. Her face, too, was unusually pale now. Her eyes, however, shone with anger, with impotent hatred. "A good shot, the professor's," Egor thought inspired. "This little witch would now burn us alive, if she only could." He looked into her eyes and could not withstand the fascination, the forces unleashed by Simina's humiliation.

Mr. Nazarie noticed that the nanny was looking intrigued at the door. He turned and saw Mrs. Moscu, frowning, thoughtful, hesitating.

"Strange !" Mrs. Moscu uttered. "Sanda is no longer in her room. I wonder where she could have gone !"

Egor and Mr. Nazarie both jumped up at the same instant and ran to Sanda's room without a word.

"If we only had a decent light, a flashlight," Egor whispered as he ran.

He could think of nothing except that flashight, so very practical, that he didn't have on him.

Sanda's room was dark. Egor struck a match and looked for the lamp. The wick was dry and cold. His hands were slightly shaking. The flame too, shook, yellow, choking in smoke.

"We shouldn't have left her alone," Mr. Nazarie said. "I don't really know what to think."

The professor had spoken with deep sincerity, but Egor did not reply. He had placed the lamp cover and was now carefully raising the wick. When the flame was full, Egor raised the lamp and prepared to leave the room. He seemed to see something indistinguishable in bed. He took a step, holding the lamp high over the bed. He found Sanda lying on the bed, half dressed, her eyes open, looking at him.

"What's happened ?" she asked with difficulty.

Her cheeks were flushed, her breath came quickly as if she was just waking from a great fright or had just stopped running.

"Where have you been ?" Egor now asked.

"Right here."

It was easy to see that she was lying. Her color rose as she spoke and she cupped her hands.

"It's not true," Egor flew at her, "Mrs. Moscu was here a few minutes ago and didn't find you."

"I was asleep," Sanda said. "You woke me."

Her voice shook. The look in her eyes was tearful, imploring. They were begging into Egor's eyes, but they also turned to Mr. Nazarie who stood frowning at a decent distance from the bed.

"Look at yourself, you're still dressed," Egor spoke again, "you haven't even had time to take off your shoes !"

He pulled the cover off the girl's body. There was no possible doubt. Sanda had tumbled into bed and covered herself just a few minutes before. But how did she come and from where ? "This room feels heavy every time I come into it," Egor thought.

"Sanda, where have you been ?" he asked again, his face close to the girl's head. "Tell me where you've been, tell me, my love ! I want to save you ! Do you understand that I mean to save you ?"

He had spoken these last words in despair. The lamp shook in his right hand. Sanda was frightened and nestled near the wall, her fingers clinging to her nouth.

"Do not come near me, Egor !" she cried. "I'm afraid of you ! What do you want ?"

Mr. Nazarie, too, was afraid. For the light shone sideways on Egor's cheek and his eyes burnt with anger.

"What is it that you two want from me ?" she asked again.

Egor gently placed the lamp on the bedside table, then stooped still lower over the girl, took her by the shoulders and began shaking her. He felt the same resistance as at sunset. "She is being taken away from here, she is bewitched too..."

"Wake up, Sanda," he spoke tenderly, "the doctor will soon be here. Why won't you tell me where you've been ?"

Sanda was still shivering ; with cold, with fever. She was biting her lips, wringing her hands.

"Do you love me, Sanda, tell me, do you love me ?" Egor asked again.

The girl began to kick and toss. She wished to bury her head in the pillows, but Egor got hold of it and forced her to look at him, while he kept repeating the same exasperating question.

"I'm scared ! Shut the door !" Sanda suddenly yelled, trembling.

"There is no one at the door," Egor calmed her. "You can see for yourself that it is closed."

He stepped aside that the girl could see the door. Sanda looked up for a second, then buried her face in her hands. She cried, choking as in prolonged, interrupted sighing. Egor sat on the bed by her.

She looked into his eyes, briefly, as if ready to reveal some secret, but she buried her head in her hands again, exhausted.

"Where have you been ?" Egor asked in a whisper.

"I can't tell you," the girl wept, "I can't tell !"

She curled around Egor's body, close to him, frightened, delirious. His warmth was soothing and his masculinity reassuring. But suddenly she drew away as if something pierced her body, frightened, and sought the wall again.

"I don't want to die, Egor," she yelled with unbelievable strength. "I don't want to be killed, too !"

Both men stretched out their arms to catch her as she was fainting.

## X

When they were near the door, ready to leave, Mr. Nazarie turned to Egor saying :

"I feel as if I've been dreaming ever since this morning."

"I wish you were right," Egor said, "but I'm almost sure that we're not dreaming. Unfortunately," he added in a graver tone.

They wished each other good night and separated. Egor locked the door, then went up to the window and closed it. He was moving about the room with utmost care, supervising each gesture, as if preparing to go to bed under the unseen gaze of a hidden presence. He was no longer afraid, but his flesh was weary, his blood sick, as after a fever. He had in mind to stay awake a good bit of the night. The clock would soon strike two ; one more hour and he could safely go to bed, for at daybreak he would be safe from all dreams.

However, as soon as he put on his pyjamas, he couldn't resist any longer. He shook his head, slapped his body several times, but couldn't get rid of that heavy weariness that had suddenly crept into his veins. He fell asleep, the lights on, his arms above the bed cover. His head lay sideways on the white pillow. Above him, a few unseen mosquitos were buzzing up the ceiling.

He suddenly found himself in a large drawing room with gilt walls, huge chandeliers hung with arrow-shaped crystal ornaments. "Yes, it's the beginning of the dream," Egor thought tossing about, trying to escape, but he was genuinely surprised seeing so many unknown people, so elegantly dressed, the women particularly, wearing long evening dresses, slim in the waist.

"Vous êtes à croquer !" he heard a man's voice beside him.

Then the laughter of women. "Wherever have I heard the same words ?" Egor asked himself quite perplexed. "Or maybe I read them somewhere, long ago." But he remembered that everything was just a dream and calmed down. "If only I could wake up soon..."

Strange and well-known music was unexpectedly about him. An old melody, of melancholy mirth, bringing hazy memories of childhood and dreams rather than of actual incidents. He started carefully making his way among those well-dressed couples. He realized that people around were dancing. He kept out of the dancers' way, slipping along the walls. "Yes, this is roughly 1900. How surprised these people must be seeing my dress." He considered himself rather shyly and found it difficult to identify himself ; he didn't recognize these clothes, had never worn them. The same instant, however, he thought there was no point in these perplexities. They were speaking French next to him. The voice of a young woman, conscious of being listened to and voices of unseen men. "She knows I'm here," Egor thought with delight. He took a few steps to the mirror, that he might see the woman's face. She, too, looked at him. Very red lips and a slight dark shade above the mouth. He didn't know her. Maybe she wanted him to be introduced, she had smiled at him, but the whole strange company was gazing at him. He didn't know anyone in this drawing room that he had unintentionally entered. He passed on into another room. Tables covered with green cloth. "They're playing cards," Egor quickly thought, "I'm not interested." He wondered, however, since he heard none of the words they were speaking.

He went back into the dancing hall. It was warmer now. The women fanned themselves with big silky fans. He felt someone piercingly watching him from a corner. He turned round. The face seemed familiar. But he couldn't remember the name. Then a sudden flash of light : Radu Prajan. What can he be doing here ? And so much changed, too ! How absurdly dressed! His friend considered him attentively, never blinking. You could see that this party of rich, pleasure-seeking people was no place for him. No one talked to him. Egor made for the sofa against which Prajan was leaning. He understood what his eyes were saying : hurry, come as soon as possible, as near to him as possible.

How difficult, though, to walk through the ballroom. New couples continually crossed Egor's path. He elbowed his way through, politely excusing himself to begin with ; later, annoyed by so many impediments, he shoved people, stepping on ladies' shoes, thrusting his arms out. The few meters separating him from Prajan now seemed absurdly long. He had long been struggling to reach him, yet Prajan was equally far away, looking constantly into his eyes, waiting. He clearly understood his summons.

He suddenly felt a woman's arm round his waist. That moment the couples around him became misty, all at once. He turned his head to look at Prajan. He could only see his eyes. He had risen very high up and his disguise now seemed even more ridiculous, more absurd.

"Come, look at me, my love !"

Miss Christina had spoken close to his ear. He felt her warm, enticing breath and recognized the heavy smell of violets. He could feel the former terror and disgust, too.

"You're not keen on our parties, Egor," Miss Christina added.

Every word stupefied him. Each sound projected him into a different space, a different atmosphere.

"This is our own house, my love !" Christina said.

She had now taken him by the hand, her other arm pointing to the walls of the room they were walking through. Egor recognized the dining room. Nothing was changed ; the furniture looked more fresh, less somber.

"Will you come to my room ?" Christina suddenly asked.

She tried to make him climb the stairs by force, but Egor resisted. He drew near the window, made an effort and said :

"You're dead. You know you are dead."

With a sad smile Miss Christina approached Egor again. She was now white in the face, maybe bathed in the light of the moon. "A sudden, unexpected moon," Egor thought.

"But I'm in love with you, Egor," she murmured. "It's for you that I've come all this way, from afar."

Egor regarded her with hatred. If only he had the strength to shout, to wake up. As if she read his thoughts, Christina gave a sadder, more desperate smile.

"You're always here," Egor spoke, "you don't come from any other place."

"You'll never understand, my love !" Christina whispered. "For I don't want to destroy you, I don't want your blood... I just want you to let me make love to you, sometimes !"

She had spoken so passionately, ravenously starving for love, that Egor was frightened. He tried to run away. It seemed he was running along an endless corridor, never seen before, sinister. In a few seconds he thought he was alone. Frightened, tired, he breathed heavily. He began to walk at random, dizzy, not knowing where he was going. His thoughts were scattered, his will power blind. The corridor stretched on like a tunnel in a coal mine. He suddenly felt a vague smell of violets blowing into his face. Egor hesitated a moment then momentarily decided to open the first door he came to. The blood was violently throbbing in his temples. He stopped, his head against the door, listening. Would he again hear Miss Christina's step? The silence persisted for long seconds. Worn out, Egor turned his head. He was in his own room. Unwittingly he had entered his room. Everything was there : the box of cigarettes on the table, as well as the glass where the last drops of cognac evaporated. And yet in such queer light all these things appeared... as if perceived in a mirror.

Egor threw himself on the bed. "If I could only fall asleep soon," he thought. But the smell of violets was there too ! This time he had no strength to oppose, to run away, Miss Christina was right by his side as if she had long been waiting for him, sitting on the bed.

"Why do you run away, Egor ?" she asked looking him fixedly in the eyes. "Why won't you let me make love to you ? Or, maybe, you really love Sanda, do you ?"

She ceased, still looking at him — sadly, impatiently, or was it menacingly ? Egor found it difficult to understand. He could hardly read that face, so much alive, yet so frozen. The eyes, too, were too big, too unmoving, like two crystal rings.

"If Sanda is dear to you, she won't be anymore... she will not live long, poor, thing."

Egor sat up in bed. He wanted to put out his arms, to menace, but he only found the strength to hold her eyes.

"But you are dead, Christina !" he shouted. "You can no longer love !"

Christina laughed. It was the first time he had heard her laugh. Just as he had imagined she would, a few days ago when looking at her picture : a girl's laughter, sincere and pure.

"Don't you appraise me quite so soon, my love !" Christina exclaimed. "I come from other climes. Yet I am still a woman, Egor ! And since there have been girls falling in love with evening stars, why shouldn't you fall in love with me ? !"

She waited a few seconds, waited for Egor's reply.

"I cannot," he said at last. "I am afraid of you !"

He was then ashamed of this cowardly avowal. He ought to have resisted, telling her repeatedly that she was dead, while he was alive... Christina put out her hand to caress him. Egor again felt that unseemly touch which froze the blood in his veins.

"One day, you shall take me in your warm arms," Christina spoke softly.

The voice was intimate, very low. Her body had drawn very near.

"You will then make love to me, Egor. Don't think of Sanda any more, you won't see her again."

She ceased again, stroking him as before.

"How handsome you are ! So warm and strong. I'm not afraid of you. No matter where this love is to lead me, I'm not afraid. Why do you hesitate, Egor, you who are a man ? !"

Egor tried once more to fight free of Christina's spell, to stop the dream. The smell of violets made his head turn, the proximity of Christina's body left him limp. He only succeeded in drawing away from her towards the wall.

"I love Sanda," he murmured, "and my prayers are to the Lord God and to Holy Mary, Mother of God !"

He had begun in a whisper but the last words he said loud enough. Christina jumped from the bed where she had been sitting and buried her face in her hands. She stood there a long time, away from him.

"I could have frozen your thinking and dried up your tongue," she said. "I could have you in my power any time, Egor ! I can easily bewitch you, do anything I like with you. You would follow me like the others have. And there have been many, Egor. I am not afraid of your prayers. You're only a living human being. I come from other climes. You won't understand, no one can understand. But you, my love,

I did not mean to kill, I meant to wed you. You'll soon see me differently and then you'll love me, Egor. Last night you weren't so afraid of me, nor shall you be now, my love; you'll wake up now, when I'm telling you to, you'll wake up."

It was late when Egor realized that he had been long lying open-eyed, with no thoughts, no memory. He suddenly remembered Christina. "I woke up at her command," he understood. He knew where he had left her in his dream: in the middle of the room, standing upright, gazing on him with those glassy eyes. He suddenly turned his head. Miss Christina was no longer there. "So it was a dream, I've just been dreaming." His blood again rushed from all sides to his heart. A weary enchantment invaded his flesh, as if he'd won a tough battle and his muscles were ready for rest.

The smell of violets was still strong in the room. And in a few seconds Egor was aware of something unseen and unknown about him. It was not Miss Christina's presence. He felt being watched by someone else, the terror of whom he hadn't yet experienced. Fear now took on a different aspect; as if he had suddenly awoken in a strange body, sick of his own flesh and blood, as well as of that cold sweat that he felt, but that was not, however, his own. The pressure of that strange body was impossible to bear. It throttled him, left him no breathing space, exhausted him. Someone was by him, looking at him, and the gaze was not Miss Christina's.

He was never to remember how long that slow throttling was, the nausea that had confused his whole body. Occasionally, he could feel the smell of violets deep in his nostrils, vying with the other one's terror, with that obscure presence. The memory of Miss Christina now seemed far less frightening. Compared to the frozen frenzy of the other one, Miss Christina's presence was infinitely more soothing, more gentle.

Suddenly, against hope, he felt free. He could at last breathe normally, deeply. The other presence had completely vanished. The smell of violets now grew with renewed force, warm, feminine, wrapping him round. He was no longer afraid of it. Egor opened his eyes wide, searching the darkness around. When had she approached, what immaterial steps had brought her so near the bed? She was now smiling. Gazing, as before, in the dream, smiling on him. Her face seemed illuminated from within, for Egor could see the broken line of her smile, the thin nostrils, the eyelashes slightly lowered. "You see, you're no longer afraid of me now ?" her eyes seemed to say. "There are things more fearful than my approach, Egor. I brought here the terror of the other one, more cruel and devilish than I am."

"She makes me read her thoughts, she commands me what to think," Egor understood. "Yet why doesn't she speak, why doesn't she come near me ? I couldn't resist now."

Whose thought was this, entering his mind almost unaware ? Had he actually been thinking that he wouldn't be able to defend himself, or was it Miss Christina ordering him to think that, preparing him for new developments ?

Christina went on smiling. "You see, you're no longer afraid of me," her eyes seemed to say. "The steps of terror go down a long way, my love. You'll cling to me, you'll embrace me, at my breast you'll find the only hope, the only salvation, Egor !" Egor could hear all these words ever so distinctly, words that her lips were not uttering, but her looks were speaking.

"You'll love me," her eyes seemed to say. "You saw how easy it's been to throttle you with terror. Someone came near you and it was enough, you lost control. Someone you don't know, but will always remember. There are hundreds and thousands like him and they're all under my orders, Egor, love. You'll fall into my arms ! My loins shall be so warm for you, dearest !"

One thought after another, no haste, normally, clearly did Egor watch himself thinking. Miss Christina, of course, knew all that was going on in his mind ; seeing him worn out and sobered down, she took a step towards him. Then another one, until she was very near. And it was no dream any longer. Egor distinctly felt that unreal body moving in space, pushing the air about it, warming it. "I shall once come naked into your bed and ask you then to hold me tight in your arms, my love," Egor surprised himself in thinking. "Get used to me being by your side, Egor. See, this is my hand that strokes you and you're not frightened, it brings you joy, this hand does ; can you feel it now, gently resting on your cheek ?"

But Egor no longer felt anything. As Miss Christina's hand touched his cheek, his blood seemed to run havoc, his breathing rattled low down in his chest. His face white, his brow frozen, he lay limp in bed.

## XI

The doctor was detained for dinner. When Mr. Nazarie entered the dining room, Mrs. Moscu stood up and solemnly introduced the bald young man in hunting attire.

"Doctor Panaitescu, a distinguished scientist and an untiring apostle," she said. Then turning to the doctor, she added, putting her arm out : "Professor Nazarie, a glory of Romanian science."

Mr. Nazarie looked down. He was tired, nervous, he seemed to be dreaming. He shook the doctor's hand and sat down. He was struck by Egor's white face, by his dark-ringed eyes. He began reproaching himself for his callousness ; he had left early that morning, to inspect the diggings in the northern part of the village and had not seen his companion. He now found him changed, exhausted. He sought his eyes to understand by his look whatever may have happened. Egor's brow was low, thoughtful, perhaps just sad.

"The professor is busy with archaeological digging in our village," Mrs. Moscu went on. "It is an honor to have him as a guest."

"Did you find anything of interest so far, professor ?" the doctor asked.

"Oh, we're just starting work," Mr. Nazarie murmured.

Simina was expecting him to continue ; to speak long and fast, happy to get the opportunity, but Mr. Nazarie was in no mood to talk that day. He asked, giving the doctor an inquiring look :

"What is your opinion concerning Miss Sanda ?"

The doctor shrugged, then quickly recollected himself. He gently stroked his forehead, his hand advancing to the top of his head as if he were himself shocked by that shining, dry pate that his fingers touched.

"It's difficult to say," he hesitated. "Anyhow it's none too serious. Excessive anemia and, possibly, a touch of flu. Quite a strange type of flu, as a matter of fact. At first I thought it might be an intermittent fever."

He spoke stumbling over every word, pausing long after every sentence. "Maybe he's not even thinking of the patient," Mr. Nazarie thought considering, in spite of himself, the doctor's hunting outfit. The doctor noticed his look and promptly blushed.

"You're probably surprised at this tunic," he said, taking hold of a button and twisting it. "It's quite a comfortable suit. The days are so fine so I thought it would be a good thing... I am no inveterate hunter, you know, but I do like to go out into the fields with a gun. Intellectuals, you can well imagine, are condemned, it is seldom that we can... But I have no dog and by myself it is of course more difficult."

He began to eat, ill-at-ease. Mr. Nazarie had long been busy with his plate.

"When do you go shooting, doctor?" Simina amiably asked.

The doctor answered by a vague gesture of his hand. He was, however, quite content that someone had spoken of shooting. He no longer felt alone, ridiculous, compromised at this meal in such strange company.

"Would you take me along?" Simina asked again, more eagerly. "I've never been and I would so much like to go shooting once, or at least to look on..."

"Gladly, with pleasure, why not?" the doctor promised.

Egor looked up and slowly gazed at Mrs. Moscu and then at Simina.

"Not at all the thing for a little girl like yourself to go shooting," he said severely. "To see innocent animals dying, to see that much blood."

In saying these last words he looked into her eyes, but Simina didn't appear to be embarrassed at all. She lowered her eyes like any well-bred child when snubbed by her elders. Not for a second did she let Egor think that she had gathered other meanings in his speech, something the others did not understand.

"In fact it's not the best entertainment for a child," the doctor said conciliatorily. "Later, when you're grown up..."

Simina smiled. Mr. Nazarie recognized her ever-present smile, triumphant, contemptuous, yet discreet. He was beginning to be scared of her, intimidated, sometimes paralyzed by her intensely serious, crushing gaze. Owing to what unnatural perverse force did that cold irony show on the angelic oval shape of her face?

"I am glad that our young lady Sanda shall soon get well and force Egor to paint," Mr. Nazarie suddenly spoke in order to divert the discussion.

Egor turned to him, his face bright. His lips, however, were slightly trembling. He was unusually pale, too. "I wonder why no one should notice such a change." That same instant he spied Simina's cold, hard eyes and he blushed ; it was as if she had heard him or read his thoughts. "Simina is the only one to notice," he thought, upset.

"Within a few days she will be all right again, won't she, doctor ?" Egor asked.

The doctor shook his head vaguely, benevolently.

"What about the shooting ?" Mrs. Moscu seemed suddenly to remember. "You haven't told us anything about it. I can hardly wait for a piece of venison. What fresh, tasty meat, what fine meat !"

Her eyes were alight for a few seconds, and her outstretched arm shivered as if ready for the juice of that unknown venison.

It was then that Egor first realized that the nanny had come into the room, waiting attentively by the door. The woman who attended at meals was a newcomer. "Maybe she's supervising her," Egor thought in order to calm his nerves. He deeply disliked the presence of nanny. He had the painful, yet vague sensation that she was making fun of him, that she and Simina constantly exchanged glances, that they both knew what was happening in his dreams...

"Honored hostess," the doctor began in a dignified manner, "shooting is not, of course, my highest achievement. I hope, however..."

That moment the nanny approached Mrs. Moscu's chair saying :

"The elder young lady wishes to see you."

"Why didn't you say so from the first ?" Egor asked angrily, rising.

The nanny said nothing. She looked at Simina biting her lips. Mrs. Moscu rose quite perplexed. Egor had left the dining room before she could even say a word.

Sanda was waiting for them, her head propped against pillows, quite collected. She gave a start as Egor was first to enter.

"What is it ?" he asked anxiously.

The girl gave him a long, loving look. She seemed to be afraid of this great happiness, that she could no longer enjoy, since it was coming too late.

"It's nothing, Egor," she murmured. "I want to see mother... to ask her to read to me," she quickly added.

Egor was upset. "Absurdly lying, thoughtlessly getting herself tied up. This morning she felt tired of reading. Now she calls her mother from the dining room to read verse to her."

"This is no place for Mrs. Moscu," he said severely, "no place for her at this hour."

He went up to the door and turned the key. The blood rose to his cheeks, but a decision was taken. He had to find out, at any risk.

"Please tell me now," he gently added.

Sanda looked at him in terror. She was a prey to so many thoughts, so many feelings that she no longer realized what was happening. She hid her face in her hands. A second and she felt Egor's hand on her brow.

"Tell me, dearest," he whispered. He waited. Sanda continued holding her face in her hands. Her breast was heaving, her shoulders were trembling.

"For I, too, have many things to tell you," Egor added. "The doctor has revealed the secret of your illness."

Sanda's body gave another jerk. She raised her head and looked at Egor trying to understand.

"But before that," he continued, "I want to ask you something. Do you often see Christina? I'm asking you because I see her."

The room swam before her eyes. Egor suddenly pounced on her, taking her hands, pressing them. The imprint of his fingers hurt her, a violent, keen pain.

"I see her myself," Egor again spoke, "just as you all do. But this madness is not going to last long now, Sanda. I will pierce the ghost's heart. With a pointed wooden stake I will pierce it !"

His words had been so loud that he shuddered hearing them. He had uttered them in spite of himself. The thought had come on the spur of the moment, the thought of speaking clearly and brutally to Sanda, once and for all.

"I was rather thinking of you, my love," she suddenly began in a toneless voice. "I was thinking that you have nothing to do with all this, that you must get out of here, leave as soon as you can."

"However, yesterday you begged me to stay," Egor said.

"That was my mistake," Sanda continued. "Had I only imagined... but I love you, Egor, I love you !"

She wept. Egor relaxed his grip that he might stroke her head, her cheek.

"I, too, love you, Sanda ; I did it for your sake."

"Don't do anything, Egor," Sanda interrupted, "or it will be worse for us. For you, most of all. It's about you I was concerned. If you could just leave, go far away, that's what I was calling mother for ; to tell her that in her absence you'd been impertinent... to say that I can no longer receive you in my room ; to ask her to throw you out."

She began sobbing. Egor had listened calmly, caressing her with the same brotherly gesture, He had expected graver, more maddening news. "That's what Christina ordered her to do, put me out. She thinks she's doing it for my sake, to save me..."

That moment someone tried the door handle. Sanda gave a start. Her face had suddenly turned red. "Modesty, which means that she is not yet lost, not thoroughly bewitched," Egor thought.

"Why did you lock the door ?" said Mrs. Moscu.

Egor rose and went to the door. He chose his words very carefully.

"Sanda asked me to lock the door, dear Mrs. Moscu. She wants to be alone for a while. She's afraid of any member of the family... She had fallen asleep and seemed to see aunt Christina, her dead aunt."

Mrs. Moscu said no word. She continued to stand by the door, trying to understand.

Egor went back to the bed, took Sanda's hand and whispered into her ear :

"They'll think we locked ourselves in here because we are in love. They'll think whatever they please, but this is compromising for you, it demands that you accept me as a fiancé. We must get engaged, now, Sanda."

Mrs. Moscu shook the door handle again.

"But this is not done !" her voice said, slightly altered. "What are you doing in there ?"

Sanda was ready to get out of bed and open the door, but Egor pressed her down with both arms.

"Mr. Paşchievici !" Simina's voice called.

Egor went to the door again.

"Sanda is now my fiancée," he said calmly. "She asked my protection and won't let me open the door. She wants to stay here, alone with me."

"A funny engagement, locked in the bedroom," Simina said loudly.

Sanda wept burying her head in the pillows. Egor could hardly control himself.

"We are ready to leave within the hour, Mrs. Moscu," he said, "for Sanda is now quite restored."

He heard the steps receding along the corridor. He turned to the bed. He pressed his temples with both hands. "What have I done ? What have I done ?!" How did he suddenly find so much strength and madness to make this decision ?

"Do you feel sorry, Sanda ?" he asked, stroking her brow ; "do you feel sorry for being my fiancée in spite of yourself ?"

The girl stopped crying, gave him a frightened look, then put her arms around his neck. It was her first gesture as a lover. Egor again felt strong, powerful, happy.

"Are you actually sorry ?" he asked once more in a trembling voice.

"If only I weren't dead before that !" Sanda whispered, shuddering.

## XII

A few hours later Egor met Mr. Nazarie in the dining room. He seemed much upset, his eyes bewildered, his gestures impatient, precipitated.

"What's going on ?" he asked under his breath. "Mrs. Moscu has locked herself in her room, you locked yourself in Sanda's room, the little girl has disappeared... What's going on ?"

"I don't quite know what has happened," Egor said wearily. "I only know I got engaged to Sanda. I love her, I want to take her away as soon as possible."

He was moved, disturbed. Mr. Nazarie was wringing his hands.

"I'm afraid on her account, I fear for her life," Egor added in a whisper. These people, mad as they are, are quite capable of throttling her."

Mr. Nazarie well knew that Egor was lying, that it was not Mrs. Moscu's madness that worried him. He nodded, however, as if convinced.

"A very good thing, this engagement," he said. "It shall put a stop to all misunderstandings. No one shall have anything to say."

Egor could not help a gesture of impatience and fear.

"We got engaged and there she is fainting," he spoke in a strangled voice. "Sanda's been in a swoon for the last half hour. And I can't do anything. What could I do ?"

He began pacing the room and smoking.

"We ought to leave this place, run away as fast as possible, while there's still time. But the doctor must see her. Where is the doctor ?"

"He's gone shooting," Mr. Nazarie shyly said. "He left right after our meal. I didn't know anything, either. The housemaid told me. But he said he would be back in the evening."

Egor sat down, thoughtfully finishing his cigarette.

"I locked her in," he said suddenly, fumbling in his pockets. "Here is the key to her room."

He produced it triumphantly. "There's a strange glint in his eyes, too," Mr. Nazarie thought, "Goodness knows what he's been up to."

"If only they didn't get in by the window," Egor said looking into empty space. "Especially now, when sunset is near."

"So what do you intend to do ?" Mr. Nazarie asked.

Egor smiled a secret smile. He seemed to hesitate in confessing his entire plan.

"I'm going to look for Simina," he finally spoke. "I have an idea where she must be hiding, the little witch."

"I should hope you won't fight a child," Mr. Nazarie said, "I mean you won't hurt her."

Egor suddenly got up and took the professor's arm. Gravely, solemnly, he gave him the key of Sanda's room.

"You know which room is hers," he said. "I ask you to keep an eye on her till I come back. Lock yourself in, from the inside. I'm afraid of them," Egor added. "To think I've left her alone all this time."

They left the dining room making for Sanda's room. The house seemed deserted. They did not meet anyone, no sound from anywhere. A window still had drawn blinds, as on a midsummer afternoon. The silence there, in the shadow, was more depressing.

"Wait for me here and don't open the door, except for me, no matter what happens," Egor whispered unlocking the door.

Mr. Nazarie went in, disturbed. Nothing serious has happened in this room, so he realized cursorily glancing everywhere. Sanda seemed to be plunged in deep sleep, her breathing light, inaudible.

★

Egor dashed straight to the old stable. It was almost dark inside. The glass panes were now dimmer. Egor made his way to Miss Christina's coach. He looked carefully in every corner, but did not find Simina's small body. "She's hiding elsewhere," he thought. He began inspecting the coach; it was old, shabby, corroded by rain, the cushions shrivelled up. He stood undecided a few seconds, thinking of Simina, wondering where to look for her.

As he walked out of the stable, the sun was sinking far away beyond the border of the fields. "It will soon be dark," Egor thought with fear. "The mosquitos will be swarming." He didn't know which way to go. He started walking thoughtfully with a swinging gait to the servants' quarters. He couldn't see anyone. The place seemed empty and the loneliness more frightening among so many walls and so many tools. People had recently been there. You could see traces of fire, ashes and half-burnt brushwood. You could also see dry linen dusters, forgotten earthen pots, cattle dung and seeds. In spite of all, the silence was so absolute that the place seemed deserted. No dog barking, no bird in sight.

Egor reached the entrance of the cellar; he had been inside on the first day of his arrival. He had gone down with a group of guests. Sanda had shown them the steps dating from the time of Tudor Vladimirescu and the walled-in nook at the far end where one of their ancestors had been hiding, staying three weeks under ground. A faithful servant would bring him, at night, a pot of milk and a loaf of white bread. Sanda had shown them the hole where the servant crept in. How long it was since that warm, clear autumn day when Sanda's eyes sparkled playfully and you could hear so many young voices on the steps of the cave. It seemed weeks separating them from that happy time, yet only a few days had gone by.

He lit a cigarette and went on his way to the kitchen. He seemed to hear light footsteps behind him. He turned his head. No one. The sounds had bean clear, however, quite definite, and they were not like sounds in the night, but live steps. He waited a few seconds, intently, trying to make as little noise as possible ; Simina's figure appeared at the mouth of the cave. Seeing Egor, the little girl was startled, but she put her hands behind her back in a seemly way and came up to him.

"I am no good at labels," she said looking him right in the face. "Mother sent me to fetch a bottle of mineral water from the cellar and I couldn't manage. So many labelled bottles. And I didn't dream it was so dark in there."

"Since when does Mrs. Moscu send you to fetch bottles of mineral water ?" Egor asked. "There are plenty of servants in the house."

Simina shrugged and smiled.

"I don't know what's up, but there is only nanny left. The others say they've gone grape cutting, it's vintage time."

She stretched her bare arm northward, pointing over the acacias.

"There was a new housemaid, too," she added, "but she fell ill. It's so difficult to do all the work without help."

Egor approached and stroked her hair. She had soft, nice smelling, warm hair. Simina welcomed the fondling, lowering her lashes.

"I shall be sorry for you, Simina, in leaving you here to work without help," Egor said, "we're leaving tomorrow morning, Sanda and I."

The little girl slowly drew away from Egor's caress, controlling herself. She looked up at him, surprised.

"Sanda is ill," she said, "and the doctor won't let her."

"She hasn't been ill exactly," Egor interrupted, "she was actually frightened. She thought she saw her dead aunt."

"That's not true," Simina said quickly.

Egor laughed. He threw away his cigarette, smoothed the hair on his brow. Plenty of hurried gestures as if he were trying to prove to Simina how absurd her interruption had been.

"After all, that's neither here nor there," Egor added, "tomorrow we're leaving."

Simina put up a smile.

"Mother is certainly waiting for me to bring the bottle of mineral water," she said thoughtfully. "Would you kindly help me ?"

"She's laying a trap," Egor thought. A shudder passed through him as she pointed to the entrance of the cellar. But the girl considered him with such contempt that he was ashamed of his fear.

"I shall be glad to," Egor said, making his way to the cellar.

Simina's invitation relieved his apprehension. Maybe she had actually been in the cellar to look for a bottle of mineral water.

"Do you know where the bottles are ?" he asked, going down the stone steps.

He could hear Simina's excited breathing as she followed him. "If she's so excited, that means I've fallen into the trap," Egor thought.

"They are farther on, farther on," Simina answered.

Egor had come to the bottom of the steps. He could feel the damp sand of the cellar under his soles.

"Wait, I'll strike a match," Egor said.

Simina grasped his arm. The movement had been sudden, commanding.

"There's still light enough to see," she said. "Or maybe you are afraid ?"

She was laughing. Egor felt the same shudders of terror along his spine, the same as on the previous night. It didn't sound like Simina's normal laughter. Her voice, too, changed — commanding, sensual, feminine. Egor clenched his fists. "I've been a fool," he thought. He struck the match, however, and looked severe, threatening Simina. The little girl burst out laughing again.

"Egor, our brave Egor !" she said with infinite contempt.

She then blew out the light and walked ahead showing the way.

"Simina, when we get out, I will box your ears !"

"Why not do it now ?" Simina answered, stopping and putting her hands behind her back. "Just you dare !"

Egor started to tremble. A strange fever was getting hold of his body. "That's probably how it begins. That's how all madness begins."

"If you are frightened you're free to go back!" Simina spoke again.

How strange that unknown voice sounded on her small red lips! Egor felt the poison in his blood; an insane beastly appetite coursing through his body. He closed his eyes trying to remember Sanda's face. He only saw a wave of crimson steam. He only heard the little girl's bewitched voice.

"Come on, don't be afraid," she spoke again.

Egor followed her. They entered the third partition. You could hardly see old rotten cupboards against the walls. A barred glass pane still glimmered a filthy, weary light. Bags and torn rush baskets in one corner.

"What is the matter?" Simina asked, approaching him.

She took his hand. Egor acquiesced, breathing heavily. His eyes grew dim. He was suddenly in a dream dreamt long ago, vainly trying to remember when he had come out of it, when he had started a new life. "How snug this is, how snug by Simina's side!"

"Sit down!" the little girl commanded.

That's what he ought to have done from the first, throw himself on the bags and rest. His limbs were burning, his hands shaking. He felt Simina's body close.

"Is she here?" Egor asked almost in spite of himself.

"No. It's still too early," the little girl whispered.

"But this is where she dwells, isn't it?" Egor asked, as if in a dream.

Simina hesitated for a second. Finally, she smiled: there was nothing to be afraid of. Egor could no longer resist. His mind, too, was now wandering.

"She's here, close to us!" Simina whispered is his ear.

Egor was trembling violently, shaken by a fever.

"Are you not afraid?" he asked again.

Simina laughed and raised herself to stroke his hair.

"It's good to be with her; I am not afraid. Nor shall you be afraid!"

"Simina, don't leave me alone!" Egor yelled, holding her tight.

He hugged her hard, blindly.

"Calm down," Simina whispered.

Then, after a second, she put her mouth to his ear.

"Don't lock your door tonight; she'll come in person. She'll come to you, naked."

She laughed, but Egor no longer heard her excited laughter. Everything was dancing before his eyes, playing havoc with his mind, with his memory.

"What a fool you are, Egor!" Simina said again. "And so weak! Were I to leave you, you would die from fear!"

"Don't you leave me, Simina!" Egor rattled in his throat, inaudibly. "Forgive me, Simina! Don't leave me alone!"

He began kissing her hands. Cold sweat was running down in drops from his forehead. His breathing grew difficult and hot.

"Not like this, Egor, not this way!" Simina murmured. "You shall kiss me as I want you to."

She pressed her mouth on his, biting into his lips. Egor felt unspeakable happiness, heavenly and holy, in his flesh. His forehead backwards, he abandoned himself to that kiss of blood and honey. The little girl had crushed his lips, wounding them. Her unripe body remained cold, slim, fresh. Feeling the blood, Simina lapped it thirstily. But she soon sprang to her feet.

"I don't like it, Egor. You can't kiss, you're a fool!"

"Yes, I am," Egor murmured dumbfounded.

"Kiss my shoe!"

She stretched her foot. Egor seized the little girl's leg and began kissing it.

"The shoe, I said!"

What delight in that unthinkable humiliation. In that warm poison! Egor kissed her shoe.

"You're a fool! I would like to thrash you! And there is nothing here, there's no whip here!"

Egor began to weep, his head limp on the sack.

"Don't weep, you're a bore!" Simina yelled. "Take your coat off!"

Egor undressed slowly, without a thought, his face smeared with dust and tears, a few marks of blood round his mouth. The smell of blood had maddened Simina. She approached the man's bare chest and began scratching, biting. The deeper the pain in the flesh the sweeter Simina's nail or mouth felt. "And yet, I ought to wake from this dream," Egor thought once more. "It's time for me to wake up, or I shall go mad. I cannot bear it any longer, I simply cannot !"

"Why don't you groan ?" Simina asked. "Why don't you struggle ?"

Her scratching was now furious, vehement. But Egor had no reason to groan. The humiliation dripped in delights he had never thought possible for a human being to taste.

"You are a coward!" Simina spoke. "You're just as musch of a coward as the others ! I can't think how she ever fell in love with you."

She stopped abruptly. As if she were afraid too. She was listening.

"Is anyone coming ?" Egor asked sleepily.

"No. But we must go back. Maybe Sanda has died."

Egor woke up, terrified, his hands on his temples. A fearful pain, like a drill in his brain. He realized where he was, he remembered everything quite clearly, but he couldn't remember how he got there, how he had suffered it all.

A fearful loathing for himself, aversion to Simina's body, disgust of life. But there was no strength left in him. Not even the strength to look into her face.

"Don't forget what I told you," Simina added setting her dress right. "Don't lock your door."

"She doesn't even take the trouble to challenge me," Egor thought, "she knows I shall lack the nerve to tell, to expose her."

Simina waited for him to get up from those bags, to put on his coat. She wouldn't help him. She just looked on, distant, contemptuous, smiling a wan and bitter smile.

## XIII

Mr. Nazarie was impatiently counting the minutes. The dark was descending in Sanda's room. He had gone to the window, wondering at his presence there, by the side of a patient in lethargic sleep. He had gone to the window to catch the remaining light of the evening ; you could see there the opal-colored sky and a few tall tree branches. Outside, the mosquitos, vainly trying to pierce the pane, were swarming as usual. Mr. Nazarie considered them, vaguely anxious. Dusty swarms they were, crowding and dispersing to the sound of unperceived music ; their flight, thwarted by the window pane, rendered them more threatening. "If they were all to invade the room in a swarm..." His thought was arrested. He suddenly turned his head to Sanda's bed. The silence oppressed him, disturbed him. "Such endless sleep," he thought. "She doesn't even breathe... What if she has died without my knowing it ?"

He clenched his hands, feeling his wet fists, cold fingers, and hot palms ; fever, terror. "Yet she couldn't have died by my side, I should have heard her dying. People don't die like that, suddenly, in their sleep. They groan and struggle, they fight. Death comes in black garments, with a long silver scythe... not like that, all of a sudden."

Mr. Nazarie took his temples between his palms. Sanda was lying on her back and you could still see her face in the dusk of the room. "If only the doctor came back," Mr. Nazarie thought hopefully. "If I only had the nerve to go up to the bed, to touch her cheek, to feel it..." Maybe the cheek would be too cold, or he may imagine it was too cold. He could still run away. He was still strong enough to run away.

He took a step to the door. A strange sleep, no dreams in it ! She doesn't even moan with pain, not a stirring in her body. Her breast not heaving. Or, maybe, the lips have moved, calling him repeatedly, he never hearing ?... "If I leave now, it will be darker in the corridor. Maybe there's someone else behind the door, waiting for me. That's how it always happens ; they stand by the door, the ear against the panel, hardly breathing — and they listen hour after hour, watching. To see what you are going to do... That's the way. Someone standing by you, unheard and unfelt, looking on, reading your thoughts, waiting, to see what you are going to do."

"Egor has long been gone. He left and locked me in, here by Sanda's side." Mr. Nazarie knelt by the door. He, too, put his ear against the panel. Not a sound. But the silence frightened him even more, that stark loneliness. Why is no one walking along the corridor, why doesn't any object fall in this house, why don't any dogs bark in the fields ? As if the whole house house had emerged out of the void, or descended out of a forgotten dream. For the heavens had grown old too, distant, cold. Egor stays somewhere outside, or maybe he left for good.

The dark was thick now. Mr. Nazarie's eyes watched in wonder the dark coming down, cloud after cloud, penetrating through the window, crushing all transparency, dulling the bright glass pane. "I ought to light the lamp." Yet the light stirs the shadows into life, the flame of the match trembles. "I'd rather stay like this, completely still. Listen for the others. Never move."

He seemed to hear a deep breath from nowhere ; a single deep endless breath. Mr. Nazarie plugged his ears with his fingers. "I must stay in my right mind, not lose my right mind. ... One, two, three, four... Our Lady, Mother of God !" However the breath could still be heard, stronger, coming as it were, out of his own heart, from between his temples, sounding victorious though he was pressing his fingers tight. He dare not look at Sanda. He backed against the wall. "Maybe she can't see me here. Seeing me suddenly by her may frighten her, or maybe she won't see me, she won't know she's dead, will not realize it."

He suddenly heard someone calling him.

"Professor !"

The voice came from another direction. The long heavy breathing was now pounding with heavy fists upon the door.

"Open the door, professor !"

The voice came from afar. He heard it altered, muffled, as if coming from some bottomless pit. He suddenly removed the fingers from his ears. The pounding on the door grew more violent. He approached.

"Professor !"

He fumbled and there was the key. Strange ! Whoever put it there, inside the door, without his knowing it ?

Simina came in. She stood before him, a shadow dressed in white. She stopped on the threshold, waiting.

"Is she dead ?" she asked.

"I don't know."

The little girl went up to the bed and put her ear to Sanda's breast. She listened long, intently.

"Where are you ?" she asked again.

"Here, by the door," Mr. Nazarie quietly answered. "Can't you see me ?"

Simina gave no answer. She went near the window as if expecting to find a well-known face, brow against the window, striving to look inside, waiting. Mr. Nazarie saw Simina's white figure clinging to the window and began to shiver.

"Where is Egor ?" he asked in fear.

"I don't know. I left him outside. He's waiting for the doctor. Why did you lock yourself in ? Or have you, too, become engaged to Sanda ?"

Mr. Nazarie put his head down, ashamed. He dare not go. It was still too dark in the corridor, Egor was far away, outside.

"How is she ?" Mr. Nazarie asked again.

"She's alive. Her heart is beating."

Simina had spoken under her breath. But then she began to laugh. She took a few steps.

"Are you afraid ?"

"No, I'm not," Mr. Nazarie said dryly.

"But you didn't go near her, you were afraid. Where are you ?" she asked once more, roughly, "I can't find you."

"I am here, by the door."

"Come this way, to me."

Mr. Nazarie obeyed the order. The little girl caught his arm and took his hand between her own small, cold ones.

"Professor," she whispered, "I don't know what will happen to mother. We have to protect her. Would you please look for Egor and go upstairs to her room, both of you."

Mr. Nazarie started shaking. The little girl's voice was altered, hardly recognizable, as if out of old memories, of dreams forgotten.

"I'll try to find him," he murmured, drawing his hand back, "but I'm afraid to walk along the corridor, knocking against the furniture. Isn't there a match in this room ?"

"There isn't," Simina said dryly.

Mr. Nazarie walked away, staggering. Simina waited for the sound of his steps to die down, then shut the door, turned the key in its lock, and went up to the window. She waited a few seconds, then she climbed on a chair to reach the handle and opened the window. The darkness outside was breaking up far away ; in mid heavens, above the elm tree, a half-baked moon, pale, dead.

★

Mr. Nazarie found Egor leaning against the veranda's railings. He was looking into the void, upon the ground. He dare not raise his eyes too high up.

"Sanda hasn't yet come to!" Mr. Nazarie whispered. "Simina is in her room. She's there."

He thought Egor couldn't hear, so he grabbed his arm.

"What's the matter with you? Where have you been all this time?"

"I've been looking for her," Egor vaguely answered. "I've looked everywhere."

He sighed and wiped his face. In the slanting light of the veranda lamp, Mr. Nazarie noticed the traces of blood round his lips. Only then did he notice that Egor's clothes were in a state of disorder and that his hair hung wet upon his brow.

"What's happened?" he asked again, concerned. "What is that around your mouth?"

"A scratch. I got hurt among the acacias," Egor absent-mindedly answered, raising his arm and pointing limply to the park. "Over there!"

Mr. Nazarie gazed in terror. Whoever had lit the veranda lamp in this deserted house? They heard no steps, no voice reached them.

"Who lit the lamp?" asked in low tones.

"I don't know. That's how I found it, burning. Maybe the nanny."

"We ought to leave," Mr. Nazarie whispered again. "We'll wait for the doctor and leave with him."

"Too late now," Egor answered after a long interval "There's no point in it now."

He laid his brow upon the palms of his hands.

"If I knew what happened, if I could only understand what happened," he murmured again.

He looked up to the new moon on top of the elm.

"I thought of calling in a priest," Mr. Nazarie said. "The house, the people in it are oppressive."

Egor made his way to the big flower bed. White, sweet-smelling flowers grew there. The air, too, was purer there, as if in perpetually renewed coolness.

"Yet something's happened to you," Mr. Nazarie said, catching up with Egor.

He wouldn't have him go too far from the house. He was afraid of the dark there, of the shadows of the acacias.

"I sometimes think I'm dreaming," Mr. Nazarie spoke rather to himself.

Very anxious, he went into the adjoining room and washed his hands. He was nervous, frowning.

"I don't understand how they can leave the house so empty at such a time," he added.

They both started for Sanda's room. Mr. Nazarie held the lamp in his right hand, high above his shoulder.

"I was told that these people are fairly rich," the doctor murmured along the corridor.

Mr. Nazarie was silent. The place seemed to be altered once more. There was a different smell now in the corridor; the air fresher, warmer. The loneliness no longer oppressed him. You could hear young voices, plenty of them and very close.

"Here," Mr. Nazarie said pointing to Sanda's door.

The doctor knocked, his breathing stopped. They walked in. There was a lamp burning in the room, with a powerful wire sieve, under an enormous peach-colored lamp shade. Mrs. Moscu rose from her chair, fondly smiling on the guests. Simina was waiting by the bedside, collected, gazing on the ground.

"How is our young lady?" the doctor asked under his breath.

"She's had a very good sleep," Mrs. Moscu answered, "she's been asleep all afternoon. We could hardly wake her."

She smiled an infinitely loving smile on Sanda whose head was propped against a few pillows. The girl looked very tired, but calm, resigned. The doctor took her hand feeling her pulse. He frowned, perplexed. Perplexity then became anxiety, fear.

"Very strange, I think," he murmured. He sought Mr. Nazarie's eyes, but the professor lacked the courage to meet his. He was vaguely, pointlessly gazing into the middle of the room. "How absurdly frightened, what absurd dreams I dreamt here, just a few hours ago." Everything now seemed to be altered. Everything looked familiar, warm, normal.

"Yet, there is something I don't understand," the doctor spoke again. "I'm under the impression that the fever is rising. Have you taken her temperature?"

"I am feeling much better now," Sanda whispered.

Mr. Nazarie started. What a faint, tearful voice. Deep down he could feel the approach of death. It was a voice preparing for the great silence.

"She's been under great stress today," Mrs. Moscu intervened. "Just imagine that, quite unexpectedly, she became engaged."

She laughed looking now at Sanda, now at the two men.

"She got engaged in this very bed, to Mr. Pașchievici !" she exclaimed. "Can you imagine !"

She did not seem to mind this engagement in the least. On hearing Egor's name, the doctor again looked at Mr. Nazarie. This time he met his gaze. "I don't understand anything," the doctor was thinking. "This fellow Pașchievici is quite mad !"

"An impatient bride she is," Mrs. Moscu said. "Mr. Pașchievici promised that they would leave very soon, for the wedding at Bucharest."

"No, mother, it's not true," Sanda protested, still more faintly, "as you wish, I'll do what you wish."

Simina began to smile. The doctor considered her, unable to understand the seriousness of her face, her hard look, her crushing smile. Such a precocious child !

"It's time for dinner," Mrs. Moscu said. "Simina, go tell nanny to serve dinner."

*

When they came back to the dining room, the nanny was waiting by the door.

"There's nothing except milk and cheese," she said approaching Mrs. Moscu.

"We ought to find something else besides," Mrs. Moscu said. "Look around, there must be something left in the pantry, jam, fruit, biscuits."

The doctor heard and instantly blushed. He felt ridiculous, disgraced, offended. He had stayed for dinner without being asked. He sought Mr. Nazarie's eyes by way of assistance. He only met Simina's same distant, bitter smile. Mr. Nazarie had gone out on the veranda to fetch Egor. He had spied him slowly coming along the broad walk, without hurry. He went out to meet him, as if bound to bring him to his senses.

"Sanda is all right, I went to see her with the doctor," he told him quickly. "I even spoke with her. She is still very weak, but no longer in danger."

He took a quick look at Egor's face and clothes. He seemed to have come to his senses, for his hair was tidy, the clothes clean. His face, too, was now more aware, more manly.

"I, too, have been very unwell, but it's over now," Egor said, "however, we've got to stay together after dinner. To plan things."

Going into the dining room Egor was faced with Simina. The little girl regarded him quietly, calm, as a well-brought up child should look at a guest. "What had happened there," Egor thought with a shudder, "what actually happened, or was it all dream ?"

"Congratulations on your engagement, Mr. Paşchievici !" Mrs. Moscu said ironically.

Egor bowed. He bit his lips, controlling himself. But he could feel the sore swelling on his lower lip and shuddered. He took another look at Simina. She didn't seem to have noticed anything. She was waiting for a bidding to sit down. The nanny was late serving dinner.

Mr. Nazarie and the doctor were talking in a low voice at the doorway of the veranda. Though he realized he was being downright rude, Egor left Mrs. Moscu and Simina by themselves, and joined them. They were talking about Sanda. The doctor saw Egor coming and ceased talking, embarrassed.

"I was wondering why you came by yourself," he said at last. "Where did you leave the lady, or was she the young lady ?"

He gave a wry smile. Egor looked at him blinking, trying to understand.

"The young lady you were walking with an hour ago, in the park," the doctor explained, rather confused. "I was returning from my hunting, and I couldn't help but see you."

He smiled once more looking at the professor and at Egor, from one to the other.

"It's quite true that I took a long walk in the park, but I was alone," Egor said softly.

"Maybe this was an indiscretion," the doctor apologized.

"Not at all," Egor intervened, "but I assure you I was walking by myself. As a matter of fact you won't come upon another country house for ten kilometers round about. And the Moscu family you've met, I think, with all its members." The doctor was listening, bewildered, red in the face. He had first taken it for a new joke, as Mr. Nazarie had done about

Sanda's death. Then he thought Egor was making fun of him.

"I saw her quite clearly, anyway," he said stiffly, "I was surprised by the luxury and elegance of her apparel, too stylish, I should say, for a walk in the park."

Mr. Nazarie shuddered and closed his eyes, Egor, too, was now listening more intently, more excitedly to the doctor's words.

"Maybe that was the reason for my indiscreetly watching a couple. The outfit."

At that moment Simina suddenly appeared in their midst.

"The milk is getting cold," she politely said, inviting them inside.

The three men entered the dining room looking inquiringly at each other.

## XIV

The doctor was very tired and was the first to retire to the room that the nanny had prepared for him. The shooting had been too much for him. He had especially been upset at mealtime, by those very strange, sick people, who only spoke at cross purposes. He had been ashamed to eat two plates of hot milk and the largest piece of cheese, because he and Mrs. Moscu were the only really hungry ones. The most unpleasant meal of his lifetime, in a country house, with such a rich family, moreover. And yet, soon after dinner, Mrs. Moscu handed him an envelope containing one thousand lei. She was requiting his services in a grand style.

He disliked everything in his room, which felt as if someone had just left, someone who had long inhabited it, and left the impress of his soul everywhere. The furniture seemed to be arranged by a certain hand, fond of a certain order which he disliked. The room smelled of flowers picked long ago, now withering somewhere, possibly on top of the wardrobe, possibly in the chest facing the stove. A single picture, faded and stained by flies above the bed. A picture certainly loved by someone, since it didn't look sad or lonely as it hung there, as if part of the bed's warmth. "Someone has been staying here until the other day and they gave me the room because it was furnished with all the bed clothes at hand," the doctor thought.

He undressed in a hurry, put out the lamp and threw himself on the bed. It would be a short night for the housemaid would wake him at dawn to catch the first train to Giurgiu. What strange people these guests. And yet, so amiable ; they, too, would be up at dawn to see me to the station. They wouldn't even say goodbye. They enjoy seeing me off. Hm !

He thought he would soon fall asleep. In front of him, at the window, the moon was watching.

★

"We must both say our prayers," Mr. Nazarie said, trying to look calm. "I will help us."

In speaking he seemed to become a prey to the terror that he felt lurking in Egor's eyes.

"Do you really believe what the doctor said ?" Mr. Nazarie spoke again. "Is it possible, is such a horror possible ?"

Someone had asked the same question before, a long time ago, on a night like this. It was then colder, the autumn winds were beginning, but there was no such unseemly, petrified silence. Now their own steps in this room, with the burning lamp, were incapable of breaking such utter solitude. Any noise sunk, as if in a thick felt, charmed away.

"We must say our prayers," Mr. Nazarie spoke again, "to pluck up our courage."

Egor poured himself another glass of brandy with no answer. He was smiling, but his hand was shaking, as he replaced the bottle on the table.

"I am afraid for Sanda," he said eventually. "Maybe we shouldn't sleep tonight. We should be watching her, at least I should."

Mr. Nazarie went up to the window. It was open. The night, the dark outside were pouring in.

"Won't you shut it ? Do you want to sleep like that ?"

Egor attempted a laugh.

"I'm not afraid of the open window," he said dryly. "Nothing happens out there." He made a short gesture pointing to the garden, the moon, the sky.

"I don't even mind the moon's light," he added. "It's soon to die, as a matter of fact. The moon sets after midnight."

Mr. Nazarie could feel by his voice how dreadfully the terror was eating into him. Egor was speaking almost unconsciously. Or was he drunk ? So soon...

"I'll sleep here, with you, tonight, if you'll have me," Mr. Nazarie spoke.

Egor laughed again. He threw himself on the sofa, a lighted cigarette in his fingers. His voice was now deeper ; he was trying to make it sound vulgar, coarse.

"That's out of the question," he said. "I have to keep my promise. At any risk, I must. I will not sleep a wink tonight."

"Is this my own thought, my real thought ?" Egor asked himself in terror. "What if it were she commanding what to speak and what to do ? !" He suddenly felt everything in the room reeling and put his hands up to his head. Mr. Nazarie, eyes half closed, had begun to pray. Short, broken fragments of his words, meaningless, senselessly uttered, could be occasionally heard.

"If I could only remember what happened," Egor said after a long time, as if speaking to himself.

There was a sudden far-away, muffled noise ; both men gave each other a long look, white in the face. It was as if someone had bumped against the wall, as if a table creaked at the far end of the corridor. Mr. Nazarie then remembered, with absurd exactness, the words of the song *Les vieilles de notre pays.* He looked deep into Egor's eyes ; "it was no illusion ; he, too, heard the same."

"Some man back from the vineyards, looking for us," Egor said distinctly, obstinately

"Yes, a man's steps," Mr. Nazarie said.

He listened on. Heavy steps approaching, walking aimlessly. The man walking so blindly in the dark seemed to be carrying someone on his back.

"Has anything happened to Sanda, I wonder ?" Egor asked frightened.

He jumped up, went to the door, and opened it He stood on the doorstep with clenched finsts. Presently the doctor appeared, in a nightgown, hunting boots on his feet. He was shivering with cold. Menacingly he carried a gun in his right hand.

"Am I disturbing you ?" he mumbled walking in and swiftly closing the door. "I was not sleepy, so I thought..."

He sat on the edge of the bed, quite worn out. The boots sounded heavy, muffled on the floor.

"I was not sleepy," he added, "so I said..."

He suddenly felt ridiculous, sitting there on the edge of the bed, in his nightgown, gun in hand, trying to make it look smaller, to hide it.

"I didn't quite know where your room was," the doctor said again, shivering. "So I took this gun to keep off the furniture. It's pitch dark in the corridor."

"Is it at least loaded ?" Egor ironically asked.

"I have been using it all day. It's a good gun."

He fell silent, looking from one to the other.

"Please go on talking," he said seeing they were looking at him equally perplexed, "I hope I'm not intruding."

"Not in the least," said Mr. Nazarie, "we were just ready for bed."

"So you both share this room ?" the doctor asked in panic, yet with evident envy.

"No. This is the room of Mr. Paşchievici. It's the finest too, with a balcony," said Mr. Nazarie.

"You have a very good bed, an excellent bed," the doctor mumbled.

He was carefully surveying the bed, pale, nervous. Then, ashamed, he looked the others in the face. Egor poured a glass of brandy for him.

"Against a possible cold," he said gently, offering the glass.

The doctor grasped it greedily and drank it in one gulp. The burn did him good. It woke him up. He clutched the gun more confidently. There was so much light, such security in this room. The bed was not shaking, no piece of furniture moved, the floor did not twitch under the moon's rays. The moon did not come down right through the window, nor were there so many moths.

"Strange, I am no longer sleepy."

The doctor was beginning to be himself again. Sleep had gone, weariness too. Yet had he closed his eyes he would have felt the same slight shaking of the bed, the same insane tremour of the pillows ; the was certain he would again feel the frenzy in his room. That abnormal shaking of the bed, the terror that suddenly woke him, as if a gigantic hand had crept under the bedding, shaking him.

"I hope I haven't been intruding," he said again grasping the gun tight.

Without this gun, could he have walked alone in the dark, along that endless empty corridor ?

"We're not very talkative tonight, either of us. It's a pleasure to have you here."

"What time do you think it is ?" the doctor asked.

"A quarter past eleven," Egor answered smiling.

"To think I must get up so early," the doctor complained. "Is it far to the station ?"

"Six kilometers. You're not thinking of leaving now, are you ?"

The doctor did not reply. He was again contemplating the bed in wonder. Then he got up and began walking about the room.

"To tell you the truth I am no longer sleepy," he said, his eyes upon the ground. "I don't care for the room they've given me. It's so far away, and very old too ; all the furniture is creaking... waking you up."

Egor sought the professor's eyes, but Mr. Nazarie would not meet his gaze.

"You may have my room if you like," the professor addressed the doctor.

"And you'll sleep here ?"

"No, I'll stay with you. There are two beds in my room."

The doctor's eyes shone with joy. He suddenly approached Mr. Nazarie.

"And we've got the gun, too, don't you be nervous," he spoke quickly. "We'll sleep with the gun by our side. If only I could go to sleep," he said in a lower voice, "sleep has now gone."

*

In the doorway, Egor asked :

"Frankly speaking, what is your opinion concerning Miss Moscu ?"

The doctor blinked.

"I believe she won't live much longer," he said without thinking.

"She is my fiancée," Egor sharply said, looking into his face.

"Quite so. It is, in fact, strange," the doctor murmured. "Maybe, however..."

Egor stood long by the door, listening to the receding steps. He was suddenly quiet, by what miracle? He was calm, clear-headed; he felt strong and fearless. He put his hands in his pockets and began thoughtfully pacing the room. Nearly twelve o'clock, he remembered. But the time is unimportant, these old, ancient superstitions were of no importance. It was his strong hope and faith, his great love for Sanda that kept him lucid and strong.

No more noises, no more steps. The moon was sinking somewhere beyond the park. Egor felt alone, which now gave him strength and courage. "If only I wasn't dreaming," he thought with a frown. "Or, maybe, who knows? if I could only wake the sooner." He slapped his arms together. He was not asleep. Here, this is the lamp burning, the dark coming in through the window, this is the chair, the table, and the bottle of brandy almost empty. Everything was normal in his room. Just as in the daytime, just as in a dream...

He was pacing again with long rhythmic steps. "I have to wake up at some point," he thought. "If I'm really asleep, I must wake up, I'll hear her voice, I'll smell the scent of violets, and I'll wake up."

Yet he didn't hear anything. The same cold sharp air pouring through the window into his nostrils and sometimes the smell of brandy and a slight memory of tobacco. Everything was actually happening in his room.

He passed by the door several times, but could not decide to lock it. Better like this, unlocked. "As I was told in my dream. If my love is stronger, if..." He wanted to continue this thought: "should the Lord God and the Holy Mother of God help me." But he was unable to finish his hopeful, firm thought. His mind went dark. He seemed to be struggling as if to wake from a dream. He stretched his arms, feeling them curved, slightly shivering. He was not dreaming. Tonight something different is going to happen.

He made up his mind: he would not lock the door. He would only close the window. It was getting cold as a matter of fact. It was really getting too cold.

Very quietly he sat down by the table, serenely propping his chin in his hands, looking at the door, scowling with a youthful light in his eyes.

## XV

Time was passing very slowly. At last, Egor realized that his cigarette was burnt out on the cold edge of the ash-tray, a cigarette he had lit a long time ago, possibly without knowing it. What had he been doing in the meantime, where had his thoughts rambled ? The lamp was lightly smoking as if under a strange breath that he himself did not feel. Yet there was no one in the room beside himself, no one had yet come. The room stayed as it was at the beginning — whole, petrified,deserted. Egor was surprised to find himself seated at his table, apathetic, with no memories. He was not even calm. Endless indifference occupied his mind ; no miracle would have shocked him. As if he had suddenly awaken into some unusual dream, in which dreams are dreamt by several people in common, people that you do not see, but somehow guess to be beside you.

He rose, however, went up to the lamp and lowered the wick. He realized that the room had turned very cold, yet he did not feel the cold inside himself ; he just noticed it around him, as you record a thing that is there. He walked up to the window, found it closed and put his brow against the pane for a second, looking out into the night. He then thought he heard a groan, very far away. Was it a groan or the creaking of dry wood under human steps ? He turned around from the window, listening, his head slightly raised. "Don't lock the door tonight," he accurately remembered Simina's words. As if she couldn't have come some other way, in a dream, through the windows. Someone had been groaning, no doubt, far away, in his sleep ; maybe Mr. Nazarie, or perhaps the doctor.

Egor sat down again by the table. "It's useless to deceive myself ; no use telling myself it was just a groan that I should no longer hear her steps ; all in vain." The floor no longer gave a muffled creak, nor did the wooden chests shake. You could now hear distinctly the sound of light swift steps along the corridor. "If only I could wake up," Egor thought with a thrill. He then realized that he was again deceiving himself, as if all that was happening was only a dream.

He was suddenly sorry to have done nothing in the meantime, that he hadn't prepared himself, content to wait. Worn out, he felt time fleeing ; seconds were running into each other, hopeless, never to return, heavy, empty, senseless. The footsteps had been heard a whole eternity. Sounds hardly reached him, muffled, hushed. A gentle shuffle of a slipper in front of the door, then a few seconds silence. "Someone is waiting outside, waiting and hesitating, or is the door actually locked ?" Egor hoped, shaking. "Maybe I locked it in my sleep. And she won't dare come inside."

He then heard a few brief, rapid knocks, the knocking of an excited woman. Egor rose, but stood with both hands propped against the table. He was very pale, his eyes burning under a spell in their sockets. His eyes were bluish-grey, hard, feverish. The knocks came again, more impatient.

"Come in," Egor moaned.

His throat was dry, he lacked breathing space. The door opened slowly and Miss Christina stood in the doorway. She looked Egor straight in the face. She held him thus a few seconds. Her face was then lit up by an incomparable smile. She smoothly reached for door and turned the key in the lock.

★

Eyes open, looking up into the dark, Mr. Nazarie was breathing evenly, soundlessly listening to what was happening to his room mate. The doctor, was he awake ? was he looking for something on the table, fumbling in the dark, striking objects, then clutching them tight in his fists, to stop them from shaking ? The sounds were muffled, stopped dead as if by some invisible hand. They exploded with raw, painful sonorousness, but soon died as if smothered in felt ; the silence then seemed more unnatural, more threatening.

His lips tight, Mr. Nazarie listened, not daring to move, to wipe the cold beads of sweat off his brow. When was it that he had sweated so much, his whole body in a cold sweat ? Maybe the doctor had a bad dream and was now walking about the room unable to wake up. The moment he woke up, he would give such a yell of terror, in this darkness closing in on him on all sides.

Then he heard, right there by his side, a claw scratching at the wall, slowly, smoothly trying some means of penetrating into it. Mr. Nazarie jumped in the middle of the room ; his jaws were clenched, his hands cold. He bumped against a rigid body. The doctor moaned and shuddered as Mr. Nazarie grasped his arm.

"What were you doing here?" Mr. Nazarie asked in a strangled voice.

"I thought there was someone walking about," the doctor whispered. "I thought someone was scratching the wall on the outside. Did you hear anything?"

"There may be some bird in the next room," Mr. Nazarie said.

Yet he was sure there had been no bird. The claw had scratched too firmly along the wall, rigidly.

"Were you trying to find anything on the table?" Mr. Nazarie asked. "You gave me quite a shock."

"Not me," the doctor confessed, "those are ghosts, evil spirits."

He was delirious. His hands were shaking. He wished to look for the gun that he had propped against the bed, but was afraid of going away from Mr. Nazarie. He had taken him by the arm and was clinging to him.

"Have you got a match?" Mr. Nazarie spoke with some difficulty.

"The box is on the table."

They both came up trying to avoid bumping against the chair. Mr. Nazarie fumbled carefully, found the match box. As he struck a match, his hand shook.

"Maybe we got scared for no reason," he whispered.

"No, I am positive, positive."

The doctor was senselessly mumbling. He had taken hold of his nightshirt in his left hand, pressing it above his heart; the hand looked petrified, in a spasm.

"We ought to leave," the doctor said after a while trying to control himself. "I can't stay any longer in this room."

"Daylight will soon be here," Mr. Nazarie calmed him. "We'd better wait."

They exchanged a look, each horrified by the other's terror.

"In the meantime we could pray," Mr. Nazarie added.

"I keep praying continually," the doctor whispered, "but it doesn't help, I keep hearing the same noises."

The lamp was burning low. The silence was so compact that their breathing sounded like a sick man's snoring.

"Can't you hear anything now?" the doctor suddenly asked.

Mr. Nazarie gave a quick look all around. These were not the same sounds, they did not come from their room or from the next. It was a step walking about in the open, somebody stepping lightly and carefully on the gravel. He went up to the window. At first he couldn't see anything. The lamp was yet too near, its pale light was dimming the window pane.

"Still, you can hear it very well," the doctor said, coming up to the window.

His eyes got quickly accustomed to the dark. As a matter of fact, someone was actually walking in the middle of the broad alley, very carefully, someone stepping dumbly, as you do when sleeping.

"It's Simina !" Mr. Nazarie spoke upset. "Maybe she's coming to call us. Something may have happened to Sanda."

The little girl, however, was walking into the heart of the park, towards the large flower bed. The doctor's eyes followed her. He was dumbfounded.

"What on earth is she doing in the park, at night, by herself ?" Mr. Nazarie spoke in a strangled voice. "I am afraid something may happen".

He stood a few seconds by the window, trying to pierce the dark as far as Simina had got. Then he suddenly made up his mind. He went back and looked for his shoes.

"We must see where she's going," he said with concern, "find out what's happened."

He dressed in a hurry. The doctor was looking on, wildly, as if trying to understand what he was about to do.

"Aren't you coming ?" Mr. Nazarie asked.

The doctor wagged his head. He put on his boots and put his overcoat on top of his nightshirt.

"Is it possible that she didn't see us ?" the doctor wondered. "We stood at the window, the light on us and she went right past us."

Mr. Nazarie closed his eyes in terror.

"She may not have realized, maybe ?" he asked under his breath. "Could she actually be sleepwalking ? We must catch her, there's still time."

*

The iron turn of the key in the lock was the last real sound that Egor caught. Christina's steps had a different feel. They reached him full, sonorous, but seemed to come from another clime, accompanied by a melodious whisper, as if growing out of frenzy.

Christina advanced into the middle of the room. "If I could only close my eyes," Egor thought. "Don't close them, my love !" he suddenly found himself thinking the words that Christina could not utter. "Don't be afraid of me !"

He definitely felt Christina's thoughts springing up in his mind ; he could now sift them quite easily from his own thoughts and fears. He was, however, less frightened than he had thought. Christina's closeness was a weight, the air he breathed was ever hotter, more rarefied ; nevertheless, he succeeded in standing upright, no trembling of his hands, no wandering of his mind. He could see Christina's whole person, he missed no single twitch of her waxen face. The smell of violets had now invaded the whole room. Christina's breast was now deeply heaving ; she, too, was excited by the man's presence, feverishly eager at the prospect of his body. "Why not put out the lamp, dearest ?" he heard Christina's thought in his own mind. But he succeeded in resisting it. He was expecting something frightful to happen, to see Christina blowing out the light or coming too near. But Christina tarried, weighed down with emotion, looking into his eyes, occasionally glancing down at his strong arms, at the hands clutching the table. Egor made a supreme effort and sat down. "And yet you once wished to paint me," he heard Christina's thought, "you wanted to paint me in your own manner."

Christina smiled an embarrassed smile and went up to the bed. She sat down very carefully, almost noiselessly. She began to take off her gloves. She had long-drawn, soft gestures, strangely graceful. Egor's heart stopped beating for a second, suffocated with too much blood. "Why don't you help me ?" Miss Christina wondered, blushing. "Such a timid lover you are, Egor. You're right-down objectionable now, standing away from me. Don't you want to see me naked ? I haven't yet done this for anyone, my love ! But your eyes are such a temptation, they've driven me out of my mind, Egor ! What more could I give them except the snow of my body ? You know, you do know how lovely I am, you know it only too well !"

Egor tried to close his eyes. The eyelids would not obey him, his gaze was clinging to Christina's body. The girl had begun to undress. With infinite elegance she took off her hat and placed it on the bedside table, with the black silk gloves ; her calm, royal gestures did not conceal an inconceivable fear. "You shall never understand what I've done for you, Egor ! You can't appreciate my courage. If you knew the curse I'm laboring under ! Love with a mortal !" She smiled a sad smile ; her eyes seemed tearful with weary melancholy. But Egor's presence restored her. The contiguity of his manly body seemed to rout both sadness and fear. She stood up, undid her silk collar. Her throat appeared dazzling-white, velvety, tender. Exuberant and victorious, her bust was now projected against the wall's pale background. Virgin breasts they were, firm, round, grown freely and held very high by the knitted work of her stays.

"She is now going to undress," Egor shivered. Terror and nausea weighed upon him like delirious fever ; yet, with these, he also felt the sting of a voluptuous malady, of a poisonous caress, both humiliating and maddening. The blood was hotly beating in his ears, in his temples. The smell of violets was now striking him with obscure force, making him dizzy. Above the bed a vast sound of feminine swishing, of silk against the skin, and the perfume of breasts, now free, was warmly floating. "I am Lucifer from the sky," Egor heard Christina's unspoken words. She was smiling the same melancholy smile. "And I want to be your bride !" she continued. Her face was transfigured by yearning, by excitement, by hunger for his body. Her eyes were no longer as before ; they were now burning with a different fire, more turbid, softer, warmer. "Don't leave me alone, my love," Egor heard her last call. "It's cold to undress alone. Fondle me, hold me close to you, take me in your arms, Egor."

He looked and his sight grew dim. Miss Christina was taking off her blouse, slowly, almost bashfully undoing the silk laces that held her waist tight, almost iron tight. His hands began to tremble. "She is now coming closer, she will take me in those bare arms." And yet from the pitch dark aversion, the sweet poison of expectancy was dripping deep down ; love-making as never dreamt of.

"I no longer want to be a dream," Miss Christina completed his thought. "I no longer want to be cold and immortal, Egor, my love !"

⋆

Sanda was leaning against the window, her head outside in the dark, waiting. It won't be long now and everything will be over. Everything will be as it was in the beginning. As it is during sleep. The moon has now sunk very low ; it is pitch dark. No one can see her as she leans against the window, waiting. No yell will be heard. The moths and even the mosquitos are now asleep.

A few steps nearby, quite close to her, called her attention. Resigned, she turned her head. She would come first, then others would follow, shadow after shadow.

"What are you doing here in the middle of the night ?" Mrs. Moscu asked. Her mother had stealthily come into the room. She had been somewhere, possibly in the park, for she was fully dressed, a shawl wrapt round her neck.

"I was waiting," Sanda whispered.

"She won't come now," Mrs. Moscu spoke with concern. "You may go to bed."

Sanda noticed that her mother was grasping a live, dark ball in her left hand. There was a time when such a discovery would have set her trembling, would have humiliated and nauseated her. Now she was just wondering at the small creature that her mother was carefully keeping in her closed hand.

"Where did you catch it ?" Sanda wearily asked, her words whizzing, rather than spoken.

"In the nest," Mrs. Moscu murmured. "It can't fly."

"And so raw ?" Sanda unexpectedly shivered.

She put her hands up to her temples. All the sorrows, all the forgotten fears, the frenzy and nausea of the first night, they all suddenly rushed back upon her. She was shaking. The cold night had come in through the open window.

"Get into bed," Mrs. Moscu spoke in a metallic voice, "you may catch cold."

Trembling, Sanda went up to the bed. Her head ached fearfully, her temples throbbed.

"But do not close the window," she whispered to Mrs. Moscu, "she may still be coming."

★

Mr. Nazarie and the doctor stopped in the middle of the broad walk, quite surprised. Simina stood with her back to them, intently watching something invisible, among the trees.

"How on earth could she still be here?" Mr. Nazarie murmured, "A number of minutes have gone by since..."

Simina was stubbornly peering into the darkness in front of her, never turning, never hearing anything. As if she had been waiting for them to come out, to see her distinctly, that they might afterwards follow her.

"She does not realize," Mr. Nazarie was upset, "maybe she doesn't even know where she is."

Just then Simina set out, intently, with a firm step. She walked straight across the acacias, never looking for a path, not minding the dead branches in her way.

"We mustn't get lost," the doctor mumbled.

Mr. Nazarie didn't answer. He was beginning to wake from a terror that had lasted too long, and he felt giddy. He fancied that he was embarking on a senseless chase, that he was tempted into a trap, that he was going to fall soon, to slip into some hole of wet grass and darkness.

"I've lost sight of her," the doctor spoke again, stopping amid the trees. "How on earth doesn't she hear the branches cracking, nor our steps?" the doctor wondered.

"She's over there," Mr. Nazarie said dryly.

His hand pointed far away, a white shadow by a bush. That was, probably, the beginning of a new path, since the horizon became clearer, the shadows of the trees more distinct, in line.

The doctor took a few careful steps, avoiding the lower branches that hung contorted, barren, as if weighed down by some unseen burden. Frightened, he gazed at the shadow that Mr. Nazarie had pointed out.

"My eyesight is good," the doctor said under his breath. "That's not Miss Simina over there."

That moment Mr. Nazarie realized that the shadow by the bush was slowly rocking, its arms raised as if calling to someone far away, someone invisible. It was not, in fact, Simina's figure. He stood transfixed, breathless ; that was no living creature. It looked like his former fantasies, so aerial, so abnormal in its limp, raglike gestures.

"Let's go back," he heard the doctor's stern voice.

It was then that Simina passed by them looking afraid. Mr. Nazarie guessed by her wide open eyes and her tightly pressed lips that Simina was now trying to correct her mistake in bringing them here. She, probably, did not expect to meet someone else on the border of the other alley. She was now coming back bewildered and was trying to draw them to the opposite side of the park. She passed by them, then set out thoughtful, walking fast, towards the northern gate.

The doctor was ready to follow. Mr. Nazarie grabbed his arm tight.

"Let us first see what is to be found there," he firmly spoke.

Walking slowly, side by side, they approached the alley. The shade vanished for a few seconds. It seemed it was making for the opposite direction, like Simina, or possibly was hidden by some tree. The more they advanced, the more Mr. Nazarie was under the distinct impression of having once more been through the same incident, that he had once again, long ago, followed a shade with soft felt-like gestures among petrified trees.

"Nothing visible, I can't see anything," the doctor murmured.

But Mr. Nazarie was beginning to see. Simina had appeared again, a few steps away. Leaning against a tree, clinging to its trunk, she watched in terror as the two men were approaching. The little girl sought Mr. Nazarie's eyes and tried again to dominate, to command him, breaking his willpower, but Mr. Nazarie proceeded firmly, passed by her and reached the border of the alley.

"Stand still, don't move !" he spoke to the doctor.

In front of them, in the alley, a long-abandoned barouche was waiting, a lordly coach, ancient and lustreless, drawn by two sleepy horses. The driver had fallen asleep on his seat ; you could only see his white coat threadbare with wear and his shabby leather cap. He seemed to have long been sleeping up there on the driver's seat — a peaceful sleep, with no start or quiver. The horses, too, seemed to be sunk in the same deadly sleep ; they didn't move, didn't breathe ; they were waiting like sombre statues in front of the ancient barouche, waiting as if in a swoon.

Beside himself, with his eyes popping out of his head, the doctor was shaking. He grabbed Mr. Nazarie's arm in both hands.

"Do you see them, too ?" he whizzed rather than spoke.

Mr. Nazarie nodded.

"Are they alive ? !" the doctor asked again, "or is it a delusion ?"

That very moment, the shade which had long vanished from the alley, now appeared. It was a very weary old man, with sunken cheeks. His dress was that of a field hand on the manorial lands, in former times. He walked past them as if he hadn't seen them. His eyes were bent on the ground. But Mr. Nazarie felt that the old man knew of their presence, so close to him there. He had seen his eyes for just one second ; glazed eyes, weary, heartsick. The doctor covered his face with the palm of his hand. He felt like running away, but Simina's small, cold hand clung to his arm, stifling some possible outburst.

## XVI

Miss Christina was very close to him, breasts bare, hair loose, waiting. "Egor, it's humiliating," he heard her thoughts. "Put out the lamp and come close !" Egor was vainly trying to resist. He could feel Miss Christina's command in his brain, her poisonous appeals in his blood. "If she kisses me I'm lost," he thought. But at the same time he felt a mounting frenzy, a desire for that flesh so much alive and so wildly palpitating. Miss Christina's body was expecting him with such ravenous hunger that Egor was dizzily swaying as he approached the bed. With devilish lucidity he felt he was losing his mind, weighed down by nausea and voluptuousness. One more step, yet another...

Before him, before his own lips, Christina's mouth was open. When had she come so near ? He put out his arms and embraced the girl's snowy shoulders. The flesh was both so cold and so hot that Egor fell upon the bed. That fire, unlike any flame, was beyond endurance, the sensation of holding in one's hands something impossible to grasp. He suddenly felt Christina's mouth seeking his lips. Her mouth was so hot that, at first, Egor only felt an overwhelming pain in his whole body. Then the poisoned sweetness got into his blood. He could no longer resist. His breathing mingled with Christina's own and his lips were sucked in, set on fire by her mouth, sweet as a malady never dreamt of. So savage was this love-making, that tears ran from Egor's eyes, he felt the bones of his skull falling apart, the bones in his body grow soft, his whole flesh shuddering in a supreme spasm.

Christina raised her head and looked through her lashes. "How handsome you are, Egor !" She fondled him, slowly pressing his cheek against her small trembling breasts.

Egor seemed to hear a smothered, melodious voice reciting somewhere, yet close to his ear :

*"Come Arald, rest your brow upon my bosom,*
*Thou dark-eyed god, with eyes that never were !*
*Let me entwine your neck with golden locks,*
*My life, my youth, you've turned to very heaven*
*Let me just pore into your eyes,*
*Those eyes of cloying, fatal magic."*

It hadn't been her dream voice ; nor was it her unspoken voice coming straight from one's thought. Someone had spoken the bit of that poem, quite close to them. The lines sounded familiar to Egor, read long since, one autumn in high school, during a night of great loneliness. "Egor, what is the color of your eyes ?" Christina asked. She turned his head with her small hands and looked deep into his eyes, thrilled. "You God with dark eyes ! You have dark blue eyes, fearless eyes. How many women looked into them, Egor ? My mouth would soon thaw the icy look in your eyes, love ! Why did you not wait for me, why didn't you choose to love me and no other ?"

Egor was trembling, but no longer with a spasm of terror, but the yearning of his whole body, his consuming frenzy in expectation of the supreme love-making. His flesh was madly torn to shreds, lust was choking him, humiliating him. Christina's mouth tasted like fruit in dreams, like a forbidden cursed drunkenness. The most devilish figments of love did not drip with such poison, such dew. In Christina's arms Egor was experiencing the most impious joys, coupled with a sense of heavenly merging into all and everything. Incest, crime, madness — beloved, sister, angel... They fused together, coalesced and burnt up by this incendiary, yet lifeless flesh.

"Am I dreaming, Christina?" he whispered, his face white, his pupils dim.

The girl smiled. The dew was fresh on her lips; the mouth bloomed with the same smile. Yet Egor heard the answer distinctly.

"...Similarly, if I close one eye, my hand looks smaller than seen with both... In fact the world is just our soul's dream."

"So it is," a thought was running through Egor's mind, "she is right. I am now dreaming. And no one will induce me to wake up."

"Speak to me, Egor," he heard the summons in his mind. "Your voice is pain and death to me. But I can no longer be without it!"

"What shall I tell you, Christina?" Egor asked exhausted.

Why did she keep him embraced and wished him to speak, thus making him wait still longer for their supreme and full embrace? Why had she so impatiently called him, undressing in front of him, while now, only half naked, she was forgetting the light that initially offended her, his timidity, her own temptations?

"What do you want me to say?" he repeated looking into her eyes. "Are you dead or are you just a dream?"

Christina's face grew sad, even to dispair. There were no tears, but her eyes suddenly lost their glassy shine and became turbid. Her smile came very slowly and the lips no longer dispersed that poisonous smell that had wreaked such havoc on the flesh of the man in her arms.

"Why do you keep asking, Egor, my love?" he heard her thinking. "Why do you want to know if I am actually dead and if you are perishable? If you could stay with me, if you could only be my own, an extraordinary wonder would come true!"

"But I love you now," Egor moaned, "I did not want to in the beginning, I was afraid of you. But now I love you. What potion did you make me drink, Christina ? What deadly night-shade blooms on your lips ?"

Frenzy was suddenly getting hold of him ; as if blood, mind and speech had suddenly been poisoned. He began talking senseless, his brow ever closer to Christina's breasts, mumbling and kissing, madly fumbling for the snowy flesh that he wished to be dissolved into.

Christina smiled. "That's right, my love, speak of passion, go on telling me you like my body, look hard into my eyes, give yourself up for lost !"

"I should like to kiss you !" Egor spoke beside himself.

He then felt the glow of her lips once more, that frozen blissful ecstasy. He thought he was losing hold of himself, swooning, so he closed his eyes. Again he heard Christina's thought : "Undress me, Egor ! Undress me with your own hands !" He began delving into her poisoned silken wear. His fingers were burning as if crushed between blocks of ice. The blood was throbbing up to his heart. The lust Egor was now feeling threw him blindly, crazily, into voluptuous disgust. A devilish impulse towards unconsciousness, towards annihilation in a single spasm. Under his bloodless fingers Christina's body began to twitch. Yet he heard not a sigh, not a breath between her wet, parted lips. Christina's flesh was living a wholly different life ; encompassed within itself, no exhalation, no whisper.

"Who taught you to fondle, winged spirit ?" Christina's thought asked. "Why does your touch sear me, why does your kiss kill me ?" Egor undid her stays and slipped his fingers down her silent spine. He was abruptly stunned and began to shake. It seemed he was walking on the edge of a rotten pool, almost falling in. Christina gave him a long inquiring look, but Egor did not look up to her. His fingers had touched a raw, wet, warm wound ; the one warm spot on Christina's unreal body. The palm of his hand had dizzily slipped along the skin of this great enigma and turned stiff, clogged in blood. The wound was still fresh and so raw that Egor thought it had just opened a few seconds ago. The blood was gushing fast. Yet why didn't it leak through the stays, soak the dress red ?

He suddenly got up stupefied, his hands on his temples. A nauseating terror was again upsetting his whole person. "A good thing it was all a dream !" he said to himself, "and that I woke up *before...*" That moment he saw Miss Christina's half naked body lying prone on the bed, humiliated and he heard her thought : "It's my wound, Egor ! That's where the bullet struck, that's where the brute shot me dead !" Her eyes were glassy again. Her body seemed to be whiter, more distant, but the spell had vanished. Egor dizzily looked at his hand. A slight bloodstain was still on his fingers. He moaned, wild with terror and rushed into the other corner of the room, behind the table. "You are just like all the others, Egor, my love ! You're afraid of blood ! You're afraid of your very life, of your fate as a mortal ! I didn't hesitate to face the fiercest curse for one hour of love, and here you are, hesitating before a drop of blood, Egor, you poor mortal..."

Christina got out of bed, proud, sad, uncomforted. In terror Egor saw her coming up to him.

"You are dead ! You are dead !" he yelled, beginning to go into a frenzy.

Christina took a few calm steps, still smiling. "You'll look for me a whole lifetime, Egor, but shall not find me ! You'll perish yearning for me. And you'll die young, taking this lock of hair into the grave with you ! Take it, keep it !" She came nearer. Egor felt again the fragrance of her strange body in his nostrils. But he could not reach out. He could not stand the feel of her silent flesh once more. As Christina raised her arm offering the lock of hair, Egor crazily shook the table. The lamp fell on the floor, the glass funnel broke with a muffled sound flaring into a yellow blaze. A strong smell of petrol filled the room. Christina's half naked body looked more terrifying in the light of the flames mounting from the carpet and the floor. Her head was almost in the shadow. "I'm beginning to wake up," Egor thought joyfully, "I have to wake up now." Yet he couldn't understand why he was standing, shrivelled up, his hands clenched upon the wood of the table ; mostly couldn't he understand the flames creeping along the rafters, round his bed, destroying the bedding. "Miss Christina has been here in my sleep," he thought, trying to realize the meaning of so many abnormal facts. That moment it seemed that Miss Christina was going away, looking at him contemptuously, one hand putting up her flowing hair, the other hand gathering her silken wear upon her breast. He only saw her for a moment. Then, never realizing by what miracle, the room stood empty.

Among the flames, he felt alone.

## XVII

Mr. Nazarie, the doctor, and Simina stood by a long time watching the barouche with sleeping horses. Time had stopped. The leaves themselves seemed to stand still on the branches, and no bird flew across the night sky. Mr. Nazarie was looking on, no thoughts in his mind, no willpower. Since Simina had joined them he had no will to take another step. He stood by the doctor, his mind dead to the world. Simina was breathing heavily, upset, in expectation.

"You must go," she said after a long while. "She will soon be back. She will be cross with me if she sees you here."

Simina's murmur seemed to come from afar. They did their best to hear it.

"She will be cross," Simina repeated.

Mr. Nazarie began to rub his eyes. He looked thoughtfully at his companions and looked again at the barouche. The horses waited desperately, their heads down.

"A long sleep I've slept," he said to himself.

Simina smiled. She took him by the arm.

"We haven't been asleep," she whispered, "we stood here and waited for her."

"Yes, that's what we did," the doctor agreed. You could clearly see he did not know what he was saying. He had spoken the words without hearing them. He was stupefied, rigid, no sensation from the outer parts of his body ever reached him.

"She will summon you too," Simina spoke again, "some other time. She's now with Egor, she's gone to him..."

Mr. Nazarie shuddered. But there was no strength, no thought in him. Simina's spell was lulling, it didn't even allow him to be upset, frightened.

"That is an old servant of ours, Christina's coachman," Simina murmured, her arm pointing to the middle of the alley. "Don't you be afraid of him. He's kind."

"I'm not afraid," Mr. Nazarie quietly said.

At that moment he felt a freezing twinge shooting him in the back, pointing to his heart. He seemed to wake up in pain, in terror. It had suddenly turned cold and he began to shiver. Miss Christina was coming from the far end of the alley, her step brisk, her face angry. She passed by them, looking into their faces, threatening; as if she meant to freeze them, so glassy were her eyes. Mr. Nazarie rocked on his feet, as if stabbed. This was no longer the hazy terror-striking phantom, nor the oppressive presence of some unseen soul. Christina was transfixed upon them rigorously out of space, not in a dream. He could see her with frantic acuteness, quite close to him. He was particularly bewildered by her feminine way of walking, a brisk yet grieving step. Miss Christina got into the barouche, both her hands gathering the silken gear round her neck. Her dress was in disorder, her blouse undone. A black silken glove, long and delicate, fell on the carriage steps and then dropped unobserved in the middle of the drive.

Simina had been the first to run to the barouche as Miss Christina was coming. She was scared, with turbid, glassy eyes. Her pale cheeks were like Christina's nacreous face. She put out her frozen hands to her. She uttered no word. She was possibly waiting for a sign, for courage. Miss Christina gave her a very sad, very tired smile, looking into her eyes, a single look, confessing what had happened, then the barouche set off, soundless, swinging like a heavy fog over the drive. A few seconds later it vanished from sight.

Simina looked upon the ground, dispirited, engrossed in thought. Mr. Nazarie had difficulty in breathing. The doctor stood as before, stunned. He was concentrating, almost fascinated by a black spot a few meters in front of him, in the drive.

"She's forgotten her glove!" he shouted after a time, as if throttled.

Anxious, Simina gave a start. She turned her head as if wishing to be the first to reach that black spot in the road, but the doctor was already there. He bowed down trembling, and picked up the black silken glove, vaguely smelling of violets. He kept it rigidly in the palm of his hand, perplexed at the freezing and fiery thrill running through his body.

"Why did you touch it ?" Simina asked, coming up.

Mr. Nazarie was now looking on dumbfounded, his face contorted by perplexity and terror. He tried to touch that piece of dream-silk, but the glove had quickly dissolved in the doctor's palm, as if consumed by a hidden blaze. It was a handful of rot, of dusty ashes, that fell down in the middle of the drive, on the very spot where it had dropped from the barouche. Sleepy, the doctor inclined the palm of his hand and allowed it to scatter.

*

The fire was fast gaining ground in the room. The wardrobe and clothes, the bed, the curtains were now burning, but Egor stood a long time, irresolute, his hands upon the table, choking with smoke. "I ought to be doing something," he thought as if dreaming. He spied the water jug in a corner, grabbed it, jumped across the burnt carpet and began splashing anyhow. He felt empty of all strength. The water he found in the room did not even suffice to put out the fire on the floor, by the door, where he was standing. He then tried to open the door and call for help. The door was locked. "I didn't lock it," he remembered with a shudder. The terror that came upon him again strengthened him. He fumbled for the key in the lock. The iron was hot, blackened with smoke ; the key was hard to turn, a few flames had reached the wooden door, here and there, blotting the thick, yellowish old paint with soot.

Egor ran along the corridor, shouting. The dark was complete. Thin clouds of smoke, red, with the blazing flames inside, issued through the open door. He could not understand the loneliness and silence along the corridor. Had he located the professor's door, he would have kicked it to waken him, but in the dark, he couldn't tell where he was. He went down into the yard, meeting no one. He stood some time in front of the house, bewildered, trying to understand what was happening to him, still hoping to wake up suddenly, hoping that he was dreaming. He looked at his hands in the dark, but couldn't see anything. A vapid scent of faded flowers and old bed sheets reached him. In looking up he saw a glaring blaze blowing through the window of his room. The fire was fast gaining the garret. "They'll be burnt alive!" Egor panicked. He began shouting again. But he fancied there were steps behind him on the drive, and frightened, without turning, he started running toward the manorial house where the Moscu family was sleeping. Only then did he realize the danger that Sanda was in.

"If only I'm not too late !" he thought, "if I can reach her room undetected".

He had been shouting loudly, but no one had heard ; not even a dog barking. The same empty yard, the shadow of the park pressing on every side. The hands were all gone to the vineyards, so Simina had said. But how about Simina, or the nanny, or Mrs. Moscu, how was it that they didn't hear ? He looked back ; the air was beginning to grow red. The shadows of the lilac bushes and acacias nearby were now trembling in a tired, blood-red light. "The house will burn down," he thought, indifferently. "Nazarie has run away of course ; away, together with the doctor, to leave me alone, that I alone should perish. They were afraid."

He walked with slow, uselessly careful steps, around the manorial residence. "Soon they will all come, the hands from the vineyards will be back, the people in the village." The fire was burning far away, noiselessly. "There is still time, there is still time to save her, to take her in my arms and run away with her."

Then he realized that Sanda was looking at him, close by, leaning against the window, as if having long waited for him to come. She was in her nightgown, white in the face, her cheek upon the palm of her hand, as if tired of waiting, ready for sleep. Egor had a shock at the sight of her pale absent-looking face. "She knows what has happened..." He took a few steps towards the window.

"So you've come," Sanda said in a muffled voice, "mother said you wouldn't come tonight... It's late !"

She looked straight into his eyes, yet with no tenderness whatsoever. She wasn't even surprised to see him suddenly before her, in the dead of night.

"Put a coat on and come down, quick !" Egor said.

Sanda continued to look at him. She started shivering as if only just feeling the cold night air, the cold mists that stiffened her shoulders, arms and neck.

"But I won't be able," Sanda whispered shaking herself. "Don't force me, do not. I can't ! I pity them."

Egor looked at her, frightened. He understood that Sanda was not speaking to him, but to some invisible creature behind him, that Sanda had been waiting for by the window, that she feared. He went closer to the wall. What a pity he could not climb directly into her room, force her to dress, take her in his arms and bring her down in spite of herself.

"I've seen one a moment ago," Sanda added in a more toneless voice, "mother picked it up in the nest. I won't be able to do it, I pity them. I don't like it... No drop of blood..."

"Who are you speaking to, Sanda ?" Egor asked. "Who are you waiting for here, in the dead of night ?"

The girl was speechless, looking deep into his eyes, with no understanding. Somehow he was afraid to take his eyes off her, lest she should slide down unaware.

"I've come to save you !" Egor shouted, his arms up, his hands clinging to the wall.

"That's what mother, also, told me," Sanda mumbled, shaking. "But I'm afraid. Shall I come now ? Jump down ?!"

Egor was stunned. He thought that Sanda was standing on tip-toe and trying to climb into the window frame. She was, perhaps, too weak, for she struggled hard to hoist her whole body on to the high window sill. She repeated the gesture without nervousness, but tenaciously ; as if obeying some order impossible to disobey.

"What do you want to do ?" he shouted desperately. "Stay there ! Don't move !"

Sanda didn't seem to hear his words or to understand their meaning. She had now succeeded in standing, her feet on the window sill. She was waiting for a sign or, possibly, just for the courage to throw herself down. There were only four meters to the ground, but as Sanda stood rocking, head forward, the fall might have been fatal. Beside himself, Egor was constantly calling to her. He was raising his arms to her, hoping she would see and recognize him.

"Don't be afraid," said a dry voice, quite close. "We'll catch her in our arms. It's not very high up !"

He slowly turned his head. Mr. Nazarie stood by him, his face ravaged, sweating. He didn't look at him. He was just watching Sanda's sleepy movements.

"If you wish, you may go and catch her in her room. I'll stay here with the doctor."

The doctor was a few steps behind him, among the roses. He was leaning on his gun. He seemed accustomed to everything that was going on around. There was a kind of abnormal firmness in his quiet, petrified, keen attention.

"Who set the fire ?" Mr. Nazarie asked coming close to the wall.

"I did. I upset the petrol lamp," Egor murmured. "I upset it in my sleep, unconsciously... I thought Christina had come."

Mr. Nazarie came closer to Egor and took his arm.

"I saw her, too," he quietly spoke, "I saw her in the middle of the park."

At that moment Sanda's arms limply beat the air like two wounded wings. The girl tumbled down, scared, uttering no sound. She fell on Egor's chest, pulling him down to the ground. In tumbling down her body was stripped of its nightgown ; Egor, dizzy with the shock of falling, realized that he had a naked girl, fast asleep and cold, on top of him, in his arms. Sanda's hands hung limp. Her body didn't move after the shock of the fall.

"I hope you're not badly hurt," Mr. Nazarie said, helping Egor to get up.

He then put his ear to the girl's breasts.

"Don't worry," he added, "her heart is still beating."

## XVIII

The house was now burning with tall flames. They lit the park blazing over the tops of the acacias. A few crows, awakened out of their sleep, flew over the stables. The dogs were waking, too ; you could hear some muffled barking from afar.

"Let's carry her inside," said Egor, covering Sanda's almost bare shoulders with his coat. "It will be some time before she comes to."

The pain he had felt when knocked down by Sanda's fall had done him good ; it seemed to have brought him back into reality.

"Our things have all been consumed by the fire," the doctor said under his breath, his eyes on the flames.

At that moment, he was trying to remember what he had done with the thousand lei given to him by Mrs. Moscu. Is it in the pocket of his overcoat or had he left it on the table, by his watch and by the box of cartridges ?

"It will burn down to the ground," Mr. Nazarie said mournfully. "Maybe it's for the best. Maybe it will be the end of the curse."

The first human voices were then heard at the other side of the yard.

"It's the men from the vineyards, from the village," Egor said quickly. "Let's take Sanda in first."

He took her in his arms and made for the back entrance of the manorial house. The girl was dozing. Her cheek was smeared ; maybe soot or, possibly, the mud that Egor was full of. "By what happy chance had she not broken a leg, sprained no wrist in falling ?" Egor wondered. Had anything serious happened, she would certainly have come to, instantly, or fright may have plunged her into a swoon ?

"Who's there ?" Mr. Nazarie asked.

A few shadows were moving over by the servants' rooms. People were fast coming, almost running.

"It's us, Sir," a man spoke out of the dark, "uncle Marin's men, from the vineyard."

"Downright ruin," another man said coming up. "There's no time for the villagers to come, everything's burnt to ashes."

"Let it burn," Mr. Nazarie harshly answered. "Let the ghost perish !"

The men were dumbfounded. They looked at each other, confused, sleepy.

"Have you, too, seen it ?" the first man asked. "Was it the actual ghost, the young lady ?"

"Miss Christina," Egor calmly said, "it was her ! She upset the oil lamp."

He then went on, bearing Sanda in his arms, making for the door. He was beginning to be afraid of this benumbed body that he was carrying, this young heart, the heartbeats of which he could no longer hear.

Mr. Nazarie stayed behind to tell the men what had happened.

"Better like this," he mumbled. "This shall be the end of Christina."

The men were coming apace, jumping over the wall at the end of the yard or walking across the park. They came from the opposite side too, the village side, crowding in front of the fire, dumbfounded, looking on from a distance, doing nothing, crossing themselves.

"Our cattle have perished, too," Mr. Nazarie heard them. "We've lost everything this last autumn."

"...And the children who die, they turn into ghosts too," Mr. Nazarie further heard.

They were speaking to him. They dare not come too close to the house, to walk inside, to ask questions. They dare not even lend a helping hand to put out the fire. You could now hear the lower floor beams cracking and the less durable ceilings caved in with plenty of smoke.

Mr. Nazarie suddenly found himself alone facing so many unknown men, peasants awoken from sleep, still breathing heavily after running to the manor. He didn't know how to speak to them in these circumstances. He didn't know what to ask them to do and began to fear their number, their presence, ever more grave, possibly more threatening. The flames were now so tall, the men's shadows so vast, so imposing, that Mr. Nazarie suddenly thought of uprisings, but these people waited silent, tough, lost in thought ; they didn't ask anything, didn't ask for anyone's life. Or, possibly, were they asking for the real death of Miss Christina, whom the bailiff had only half killed at that time, long ago, in the great wrathful upheaval of 1907 ?

Mr. Nazarie quickly went inside, following Egor. There was now light enough reflected through the windows that he could slip along the corridor without danger. He met Egor in the doorway of Sanda's room.

"I wonder if it was wise to bring her back here," Egor said. "I believe she's asleep. But she may wake up any minute and try again."

"We shall have to watch her," Mr. Nazarie spoke. "The doctor will come. Let's call him."

"It's just that I have a little job to do with the men," Egor said, deep in thought. "And I need you, as well."

He didn't know what to do. He went inside the room again. Sanda seemed unconscious.

"Why didn't the doctor come too," Egor asked somewhat impatiently. "I don't quite realize what the trouble is, why she's sleeping such a heavy sleep."

"As if the doctor would know anything," Mr. Nazarie said engrossed in thought.

*

When the walls began to come down with a crash, the peasants drew back a few steps, their eyes still on the flames. It was as if some abandoned house were burning, they didn't seem to care, they were petrified. They walked over the flower beds, carelessly trampled the rosebushes under their feet. Practically no word was spoken. They looked on as if waiting for some long promised pledge to be fulfiled ; it had been too much desired and too long postponed to give them any joy now.

"Stand aside," Egor's voice was suddenly heard.

He seemed taller, his face drawn. The dancing flames caused his eyes to look sunken deeper into their sockets. He was elbowing his way through these silent people.

"Does anyone know how to undo spells, to charm away ghosts by magic wording ?" he asked looking round with hard eyes.

People hesitated, avoiding his eyes.

"Why, that's an old wive's tale," one man spoke, shyly blinking.

Egor could not make out whether this man was smiling or craftily looking askance. He was the sharpest of the lot, the boldest.

"And which one of you has a hatchet or a knife ?" Egor asked again. "There's a job we should finish together..."

The words struck home. The men gave a start, invigorated, excited. If there was no iron, no whacking, the ruin by fire of the cursed manorial houses did not move them.

"Come along with me," Egor said to those who had first stepped out of the crowd.

Mr. Nazarie stood by him, pale in the face, catching hold of his arm.

"What do you mean to do ?" he asked, his teeth chattering.

When he saw Egor leaving Sanda's room with a frown as if angry at the girl's mysterious swoon, irritably asking where Mrs. Moscu's bedroom was, Mr. Nazarie took fright. Has he gone crazy ? he asked himself in terror. Such a wild flame was burning in Egor's eyes that the professor dare not look into them.

"What do you mean to do with the hatchet ?" he asked once more, shaking Egor's arm.

"I need iron," Egor said, "plenty of cold iron against witchcraft."

The words were well and clearly spoken. However Egor raised his hand to his brow as if to banish too fresh a memory, an all too recent curse. He was walking with long strides, followed by the crowd of men that he had summoned.

"Who is by Sanda ?" he asked a few seconds later.

"The doctor and two women from the village," Mr. Nazarie shyly answered.

He did not like Egor's firm, tough step, his call sounding over the petrified heads of the peasants. The men reacted too suddenly to his words. In front of the fire, the iron that Egor was asking for took on a magic, revengeful meaning. Prompting people to look for their knives and follow him into the manorial household, apparently for no reason at all...

"Do you want them all to follow us inside ?" Mr. Nazarie asked, perplexed.

A number of peasants stood in the doorway, hesitating. But Egor waved to them to come in and follow him.

"Make a few torches, instantly, out of whatever you find," he prompted them.

The house was in darkness. Someone had brought a burning branch of acacia from the fire outside, but the flare was soon out and filled the room with bitter stifling smoke. Egor was impatient. There was no time, nor did he wish to look for the oil lamp. There was a light in a single room, Sanda's room, but he didn't want to go there. He caught sight of the linen curtains on the corridor's windows.

"Can't you make these into torches ?" he asked pointing them to the men.

The man with ever blinking eyelids went up to the window and tore down a curtain, wooden gallery and all. The noise seemed to be the early fulfilment of a delight promised by Egor's call. The men began breathing hard, growing slowly angry, not knowing against whom.

"Don't set the house on fire with that thing," Egor sternly spoke when seeing the unknown companion set light to the curtain.

"I'll wrap it around tight, don't you worry, Sir," the man answered.

He wrapped the curtain round a cudgel setting only the upper end alight. Another man who was standing by tore another piece of cloth and, just as carefully, set it afire. The corridor was now full of smoke and barely lit by the timid flame of the cloth. Egor took the lead going forward. They seemed to enter a cellar, so wet and stifling was the air.

The doctor came running to Egor. He wished to say something, but choking with smoke, he began to cough. They were passing by many doors, Egor attentively surveyed them, frowning, hesitating, as if laboring to remember. At the far end he bumped into the nanny. She was frightened, her eyes troubled, red with weeping.

"What were you doing here ?" Egor sternly asked.

"I was watching over the mistress," the woman tonelessly whispered. "Have you come to set the entire manor house on fire ?!"

The question sounded malevolent ; in spite of the fear in the woman's eyes, her face was derisive.

"Where is Mrs. Moscu ?" Egor quietly asked.

The nanny stretched her arm pointing to a door.

"In the young lady's room..."

She stood speechless. The men's breathing reached her now, upsetting her, rendering her dizzy.

"In Christina's room, is that it ?" Egor said.

The woman nodded. Egor turned to the men and said :

"This one, keep her among yourselves, she's almost crazy too, but don't molest her."

He was the first to enter Christina's room, without knocking. A sinister iconlight and an oil lamp were burning within. Mrs. Moscu was expecting them in the middle of the room very haughty, upright, her looks serene. Egor stood a few seconds upset by this unexpected sight, by Mrs. Moscu's white brow, by her solemn face.

"You've come for land, haven't you ?" Mrs. Moscu asked. "We have no more land."

She did not seem to see Egor. She seemed to be talking directly to the men behind him, to those rough, stubborn faces, to those eyes scared by this lordly bedroom, not slept in for so many years.

"I might have summoned the gendarmes," Mrs. Moscu continued, "I might have had you whipped. Captain Darie at Giurgiu is a friend of mine, I might have summoned him with his regiment, but I won't have bloodshed. If you've come for land, I tell you : we have none. It's been taken from us."

Egor realized that Mrs. Moscu was raving, that she thought this was rebellion at its height. He tried to stop her, lest some peasant should lose control of himself. Quite close the house was burning ; they were all stifled by smoke, choking from the smell of burnt cloth ; however, Mrs. Moscu went on speaking.

"You've roused the whole village and set fire to the house. You've forgotten I have my own children."

Egor then felt a pair of eyes transfixing him, cold, metallic, destructive. He looked up and saw Miss Christina's portrait. She was no longer smiling. She had slightly lowered her eyelids and was looking through him, a deep look, inquiring, reproachful. Egor shuddered and bit his lips. He suddenly rushed at Mrs. Moscu, getting her out of the way, pushing her upon Christina's bed. Mrs. Moscu began to shake.

"You want to kill me, do you ?" she said in a low whisper.

Egor had wrenched the hatchet from his neighbour's hand and went up to the picture. He raised his arm high, then shot the hatchet into Miss Christina's lace-wrapped neck. He fancied the eyes were blinking, the breast heaving. He also fancied that her hand was hanging limp, without feeling, from the elbow down. But it was just his fancy. A second later he raised the hatchet once more and tore Christina's blooming face across.

He could hear Mrs. Moscu's stifled yell and her pain sent the blood coursing more hotly, more savagely.

"Stop it, you'll pull down the wall," Mr. Nazarie shouted from behind.

He turned round. There were beads of sweat on his brow, black with soot. His lips were trembling. The men regarded him dumbfounded, perturbed, famished. They could hardly control themselves, for the grin of the half-torn picture was provoking, while the arms shooting up and implanting iron in Miss Christina's portrait incited them to destroy, to trample under foot, to darken the lordly bedroom with their smouldering revenge.

"Why did you kill her ?!" Mrs. Moscu suddenly yelled. "She will throttle you all !"

Trembling, Egor approached Mr. Nazarie.

"Take her away," he said pointing to the bed where Mrs. Moscu was lying. "Take her and keep an eye on her."

Mrs. Moscu was struggling. Two young men and Mr. Nazarie got her through the door the very moment when the iconlight was petering out, smoking.

"It's the ghost, the young lady !" someone said, near the window.

Once more Egor felt the fever that carried him with such force up and down that dreamlike state. He took his brow in his hands. The hatchet slid almost soundlessly upon the carpet. Someone picked it up, shaking.

"This is Miss Christina's bedroom !" Egor suddenly shouted in an inhuman voice. "Who's afraid may leave, who's not afraid let them stay here with me ! And smash !"

He was the first to rush with fists and knees upon the bedside table, then grabbed the strips of painted canvas and tore them furiously down to the ground. A few seconds later the men rushed into every corner, smashing, breaking, striking with their hatchets into the furniture, the window, the walls.

"Take care that things do not catch fire," Egor shouted like mad.

You could no longer hear his voice. Silent, breathing heavily, choking with smoke and rubbish, eyes almost closed, bumping into each other, Miss Christina's bedroom was scattered to the winds.

"Beware of fire," Egor again shouted.

He was making his way out, his arm over his eyes, slipping out. The corridor was full of people.

## XIX

He paused by a window to look at the fire. The flames were menacingly trying to catch at the roof of the old buildings.

People were constantly coming in crowds. "Now they're coming from the neighboring villages," Egor thought. He was still very upset. You could hear the fall of the hatchets in Christina's room. People were crowding in the corridor ; their deep breathing, the smell of their shirts, the giddy throbbing of their blood was everywhere. "If only they can abstain from plunder," Egor shuddered at the thought.

He found it difficult to reach Sanda's room. The girl lay still, in a swoon, her cheeks pale, her eyes closed. There were plenty of women round the bed. In a corner of the room he saw the doctor, tense, holding his gun with both hands. An old woman was speaking an incantation by Sanda's pillow.

And I saw a red gnat,
Wanting her blood to drink,
Her days to the winds to fling.
Nay, her days thou shalt not fling,
Her blood thou shalt not drink.
With a needle against evil
Shall I charm magic and harm.
With a broom away I'll sweep it,
Into reed grass shall I stick it,
In the Danube broad I'll fling it,
Clean shall Sanda henceforth be.

In her deep sleep Sanda seemed to hear her name called, for she turned in bed, tossing about. The old woman took her hand, pressing it against the cold blade of a knife. The girl moaned. Egor pressed his temples between his hands and closed his eyes. Where did these vague, muffled sounds come from, as if from some distant chasm ? It was as if the foundations of the house were moaning, as if large wooden wings were cleaving and yelling. An indefinite, sleepy rumor like a ceaseless moan was filling the heavens. The air was even more oppressive in the room. Sanda's sleep was so much like death that Egor rushed at the doctor and shook him, in fear.

"Why doesn't she wake up ?!" he asked.

The doctor gave him a long, puzzled, reproachful look. As if he couldn't believe that Egor did not understand such a simple, grave fact.

"The ghost isn't yet dead," he solemnly whispered.

At that moment Mr. Nazarie approached Egor.

"Come outside, the men have lost their heads, they want to pull down everything !"

From the corridor, you could hear heavier strokes and crumbling. Now and then, a broken window would yell out over the muffled, heavy noises.

"You must speak to them," Mr. Nazarie said, "they've laid waste to a few rooms ! You'll be held responsible tomorrow morning."

Egor again took his temples in both palms and closed his eyes. His thoughts were growing confused, his willpower was giving way.

"Better that way," he said after a time, "it's better to destroy everything." Mr. Nazarie shook him, frightened by Egor's gauntness.

"You're crazy," he howled, "you don't realize what you're doing. This is Sanda's dowry."

Egor seemed to come to his senses. Frowning, fists clenched, he rushed among the men.

"Stand back, all of you !" he shouted, "back, I say, the gendarmes are coming."

He forced his way to Christina's bedroom. Everything was ruined. The windows had all been broken, the walls pierced, the furniture maimed.

"Back, back you go !" Egor was desperately shouting, "The gendarmes are here ! The regiment has come !"

*

The plunder was slowly subsiding, as if tired. No one had obeyed Egor's orders, but a rumor was spreading that Miss Sanda was dying and the men began to draw back timidly. Into the crowded yard they came, group after group, dusty with chalk, smeared with soot, their hair hanging over their eyes. The people in the yard stood silent, frightened.

"Come along with me !" Egor said to Mr. Nazarie.

He seemed to be high strung, impatient ; his voice was harsh.

"Is there no end to this night ?!" he said looking up to the sky. "I can't even remember the time I last saw the daylight."

Far away, as yet unseen, the dawn was close. The air was cold, clear, stone still. The stars had vanished under the flaring light. Egor had taken an oil lamp from a peasant, and was carrying it carefully lest it should go out along the way. He was advancing firmly, deep in thought. Seeing that he was making his way to the stables, Mr. Nazarie was frightened.

"What do you mean to do ?" he asked in a strangled voice.

He was afraid to be so far from other people, from the glare of the fire. Afraid, because Sanda's prolonged swoon constantly reminded him of the powers of witchcraft.

Egor didn't answer. He was walking fast to the old stable. It was very dark here and the lamp threw a round, tremulous patch of light. Far away you could see the high flames flaring over the manorial house. As Egor opened the gate of the stable and took the first step inside, Mr. Nazarie began to understand. Fear, cold fear, took hold of him. He dare not look up. Egor walked straight to the far end of the stable. Miss Christina's barouche was in its usual place, unmoved.

"Is it this one ?" Egor asked, holding the lamp high that Mr. Nazarie should see more clearly.

The professor nodded, white in the face. It was the same old, sleeping barouche ; just as he had seen it, a few hours earlier, on the main drive, waiting for Miss Christina's light step.

"Yet the door was closed," Egor whispered smiling.

A confused smile, his voice uncertain, troubled. Mr. Nazarie stared at the ground.

"Let's go," he said, "Goodness knows what is happening in the house."

But Egor's thoughts seemed to be bent on something quite different. As if he hadn't heard, in the dirty light of the oil lamp, he continued to look at the old and bedraggled leather cushions in the barouche. It was, therefore, true : Miss Christina had come, the true one. He seemed to see her unnatural body on the cushions of the coach. How strange, this scent of violets still in the air !

"Come on, Egor !" Mr. Nazarie impatiently spoke.

So everything shall prove true in the end, Egor thought. Tired, he lowered his eyes. He remembered his first encounter with Miss Christina's barouche.

"Strange," he suddenly said, "very strange, that nobody should have yet seen Simina !"

They walked to the door. Mr. Nazarie was in a hurry, unwilling to look back.

"Indeed, I haven't seen her since the house caught fire and began to burn," he said, she may be hiding somewhere."

"Don't I know where to find her," Egor said smiling. "I know very well where the little witch is hiding."

Yet, in spite of all this, strange despair was breaking his heart; as if he were suddenly alone, cursed, unable to step beyond the fiery magic circle of the spell, unable to plead with his destiny, to relent.

★

The doctor had left Sanda's room. The women were still there, and Mrs. Moscu whom a few decent peasants had carried in their arms. The doctor and the crowd of people were waiting in the yard to see the fire die down. He had no thoughts, and did not even remember when he had sunk into this pleasant weariness, into this warm vacuity. He was surprised to see Egor appear again among the men, asking them to follow him. He did not hear him speak, only saw his raised arms, his sombre face. A group of peasants set out, following Egor's lead, no hurry, packed together, their eyes on the ground. The doctor followed. Someone heading the group was carrying a torch. Egor still held the oil lamp in his left hand, close to his breast. He clutched a thin iron bar in his right hand.

"Let me go down first," he spoke, having reached the cellar's entrance. "You wait here and when you hear me shout, jump in too."

Mr. Nazarie tried to stop him. His eyes were burning with lack of sleep and fever. His fingers shook as they clutched Egor's arm.

"You're crazy to go down there alone ?" he shouted.

Egor gave him a haggard look. "Where did he get the strength to command with such firmness ?" Mr. Nazarie wondered, for there was immense weariness in Egor's eyes; his dim pupils, his stiff dry lips spoke of a delirious state,

"I'll take you with me," he told the professor, "but you must have a piece of iron in your hand... As a means of defense," he murmured.

They began to go down the cellar's steps. The men remained outside, breathing more slowly, packed together, feeeling sound and alive because they were crowding together. Before plunging into the cellar's foggy darkness, Egor took a last look outside. The sky seemed to brighten far away.

"It will soon be daylight," Egor said turning to Mr. Nazarie.

He was smiling. He went down the cold steps fast enough, keeping the lamp close to his breast.

Mr. Nazarie followed him closely. When he felt the wet sand under his feet he gave a start, trying to pierce the darkness. They couldn't see anything except the wall they were walking along, with just the tremulous light of the lamp. Egor advanced firmly, straight to the far end of the cellar. The more they advanced, the lesser noise from the fire and the crumbling of the walls.

Silence reigned again here under the earth.

"Are you afraid ?" Egor suddenly asked, throwing light on Mr. Nazarie's face.

The professor blinked fast, quite blinded. What was happening to him, what crazy thoughts were sprouting in Egor's mind ?

"I am not afraid," Mr. Nazarie said. "I have iron in hand and a cross too... Moreover, it will soon be daylight... Nothing can happen then."

Egor did not answer. He walked on, frowning, lifting the iron bar in his right hand. They now entered the second partition. Egor recognized the way with terror. A slight blood-red glare was showing through a small window. "We're passing by the fire again," Mr. Nazarie thought. Very few noises, however, came from outside. The heavy vault and cold walls stifled the sounds, the murmur of voices.

"Can you see anything over there ?" Egor asked, stopping and pointing the lamp to a dark corner. "I can't see anything," Mr. Nazarie answered.

"And yet that's where it is," Egor said, more obstinately.

He set out with long, firm steps. The light began to tremble. The air here was more oppressive, more humid. The walls looked ashy and the age-old vault came down close upon their heads.

They found Simina lying prone on the soft, scratched earth. She didn't even hear the steps of the two men, and the light of the oil lamp did not seem to wake her out of her trance. Egor began to shake, approaching Simina's small tattered body.

"She is here, isn't she ?" he wispered, shaking her by the shoulder.

The little girl turned her head and regarded him without surprise. She did not answer. She clung close to the earth and vainly raked it with her nails, obstinately keeping her ear to the ground, tensely waiting. Her hands were blood-stained, her calves muddy, her dress dirty from leaves that she had crushed, running and frequently slipping in the dark.

"No use waiting for her, Simina," Egor said harshly. "Christina died once, long ago, and now she's going to die once and for all."

He rushed at the little girl furiously, brutally lifted her from the ground, and shook her in his arms.

"Wake up ! Christina is now going to hell, and the fires of hell will burn her corpse !"

A strange turbid feeling came over him as he was saying these words. The little girl was limp in his arms. Her eyes seemed glassy, and she looked at him with a haggard stare. She had bitten her lips and the blood showed. Egor began fretting. "I must make up my mind quickly," he thought shuddering, "to save them all, I must decide."

"Hold her in your arms and cross yourself !" he said to Mr. Nazarie, handing him Simina's body, drained of all strength.

Mr. Nazarie made a large sign of the cross, then began murmuring a prayer he had not known before.

Egor went up to the spot where Simina had lain, scrutinized it piercingly, as if trying to penetrate into it, to guess the dark treasure that it was guarding against nature. He then grabbed the iron bar and pressed down against it with the weight of his body.

"Is her heart here, Simina ?" he asked, never turning his head.

The little girl gave him a perplexed look. She began to struggle in the professor's arms. Egor pulled out the iron bar that had only half sunk and planted it beside, with growing obstinate fury.

"Is it here ?" he asked again, as if strangled.

A thrill ran through Simina's body. Her body suddenly stiffened in Mr. Nazarie's arms, and her eyes rolled back in her head. Egor felt his arm trembling as he was driving the bar in. "It's in now," he thought savagely. He leaned upon the bar with his full weight, howling. He felt it piercing into the flesh. He was shaking, for this slow transfixing was making him sink leisurely into ecstasy, into fearful frenzy. As in a dream, he heard Simina yelling. He fancied that Mr. Nazarie was coming up to stop him, so he grew more stubborn, fell on his knees, screwed in with his utmost strength, though the iron was wounding his hands, striking the bones of his fists. Ever deeper, further on, into her heart, into the core of her bewitched life !

A painful enchantment suddenly seized him. He saw with stupor the walls of his room, saw the bed that he was lying on and the bottle on the bedside table. The fragrance of violets was still there. And he heard the words of old, as in a song :

*"Your eyes, so glowing, make me grieve,*
*And scorching is their fire."*

Where did they suddently vanish, Simina and Mr. Nazarie, as well as the ashy walls of the cellar ? He heard a distant, sad voice calling :

"Egor ! Egor !"

He looked round. No one. He was alone, alone for all time He would never meet her again, the scent of violets would never excite him, her blood- red mouth would never kiss him.

He dropped down. The darkness was again heavy and cold. He felt as if he was buried alive in some unknown cave, unknown to anyone, with no hope of ever being saved.

Human steps, however, were approaching from other spaces. Sad music, an old-fashioned waltz tune, human steps, and a beam of light. Someone, his face quite close, asked him :

"Do you know Radu Prajan ? There he is !"

He turned his head in fear. What a new and absurd disguise ! Radu Prajan was now very much like Mr. Nazarie; he dare not come near, dare not speak to him, but only looked into his eyes, calling him, imploring him to come, that he might confess the great danger that was to come. He was carrying Simina in his arms, her hair in her eyes, her lips white.

"There now, she, too, is dead," Prajan's eyes seemed to say.

Yet, maybe, it wasn't true, maybe he was saying this, lest he should be identified. Prajan was also afraid, for he was staring, as if frozen, without even blinking...

*

He came to with many people around. They were carrying torches, hatchets and wooden pointed stakes. In front of him, on the humid earth, he saw the end of the iron bar. "So it's true !" he thought. He smiled sadly. Everything had been true. He himself had killed her ; was he to expect any hope from anywhere ? Who should he pray to, what wonder would bring close Christina's warm body ?

"You're to come up," he heard an unknown voice. "Miss Sanda is dying."

His chin dropped, without an answer. No thought. Just loneliness, his destined loneliness.

"She's dead," another voice whispered nearby.

He felt he was being raised and carried. He heard that voice again, very close to his ear.

"Miss Sanda is dead ! Please come up, it's a calamity."

Whoever had spoken so closely, in this his great loneliness, in this dark night where no one and no rumor could ever penetrate ?

They were carrying him in their arms. The rooms around him changed, as if bewitched. He first passed through a large ballroom with gilt chandeliers, bedecked with hanging crystal arrows. He came across elegant couples, seemingly that minute arrested in their dance, watching him perplexed and surprised. Men in black suits, ladies with silken fans... Then a strange room with lots of green baize tables, and strange people playing cards without speaking to each other. They all looked upon him in surprise, as he was carried aloft by certain invisible men. There, he's now climbing the steps into a dining room with old wooden furniture. Here's the beginning of the corridor. Yet the corridor became instantly blurred, and out of the blue haze a gigantic flame suddenly shot up, somewhere quite close. Egor closed his eyes. "So, it's true," he remembered.

"The fire is now spreading to the other house, too !" he heard a voice saying.

Egor tried to turn seeking the man who had spoken so close to him. He only saw a wing of blazing fire, no beginning and no end to it. He closed his eyes.

"Alas for the gentry ! The way it has gone to waste."

It was the same unknown voice, which seemed to come from beyond the boundaries of sleep.

# DOCTOR HONIGBERGER'S SECRET

One morning in the autumn of 1934 I received, by hand, a rather strange letter, the messenger saying that he was expecting an immediate reply. A lady whose name, Zerlendi, I had never heard, wrote asking me to visit her that very afternoon. It was a correct, excessively polite letter as befitting an old-fashioned lady addressing an unknown person. "I hear you have recently returned from the East and I think you would be interested in examining the collections amassed by my husband," she wrote among other things. I confess that I have little interest in the contacts I was asked to make because I had spent a few years in the East. I had to give up a friendship that promised to be thoroughly agreeable, because I would not tell platitudes about "the mystery of Asia", about fakirs, miracles, or adventures in the jungle, sensational details that my companion expected me to enlarge upon. Mrs. Zerlendi's letter mentioned oriental collections without specifying their nature or source, which was enough to stir up my curiosity.

I was actually interested in the lives of those Romanians who had been possessed by a passion for the East. Sincerely speaking, I ought to say that several years before this I had discovered a case of books about China in one of the second-hand bookshops on the banks of the Dîmbovița. These books had long been studied, annotated, sometimes even corrected in pencil, by the buyer, whose signature I found time and again on the fly-leaf of most of them : Radu C. This Radu C. had been no amateurish reader. His books, now in my possession, proved that he had undertaken a serious methodical study of the Chinese language. He has actually annotated the six volume of *Mémoires Historiques* by Se-Ma Ts'ien, translated by Edouard Chavannes, correcting all printing mistakes in the Chinese texts ; he knew the Chinese classics in the Couvreur editions, was a subscriber of the T'oung Pao publication and had acquired all the volumes of *Variétés sinologiques* printed in Shanghai before the war. I became interested in this man as soon as I assembled part of his library, though I did not find out his full name for a long time. The bookseller had acquired several hundred volumes in 1920 ; a few illustrated books he had sold immediately, but found no customers for this collection of synecological texts and studies. So I was wondering whoever that Romanian might have been who had so seriously set to work on the Chinese language, leaving nothing, not even his full name behind. What obscure passion led him to that faraway land ? He did not want to approach *the language* as an amateur, but he meant to learn it, while he strove to understand the history of the country. Did he ever reach China, or did he prematurely perish in some hide-out during the war ?

These questions that I was asking in sadness and perplexity while looking through his books at the bookshop on the river bank were to be answered much later. The very answer, in fact, was wrapped up in unexpected mysteries. But that is a different story, quite distinct from the incidents I am now going to relate. I remembered, however, this Radu C. and a few more oriental scholars or connoisseurs who had lived in perfect anonymity here în Romania, so I decided to accept the invitation of the unknown lady.

That very afternoon I stood in front of the house on S. street. I stopped in front of number 17, and recognized one of those houses that I could never pass without slowing down and gazing at it; I was anxious to guess what was going on behind those time-worn walls, who was living there, fighting what destiny ? The street is in the very centre of Bucharest, close to Calea Victoriei. By what miracle did the residence at number 17 manage to stay intact, with iron gates, gravel in the yard, with full-grown acacia and chestnut trees darkening part of the façade with their shade ? The gate was slow to open. A pool where the water had long been dry stood beside rich beds of autumnal flowers. There was a different air here. A world that had slowly died out in other fine districts of the capital had decently survived here, away from the agony of decay and poverty. It was a residential dwelling from the old days, but well-preserved, except for the damaged façade too soon impaired by the damp shade of the trees. The main entrance was protected by an awning of frosted glass, in the fashion of about forty years ago. A few stone steps green with moss, laden with large flower pots on every side, led up to a gloss porch with colored upper windows. No name to be seen by the bell.

I was expected. A halting old maid opened the door instantly and showed me into a vast drawing room. I hardly had time to have a look at the furniture and pictures around me before Mrs. Zerlendi appeared from behind an oak door. She was a woman past fifty whom you could hardly have forgotten had you met her but once. She was not aging like everybody else, this lady. Or maybe she was aging like women of former centuries, secretely understanding that in death they would approach the great illumination of all understanding, by no means the end of an earthly life, the gradual shrinking up of the flesh and its final dissolution into the earth. I have always considered people as falling into two categories : those who hold death to be an end of like and of the body and those who imagine it as the beginning of a new spiritual life ; therefore, I never attempt any judgment of a man I meet, before discovering his sincere opinion with regard to death. The most brilliant intelligence and the most captivating charm may otherwise be misleading.

Mrs. Zerlendi sat in an armchair motioning me to a high-backed wooden chair, with a gesture devoid of that familiarity of women of a certain age.

"Thank you for coming," she said. "My husband would have been delighted to meet you. He, too, loved India, maybe more than his medical profession would allow."

I was prepared to hear a long story, glad to be able, meanwhile, to consider attentively the very strange face of Mrs. Zerlendi. But my hostess stopped after a few moments and asked, her brow slightly inclined towards me :

"Do you know the life and writings of Doctor Johann Honigberger ? My husband fell in love with India owing to the books of this Saxon doctor from Braşov. He had probably inherited an interest in history, for history was a craze in the whole family, but he began with India when he discovered Doctor Honigberger's works. As a matter of fact, he kept collecting material a few years running and even began work on a monograph of this Saxon doctor. He was a medical man himself, and thought that he could write such a monograph."

I confess I knew very little about Dr. Johann Honigberger. I remembered having read, many years before, his main book "Thirty Five Years in the East", in an English version, the only one available at Calcutta. In those days I was busy studying the Yoga philosophy and techniques. I had consulted

Honigberger's book for the details of these occult practices that the doctor had apparently been closely familiar with. As the book had come out in the middle of the last century, I suspected that the author had been devoid of a critical attitude. I did not know, however, that this doctor, who had been a name in Oriental studies, belonged to an old family in Brașov. It was this particular detail that I was now interested in.

"My husband actively corresponded with diverse medical men and scholars who had known Honigberger. The doctor died in 1869 at Brașov, just after he returned from his last voyage to India ; but there were plenty of people still living, who had met him. One of his sons was a magistrate at Iași. He was the son of the doctor's first marriage. My husband did not get to know him, though he frequently went to Iași to look for certain papers..."

I couldn't help smiling. I was surprised at the precise details of the Honigberger biography that Mrs. Zerlendi knew. Maybe she guessed what I was thinking, for she added :

"These things meant so much to him that they remained imprinted in my memory. These and a lot more..." she suddenly ceased, looking thoughtful. Later on I had the opportunity to check the many precise things that Mrs. Zerlendi knew about Dr. Honigberger. One entire evening she told me about his first residence in India, after spending four years in Asia Minor, one year in Egypt and seven years in Syria. It was obvious that Mrs. Zerlendi had repeatedly consulted her husband's books and mansucripts, as if anxious sometime to complete the work he had left unfinished.

The truth is that you could hardly escape the mysterious charm of the Saxon doctor, a doctor by his own determination, since officially he only possessed an apothecary's diploma. Honigberger had spent the better half of his long life in the East. He had once been physician to the Court, apothecary, head of the Arsenal and admiral of Ranjit-Singh, the Maharaja of Lahore. Repeatedly he amassed considerable fortunes and lost them. Though a high class adventurer, Honigberger had never been an impostor. He was a man well-informed in many sciences, profane and occult. His ethnographic, botanical, numismatic and art collections became the valuable property of many illustrious museums. It was easy to understand why doctor Zerlendi, with his passion for our own historical past, as well as for the history of medicine, dedicated so many years of his life to restore and decipher the real biography of Honigberger.

"For he had come to the timely conclusion," Mrs. Zerlendi once confessed, "that Honigberger's life held many secrets, in spite of all the books written about him. He couldn't understand, for instance, his last voyage to India in 1858 when hardly able to go on from day to day, just back from an expedition in tropical Africa and gravely ill. Why had Honigberger gone back to India, worn out as he was, and why did he die as soon as he set foot in Brașov? my husband would often wonder. Likewise the doctor's so-called earlier botanical research in Kashmir he considered suspect. He had reason to believe that Honigberger had actually been not only in Kashmir but had crossed over into Tibet or had anyway inquired into the science of occult pharmacopoeia in one of those Himalayan monasteries and that the botanical research had been a mere pretext. These things, however, you'll judge for yourself," Mrs. Zerlendi added.

I must confess that having seen the books and documents concerning Honigberger, so carefully collected by Mrs. Zerlendi's husband, I, too, became inclined to believe that the life of the Saxon doctor was wrapped in mystery. Yet all that followed my first visit to the house on S. street went far beyond the Honigberger mystery.

"So, I thought," Mrs. Zerlendi resumed after a long pause "that it would be a pity to abandon all this work. I have heard about you and read some of your works, especially those referring to India and Indian philosophy. I can't say I thoroughly understood them, but one thing I did understand : that I could confidently address myself to you."

I tried to confess that I was flattered, etc., but Mrs. Zerlendi continued in the same voice :

"For many years, practically no one has entered this house, except for a few friends who do not possess the special training that my husband had acquired. So there has been no change in his study and library since 1910. I have been abroad a long time and in coming home I have refrained from mentioning my husband's name very often. His medical colleagues used to consider him possessed by obessessive mania. The library that I am now going to show you has been visited by only one person among those who might have valued it : by Bucura Dumbravă. I wrote to her, as I have to you, that I had a rich oriental collection and she came after much postponing. I believe she was very interested. She told me that here she could find books that she had applied for a the British Museum. But she had no time to examine it at her leisure. She made a few notes and promised to come again on her return from India. As you possibly know she was going to a conference in theosophy in India, but she never set foot on Romanian soil again. At Port-Said she died..."

I couldn't say if Mrs. Zerlendi was attributing some secret meaning to this death on the verge of homecoming. She was again silent, considering me with uncommon attention. I felt that I was bound to say something, so I told her that mystery is so present in our existence, that there's no use looking for it afar, at Adyar or Port-Said, for instance. Mrs Zerlendi gave no answer. She rose from her armchair and asked me to accompany her into the library. Walking across the drawing room, I asked her if her husband had ever been to India.

"Difficult to say," she whispered, hesitating, yet trying to smile.

## II

I have seen many libraries belonging to rich and scholarly people, but none delighted my heart like the one on S. street. As the solid oak door opened, I stood transfixed on the threshold. Here was one of those vast rooms seldom found even in the wealthiest homes of the last century. Large windows looked upon the back garden of the house. The curtains had been drawn shortly before our arrival. The clear autumn twilight gave added solemnity to this high ceilinged hall, its walls practically lined with books. A wooden gallery ran a good way round the library. There were possibly thirty thousand volumes, mostly in leather bindings, covering the most diverse fields of study : medicine, history, religion, travel, occult sciences, Indian lore. Mrs Zerlendi led me straight to the shelves occupied exclusively by books about India. Seldom have I found in a private collection such valuable books in such numbers. Much later, having spent a whole afternoon gazing at those endless shelves, did I actually realize what treasures were housed there. Hundreds of volumes dealing with voyages to India, from Marco Polo and Tavernier, to Pierre Loti and Jaccolliot. It was obvious that Doctor Zerlendi picked up any kind of book issued about India. Only thus could I understand the presence of certain impostors, for instance, Louis Jaccolliot. There were, moreover, complete sets of the *Journal Asiatique* and of the London *Journal of the Royal Asiatic Society,* not to mention the acta of many academies, hundreds of scholarly papers on the languages, literature and religion of India. Anything of importance in the field of Indian lore published in the last century was there, from the great Petersburgh dictionary, down to the editions of Sanskrit texts issued in Calcutta or Benares. The volumes of Sanskrit texts were a great surprise.

"He began to study the Sanskrit language in 1901," Mrs. Zerlendi said in answer to my surprise, "and learnt it systematically as much as you can learn far from the living centers of a language."

In fact there were on those shelves not only elementary books or texts usually acquired by an amateur, but books that only a man who was thoroughly familiar with the secrets of the Sanskrit language could have ordered. For instance, I came across difficult commentaries like the *Siddânta Kaumudi,* which showed an interest for the nuances of Sanskrit grammar ; or the bulky treaty of Medhaditi on the Manu laws ; or those ticklish sub-commentaries to the Vedantic texts only issued by the Allahabad and Benares presses ; or numerous texts concerning the Indian rituals. I was particularly struck by the volumes of Indian medicine, and by the treatises of mysticism and asceticism. I knew from my own limited experience that these texts are difficult and profound, impossible to understand without an extensive commentary ; they are often only half understood unless orally explained by a teacher.

I turned to Mrs Zerlendi in wonder. I had been excited in entering the library, expecting to find a complete file of doctor Honigberger's life and work. I was discovering the library of a scholar in Indian lore, that in its immensity and diversity could have stirred the jealousy of a Roth, Jacobi or Sylvain Lévi.

"He went as far as this starting from Honigberger," Mrs Zerlendi said, understanding what I was thinking, and taking me to another section of the library where I was soon to discover the books and documents about the Saxon doctor.

"But how did he find the time to amass so many books and how did he manage to examine them all ?" I exclaimed equally bewildered.

"A good number were a family inheritance, particularly the history books," she added. "The rest he bought himself, especially in the last eight years. He sold a few landed properties," she uttered the last words with a smile, without the slightest trace of regret.

"All the dealers in secondhand books in Leipzig, Paris and London knew him," she went on. "And the fact is, he knew what to buy. He would occasionally buy whole libraries from the family of deceased oriental scholars. But, of course, he had no time to read everything, though in his last years, he would sit up all night, only sleeping two or three hours."

"That, very likely, shattered his health," I said.

"On the contrary," Mrs Zerlendi answered. "He had an enormous capacity for work. He kept a special diet, moreover : he ate no meat, did not smoke, did not take alcohol, tea, coffee..."

She seemed to be on the point of adding something else, but she stopped somewhat abruptly and beckoned me to the other end of the library where "The Honigberger corner" stood. All the books of the Saxon doctor were there, as well as a good many works on his prodigious life. In a corner, a copy of Mahlknecht's engraving, the famous etching presenting Honigberger dressed as a counsellor of Ranjit-Singh. Doctor Zerlendi had assembled in bandboxes countless letters of Honigberger addressed to the scholars of his time, copies of portraits and etchings of his family and contemporaries, and maps on which he had traced the itineraries of all Honigberger's voyages to Asia and Africa.

I was sadly looking through these papers, the importance of which I was only later to realize, wondering that such a man had lived in our town, only a quarter of a century before, without anybody even dreaming what treasure he had brought.

"And why didn't he write this book on Honigberger ?" I asked.

"He had begun writing," Mrs Zerlendi spoke after a long hesitation, "but he suddenly ceased working, never giving the real reason. As I was saying, he carried on a considerable correspondence in his search for information and unpublished documents. In 1906, on the occasion of the Exhibition, he got to know a friend of Constantin Honigberger, the son of the doctor's first marriage, who possessed a few letters and several papers, accidentally fallen into his hands. That same autumn my husband went to Iași ; on his return he was quite upset. I do not think he got hold of the original papers, but he had had all those documents copied The fact is that from that moment he stopped writing, his interest being intensely focused on Indian philosophy. In the course of time, Honigberger was definitely abandoned, and during the ensuing years my husband exclusively dedicated himself to the study of the Sanskrit language."

Smiling, she pointed to the shelves I had first considered in wonder.

"He didn't ever confess what led him to abandon the results of such long years of eager study, did he?" I asked.

"He gave me a few hints," Mrs. Zerlendi began," "for since he was back from Iași he had grown less talkative. He once told me it was essential for him to become thoroughly acquainted with Indian philosophy and the occult sciences in order to understand part of Honigberger's life which had thus far remained obscure, buried in legend. As he embarked upon the study of the Sanskrit language, he developed an interest in the occult sciences. This, however, is an episode that I am vague about, for my husband never spoke about this ultimate passion. I could only surmise his fierce interest in these studies judging by the books he was constantly ordering. As a matter of fact you may judge for yourself," Mrs. Zerlendi added, leading me to a different section of the library. Hard to say, but here my surprise was still greater. Mrs Zerlendi's confessions since I entered the library and the things I saw greatly surprised me and actively contributed to my bewilderment, so that I examined the new shelves in wonder and admiration, quite speechless. It was obvious at first sight that the doctor had made a good beginning in his collection of occult lore. There were no vulgarizing works that the French bookshops threw on the market at the end of the last century. Even the majority of theosophist books, mostly mediocre and equivocal, were absent. Just a few of Leadbeater's and Annie Besant's books, as well as the complete works of Mrs. Blavatsky, which, as I discovered on another occasion, Doctor Zerlendi had very carefully perused. On the other hand, except for Fabre d'Olivet and Rudolf Steiner, except for Stanislas de Guaita and Hartmann, the library was extremely rich in the classics of the occult, of hermetism and traditional theosophy. Ancient editions of Swedenborg, Paracelsus, Cornelius Agrippa, Böhme, Della Riviera, and Pernety stood side by side with works attributed to Pythagora, with hermetic texts, with collections of the famous alchemists, both in the old print of Salmon and Manget, as well as in the modern edition of Berthelot. Those forgotten books of physiognomy, astrology and palmistry were also present.

Later on, having the opportunity to examine these shelves at leisure, I was to discover extremely rare works, as for instance *De aquae vitae simplicity et composito* by Arnaud de Villeneuve ; or Christian apocripha, the *Adam and Eve* for instance, that Strindberg had long been looking for. A firm intention and a definite goal seemed to have had impelled doctor Zerlendi to build up this library richly furnished in occult works. I gradually realized that no important author, no essential book was missing. No doubt, the doctor had sought no mere superfical information to assimilate the essential elements of occult doctrine and terminology, to express himself competently in Honigberger's biography that he was to write. His books proved his attempt at a personal conviction of the truth so well concealed in the hermetic tradition. Otherwise it would have been useless to read Agrippa von Nettesheim and the *Bibliotheca Chemica Curiosa*.

It was exactly the doctor's keen interest in the occult, plus his passion for Indian philosophy, particularly for the secret schools of thought in India, that aroused my vivid interest. Expecially since Mrs Zerlendi had led me to understand that this new and last passionate interest of her husband's had flared up as a result of his visit to Iași.

"Very likely, he didn't confine himself to reading about occultism ; the doctor must have attempted a certain amount of practice, no doubt."

"I rather believe as much," Mrs Zerlendi said after a brief hesitation. "He never confessed anything, but his last years were practically spent in this study, or by himself at one of our country estates in Oltenia. As I was saying, he never showed signs of fatigue in spite of his almost ascetic way of life. On the contrary. I may say that he was feeling better than ever before."

Nevertheless he died, I was thinking while listening to Mrs Zerlendi's timid explanations. The room was now practically dark and the hostess crossed it to turn on the light. Two enormous chandeliers with innumerable pendant crystal arrowheads flooded the library with strong artificial light, a bit too strong. I could not tear myself away and lingered in front of the shelves with books on occultism.

Mrs. Zerlendi came back, having first closed one of the windows, the one looking out on a stone balcony, and pulled a golden-green velvet curtain.

"Now that you have seen the collections in question," she began, "I may reveal my full intentions. I have been wondering for years if I was not to blame concerning the fruit of my husband's work, concerning these drawers full of papers and letters collected at the time when he was interested in Honigberger's biography. I have no definite knowledge of what he intended to study during his last years, but the inquiries he had begun were due to the same necessity of understanding Honigberger. When I heard about you having spent so many years in India studying its religions and philosophies, I thought that you could possibly know what my husband intended to study and that Honigberger's life would have no secrets for you. This labor will not be useless," Mrs. Zerlendi added, lightly pointing to the Honigberger section. "Maybe you'd find it interesting to write the Saxon doctor's life that my husband was unable to conclude. I would die comforted," she went on, "knowing that my husband's research was of use to someone and that the biography he had set his heart on would eventually see the light of day."

I did not know what to say. So far I had never undertaken to write by order, in a field unfamiliar to me. Practically all the books I had written were got up in haste, under pressure of circumstances, but I always had my own choice,

whether I was starting a novel or a philosophical treatise. However, I was aware that my hesitation could not go on indefinitely.

"Mrs. Zerlendi," I began, "I am flattered by your confidence. Let me sincerely confess that I'm happy at the mere thought of being able to return to this library without inconvenience to you. I'm not sure, however, of ever succeeding in carrying out what your husband began. In the first place, I am no medical man, and I'm ignorant of the history of medicine in the 19$^{th}$ century. Secondly, quite a number of things that your husband was familiar with are quite unknown to me. Yet I can promise this much : that Honigberger's biography shall be written and published. I might collaborate with someone competent in medicine and its history in the 19$^{th}$ century."

"I have thought of that," Mrs. Zerlendi said, "but the medical side is not primarily important, distinguished specialists may be found any time to collaborate ; the orientalist side of the biography is the essential one. Had I not known my husband's fervent wish that Honigberger's biography should also be written by a Romanian, for biographies compiled by foreign writers exist in plenty, I should have contacted a specialist in England or Germany, where Honigberger is especially well-known." She suddenly stopped speaking, and after a few moments' silence, she looked up into my eyes. "Besides, to tell you the truth, there is one more thing that may seem to you rather too personal : I wish to see this biography being written by my side. There are certain incidents, obscure enough in this man's life, you'll see, and I keep hoping that someone, some day, shall clarify them for me."

## III

Only later, after attentively reading the manuscripts and documents as collected, classed and annotated by the doctor, did I realize how right Mrs. Zerlendi had been about those obscure episodes in the life of Johann Honigberger. I went back to the house on S. street a few days later, after which I began spending at least three afternoons a week in the

library. That long autumn was unspeakably fine and warm. I would come at about four and stay late into the evening. Mrs. Zerlendi would sometimes greet me in the drawing room. Usually, however, we met in the library ; she would come in long after I had been seated at work, walking with the same unobtrusive grace up to my desk, putting out the same unusually pale hand from a black silk sleeve. Soon after, came the old parlor maid with Turkish coffee and comfits on a tray. Mrs. Zerlendi was always present when my coffee was brought. No doubt she thought that her presence would not inconvenience me during that space of respite when I interrupted work, the file of manuscripts open in front of me.

"How are you getting on ?" she would ask. "Do you think my husband's papers might be of use ?"

I was, however, getting on slowly enough. Maybe it was my own fault too, for I had not been content in just examining the Honigberger archives, but, in parallel with their perusal, I was trying to examine the many shelves of Indian and occult books, an endeavor that I was most keen on and that required plenty of time. After my fourth visit to the house on S. street I had come to realize how much of Honigberger's biography the doctor had completed. The final manuscript ceased upon Honigberger's return to Alep in 1822, where the Saxon doctor had introduced the new methods of vaccination. But there were a few more rough copies dealing with the seven years he had spent in Syria. All these papers hardly covered a quarter of the actual biography, since Honigberger's life only became interesting after he had reached Ranjit-Singh's court. About other periods in the life of that adventurous doctor, I only found documents carefully classed in chronologically ordered files. Every file bore the date, the localities, and the number of respective testimonies. Sometimes a year would be queried or references to some other apocryphal file. Because Doctor Zerlendi had reached a conclusion revealed in a note to the first chapter : that many statements of Honigberger's, as accepted by contemporary biographers, were based on false data or on documents intentionally falsified later on. I couldn't grasp Honigberger's object in mystifying an existence that had been actually fabulous, developing under the sign of mystery and adventure.

"You haven't yet reached the secrets that my husband was talking about, have you ?" Mrs. Zerlendi once asked.

I found it difficult to answer. I could guess what explanations the old lady expected and I didn't know if I should ever be able to reveal them to her. Cases of "apparent death", of yogic trance, of levitation, of incombustibility or invisibility that Honigberger referred to and Doctor Zerlendi had specially investigated, all these were very difficult to explain to anyone who had no theoretical understanding of their possible realization. As to Honigberger's mysterious voyages to Kashmir and Tibet, to his inquiries into magic pharmacology, or his possible participation in certain initiatory ceremonies of the Vallabhacharya sect, I was not clear myself. If doctor Zerlendi had had some definite information concerning these obscure episodes, he had not included them in the files of his biography.

"Secrets I come across constantly," I would evasively answer. "I am not yet up to reading anything into them."

Mrs. Zerlendi sat for some seconds, looking into the void; then she would gradually take herself in hand and walk out of the library with a melancholy step. When she stayed longer she would ask me about my travels in India ; she was especially interested in the Hymalayan monasteries that I had come across, things that I don't quite like to talk about. She never let out anything about her life or family. I never found out the names of her friends that she sometimes mentioned.

What I discovered subsequently was purely accidental. Three weeks after my first visit I came earlier than usual. It was a rainy day, depressing autumnal rain. The old maid servant opened the door after some delay. Mrs. Zerlendi was unwell, she said. I was to come in, and she had even lit a fire in the fireplace. I walked in timidly. The library looked different in the miserable dull light of the autumn rain. The fireplace did not properly heat the immense room, but I sat down to work, quite stubbornly. It seemed to me that Mrs. Zerlendi's state would be soothed by the idea that I was working in a room nearby and that someday, not so far away, I might be able to clarify some of the "mysteries" that her husband had brought to light.

Half an hour after my arrival, the door of the study opened and a young lady entered, cigarette in hand. She didn't seem at all surprised to find me at the desk, the files open in front of me.

"So it's you !" she said coming up.

I rose and told her my name.

"I know, mother told me," she added cursorily. "Let us hope you'll have better luck."

I smiled an embarrassed smile, not quite sure of her meaning. Then I began speaking about what I had found concerning Honigberger. The young woman considered me with some irony.

"These things we have known for some time," she put in. "The others have gone that far. Poor Hans was even further advanced, so they say."

I must have looked quite amazed as the young lady laughed. She stubbed her cigarette in a copper ashtray and came closer.

"You thought that these mysteries had been waiting for you for almost a quarter of a century to unravel, didn't you? An error, my dear sir. Others have had a try before you. Father was, of course, a man well-known and this case did not soon vanish from the minds of a fairly large group of pre-war persons."

"I am not to blame for the error you find me in," I replied, trying to seem by no means upset. "Mrs. Zerlendi chose to reveal just certain things, keeping quiet about others. As a matter of fact, my commission is limited. I am here to appraise the documentary material concerning Doctor Honigberger's biography."

The young woman gave me a direct look as if she found it difficult to believe me. I then had a better look at her. Tall, slim, almost thin, her eyes feverish with a smothered light and a twitching mouth. She didn't wear make-up, a fact which added a few years to her more than thirty.

"I did think that mother was keeping certain things from you," she began in a less strained voice. "Maybe you would have been disappointed from the very beginning had she told you that your present work had been done by three other people. The last being a German officer who stayed in Bucharest after it was occupied. We used to call him poor Hans because his fate was actually a tragic one. He died in a shooting accident when out hunting, on one of our country estates. He maintained that he was beginning to understand

Honigberger's "mysteries" that father was referring to, but that his Romanian was insufficient and he had to go on learning. I can't say I understand the connection between Honigberger's "mysteries" and his perfecting his knowledge of Romanian. My opinion is that he hadn't found out very much either."

"What you're telling me," I began "does not discourage me in the least. It binds me more, on the contrary, to this Honigberger who, a mere few weeks ago, was simply the name of an adventurous traveler."

The young woman smiled again, sat down in the armchair by the desk and continued to give me a searching look.

"Mother is not so interested in Honigberger as you might imagine. And quite rightly, too. She is primarily interested in finding out what happened to father..."

"I could realize that," I interrupted. "Are as I never was so bold as to ask her, I will now ask you to make things clear. What did your father die of and in what circumstances?"

The young woman had a few moments' hesitation, looking down. As if asking herself if she might tell me the truth or whether it would be better that I should find it out myself from other sources. Finally she got up slowly and spoke :

"Father did not die. Anyway, we don't know if or when he died. On 10 September 1910, he vanished from the house and no one has seen or heard anything since."

We were both silent, looking at each other. I couldn't think of anything to say. I didn't even know if she was telling me the whole truth, or if she was keeping back certain painful details. She opened a small amber cigarette case and took out a cigarette.

"Of course he must have gone East, to India," I said in order to break the silence. "On Honigberger's traces."

"That's what we thought. Rather our friends thought so, for I was then a schoolgirl in the 2nd grade and did not quite understand what had happened. I was back from school and found them all in a terrible state, in terror. Father had vanished that very morning, or possibly during the night."

"He very likely meant to leave unexpectedly," I said. "He could figure the difficulties he'd have to face had he trusted anyone with his intentions."

"Quite so. Yet it's hard to believe that he could have left for the East with no passport, no money, no clothes..."

I didn't quite grasp this, so she insisted :

"The truth is that father has vanished in the proper sense of the word. And he vanished taking no suit of clothes, no hat, leaving all his money in the drawer of the desk. He took no identity papers, got no passport and wrote no letter to mother or to any friend. It's difficult to imagine how strange this disappearance looked to those who knew the circumstances. For some years father had been leading a life strange enough, almost ascetic. He never saw anyone. His days and nights he spent in this study and in his bedroom where he only slept two hours every night, on a wooden bed with no mattress or pillow. He went about scantily dressed, a pair of white trousers, sandals and a shirt of flaxen material. Such was his indoor attire, summer and winter. Dressed like that he would never have gone out. Yet, it was thus that he disappeared. We couldn't make out if he disappeared during the night, right out of this study, or after retiring to his own room. The house was asleep at the time when he usually stopped work : three in the morning. Two hours later, at five, he woke up, showered and remained a long time shut up in his room, meditating. At least that's what we believed, for he wouldn't tell mother anything. He had become detached from the world, from his own family. When I met him, which was seldom, I felt that his love was still there, but it was another kind of love..."

"The inquiries did not lead anywhere, did they ?" I asked. "He couldn't be traced anywhere ? It's incredible that a man can disappear, leaving no trace whatsoever."

"Nevertheless, things happened just like that. We found no sign revealing his preparations for travel. Here, as well as in the bedroom, things were in perfect order ; the books and notebooks were left on this desk, as usual; in the bedroom we found his watch on the bedside table, his keys and a purse with small change. As if he had vanished within seconds, no time to pick up his belongings, no time to write a word of explanation or an excuse..." The young woman suddenly stopped her confession and put out her hand.

"Now that I've told you what you should have known from the start, I'll go. I'll just ask you to say nothing to mother concerning our talk. She has certain superstitions, and I don't wish to distress her by making light of them."

## IV

She was gone before I summoned the courage to detain her and ask her to explain the many obscure episodes of her confession. How was it, for instance, that there hadn't been more talk at the time concerning this mysterious disappearance ; or what happened to the other men that Mrs. Zerlendi had asked to examine the library, and who, the young lady passingly intimated, had not been lucky. I sat down at the desk somewhat bewildered by the things I'd heard. I couldn't collect my thoughts. I was now looking at the files facing me and at the books piled up on all sides with a new feeling. The appreciation of the bibliophile and Indian scholar had been displaced by a complex feeling difficult to explain, of mixed apprehension, mistrust and fascination combined. I could hardly believe the things my visitor had told me. In spite of that, and in the light of her revelations, I could understand the old woman's reticence in speaking openly ; her caution never to mention her husband's death, her painfully controlled curiosity.

I was thinking that Doctor Zerlendi's disappearance had seemed so unlikely, possibly because the man had been long planning it in minute detail, devoured as he was by his yearning to reach India and finally to break all connections with the life he had been leading. Yet it was this very skilfully planned departure, the secrecy of its preparations, his boundless passion for the secrets of India that was captivating. I had never heard of such an attempt at leaving abruptly, no farewells, no parting letters, leaving no trace whatsoever. Considering what I had heard, the Honigberger file still open on my desk seemed of small interest. I turned to the shelves of Indian lore where I knew the drawers with his manuscripts and index cards were also to be found, the evidence of his year-long studies. I opened the first drawer and began very carefully to inventory it, examining one notebook after another.

There were rough notebooks of exercices in Sanskrit. Sadly pensive, I recognized the problems and declensions that I had once fought with. You could notice the doctor's awkwardness in writing the Sanskrit characters. His patience had been, no doubt, enormous ; scores of pages in the rough notebooks were covered with the declensions of one and the same word, obstinately repeated like a collegiate pensum.

Another notebook contained already whole sentences, mostly from *Hitopadesha* and *Panchatantra,* with a literal and free translation on the next page. I delved into scores of such rough notebooks, pages covered to the last by exercises, conjugations, declensions and translations. A fat notebook with an alphabetic index contained the transcription of the new words that the doctor came up against in his exercises. In some notebooks, on the flyleaf, certain data were inscribed. possibly the amount of time put in the study of the material included. I realized once more the doctor's labor in the learning of Sanskrit. A notebook of there hundred pages had been covered with exercises in less than a fortnight.

During that rainy autumn afternoon I found among the manuscripts in that drawer nothing but the evidence of a frenzied passion for the study of the Sanskrit language. A mere note on the first page of a notebook momentarily caught my attention. A few words, yet to me thrilling. *Shambala* = *Agartha* = the unseen country. All the other pages were covered with the same scholastic exercises.

The following day I came earlier than usual. Never before had I entered the library so excited and eager. I had spent most of the night thinking over what Mrs Zerlendi's daughter had confided, wondering what agent from the beyond had driven the doctor to take such a brutal step, such a cruel severing from family, friends and country. As soon as I was inside the study I walked up again to the drawers I had examined the previous day, took a large armful of notebooks, files and rough notes and sat down at the desk. This time I was working in great concentration. The Sanskrit lettering in the notebooks was getting ever more firm, becoming cursive. Half an hour later Mrs Zerlendi came in. She was pale, weak, though she had only been ailing for two days.

"I am glad to see you working with such zeal," she said seeing the pile of notebooks. "These papers have not been examined by anyone," she said with a slight blush. "You must not mind what my daughter told you yesterday. Smaranda is an odd character. Her imagination perceives connections between things that are totally alien. She was a mere child at that time. And since Hans, her fiancé, died owing to imprudence while hunting, and since he too had begun to investigate these notebooks, Smaranda has consequently elaborated a whole theory. She thinks that everything connected with Honigberger lies under a curse and those who examine the archives, my husband included, are subject to all kinds of misfortunes ; exactly as it is supposed to have happened to the explorers of Tutankhamen's tomb. But that is mere fantasy and she began to believe these things after reading some book or other about Tutankhamen."

As I listened to her, my perplexity increased. For now I didn't know what to believe, and on whose side the truth lay. Mrs. Zerlendi had spoken somewhat awkwardly about her daughter. Yet how did she know what the daughter had told me, I wondered. She couldn't have been eavesdropping, could she ?

"Smaranda was disconsolate after the death of Hans in 1921," Mrs. Zerlendi continued. "Maybe it's owing to this grief that she is sometimes not conscious of reality."

"But the young lady...," I tried to protect her.

"No need to say more," Mrs. Zerlendi intervened. "I know what she thinks and what she suggests, particularly to those that she meets in this study."

Mrs. Zerlendi's explanations seemed to me rather incoherent. She hadn't said a word about her husband. She didn't say he was dead, though she never mentioned his disappearance. She just tried to justify herself in face of Smaranda's accusation that she had summoned other people before me to unravel, in one way or another, the Honigberger mysteries which could have been her own husband's as well.

"That's what I wanted to tell you," she whispepred in a tired voice. "You will now forgive me if I go back to my room. I am not quite well yet..."

Left alone, I smiled. I was thinking that Smaranda would come in any moment asking me not to believe Mrs. Zerlendi's words, but I was eagerly curious, so I soon went back to the examination of the notebooks. It was late afternoon and I was still dipping into them and only came upon translations, exercises, interpretations and grammatical commentary. One notebook containing annotations on the Vedanta and Yoga philosophies I found more interesting and laid it aside. I then took up a notebook with black covers. It too bore a sign and a number like all the others, no different from them in any way. The first page was covered with a transcription of some passages from the *Upanishad*. I might have thought, no doubt, that the following pages contained somewhat similar texts if my eyes had not registered the first line of the second page : *"Adau vāda āsit, sa cha vāda ishvarābhimukha āsit, sa cha vāda ishvara āsit !"* For one moment I did not realize the meaning of the words and I was about to turn the page when the translation of the sentence I had just read flashed across my mind. It was the prologue to St. John's gospel : "In the beginning was the Word, and the Word was with God, and the Word was God." I was surprised that the doctor should have transcribed this quotation in Sanskrit, so I read on to understand the intention. The next moment an emotional shock sent the blood throbbing into my cheeks. The words I was now reading in the alien garb of Sanskrit were Romanian words. "I open this notebook on 10 January 1908. He who shall succeed in reading it to the end will understand the precaution disguising my writing. I do not want my thinking to come under the eyes of 'just anyone'."

I now realized why the doctor had transcribed the quotation from St. John's gospel at the top of page 2 : to warn that what followed were not Indian texts. He had taken every precaution that no profane researcher should have even a slight inkling of the contents of the notebook ; the same type of notebook as all the others, same file number, same Sanskrit writing.

Under the stress of emotion I did not dare to read on. It was getting late and I had to leave in a few minutes. Were I to call Mrs. Zerlendi and read to her the contents of the notebook, I should possibly have done so against the author's wishes. I had to be the first to decipher it before making it known to others. But there wouldn't be time enough to go through it tonight, I despaired.

The drawing room door then opened and the servant came in. She looked more sullen than usual, sterner. When I saw her coming up to me, I looked into the notebook that I had opened at random. What I then read caused me actual pain, unable to be alone for a few hours on end, to *realize* all that had happened.

"Tomorrow and the day after we're cleaning the house," she said. "That's what I came to tell you. No use coming all the way here. Once I begin cleaning, it takes me at least two days."

I nodded, thanking her, but the woman was inclined to talk. She came up to the desk and pointed to the notebooks.

"All these devilish things upset the mind," she said meaningfully. "You'd better tell the lady that you can't make heads or tails of them and make the best of your youth for it's a shame to waste it..."

I looked up and gazed at her searchingly.

"That's what finished the doctor," she went on.

"Did he die ? I quickly asked.

"He went into the wide world and perished," she repeated in the same voice.

"Have you actually seen him dead ?" I insisted.

"No one has seen him dead, but he perished in the wide world, no candle burning by him... leaving the house deserted... Don't you listen to what the lady says," she added in a lower voice, "she, poor thing, is not in her right mind either. Two years later her own brother, the prefect, perished too; he had brought a Frenchman, a French scholar, here..."

"Hans," I said.

"No, master Hans came later. He was no Frenchman either. He came later, after the war... He, too, died young..."

I couldn't think what to say. I sat speechless, looking at her. That minute I was myself under a strange spell, never before experienced. The servant was rubbing the palm of her hand against the edge of the desk.

"That's why I came," she spoke after a while, "to tell you that we're cleaning the house, some two days..."

She went away limping through the same door leading into the drawing room. I looked at the notebook again. It was most unfortunate to part with it now that I had found it and to come back three days later. Almost unconscious of what I was doing, I picked it up, put it inside my coat, shaking in all my limbs. I stayed on a few more minutes to control my excited breath ; I replaced the other notebooks and tiptoed out, lest I should meet someone who would guess my thoughts and my guilt.

## V

That night I stayed locked up in my room, the blinds down so that the light of my lamp should encourage no friend to disturb my solitude. As the night wore on, the time and palce where I was seemed to dissolve into a kind of hazy mist, my whole being entirely overcome as I was deciphering, page after page, Doctor Zerlendi's notes. Reading them was not exactly easy work. To begin with, the doctor took pains to write with the utmost attention, for every sound of Romanian could be hardly transposed in Sanskrit writing. Yet, after a few pages, the transcript became ever more approximate, and it was rather a matter of guessing than of reading every word. Whether because of the excitement I felt, or the haste with which I worked, Doctor Zerlendi's handwriting provided no pleasant experience. Little by little, the sentences became shorter, the words more technical, resembling a conventional cipher language. On the verge of his final experiments, the doctor had been anxious to preserve his secret by exclusively using the Yoga terminology, inaccessible to those who had not intently studied that obscure science.

"Honigberger's letter to J. E. was to me the most definite confirmation." Thus Doctor Zerlendi wrote at the begining of his private diary. He did not say who J. E. was, nor anything about the contents of the letter that Mrs. Zerlendi had vaguely mentioned in one of our talks. "As early as the spring of 1907, I began to think that everything Honigberger had written concerning his memories of India was not only authentic, strictly speaking, but represented just a tiny part of what he had seen and succeeded in accomplishing." A series of references to Honigberger's work followed: cases of fakirism, levitation, apparent death, live burial, etc., facts that he rightfully considered authentic. "I began the first experiments on 1 July 1907. Weeks before I had undertaken a severe self-examination and given up smoking, alcohol, meat, coffee, tea, and all the rest. I am not trying to go over the history of that painful preliminary period which lasted six months. Iron determination was needed, for I was several times on the point of giving the whole thing up and returning to my historiographic amusements. Fortunately, Honigberger's letter proved that these things could be done and that kept up my spirits. However, I did not imagine that one could go so far and, relatively speaking, with so little trouble. Because it's only as you acquire the first powers that you begin to realize the greatness of man's ignorance and the sorry illusion that tricks him day by day, down to the hour of death. The determination and energy consumed by man to satisfy his social ambition or scientific vanity are even greater than those required to gain that extraordinary thing : his own salvation from nothingness, ignorance, and pain."

The doctor describes, in sufficient detail his first experiments on 10 January 1908 and the following days. As far as I could understand he was already familiar with Yoga literature, especially with Patanjali's treatise and with his commentaries ; he was familiar with Indian ascetic and mystical philosophy, but he had never tried to put them into practice. He seemed to have tackled right away that difficult experiment of rhythmical breathing, pranăyama, obtaining no encouraging results for a long time.

"On July 25 I fell asleep during such an exercise," he notes in his diary, after mentioning that a few days before, a cough of unusual violence had choked him. "For some time I had been doing these exercises after midnight, then at daybreak, the only results being a fearful thoracic pain and fits of dry coughing. After a fortnight's efforts, I realized that I did not achieve anything because while trying to synchronize my breathing according to Patanjali's text, I was forgetting to concentrate on a single object. The resistance I encountered was due to this mental lapse that, at the time, I did not realize. I tried Honigberger's advice again. I plugged my ears with wax and did not begin prānāyama until after praying for a few minutes. I achieved a state of unusual mental calm. I can still remember the first sensations : it was as if I were in the midst of a stormy sea which was rapidly calming down into an endless blanket of water, with no wave or shiver. An uncomparable feeling of plenitude followed, similar to the one you have after listening to a great deal of Mozart. I went through the same experiment the folowing days, but I was unable to go beyond it. I came to after fifteen minutes in a state of vague reverie, though I knew that this was not the expected result of the exercise. Somewhere along the way I had lost control ; I had been overwhelmed by the spell that my own mind had created. I repeated it again but, after a certain amount of time, the result was the same : day dreaming, sleepiness, or unspeakable mental placidity."

What upsetting confessions for me ! I had tried some of the experiments that the doctor had so tenaciously insisted on and had been faced with the same difficulties, but he had been luckier and anyway more obstinate. In the early days of September 1907, almost unconsciously, he took a great step forward in these breathing exercises, namely the perfect equivalence between inhalation and exhalation: "I began, as usual, by holding back my breathing for 12 seconds," which meant that he had succeeded in inhaling 12 seconds, keeping back his breathing 12 seconds, and exhaling in as many seconds. "The object of my meditation was, on that day, fire." He had, no doubt, concentrated on a receptacle with live coal, trying to penetrate the essence of "fire", to find its equivalent in the whole cosmos, at the same time assimilating its "principle", identifying it with the countless processes in his own body, reducing the infinity of combustions that make up the universe, as well as every separate organism, to the one incandescent element in front of him.

"I don't quite realize how it happened, but after a time I found myself sleeping, or, more exactly, I woke in a sleep without my falling asleep properly speaking. My body, all my senses, sinking into a sleep ever more profound, but my mind never ceasing its activity for a moment. Everything was asleep within me, except for my mind. I went on meditating about fire, at the same time hazily realizing that the world around me was thoroughly changing and that, had I stopped concentrating a single moment, I would have naturally become integrated into this world which was the world of sleep."

As he later on confesses, Doctor Zerlendi had on that same day accomplished the first and possibly the most difficult step forward in achieving his goal. He had accomplished what in technical terms is called continuous consciousness, namely a passage from waking consciousness to that of a sleeping state without any hiatus. An ordinary man's consciousness is brutally split by sleep. No one preserves the continuity of the mental flux when asleep, no one realizes the fact of being asleep, only sometimes realizing to be dreaming, and no one continues to think lucidly while sleeping. We only remember a few dreams and certain indefinable fears from the world of sleep.

"The most frightening thing about my discovery that I was awake while sleeping was a feeling that the world around me was thoroughly changing, in no way resembling the world of diurnal consciousness. I find it very difficult to specify the way I was feeling this change because I had projected my whole mind directly upon the fire, while my senses were asleep. I seemed to be in a different space ; it was not necessary to look to see the objects, forms, and colors in the room gradually changing. What happened then is impossible to describe ; I will, nevertheless, try to do so as well as I can because no one, as far as I know, has dared to reveal in writing such an experience. I was constantly gazing into the fire, not as a pretext for some hypnotic trance, since I have studied hypnosis as far as to know its technique and effects. While gazing, I was thinking about fire, assimilating it, my mind searching my own body, identifying all its combustions. It was therefore no rigid thought, but merely a thought that was one. I mean not disseminated several ways, not solicited by several objects, not caught by any external stimulus or by any memory, a flare-up of the unconscious. This single thought had just one point of support in the fire ; by means of it, however, I could penetrate wherever fire was to be identified. Hypnosis was therefore entirely excluded, the more so as I was permanently in a state of lucidity ; I knew who I was, why I found myself in that posture, why I was timing my breathing, and to what end I was meditating on the fire. Nevertheless, I did realize that I found myself in a different space, in a different world. I was no longer conscious of my body ; just a faint heat in the head, a heat which in time also disappeared. Things looked as if they were continually flowing, but their profile was not much altered. To begin with you might have said that you saw everything through water in continuous movement, but the comparison was by no means exact. As a matter of fact some things were gliding more slowly, others more rapidly, but it was impossible to tell where they were gliding to and by what miraculous process their essence never dried up as they overflowed their natural boundaries. In trying to render my vision more precise, I realized that this was no overflowing of the boundaries of the objects, but the boundaries themselves in permanent motion. Still more striking was the fact that all these objects came together and drew apart in spite of themselves. Though I did not look, I knew that these objects were there : a bed, two chairs, a carpet, a picture, a bedside table, etc. I was under the impression that they would all come together in a single spot the moment I would lay my eyes on one of them. This was not an impression, an illusion ; it was like the definite feeling of a man immersed in water, that he could advance or get out of the water. It was something I knew, never realizing if I had ever experienced it. I was also under the impression of being able to see far beyond the walls of my room. I can't say that things had become transparent. On the contrary, besides their permanent gliding and curious mobility, objects were the same as before, as if answering my possible desire to contemplate them. All the same I could look beyond them, although, let me repeat, I was not trying to see. In any case, not through them but beyond them. They stood there before me, yet I knew I could see farther, while they remained in their respective places. In a way this sensation was like that of a man contemplating his whole house from the corner of one room. He doesn't see through walls, yet he does see everything he knows to be in another room, or in the entire house, without feeling that his eyesight has penetrated through the walls..."

## VI

The doctor was writing all this having countless times repeated the experiment of the continuous consciousness during sleep. Judging by the legible handwriting of this excerpt it seems that he had carefully drafted the above description, afterwards transposing it into Sanskrit letters ; this he did not repeat later on when he became content to jot things down in his notebook.

"After a while I felt a desire to penetrate more thoroughly into the world of sleep, to explore the unknown space around me. I dared not, however, take my eyes off the live coals. A strange disquietude, I may almost say a mounting terror, was threatening me. I don't know what caused me to close my eyes suddenly ; by no means weariness because, let me repeat, I felt that I was sleeping though my mind was more alert than ever. I was stunned to find, eyelids closed, the same vision as when open-eyed. The live coals alone seemed to have changed : they too flowed like all the other objects around, while their brilliance was more intense, though as it were, less vivacious. After a few minutes' hesitation, I opened my eyes again. I realized it was useless to gaze, to turn my eyeballs in the direction of a certain corner of the room ; I could see in whatever direction I wished, I could see wherever my thoughts would turn with or without my open eyes. I thought of the garden behind the house and saw it that very minute, as if I were there. How amazing ! Like an ocean of vegetal sap in ceaseless tumult. The trees were almost hugging each other, the grass seemed to tremble like a sheaf of algae, the fruits alone were more calm, as if in a long slow swinging state.

The next moment the mirage of this vegetable tempest disappeared. I was thinking of Sophia and I actually saw her in the large bed in our bedroom, asleep. A dark violet aura was floating round her head ; her body seemed to be continually scaling since innumerable layers of skins were dropping off her, vanishing as soon as they dropped off her limbs. I sat a long time, looking at her intently, trying to understand what was going on. I then spied a timid flame fluttering now above the heart, now lower, down the belly. Suddenly I realized that Sophia lay by me. It was a frightful moment because I saw her asleep in bed and saw her, at the same time, by my side, looking in wonder into my eyes as if trying to ask a question. Her face showed unspeakable surprise. Maybe I looked different than what she had expected, maybe I was quite unlike those beings that she had met in her dreams. Only later, having repeated the experiment several times, did I begin to realize that the faces I saw around me were a projection of the conscience of various people during sleep." I must confess I don't understand what Doctor Zerlendi meant, however, I preserved this fragment because of its possible interest for the students of occultism. A sadhu that I had joined on my wanderings in the 1930ies, at Konarak, had told me — if it is true I can't say — that it is thrilling when, during certain yoga meditations, you come up against the spirits of sleepers who wander about, like shadows, in the state of sleep. They seem to look at you anxiously, unable to understand how it is possible to meet you there, lucid and wakeful.

"A few moments later the space around me changed abruptly. Fear had reawakened me. For some time I kept the position I was in since the beginning of the experiment, and counted the seconds again : the breathing rhythm was the same : 12 seconds."

The change from the consciousness of dreaming to that of being awake had been abrupt : the continuity had been broken by fear. It was only after several experiments, repeated on the following day, in the utmost secrecy, that the doctor succeeded in returning to diurnal consciousness with no hiatus whatever, by sheer willpower which he expressed by thinking : "I am now returning." He decreased the breathing rhythm from 12 to 8 seconds, gradually awakening from his sleep.

Concerning the experiments that followed, the notes are somewhat brief, either because the doctor did not want to say more, or because he couldn't, failing to find an adequate description. Somewhere he actually confesses : "The unifying of consciousness is achieved through continuous progress, namely without any kind of hiatus, from a waking to a sleeping state with dreams, then to sleep without dreams and, finally, to a cataleptic state." Unifying these four states presupposes, paradoxical as it may seem, the unifying of the conscious with the subconscious and the unconscious, a gradual illumination of the obscure and impenetrable zones of psycho-mental life. This, as a matter of fact, is the goal of preliminary Yoga techniques. All Indian ascetics I have known who were willing to give me any information, considered this stage of unifying the states of consciousness of utmost importance. He who did not succeed in this experiment found no spiritual gain in the Yoga practices. There were very few details concerning the transition from sleep with dreams to deeper sleep, with no dreams : "I have succeeded in establishing a greater interval between inhaling and exhaling : about 15 seconds, sometimes almost 20 seconds." Which means that he was breathing once a minute ; for 20 seconds he abstained from breathing, 20 seconds he inspired, 20 seconds he expired. "I was under the impression of returning into a spectral world where I saw only colors, not contoured into shapes. Colored spots rather. A sonorous universe dominated the world of shapes. Each colored spot was a source of sound." As far as I can understand, the doctor tried, in a few brief lines, to suggest that the sonorous cosmos only becomes accessible to the initiate after prolonged meditation on sounds, on those "mystic syllables" in the treatises on Mantra-Yoga. It seems to be a fact that after a certain level of consciousness only sounds and colors appear, the actual shapes vanishing as if by magic. Yet Doctor Zerlendi's indications are too vague to form a basis for further experience.

The more astounding the results of Yoga technique, the more reticent the doctor's confessions. About penetrating the cataleptic state he only made this remark : "As a result of my last experience, I began to read the thoughts of any man I was concentrating on. I tried this on Sophia who at that time was finishing a letter to the administrator. I could well have read the letter, but did not do so. I stood there by her and heard all her thoughts, not only those she was expressing in the letter. It was as if I was listening to her speaking."

However remarkable, Doctor Zerlendi did not attach much importance to these experiments. "You may reach the same results without very rigorous austerity, but only with maximum mental concentration ; though I realize that modern man is no longer capable of such a mental effort. People are dissipated and in a state of continuous evanescence. Asceticism does not help to acquire such forces, only to avoid falling prey to them. Exploring unknown states of consciousness may be so enticing as to incur the risk of spending a lifetime without reaching an end. It is a new world, but nevertheless a world. If you are content to explore it with no purpose of going beyond it, as you tried to transcend the waking states, it would be like if you learned a new language and set out to read all the books written in that language, without ever attempting to learn another language."

I cannot decide what stage of technical perfection the doctor reached when he began writing his diary. Some twenty pages were completed on the 10, 12 and 13 January 1908. They contain a kind of short reminder for a possible reader of the preliminary stages, with no mention, however, as to how far these preliminaries extended. The initials J. E. occur several times. "This, I believe, was J. E's fatal mistake. He did not realize the unreal character of the phenomena that he had discovered in the spectral world. He believed it was the ultimate frontier that the human spirit could reach. He considered his experiment as of an absolute value, while, in fact, he was still dealing with phenomena. That is the explanation of his paralysis. Honigberger probably succeeded in reanimating certain centers, but could do no more. He was incapable of curing his amnesia." This is a difficult excerpt ;

J. E. was, very likely, unable to control his consciousness to the very end and became a prey to his own discoveries in the supernatural world. I remember that all the occult Indian treatises mention the new cosmic strata that the ascetic enters by means of the Yoga technique as being just as "illusory" as the cosmos that is accessible to any man in his normal condition. On the other hand, I cannot be sure that the "centers" he refers to are nervous centers or the occult plexus known in Yoga and other traditions.

Anyway, it looks as if this J.E., under Honigberger's direct influence, had attempted an initiation in Yoga and had utterly failed, the cause being what Doctor Zerlendi surmised, or a constitution unfavourable to the techniques that he was trying. Referring to a complicated and obscure experiment of projecting consciousness out of the body in a cataleptic state, the doctor further notes : "I succeeded in this attempt because, I may say exceptionally, I possessed an Asiatic sensorial condition. I don't believe that a European could succeed. He is not conscious of his body below the diaphragm, and even this is rare enough. As a rule, he is only conscious of his head. I have only just realized this, in seeing them as they never saw themselves ; no one can withhold anything from me."

The excerpt is cryptic enough. I am inclined to believe that "an Asiatic sensorial condition" may mean the diffuse consciousness that people have concerning their own body, which differs from one race to another. I know that an oriental, for instance, feels his own body in a way different from ours, the Europeans. When touching the foot or the shoulder of an oriental, he has the same feeling of injury that we feel if someone strikes our eyes or mouth with the back of his hand. As regards the expression "below the diaphragm" it would refer to the incapacity of occidental man to possess the entire awareness of his own body. Indeed there are few among us who feel their body as a whole. Most of us only feel certain sections — the forehead, the heart, the legs, and this only in certain circumstances. Just try to feel your legs, for instance, in a state of complete relaxation, lying at leisure in bed shall we say, and you will see how difficult that is.

"I have unified, easily enough, the two elements down to the heel," the doctor writes on in connection with the same experiment. "That moment I had a definite sensation of being completely spherical, of having turned into an impenetrable bubble, perfectly impermeable, with a full sense of autonomy, of invulnerability. Myths referring to primitive man as conceived in the shape of a sphere are of course derivative from this experiment of unifying the elements." I dare not state that it is a matter of the positive-negative elments of occult European therapeutics. More probably the doctor referred to the two fluids of a type very difficult to understand precisely, perhaps similar to occult Indian tradition, where the currents that run through the human body are identified by the Yoga and Tantric doctrines with the moon and the sun. But, as I say, I dare not definitely state anything, the stages of the initiation he tried being only fragmentarily known to me.

## VII

Doctor Zerlendi's notes became ever more sparse during the months of February, March, and April 1908. The few pages written during this interval are quite cryptic, mostly referring to previous experiments. The doctor's interest in his private diary is obviously decreasing. In the beginning he was striving to describe his experiments as accurately as possible, but soon his interest in such confessions faded. Maybe he realized how inaccessible these things are for a possible uninformed reader in whose hands this notebook may fall. Or, maybe, he was becoming ever more detached from this world, so that communicating his experiments was no longer of any interest to him. Anyway, in this space of time, he practically never registers his experiments or thoughts of a particular day. He constantly goes over incidents of former days or weeks. I am inclined to believe that his findings were too interesting to be registered daily. Particularly when trying a new experiment, he became so involved in it that he mentioned it much later and only very succintly. "Results uncertain concerning mukasana, attempted at dawn," he mentions sometime in April. Several pages would be necessary to explain this ciphered sentence relating to a certain position of the body, that is why I don't even try to attempt it. Such technical references regarding the position of the body during the Yoga meditation, regarding breathing exercises or ascetic physiology, are to be abundantly found in Doctor Zerlendi's notes. As a matter of fact, I have given a certain amount of information concerning such practices in my book on Yoga and I won't repeat them in the present tale.

By the end of 1908 the diary seems to hold his interest again. Hitherto sparse and technical notations are followed by a long confession. "Among other important things that Honigberger revealed to J. E., was the existence of Shambala, that miraculous country which, tradition has it, lies somewhere in northern India, only accessible to the initiates. Prior to his madness, J. E. believed that this unseen land could, nevertheless, be accessible to the uninitiated. In one of his papers that I found in Iași, he had jotted the names of two Jesuites, Ștefan Cacela and Ioan Cabral, who, so he maintained, had reached Shambala. I got hold, with some difficulty, of the works of these two Jesuit missionaries and realized that J. E.'s statemenets had no basis. Cacela and Cabral are actually the first Europeans to have heard of Shambala which they mention in their writings. In Bhutan, looking for a way to Kathay, they heard about the existence of this fabulous land, which the local inhabitants believed to be located somewhere in the north. They set out to look for it in 1627, but they only went as far as Tibet. The did not find the fabulous country of Shambala. In contrast with J. E., as soon as I read Honigberger's confessions, I firmly believed that it was out of the question to identify Shambala with any territory geographically situated in the center of Asia. Maybe this conviction of mine was influenced by the Indian legends concerning *Agarttha,* as well as those about the "White Islands" in Buddist and Brachmannical mythology. Actually, I never came across an Indian text stating that you could reach thehse lands except by supernatural powers. All testimonies speak of Buddha's or other initiates "flight" to these lands hidden to profane eyes. It is well-known that "flight," in symbolic and secret languages, signifies man's capacity of transcending the universe of sense, acquiring thereby access to unseen lands. What I knew about Honigberger led me to believe that he had penetrated into the Shambala owing to the Yoga technique that he had mastered as early as 1858 ; yet the mission he had been entrusted with had probably failed. That explains why he returned from

India so early and his death soon after his return, leaving that most important document in the hands of an amateur like J.E."

The pangs in my heart after reading the above pages! The memories that suddenly invaded me in the dead of night as I came across those two names: Shambala and Agarttha! I had once myself started looking for the unseen country, never to come back into the world before knowing it. An old, forgotten wound that I had long considered healed began to bleed anew, reminding me of those months spent in the Himalayas, close to the Tibetan frontier, on the holy road of Bhadrinat, inquiring from hermit to hermit if they had possibly heard of Shambala, if they were aware of anyone who should know its mystery. Who can tell if, at long last, in my hut on the left side of the Ganges, from that kutiar overgrown by the jungle which I had long given up thinking of as an earthly paradise — who knows, if absolution had not come for me there, if, after years of attempts and preparations, I might not have succeeded in finding the road to the unseen land. But it was written that I should never find it, only remember it during my melancholy moods...

Still more cruel are the qualms of conscience for he who has abandoned the quest, in hearing that the road he had taken was the right one. Doctor Zerlendi's statements strengthened all my suppositions since what followed happened just as I thought it was bound to happen to him who was avidly seeking Shambala. "The image of the unseen territory that Honigberger had penetrated was constantly clear in my mind. In fact I knew that this territory was unseen only to the eyes of the profane. To be more precise, it was simply a land inaccessible geographically, that you could only discover after exacting spiritual preparation. I imagined this Shambala hidden from other people not by natural obstacles, high mountains or deep waters, but by the space it was part of, a space differing in quality from the profane. This belief I verified with my first Yoga experiments, when I realized how different is the space of profane experience from that of other human perceptions. In the present notebook I had even begun the detailed description of these experiments, but I soon realized that they were impossible to describe. He who knows them will say that I am right. I go on writing these notes though, because a confirmation of an ancient truth that no one believes in nowadays is, however, necessary from time to time. Honigberger himself, in my opinion, was allowed to return from Shambala, in order to try and render active again in the West certain centers of initiation which had been languishing since the Middle Ages. His sudden death confirms this belief of mine ; no doubt he did not know how to accomplish his task or discredited it from the start, that's why he died so mysteriously. As for myself, though I haven't yet reached the final stages, I feel an unseen influence upon me, someone is guiding and helping me, and this gives me confidence that in the end I will succeed."

Concerning this unseen influence the doctor does not say any more. The occult, especially the oriental occult tradition, has plenty to say on the subject and all that followed leads me to believe that the doctor was not misled by some illusion when he mentioned it. His Yoga fulfilment progresses very rapidly. The summer of 1908 he spent by himself on one of his estates and later on, back in Bucharest, he went through some of his experiments again. Some may be identified almost exactly. For instance, he mentions somewhere a strange vision that he had after certain meditations ; he seemed to see all things upside down or, more accurately, the very contrary of what they were in reality. The solid objects he saw as having no consistency and vice versa. "The vacuum" he saw as "dense" while the dense things looked vacuous. Yet there was one more thing that Doctor Zerlendi did not clearly explain : the world in its entirety, he saw, to quote his manuscript, as being "completely the opposite of how it appears to a man in a waking state," never explaining what he meant by the phrase "completely the opposite." In fact, this is an expression closely resembling the severe formulas of the mystics or of the books of ritual ; each of these texts mentions the other world or the world as known in ecstasy, as being "completely the opposite" of the one which we see with our bodily eyes.

The doctor's confession about a "return" to the visible world after prolonged contemplation is equally strange. "To begin with I felt as if I were spinning around, as if I were going to fall at the first step. I no longer had the normal confidence, as if I had to become familiar again with a three dimensional space. That is why, for a long time, I dared not even move. I was literally petrified, waiting for some miracle to happen, that I might recapture the confidence I had before falling into this trance. I now understand why, after ecstasy, the saints would stay for hours or days without moving, giving the impression that their spirit was still lost in godliness."

On 11 September he writes : "Several times I have tried the cataleptic trance. 12 hours the first time ; 36 hours on my second and third attempts. I would tell the forester that I was going to the mansion and then lock myself in my room, certain that I would not be disturbed. For the first time I personally experienced the sensation of stepping out of time. For although my spirit was active, my body no longer participated in the passage of time. Before inducing the trance I shaved, and at the end of 36 hours my face was just as smooth as in the moment I had fallen into the trance. This was quite natural because man is conscious of time by his breathing rhythm. For any man, a number of seconds elapses between an inhalation and an exhalation ; life to man coincides with time. I first achieved the cataleptic trance at 10 in the morning and woke up at 10 at night ; throughout that time my body lay in what some call apparent death, without the faintest breathing. The inspiration of air at 10 in the morning was completed, so to speak, by the expiration of 10 at night. During that interval my body was outside time. To the body, the 12 hours were reduced to a few seconds — the deep morning inspiration and the slow expiration before awakening. In human terms, in 24 hours my body grew older by only 12 hours ; life was suspended without endangering the organism."

The experiment achieved by Doctor Zerlendi is, as a matter of fact, quite common, though insufficiently studied up to now. "Apparent death," which was the rage in Honigberger's time, seems actually to be an exit out of time. That is the only explanation how, after ten or a hundred days, the body preserves the same weight and a freshly shaven face stays as clean and smooth. Yet these are states that categorically transcend the human condition and about them we can have no understanding. The boldest imagination cannot adequately conceive such an "exit from time". The allusions we find in the confessions of certain saints or in the occult oriental writings are unintelligible to us. I have myself collected such precious confessions, most of them allegorically expressed, but they remain for me seven-sealed secrets. Death alone will shed a new light on this problem for some of us.

"To me, the one astounding fact is that people will not learn anything from such experiments. Most scholars have been content to deny the authentic character of these incidents — attended, as a matter of fact, by hundreds of witnesses — preferring to maintain their old positions. It is as if you were content to cross the water only by swimming, never attempting to cross the sea, simply because you don't believe in crossing the water in a boat."

## VIII

The diary stops in September 1908 for a hiatus of four months. The first ensuing notes date from the beginning of January 1909. They cannot be transcribed here owing to their technical character. They are rather simple enunciations of metaphysical principles and recipes for Yoga practices. Some of these seem to make no sense. "26 January. Experiment of darkness. Each letter taken up again from the beginning." He was no doubt referring to previous exercises, probably meditations on sounds and letters, the so-called mantra-yoga, about which, however, I found no reference. What is the sense, however, of the "experiment of darkness" ?! Further on : "5 February. Recently samyama on the body. Unbelievable, yet true." This note may have a sense if the doctor refers to a certain text of the Patanjali which says that by samyama upon his own body, the Yogist becomes invisible to other men's eyes. By samyama, Pantajali refers to the three final stages of Yoga achievement which we cannot dwell on here. Nevertheless, I find it difficult to believe that as early as February 1909, the doctor should have achieved this miracle. How then can I understand his subsequent bewilderment ? How can I account for the following 18 months during which, though few things are related, we know that he was constantly striving to acquire this very possibility of becoming invisible ?

As a matter of fact, the difficulties of the text keep increasing. Certain notations seem directly contradictory. "March. I have taken up certain texts of the Upanishad. Amazing progress in understanding the original text."

How can I understand this confession ? After everything he had achieved, a reading of the original text of the Upanishad could no longer have been of much importance. What was the sense, moreover, of a study in the Sanskrit language, by a man who had assimilated more than a dead science ? Except if he possibly went back on his traces or slackened his Yoga fulfilment owing to some "influence" that he doesn't mention at all. Maybe he was not pursuing this study in a bookish sense, reading and meditating about the text, but successfully coming to a mysterious understanding simply by an exact pronunciation of sacred words, considered in India to be a revelation of the Logos. Elsewhere he actually mentions certain very obscure exercises of an "inner utterance" of a sacred Indian text. Then, early in the summer, he writes about the identification of "mystic letters" with certain rarified states of consciousness (it would be nearer the truth to say "super-consciousness").

At the same period he relates the "occult vision" that he acquired by "reactivating the eye between the eyebrows", an eye, by the way, mentioned by the Asiatic mythologies and mysticism, which would render the man possessing it capable of seeing at immense distances. Concerning this "eye of Shiva", as named by the Indians, references are contradictory or, anyway, extremely obscure for a non-initiate. There are some who hold that the "eye of Shiva" lends a sense of direction in space, thus being a kind of sixth sense ; others, more numerous, maintain that this new vision which comes to the initiate by means of this "eye" has no connection with the world of shapes and illusions, but solely refers to the spiritual world. Through the "eye of Shiva" man may directly contemplate the spiritual world ; in other words he gains access to super-sense layers. Yet Doctor Zerlendi gives no precise information concerning this mystery. Could not — or was not allowed to ?

A long interval of silence again follows, the limits of which are impossible to identify because the notations immediately following bear no date. These jottings are actually impossible to decipher. I presume that they refer to what Doctor Zerlendi meant by "impersonal consciousness", because I came across the following paragraph : "Most difficult, more precisely impossible to reach nowadays in the West, is an impersonal consciousness. A few mystics alone achieved such a consciousness in the last centuries. All the post-mortem difficulties facing man, all the infernos and purgatories where the spirits of the dead are said to suffer tortures, are due precisely to the inability of achieving while still alive an impersonal consciousness. The soul's drama after death and the atrocious purifying that it suffers are simply the stages of a painful transition from the personal to the impersonal consciousness..."

The page immediately following the above confession was torn from the notebook. I come upon a note dated 7 January 1910. "Maybe I have been punished for my impatience, but I used to think that you are allowed to shape your own destiny. I am no longer so young and I am not afraid of death. I know well enough the span of life that I am bound to live through, but I thought it my duty to hurry because I am no longer a help to anyone here and have plenty to learn over there."

A few days later : "I now know the road to Shambala. I know how to get there. I may say one more thing : three people from our continent have quite recently got there. Each one set out alone and got there by personal means. The Dutchman even traveled under his own name as far as Colombo. I have learned these things in my long trances when I actually see Shambala in all its glory ; I can see that green wonder amidst the snow-capped mountains, those queer houses, those ageless people who talk so little among themselves though perfectly understanding each other's thoughts. If it were not for them praying and thinking of all the others, the whole continent would be shaken by the numerous demonic forces that the modern world has set loose from the Renaissance to this day. Can the fate of our Europe be sealed already ? Is there nothing to be done for this world run by obscure spiritual forces, leading it blindly to a cataclysm ? I fear that Europe will have the fate of Atlantis and perish soon into the sea. If people only knew that it is only due to the spiritual forces emanating from Shambala that this tragic change of angle in the axis of the globe is constantly being postponed; geology has already predicted it, it shall knock down our world into the waters and raise goodness knows what new continent..."

Fear of a tragic end of our continent figures in other pages of the diary. I gather that the doctor begins to see ever more clearly the succession of cataclysms in store for Europe.

As a matter of fact, this coincides with a whole series of prophecies, more or less apocaliptic, relating to Kaliyuga, the dark age that, as they say, we are rapidly approaching. Throughout the whole of Asia legends with regard to the imminent end of the present world are circulating under widely different forms. Doctor Zerlendi, however, mentions a possible "change of the globe's axis" which would be the immediate cause of the disaster. As far as I can understand he holds that such a change of axis would imply a seismic catastrophe, certain continents sinking or changing their actual profile, other continents emerging from the waters. The fact that he mentions the name of Atlantis several times leads me to believe that he considered the existence of that continent to be a reality, the disappearance of which was to be accounted for by some unknown spiritual degeneration of its inhabitants. What I consider worth noticing in these tragic prophecies is that they were conceived a few years before the first World War when the world was still basking in the illusion of infinite progress.

Then suddenly, on 11 May 1910, he turns again to the Yoga exercises leading to the invisibility of the body. It will be easily understood why I do not transcribe these stunning confessions. In reading Doctor Zerlendi's lines I was a prey to strange panic. So far I had scanned a sufficient number of documents, more or less authentic, concerning this Yogic miracle ; yet things had never been said so clearly or so minutely. When I began this tale I was still undecided whether or not I would transcribe this terrifying page. Having reached this point after so many weeks of wavering and trouble, I realize that such a thing cannot be confessed. Those who understand what is meant by "samyama upon one's own body" will know where to seek further information.

## IX

It seems, however, that the experiment of invisibility was not devoid of dangers. The effort of rendering one's body invisible to others, of a retreat out of light, causes such a commotion in the entire organism that, after such an experiment, the doctor was unconscious for several hours. "Very likely, I will not choose this way to reach Shambala," he wrote in June 1910. "The time of my final departure draws near, but I do not yet know if I will be strong enough to leave, unseen to others."

Later, during the same month : "I am sometimes afraid of the forces that I have concentrated within myself. My willpower is firm, yet I find it difficult enough to control these forces which have so far helped me to penetrate into invisible worlds. This morning in my room, while in contemplation, I suddenly felt the atmosphere growing rarified and my body perceptibly losing weight. I was unintentionally levitating and though I was trying to cling to objects, I soon felt the top of my head touching the ceiling. The scary thing is that this occurred with no effort of my will, simply owing to the forces of contemplation. I had almost lost control and a single lapse of concentration would have caused me to fall down to the floor."

I have heard of such strange occurrences when a man trying to dominate the occult powers fails at a certain moment to preserve a clear mind and his entire willpower ; he then risks falling into the hands of the magic forces unleashed by his own meditation. I had been told at Hardwar, that the adept Yogi is exposed to the most fearful dangers not at the beginning, but at the end of his training when he gains control of murderous forces. The world of myths, as a matter of fact, reveals the fact that those who "fell" most abominably were those who had come nearest to divinity. Lucifer's arrogance is another form of obscure forces unleashed by one's personal perfection, which finally succeed in destroying oneself.

Later on, 16 August : "Fearful detachment from the world. A single thought gives me a thrill : Shambala. I don't want to make any preparations before leaving. My will was written the year that Smaranda was born. Any other note written now, on the eve of my departure, would look suspicious."

Then, possibly on the same day, a few hurried lines : "I think that this notebook might fall into the hands of someone who might destroy it. My effort to confess certain exceptional things would, in that case, be in vain. But I don't regret it..." There follows a whole line, blotted out, that I have only partially been able to decipher. "If he who may read and understand... will try to make use... grave...

he won't be believed." On the eve of his departure, the doctor, no doubt, had intended to address a few counsels to that eventual reader, warning him, at the same time, of the risks he might incur in case of a thoughtless confession. I cannot think what determined him to give up those intended counsels and to strike out the phrase he had begun. I respected, however, his wish, not revealing his most important experiment.

19 August: "I found myself again invisible and my terror was greater since I had not done anything to obtain that state. I paced the courtyard for hours, by chance realizing that I was invisible. The servants passed by me without seeing me; at first I thought they were inattentive, but looking around I did not see my shadow. I followed one of the fieldhands who was walking to the stables. It was as if he had felt something uncanny behind him, for he kept looking back with troubled eyes and finally quickened his pace, making the sign of the cross. Despite all my efforts, I could not become visible before midnight when I woke up in bed, a wreck. I think that the extreme weariness that followed was chiefly due to my efforts to become visible again, because I became invisible by chance, against my wishes, not realizing what was happening."

This is the last long note in the doctor's diary. What follows is, however, no less striking. "12 September. I can no longer become visible since the night before last. I have taken this notebook and pencil and am writing on the stairs that lead to the attic. I will afterwards conceal it among my study notebooks. I shudder to think that I might still mistake the path to Shambala..."

This note is dated two days after his disappearance. Had anyone then deciphered the manuscript and read the freshly written page, he would have understood that the doctor was still in the house, quite close to his family...

## X

On the third day, having decided to return the notebook and read it all to Mrs. Zerlendi, I went to S. street. I was met by the old servant. The lady was ill, she told me, and the young lady had gone to Paris.

"But why so suddenly?" I wondered.

"That is her way," she answered, almost without looking at me.

Obviously, she was in no mood to talk. I left my card saying that I would call within a few days, for news of the lady's health, but I could only call a week later. The entrance gate was locked and I tried to open it several times and vainly pressed the rusty electric bell; the servant showed up. She crossed the garden with difficulty. The late flowers had withered almost overnight; she came up to the gate grumbling.

"The lady has gone to the country," she said almost turning to go. But she stopped adding: "She didn't say when she would be back."

That autumn and winter I stood several times before the gate in S. street. It was always locked. If I was lucky, I received an answer:

"There is no one at home."

But sometimes the servant would not even come out to answer. I then wrote several letters to Mrs. Zerlendi, never receiving an answer or any confirmation that she had opened my letters. It was impossible to understand what had happened. Mrs. Zerlendi had no way of knowing that I had found and taken away her husband's diary. I was certain that no one had seen me concealing it inside my coat. Even if spied on through theh keyhole, I couldn't have been detected; for I had hidden the notebook while standing by the shelves, surrounded by other notebooks of the doctor.

At the end of February 1935, as I was passing along S. street, I saw that the gate was open and walked in. To tell the truth, I was quite nervous as I pressed the door bell. I was expecting to be met by the same sullen old woman, but to my surprise the door was opened by a young servant. I asked if there was anyone in. "Everybody is in," she answered. I gave her my card and entered the drawing room. A few minutes later the door leading into the bedroom was opened and Smaranda stood before me. I hardly recognized her; she looked ten years younger, her face was agreeably made up, and the color of her hair was different. She considered my card again, in some wonder, before putting out her hand. She pretended that she did not know me. She told me her name as if I were an unknown visitor.

"Why are you here?" she asked.

I answered that I had been working for some time in Doctor Zerlendi's library, and that Mrs. Zerlendi knew me well enough — she herself had asked me to consult her husband's archives. I also added that I knew her, Smaranda.

"I think there must be some confusion," she replied with a smile. "I'm sure we have never met. As a matter of fact, I know very few people in Bucharest and I'm sure I should have remembereed your name and face."

"Nevertheless, Mrs. Zerlendi knows me quite well. I had been working for weeks on end here, in the library," I insisted, pointing to the heavy oak door.

Smaranda watched my gesture, then looked at me in wonder, as if hardly believing her eyes.

"What you're telling me is rather strange," she added, because my father's library actually was there once. But this was so many years ago. Under foreign occupation that library, which was exceptionally well endowed, was dispersed..."

I laughed, at a loss for an answer.

"I find this very difficult to believe," I said after a long pause during which I looked her straight in the eyes to let her understand that I was aware of her acting. "Only two months ago I worked in this library. I know it, shelf by shelf and I can tell you from memory everything that is in it."

I wished to go on, but Smaranda made a dash for the bedroom door and called :

"Mother, come here a minute, please !"

Mrs. Zerlendi appeared, leading a little boy by the hand. I made a low bow, but saw in her eyes that she did not want to recognize me.

"This gentleman says that he had been working for some two months in the library," she said pointing to the massive oak door.

Mrs. Zerlendi considered me in offended wonder, then patted the child's head whispering, "Hans, run along and play..."

"You wrote me yourself and asked me to come, you yourself showed me the library, didn't you ?" I began in exasperation. "You even asked me to continue Doctor Honigberger's biography that your husband had been working on," I added.

Bewildered, Mrs. Zerlendi looked back and forth at Smaranda and myself. She was putting on an act, and I felt the blood rushing to my cheeks.

"My first husband, Doctor Zerlendi, was interested in the life of a Saxon medical personality, but I must say, sir, that I don't quite remember the name. My first husband died 25 years ago and the library no longer exists since the war..."

As I was standing, quite stunned, with my eyes on the door that I had opened so often only two months before, Mrs. Zerlendi added :

"Smaranda, show this gentleman the room..."

I followed her, as if in a dream, and I couldn't believe my eyes when I entered the library. Only the chandelier and the curtains were still there. The desk, the shelves of books, the large carpet, everything was gone. That vast room was now a kind of living room, with two tea-tables, several couches, a bridge table, and a few skins in front of the fire. Where the bookcases had been, there was a fairly old wall paper partly covered with pictures and old weapons. The wooden galleries that had occupied three walls were gone. Astounded, I closed the door.

"You're right," I said. "The library has been dispersed. If I only knew who bought it," I added, "I would have been interested in examining more closely the Honigberger case..."

"But, my dear sir," Mrs. Zerlendi spoke, "the library was dispersed more than 20 years ago..."

"The most significant thing is, however, the fact that you don't recognize me."

I fancied that Mrs. Zerlendi's hand was slightly shaking, but I could not be sure.

"We are even more surprised, sir," Smaranda began. "To say the least, it is strange that someone should recognize a room that used to be a library 20 years ago, a room that, to my knowledge, has not been visited by strangers recently..."

I was ready to leave when I realized that for unknown reasons, they both refused to recognize me. Were they both acting so because of some invisible influence from beyond ?

"I wonder if the lame old servant with whom I spoke several times during the last weeks would be able to recognize me ?" I said.

Mrs. Zerlendi quickly turned to Smaranda.

"He means Arnica," she whispered in terror.

"But Arnica's been dead for 15 years," Smaranda exclaimed. "How could he have met her a few weeks ago ?"

I was losing control of my mind and my eyesight was growing dim. Had I stayed a few minutes more I would have fainted right at their feet. I mumbled a few words of excuse and left, hardly daring to look up. After long wandering in the streets, having recovered, I felt the significance of this astounding incident, but I never dared confess it to anyone, nor shall I do so in this tale. Even so, I've led a trying enough life oppressed by the mysteries that Mrs. Zerlendi urged me to examine without the doctor's consent...

*

A few months after the above related incidents, I was again passing along S. street. The building at number 17 was being pulled down. The railings had been partly wrenched, the pool was filled with iron and boulders. I stood watching a long time, to catch a look, maybe, of one of these two women, and find out something about their strange behavior. But there was no one except the workmen and a supervisor who was pressing them to hurry up. At long last I made for the end of the street, almost grieving about this secret that I could not solve. I thought I saw the little boy whom Mrs. Zerlendi had brought into the drawing room. I called :

"Hans," I said, "how nice to meet you, Hans !"

The child considered me with false, yet perfect wonder.

"My name is not Hans," he replied politely enough. "My name is Ştefan..."

So he walked on, never looking back, aimlessly, bored at finding no playmate.

## THE GYPSIES

It was stifling hot in the tram. Quickly stepping along the passage he said to himself : "You're in luck, Gavrilescu, old man !" He had caught sight of an empty seat by an open window at the other end of the car. Having sat down he pulled out his handkerchief and took his time mopping his brow and his face. Then he wound the handkerchief round his neck, under the shirt's collar and started fanning himself with his straw hat. An old man facing him had been eyeing him intently, as if trying hard to remember where he had seen him before. The man was carefully balancing a tin box on his knees.

"It's terribly hot !" he suddenly said. "We haven't had such heat since 1905 !"

Gavrilescu nodded and went on fanning himself with his hat.

"Hot indeed", he said. "But an educated man will easily stand everything. Take Colonel Lawrence. Do you know anything about Colonel Lawrence ?"

"No idea."

"A pity. Not that I know a great deal myself. Had he got in this car I would have asked him one or two things. I like talking with educated people. Three young men, sir, no doubt students, distinguished students, were all waiting at the tram-stop and I listened to their talk. They were talking about a certain Colonel Lawrence and his adventures in Arabia. What a memory they had ! They were quoting whole pages out of the colonel's book. There was a sentence I particularly liked, a very fine sentence, about the heat this colonel was up against somewhere in Arabia. A pity I can't remember the sentence word for word. That terrible burning heat of Arabia struck him like a sword. A blow on the top of his head and he was speechless."

The conductor had been listening with a smile, then handed him a ticket. Gavrilescu placed his hat on his head and began searching his pockets.

"Sorry," he mumbled after a couple of seconds, unable to find his wallet. "I never know where it is."

"That's all right," the conductor said with unexpected good-humor. "Plenty of time. We're not nearly there."

Turning around to the old fellow he gave him a wink. The old man blushed, nervously clinging to the tin box with both hands. Gavrilescu handed him a bank note and the conductor began to count out the change, smiling.

"A scandal !" the old man mumbled after a few seconds. "It's unthinkable !"

"It's the talk of the town," Gavrilescu said fanning himself again with his hat. "Looks like a fine house, though, and what a garden !... what a garden !..." he repeated admiringly, shaking his head. "There, you can just see it," he added stooping somewhat to see it better.

A few men stuck their heads against the windows, as if by chance.

"It's disgraceful," the old man spoke again, sternly looking straight on. "It should be stopped."

"These are old walnut trees," Gavrilescu went on. "That's why it's so shady and cool. I hear that walnut trees grow big enough to give shade only after thirty of forty years of life. Could it be true ?"

The old man pretended not to hear. Gavrilescu turned to one of the other passengers who had been looking pensively out of the window.

"Old walnut-trees," he said, "at least fifty years old. That's why there is so much shade. It's a blessing in this sultry heat. These people are lucky..."

"These women," the passenger said, never raising his eyes. "They are gypsies..."

"So I have heard," Gavrilescu went on. "I take this tram three times a week, and believe me, every single time there's been talk about them, about these gypsies. Does anyone know them ? I wonder : where did they come from ?"

"They came long ago," the fellow-traveller said.

"They've been here for twenty-one years," someone put in. "When I first came to Bucharest, these gypsies were here already. The garden, however, was much larger. The school had not yet been built..."

"As I was saying," Gavrilescu began anew, "I regularly travel this way, three times every week. As bad luck would have it, I give piano lessons. I say : as bad luck would have it," he added with a smile, "since I was not cut out for it I have an artistic disposition..."

"If that is the case, we've met," the old man suddenly said, turning to him. "You are Mr. Gavrilescu, piano-teacher. I have a young niece. You taught her five or six years ago. I was wondering where I had seen your face. It looked familiar."

"Yes, that's me," Gavrilescu said. "I give piano lessons, I often take the tram. In the spring time, when it's not too hot and there's a breeze, it's a real pleasure. As I was saying, I ride three times a week in this tram and I always hear people talking about the gypsies. I have often asked myself : Suppose they are gypsies ; how did they come by so much money, I ask you ? A house like that, quite palatial, with gardens and old walnut trees, why it's worth millions."

"It's a scandal !" the old man exclaimed again, looking the other way in disgust.

"I asked myself another question," Gavrilescu went on. "Considering by my own earnings, a hundred lei per lesson, you'd need ten thousand lessons to make a million lei. But, mind you, things are not that simple. Suppose I had 20 lessons a week, it would take 500 weeks. That is almost ten years. And I would have to have 20 pupils and 20 pianos. Not to speak about the summer holidays when I am left with two or three pupils, or about the Christmas and Easter vacations. All these hours are lost, aren't they ? So it isn't a question of 500 weeks at 20 hours per week, nor of 20 pupils with 20 pianos, but of much more, considerably more than that !"

"Quite true," one of the other passengers said. "Nowadays there is no great demand for piano lessons..."

"My word," Gavrilescu suddenly exclaimed, knocking his hat against his brow. "I could feel that something was wrong but I couldn't tell what. My briefcase ! I forgot the briefcase with my music. I had a chat with Mme. Voitinovici, Otilia's aunt, and left my briefcase behind... Bad luck !..." he added, extracting the handkerchief from under his collar and stuffing it in his pocket. "In this heat I must get off and catch a tram back to Preoteselor street."

He looked round in despair, as if expecting someone to stop him. Then he suddenly got up :

"Glad to have met you," he said raising his hat, and bowing slightly.

Then he quickly stepped out onto the platform, just as the tram was coming to a stop. After getting off, Gavrilescu was aware of the same torrid heat and the smell of melting asphalt. He crossed the street to wait for a tram going in the opposite direction. "Gavrilescu, my good man," he whispered, "mind what you're doing ! It does look a bit like old age. You're growing soft, you're losing your memory. I say it again : be careful, you've no right to do that. 49 years of age is a man's prime of life..." Yet he felt tired, exhausted, and sat down on a bench in the glaring sun. He pulled out his handkerchief and started mopping his face. "This reminds me of something," he said to himself. "Just a little effort, man, a little mental effort. Somewhere on a bench, without a penny in your pocket. It wasn't as hot as this, but it was a summer day..." He looked round at the empty street, closed shutters, lowered blinds, houses which appeared to be deserted. "People going away on holiday," he thought. "One of these days Otilia will be gone too." It was then that he remembered : it was in Charlottenburg. He was sitting, as now, on a seat in the sun, but in those days he was hungry, without a penny in his pocket. "When you're young and an artist everything seems easy to put up with," he thought. He got up, took a few steps up the street to see if a tram was in sight. As he walked, the torrid heat seemed to abate. He came back, leaned against the wall of a house, took his hat off and started fanning himself.

A fevo hundred meters up the street there loomed something like a shady oasis. From a garden, dense leafy lime-tree branches were hanging over the sidewalk. Gavrilescu considered them, fascinated, yet hesitating. He looked once more up the tram rails, then set out with long firm steps, keeping close to the walls. Once there, the shade didn't seern quite as dense. You could, however, feel the cool of the garden. Gavrilescu began to breathe in deeply, slightly tilting his head back. "It must have been heavenly a month ago, with the lime-trees in bloom," he pondered in a dream. He went up to the wrought-iron gate and inspected the garden. The gravel had been recently watered. You could see the round flower-beds and, at the back of the garden, a pool of water. That very moment he heard the tram squeaking and rattling by. He turned to look at it. "Too late," he thought smiling. "Zu-spät !" he added, raising his arm and waving his hat at it for quite a while, just as he used to do at the North station when Elsa left for a month's stay with her family in a village near Munich.

Then, quietly, sedately, he walked on. Having reached the next stop he took off his coat and was preparing to wait when a slightly bitter smell suddenly reached him, a smell like walnut tree leaves squashed between one's fingers. He turned and looked around. He was quite alone. As far as the eye could see, the sidewalk was deserted. He dared not look at the sky, but felt the same white, incandescent, blinding light on top of his head and could feel the fiery glow of the street slapping his mouth, his face. So he set out, quite resigned, his coat tucked under his arm, his hat pulled down upon his forehead. Seeing from afar the dense shade of the walnut-trees he felt his heart pounding and slightly quickened his step. He was almost there when he heard the tram metallically groaning behind him. He stopped and gave it a long farewell with his hat. "Too late !" he exclaimed. "Too late..."

★

In the shade of the walnuts it was unnaturally, unbelievably cool. Gavrilescu stopped for a moment, puzzled, smiling. It seemed as if he were suddenly in a mountain forest. He looked around perplexed, almost respectfully, contemplating the tall trees and the ivy-covered stone wall. An infinite sadness came over him. For so many years he had ridden past this garden, never once moved by curiosity to get off the tram and consider it closely. He was walking slowly, his head slightly tilted back looking at the tall tree-tops. Suddenly he found himself in front of the gate. There, as if she'd been hiding on the look-out for him, a young, beautiful, very dark woman stepped up ; she was wearing a necklace of gold coins and large golden earrings.

Taking his arm she whispered :

"Coming to the gypsies ?"

She smiled a broad smile, her eyes danced, and seeing that he was hesitating, she gently took his arm and pulled him inside. Gavrilescu followed her quite bewitched ; yet after a few steps he stopped, as if to ask a question.

"Don't you want to go to the gypsies ?" she asked once more, her voice still lower.

She gave him a brief, deep, direct look, then took him by the hand and quickly led him to a small old house which he could hardly have suspected, hidden as it was among large lilac and elder clumps. She opened the door and gently pushed him in. Gavrilescu entered a strange half-light as if the windows were of blue and green glass. He heard the tram coming, as if from afar, and thought the metallic rattle simply unbearable. So, he put his hands to his ears. As the noise died out he discovered an old woman, quite close to him. She was sitting at a low table in front of a cup of coffee. She was considering him with interest, as if waiting for him to wake up.

"Your heart's desire, what shall it be today ?" she asked. "A Gypsy, a Greek, a German girl..."

"No, no," Gavrilescu intervened with a gesture of defence. "Not a German girl."

"Well then, a Gypsy a Greek, a Jewess shall we say," the woman went on. "Three hundred lei," she added.

Gavrilescu put on a grave smile.

"Three piano-lessons !" he uttered searching his pockets. "Not counting the tram fare both ways."

The old woman sipped her coffee and sat pondering.

"You're a musician, aren't you ?" she suddenly said. "Then you'll be satisfied."

"I am an artist," Gavrilescu said, while extracting several damp handkerchiefs from one of his trouser pockets and methodically inserting them, one by one, into the other pocket. "I am now, unfortunately, a piano-teacher, but my ideal has always been pure art. I live for the spirit... I beg your pardon," he stammered placing his hat upon the small table and beginning to put in it the objects that he had taken out of his pockets. "I can never find my wallet when I want to..."

"No hurry," the old woman said. "Plenty of time. It's not yet three o'clock."

"I apologize for contradicting," Gavrilescu said. "I'm afraid you're wrong. It should be almost four. At three I had just finished my lesson with Otilia."

"Then the clock must have stopped again," the old woman said deep in thought.

"Ah, there we are at last," Gavrilescu burst out, triumphantly producing his wallet. "It was in the right place..."

He counted the bank notes and handed them to her.

"Take him to the hut," the old woman said looking up.

Gavrilescu felt his hand being taken, and on looking around, scared, he was faced with the girl whom he had met at the gate. He followed her nervously, carrying under his arm the hat filled with various objects.

"Mind you, remember them well," the girl said. "Don't get them mixed up : a Gypsy, a Greek, a Jewess..."

They walked across the garden passing the tall building with the red-tile roof that Gavrilescu had seen from the street.

She stopped and, briefly looking him deep in the eyes, burst into a short fit of silent laughter. Gavrilescu had just begun removing the various objects from his hat into his pockets.

"Ah," he said, "I have an artistic disposition. If I could have my way I would stay here in these clumps," pointing with his hat to the trees. "I love being outdoors. In this torrid heat to be able to breathe the cool fresh air, as if one were in the mountains... Where are we going ?" he asked, seeing that the girl was walking up to a wooden fence and opening the gate.

"To the hut... That's what the madame said..." She took his arm again and led him on. They walked into an untended garden, with roses and lilies overgrown by weeds and briar bushes. It was hot again and Gavrilescu hesitated, somewhat disappointed.

"I have been cherishing hopes," he said. "I came for the cool, for nature's beauty..."

"You wait until you get inside," the girl cut him short, pointing to an old half-ruined cottage that could just be seen at the back of the garden.

Gavrilescu put his hat on and sullenly followed her. But upon entering the passage he felt his heart pounding ever more violently, and he stopped.

"I am nervous," he said. "I don't quite know why..."

"Don't drink too much coffee," the girl whispered as she opened the door and pushed him in.

It was a room, the limits of which he could not see, for the blinds were drawn, and in the half-dark, the screens and walls looked alike. He entered stepping on the carpet which became ever thicker and softer ; it seemed as if he were walking on mattresses. With every step his heartbeat became faster and faster, until he was afraid to go forward and stopped. That moment he felt suddenly happy, as if young again, on top of the world, as if Hildegard, too, were his own.

"Hildegard !" he exclaimed, addressing the girl. "I have never given her a thought these twenty years. She was my great love. The woman of my life !"...

Yet, turning around, he realized that the girl was gone. He was aware of an insidious exotic perfume, and heard the clapping of hands. The room grew mysteriously lighted, as if the curtains were slowly being drawn, ever so slowly, one by one, so that the light of the summer afternoon could slowly filter through. Yet there was time for Gavrilescu to notice that none of the curtains had moved. He was faced by three young women standing a few yards in front of him, clapping their hands and laughing.

"It was your choice," one of them said. "A Gypsy, a Greek, a Jewess..."

"Now let's see if you can tell who is who," the second said.

"We'll see if you can tell who is the Gypsy," said the third.

Gavrilescu dropped his straw hat. He was staring at them, quite stunned, as if he didn't see them, as if he were looking through them, at something behind them, behind those screens.

"I'm thirsty," he suddenly mumbled, putting his hand to his throat.

"The madame has sent coffee for you," one of the girls said. She vanished behind a screen, coming back with a round wooden tray on which there was a cup of coffee and a long handled coffee pot. Gavrilescu seized the cup and drank it in one gulp, then handed it back smiling.

"I'm terribly thirsty," he whispered.

"This one is going to be hot, it's from the coffee-pot," said the girl as she filled the cup. "Drink it slowly..."

Gavrilescu tried a sip, but the coffee was so hot that he burned his lips. Disheartened, he placed the cup on the tray.

"I'm thirsty," he insisted. "If I could only have a drink of water."

The other two girls vanished behind the screen and soon returned with two laden trays.

"The madame sends you jam," one of them said.

"Rose-leaf jam and sherbet," the other added.

But Gavrilescu saw the jug of water and although he saw a heavy green rimmed glass beside it, he grabbed the jug with both hands and put it to his mouth. He threw his head back and had a long drink, occasionally gulping. He then uttered a sigh of relief, placed the jug on the tray and produced one of the handkerchiefs.

"My ladies !" he burst out, beginning to mop his brow, "I've been awfully thirsty. I've heard of one, Colonel Lawrence..."

The girls gave each other a meaningful look, then they all burst out laughing. This time they were having a good, hearty laugh, ever louder and merrier. At first, Gavrilescu looked at them in astonishment. Then a broad smile lit up his countenance, and finally he, too, began to laugh. He took his time mopping his face.

"May I ask a question," he spoke at last. "I'd like to know what's possessed you."

"We're laughing because you addressed us as young ladies," one of them said. "Here we are in a gypsy house..."

"That's not true !" another exclaimed. "Don't you listen to her, she's pulling your leg. We were laughing because you drank from the jug instead of the glass. Had you drunk from the glass..."

"Nonsense ! Not true !" he other two burst out. "She's making fun of you. Let me tell you the truth : we're laughing because you were afraid."

"Nonsense ! Not true !" the other two burst out. "She's sounding you out to see if you were afraid..."

"He was afraid ! Afraid !" the third repeated.

Gavrilescu took a step forward and solemnly raised his hand.

"Fair young ladies !" he protested, actually hurt. "I see you don't know who you're speaking to. I am not just anybody. My name is Gavrilescu, an artist. Before I unfortunately became a sorry piano teacher, I lived a poet's dream. Young ladies," he pathetically exclaimed after a pause, "at twenty I met, fell in love with, and adored Hildegard !"

One girl offered him an armchair, and Gavrilescu sat down with a deep sigh.

"Oh!" he began after a long silence. "Why think about the tragedy of my life ? For, you understand, don't you, Hildegard never became my wife. Something happened, something terrible happened..."

The girl handed the cup of coffee, and Gavrilescu began to sip thoughtfully.

"Something terrible happened," he continued. "But what ? What on earth could have happened ? Strange, I cannot remember. The fact is that Hildegard has not been in my thoughts these many years. I had grown accustomed to the idea. I used to say to myself : Gavrilescu, my good man, the past is dead and gone. That's the way with artists, no luck. And suddenly, a few minutes ago, as I entered your house, I remembered that I once had a noble passion. I remembered having loved Hildegard !"

The girls gave each other a look and began clapping their hands.

"I was right, after all," the third girl said. "He was frightened."

"Quite right," the others agreed. "He was afraid."

Gavrilescu looked up eyeing them melancholically for a long time.

"I don't see what you mean..."

"You're frightened," one of the girls provokingly said taking a step forward. "You've been afraid ever since you walked in."

"That's why you were so thirsty," the second one said.

"And you've been changing the subject ever since," the other said. "You've had your choice, but now you're afraid of guessing which is which."

"I still don't understand," Gavrilescu tried to defend himself.

"You should have guessed from the beginning," the third continued, "you should have guessed who is the gypsy, who is the Greek, and who is the Jewess..."

"Try now since you say you're not afraid," the first one took up again. "Try to guess. Who is the gypsy ?"

"Who is the gypsy ? Who is the gypsy ?" He could hear the other voices, like an echo.

He smiled looking them up and down.

"I like that," he said, suddenly feeling in good spirits. "So that's it : you've discovered that I'm an artist, so you think that I have my head in the clouds, and have no idea what a gypsy looks like..."

"Don't you change the subject," one girl interrupted. "Guess who is who."

"So you think," Gavrilescu obstinately went on, "that I haven't the necessary imagination to guess what a gypsy looks like, particularly when young, beautiful and naked..."

For he had, of course, guessed the moment he set eyes on them. The one who took a step towards him, completely naked, very dark skinned, black haired and dark eyed, was certainly a gypsy. The second, who was also naked, but who wore a pale green veil and golden slippers, possessed an unnaturally white body which was shiny as pearls. This one could only be the Greek. The third was no doubt the Jewess : she wore a long cherry-coloured velvet skirt tightly wrapped round her body ; her breasts and shoulders were bare ; her abundant, flaming-red hair was gathered and coiled in studied style on the top of her head.

"Now guess ! who is the gypsy ? Who is the gypsy ?" the three of them shouted.

Gavrilescu got up from the armchair and pointing to the naked swarthy girl in front, solemnly pronounced :

"Since I am an artist, I accept this test, even though a childish trial, and this is my answer : You are the gypsy !"

The next moment he was taken by his hands. The girls whirled him in a reel, shouting and whistling. The voices seemed to come from afar.

"That's no guess, no guess !" he heard as if in a dream.

He tried to come to a standstill, to tear himself away from those hands that were madly wheeling him around as in a fantastic reel ; but it was impossible to set himself free. He could smell the hot scent of those young bodies and that exotic, far-distant perfume. He could feel, as an inner, but also outer sensation, the feet of the girls dancing on the carpet. He also felt that the reel was gently carrying him between armchairs and screens, to the far end of the room. Yet after a time he gave up resisting and was no longer conscious of anything.

Upon waking up he opened his eyes on the dark-skinned naked girl kneeling on the carpet by the sofa. He sat up.

"Have I been asleep long ?" he asked.

"You were just about to doze off," the girl soothed him.

"Why, what on earth have you done to me ?" he asked, putting his hand to his head. "I feel a little dizzy."

He looked around in amazement. It seemed to be a different room ; yet he recognized those screens that had drawn his attention as soon as he had come in, symmetrically disposed in between armchairs, sofas, and mirrors. He couldn't figure out how they were structured. Some were very tall, almost reaching the ceiling. You could have taken them for walls if, in certain places, they had not jutted right into the middle of the room at sharp angles. Others, mysteriously illuminated, looked like windows half covered with curtains disclosing interior corridors. Other screens were curiously and brightly colored or covered with shawls and embroideries. From their disposition, they seemed to form recesses of various shapes and dimensions. However, after considering one of the recesses for a few seconds, he came to the conclusion that it was simply an illusion, that what he saw were actually two or three separate screens fusing their images in the greenish-golden reflection of a large mirror. The moment he realized that it was an illusion Gavrilescu felt the room swaying around him, and once more he put his hand to his head.

"For God's sake, what have you done to me ?" he repeated.

"You haven't guessed," the girl whispered with a sad smile. "And yet I gave you a wink meaning that I was not the gypsy. I am the Greek girl."

"Greece !" Gavrilescu cried out, standing up abruptly. "Eternal Greece !..."

The weariness seemed to have vanished, as if by charm. He could hear his heart beating faster, a sense of singular beatitude taking possession of his whole body like a warm thrill.

"When I was in love with Hildegard," he excitedly continued, "it was our one dream to visit Greece together."

"You were a fool", the girl interrupted. "You shouldn't have dreamed, you should have loved her..."

"I was twenty, and she was not yet eighteen. She was lovely. We were both good-looking," he added.

At that moment he realized that he was wearing a strange costume : wide trousers like Turkish shalwars and a short silk yellow-gold tunic. He looked at himself in the mirror in surprise, as if having some difficulty in recognizing himself.

"We had been dreaming to visit Greece," he went on later, in a steadier voice. "No, it was more than a dream. It was almost a reality, since we'd decided to leave for Greece soon after the wedding. Then something happened. Now, whatever did happen ?" he asked after a pause pressing his hands on his temples. "It was just like this, a hot day such as this one, a terribly hot summer day. I saw a bench and made my way to it ; I then felt the torrid heat strike the top of my head, striking the top of my head like a sword... No, not quite, that's Colonel Lawrence's story; I picked it up today from a group of students while I was waiting for the tram. Ah, if I only had a piano !" he cried out in dispair.

The girl rose from the floor with a quick movement and, taking his hand, she whispered :

"Come on !"

She drew him swiftly in and out of those screens and mirrors. Eventually she quickened her pace at such a rate that Gavrilescu found himself actually running. He tried to stop for a second to catch his breath, but the girl wouldn't let him.

"It's getting late," she spoke as she ran. He had again the feeling that the voice was whizzing past as it rushed on from a distance.

This time, however, his head did not turn. Because he was running fast, he had to avoid bumping against innumerable sofas, soft cushions and trunks, small wooden chests covered with carpets, and large and small strangely shaped mirrors which confronted them unexpectedly as if they had been recently placed on the carpet. Suddenly, at the end of a passage between two rows of screens they entered a large sunny room. Leaning against a piano, the other two girls were waiting.

"Where have you been all this time ?" the red-haired one asked. "The coffee's cold."

Gavrilescu caught his breath, took a step towards her, and raised both arms over his head as if trying to defend himself :

"No, no," he said, "I won't have any more. I've had enough coffee. My ladies, despite my artistic temper, I lead a well-regulated life. I don't care to waste my time in coffee-houses."

As if she hadn't heard him, the girl turned to the Greek:

"Why have you been so long ?" she asked again.

"He remembered Hildegard."

"You shouldn't have let him," the third girl said.

"I beg your pardon, allow me," Gavrilescu said, stepping up to the piano. "This is a strictly personal question. No one can stop me. It was the tragedy of my life."

"Now he'll be late again," the red-haired girl said. "He's rambling again."

"I beg your pardon," Gavrilescu burst out. "I am not rambling at all. It was the tragedy of my life. It all came back as soon as I walked in here. Listen," he exclaimed approaching the piano. "I'll play something and you will understand."

"You shouldn't have allowed him," he heard the two girls whispering. "Now he won't ever guess..."

Gavrilescu sat intent for a few moments, then he looked at the keys and got his hands ready, as if to attack vigorously.

"I've got it !" he suddenly cried out. "I know what happened !"

He rose impatiently from his chair and began pacing the room, his eyes on the carpet.

"Now I know," he repeated over and over again, under his breath. "It was much the same as today. Hildegard had gone with her family to Königsberg. It was terribly hot. I was living in Charlottenburg and was out for a walk under the trees. They were tall, very shady old trees. The place was deserted. It was too hot. No one ventured out. There, under those trees, I caught sight of a young woman, sobbing dreadfully, crying her heart out, her face in her hands. I was deeply surprised for she had taken her shoes off and her feet were propped against a small suitcase lying on the gravel in front of her... 'Gavrilescu, my good man', I said to myself, 'here's an unhappy creature indeed...' How could I suspect..."

He stopped walking and abruptly turned to the girls :

"My ladies !" he pathetically exclaimed, "I was young, I was good-looking and had an artist sensitivity. A young woman abandoned was enough to break my heart. I talked to her, I tried to comfort her. That was the beginning of my tragedy."

"And what shall we do now ?" the red-haired girl asked of the others.

"Let's wait a bit and see what the madame says," the Greek girl replied.

"If we go on like this, he will never tell us apart," the third girl said.

"Yes, the tragedy of my life," Gavrilescu went on. "Her name was Elsa... But I accepted it all. I said to myself, 'Gavrilescu, my good man, such is fate. An evil hour ! That's the way with artists, no luck'..."

"See," the red-haired girl said, "he's getting tied up again and won't be able to get out of this."

"Ah, fate !" Gavrilescu cried out, raising both arms and turning to the Greek girl.

The girl smiled at him, her arms behind her back.

"Eternal Greece !" he exclaimed. "I never had a chance to see you."

"Never mind that, never mind !" the other two shouted, coming up to him. "Just remember your choice."

"A gypsy, a Greek, a Jewess," the Greek girl said meaningfully and deeply looking into his eyes. "That was your wish, that was your choice !..."

"Guess who is who," the red-haired girl spoke, "and see what fun it will be."

"Who is the gypsy ? Who is the gypsy ?" the three asked all at once surrounding him.

Gavrilescu drew back instantly and leaned against the piano.

"So that's it," he began after a pause. "That's how things are with you. Whether it be an artist or a common mortal you hold your own : guess who is the gypsy. And why, if you please ? Whose orders ?"

"That's the game we play here, in the gypsy house," the Greek girl said. "Try and guess ! You won't be sorry."

"But I'm in no mood for playing games now," Gavrilescu fervently pleated. "I have just remembered the tragedy of my life. For, look here, now I understand it all : if that evening, in Charlottenburg, I hadn't entered a beer house with Elsa... or suppose I had entered, but had been provided with money and been able to pay the bill, my life would have been different. But it so happened that I had no money and Elsa paid the bill. The following day I tried everywhere to get a few marks to pay my debt, but no. All my friends and acquaintances were away on holiday. It was summer, it was terribly hot..."

"He's frightened again," the red-haired girl spoke under her breath looking down at the carpet.

"Listen, I haven't yet told you everything !" Gavrilescu pathetically shouted. "For three whole days I couldn't find any money, and every night I visited Elsa at her lodgings : to apologize for being unable to find the money. And we ended by going to the beer house. Had I at least been firm and refused to go to the beer house with her. But what do you expect ? I was hungry. I was young, I was good-looking. Hildegard was away, and I was hungry ! To be quite frank there were days when I would go without a meal. An artist's life..."

"And what's to be done now ?" the girls asked. "Time is getting short, getting short."

"Now ?" said Gavrilescu, raising his arms again. "Now it's pleasant and warm, and I like it here. You're young and beautiful and stand before me ready to offer me jam and coffee, but I'm not thirsty. I feel very good. And I say to myself, 'Gavrilescu, my boy, these girls are expecting something. Give them that pleasure. If they want you to guess who is who, do it. But take care ! Be careful, man, for if you get it wrong again you'll be caught in their reel and never wake until daylight..."

He smiled, went around the piano, in such a way as to use it as a protection against the girls.

"So you want me to tell you who is the gypsy. Very well, I will tell you..."

The girls fell into line, quite excited, never saying a word, looking him straight in the eyes.

"I'll tell you," he spoke after a pause. Then, abruptly, he pointed melodramatically to the young woman wearing the pale green veil and he waited. The girls were stunned, as if they could hardly believe it.

"What's wrong with him ?" the red-haired girl asked a long time after. "Why can't he guess ?"

"Something's happened," the Greek girl said." He has remembered and he's now lost, fumbling in the past."

The girl he had taken for the gypsy advanced a few steps, took the tray and the coffee cups and, passing in front of the piano, she whispered with a sad smile :

"I am the Jewess..."

Then she silently disappeared behind a screen.

"Ah !" Gavrilescu uttered, knocking the palm of his hand against his brow. "I should have known. There was something in her eyes coming down from the far past. And she had a veil, thoroughly transparent, but neverthtless a veil. Just as in the Bible..."

Suddenly, the red-haired girl burst out laughing.

"The governor has gone wrong," she shouted. "He couldn't tell the gypsy."

She passed her fingers through her hair and shaking her head, the curls fell flaming red upon her shoulders. She began a dance, slowly turning round in a circle, clapping her hands and singing.

"Tell us, Greek girl, what it might have been like," she called shaking her curls.

"Had you guessed which she was, it would have been very nice," the Greek girl spoke in a low voice. "We would have sung and danced for you leading you through every room.It would have been so nice."

"It would have," Gavrilescu repeated, with a sad smile.

"Go on, tell him, Greek girl," the gypsy shouted, stopping in front of them while she continued clapping her hands rhythmically and striking the carpet with her foot ever more fiercely.

The Greek girl crept up to him and began to speak. She was talking fast, under her breath, occasionally wagging her head or smoothing her lips with her fingers. But Gavrilescu did not understand her. He smiled and listened, a vague look in his eyes, occasionally murmuring, "It would have been fine..." The gypsy's foot struck the carpet ever more fiercely producing a muffled subterranean sound. He stood it until that strange savage rhythm seemed impossible to bear. Then, with an effort, he dashed to the piano and began to play.

"Now you tell him, too, you gypsy !" the Greek girl shrieked.

He could hear her coming closer and closer, as if dancing on a gigantic copper drum, and a few minutes later he could feel her hot breath on his back. Gavrilescu stooped down at the piano and pounced furiously as if wanting to remove the keys, to tear them away, to dig into the womb of the piano with his nails, and then even deeper.

★

His mind was empty of thought, wrapped up as he was in the new unfamiliar tunes that he seemed to hear for the first time, though they started up in his memory, one after another, like reminiscences of old. It was late when he stopped playing. Then he realized that he was alone, that the room was almost dark.

"Where are you ?" he shouted anxiously, rising from his chair.

He hesitated a few seconds, then made for the screen behind which the Jewess had vanished.

"Where are you hiding ?" he shouted again. Slowly, stepping on the tip of his toes, as if to surprise them, he crept around the screen. This might have been the entrance to a different room which seemed to narrow down into a winding corridor. It was a strangely built room, with a low irregular ceiling, slightly undulated walls, disappearing and re-appearing in the dark. Gavrilescu took a few casual steps, then stopped to listen. That very moment he thought he could hear swishing and quick steps passing close by on the carpet.

"Where are you ?" he shouted.

He listened to his echoing words trying to explore the dark. He thought he could see the three of them hiding in the corridor. He headed for them, arms extended, feeling his way. But after a while he realized that he had taken the wrong way since he discovered that the corridor was making a turn toward the left a few meters away. So he stopped again.

"It's no use hiding, I am sure I can find you anyway !" he shouted. "Better come out of your own accord !"

He then listened intently, his eyes riveted on the corridor. You couldn't hear anything, yet here the heat seemed to creep in again. So he decided to go back and wait for them while playing the piano. He remembered the direction he had come from and knew that he had only taken twenty or thirty steps. Extending his arms he advanced slowly, carefully. A few steps away he bumped against a screen and drew back frightened. He knew for a fact that a few seconds earlier the screen had not been there.

"What's come over you ?" he shouted. "Let me go..."

He thought he could again hear stifled laughter and took heart.

"Maybe you think I'm afraid," he began after a short pause, trying to seem as cheerful as possible. "Just a minute. Just a minute !"... he added hurriedly as if he were expecting an interruption. "I agreed to play hide-and-seek with you out of compassion. That's the truth : I took pity on you. I realized from the start : innocent young girls, shut up here, in a hut, at the beck and call of the gypsies. So I said : My good man, these girls want to play a trick on you. Make them believe you have been tricked. Let them think you can't tell which is the gypsy. Such is the game... Such is the game... Such is the game," he shouted as loud as he could. "And now that we've had plenty of play, come out into the open."

He listened, smiling, his right hand against the screen. That moment he heard the thud of feet scurrying in the dark very close to him. He turned abruptly with arms extended.

"Let's see who you are," he said. "What have we got here. Have I got hold of the gypsy ?"

Having grasped nothing, he stopped to listen. This time, not the slightest noise from anywhere.

"No matter," he said as if sure that the girls were just a few steps away, hiding in the dark. "Patience. I can see you don't know yet who you're up against. Later on you'll be sorry. I might have taught you to play the piano. You might have improved your musical education. I could have explained the Lieder of Schumann. Such beauty !" he fervently said. "What divine music !"

He felt the heat again, it seemed more awful than ever. He began wiping his face against the sleeve of his tunic. Then, feeling low, he turned left, constantly fingering the screen. He sometimes stopped and listened, then set out again at a quicker pace.

"Whatever possessed me to take these young girls seriously," he suddenly burst out, furiously. "I'm sorry ! I said young girls out of courtesy. You are something else. You know well what you are. You're gypsies. No education. Illiterate. Does any of you know where Arabia is situated ? Who has heard of Colonel Lawrence ?"

There seemed to be no end to the screen and as he advanced the heat became unbearable. He took off his jacket, furiously wiped the perspiration on his face and neck, then slung the tunic on his bare shoulder like a towel. His arm was groping again as he was going along the screen. This time, however, he was up against a smooth cool wall, so he clung to it with both arms extended. He stood a long time against the wall, taking deep breaths. Then he began moving slowly along the wall, never leaving it. Some time after, he was aware that he had lost his jacket. He was sweating abundantly, so he stopped, took off his shalwars and began drying his face and body all over. At that moment he thought something had touched his shoulder ; with a sharp shriek he jumped sideways, frightened.

"Let me go," he shouted. "I asked you to let me go !"...

Somebody, something, a being or an object, impossible to identify, touched his face and shoulders. So he began defending himself, madly wheeling the shalwars above his head. He was becoming hotter and hotter. He felt beads of sweat running down his cheeks and was panting. At a sudden twirl the shalwars flew out of his hand and disappeared far into the dark. Gavrilescu stood a moment with his arms raised, spasmodically closing his hands, as if hoping to find out, from moment to moment, that the shalwars were within reach. He suddenly felt that he was naked, and crouched down, his hands on the carpet and his forehead protruding, as if ready to start a running race.

He began to advance, feeling the carpet around him with the palms of his hands, still hoping he would find his shalwars. He occasionally discovered objects which were difficult to identify. Some looked like small boxes but, upon closer examination, proved to be gigantic pumpkins wrapped up in shawls. Others which seemed to be cushions or soft bolsters, became, upon investigation, balls, old umbrellas filled with saw-dust, wash baskets filled with newspapers. He could hardly decide on the nature of the objects because he was ever faced with new ones which he began to feel with his hands. Sometimes large pieces of furniture would stand in his way. Gavrilescu carefully avoided them, not knowing their shape and being afraid to upset them.

He didn't realize how long he had been crawling in the dark on his knees or on his stomach. He had given up hope of ever finding his shalwars again. It was the heat that bothered him most. As if he were walking in the garret of a tin-roofed house, one afternoon of torrid heat. He could feel the parching air in his nostrils and objects became ever hotter. His body was soaking wet and he had to stop occasionally to rest. He would then stretch as far as he could, legs apart and arms extended, sticking his face into the carpet, breathing deeply and nervously.

He once thought that he had been dozing and was waken by an unexpected breeze, as if a window had been opened somewhere, letting in the cool of the night. But he soon understood that it was something else, something quite different from what he knew. He stood transfixed for a moment, feeling the sweat on his back grow cold. He couldn't remember what happened afterwards. He was frightened by his own screams, and found himself running insanely in the dark, bumping against the screen, upsetting mirrors and all sorts of tiny objects which had been curiously placed on the carpet, frequently slipping and falling, but picking himself up and racing on. He found himself jumping over cases, going around mirrors and screens. Then he realized that he had entered a half-dark zone and was beginning to distinguish contours. At the far end of the corridor, unusually high up on the wall, a window seemed to open, the light of the summer twilight filtering through. As he walked into the corridor the heat became unbearable. He was obliged to stop for breath and wiped the sweat off his brow and cheeks with the back of his hand. He could hear his heart thumping as if ready to burst.

Before reaching the window he stopped again, frightened. The sound of voices, laughter, of chairs being pushed back on the parquet floor reached him, as if a whole group of people were getting up from the table and heading towards him. That minute he saw that he was naked, thinner than he knew he was, bones sticking out from under his skin, but his belly swollen and flagging such as he had never seen himself before. There was no time to run back. He seized a curtain at random and began to pull. He felt that the curtain was very nearly coming undone. He propped his feet against the wall and leaned back with all his weight. But something unexpected then happened. He gradually felt that the curtain pulled him its own way, with growing force. A few minutes later he was against the wall, and though he tried to set himself free by letting the curtain go, he did not succeed. Very soon he felt himself overwhelmed, tied fast on all sides, as if bound hand and foot and pushed into a bag. It was dark again and very hot. Gavrilescu realized that he couldn't stand this much longer, that he would suffocate. He tried to call but his throat was dry, as dry as wood, and the sounds seemed smothered in thick felt.

★

He heard a voice that he thought he knew.

"Go on, governor, tell us some more."

"What more can I tell," he spoke under his breath. "I've told everything. That was all. I came to Bucharest with Elsa. We were both poor. I began giving piano lessons..."

He raised his head slightly from the bolster and his eyes fell on the madame. She was sitting at that low table, the long-handled coffee pot in her hand ready to pour coffee into cups.

"No, thanks, I won't have any more !" he said, raising his hand. "I've had more than enough. I'm afraid I won't sleep tonight."

The madame filled her own cup, then placed the coffee pot on a corner of the table.

"Come on," she insisted. "What else have you been doing ? What happened next ?"

Gavrilescu sat thinking for a long time fanning himself with his hat.

"Then we started playing hide and seek." He suddenly spoke in a slightly altered voice, somewhat more sternly. "Naturally, they didn't know with whom they were dealing. I am a responsible man, an artist, a piano teacher. I came here simply curious to know. I take an interest in novelty, in things unexperienced before. I said : 'Gavrilescu, my lad, here's an opportunity to improve your knowledge.' I didn't know it was a matter of innocent, childish games. Just imagine, I suddenly found myself naked and heard voices, I was certain that one moment or another, you know what I mean..."

The madame nodded and leisurely sipped her coffee.

"The time we've had to find your hat," she said. "The girls turned the hut upside down to find it."

"Quite, I was to blame as well, I must say," he continued. "I didn't know that unless I could identify them in the daylight, I should have to search, catch, and guess in the dark. I hadn't been told anything. And I tell you, when I found myself naked and felt that curtain curling around me like a winding sheet, it was like a winding sheet, I give you my word..."

"The time we've had to get you dressed," the madame said. "You simply refused to dress..."

"That curtain was a real windingsheet, I tell you. It was skin-tight. It was wound around and so tight that I couldn't breathe. And such heat!" he exclaimed fanning himself rythmically with his hat. "It's a wonder that I'm still alive!"...

"Yes, it's been very hot," the madame said.

At that moment the metallic rattling of the tramcar could be heard.

"Ah!" he exclaimed, rising heavily from the sofa, "the way time passes! I got talking and what, with one thing and another, I forgot I had to go to Preoteselor Street. I left behind my briefcase with my music, would you believe it? I was thinking this afternoon: 'Look out, my dear fellow, it somehow looks like...' Yes, something of the sort I was saying, but I don't quite remember what it was..."

He took a few steps to the door, then turned, bowed slightly and with a flourish of his hat said:

"Pleased to have met you."

In the yard he had an unpleasant feeling. Though the sun had gone down it was hotter than in mid-afternoon. Gavrilescu took off his coat, dumped it on his shoulder, and fanning himself with his hat, he crossed the garden and walked out. As he walked away from the shady wall, the stifling heat of the sidewalk, the smell of dust and melting asphalt struck him again. He was walking dejectedly, shoulders sunk and a vague look in his eyes. No one was waiting at the stop. As he heard the tram coming, he raised his hand to stop it.

The car was practically empty with all windows open. He took a seat facing a young man in his shirt sleeves. As he saw the conductor advancing, he began fumbling for his wallet. He found it sooner than he had expected.

"It's unbelievable!" he exclaimed. "It's worse than in Arabia. Maybe you're heard of Colonel Lawrence..."

The young man smiled listlessly, then turned to the window.

"Have you any idea what time it is ?" Gavrilescu asked the conductor.

"Five minutes past eight."

"Bad luck ! They'll be having dinner, They'll thihnk I especially came so late to find them dining. Now I don't want them to think that... You see what I mean, don't you ? On the other hand, if I were to tell them where I've been, Mrs. Voitinovici, who is an inquisitive woman, will keep me talking until midnight."

The conductor who had been considering him with a smile, winked at the young man.

"Tell her you've visited the gypsies, and she'll ask no questions, you'll see."

"Oh no, not a chance. I know her well. She's an inquisitive woman. It's better not to say anything."

At the next stop a few young couples got in. Gavrilescu changed seats closer to them so that he might hear the conversation. When he thought it was proper to join in, he slightly put up his hand.

"I am sorry to contradict you. I am unfortunately a piano teacher, but that was not my calling..."

"Preoteselor Street," he heard the conductor's voice. So, getting up suddenly, he bowed and hurriedly crossed to the door.

He set out at a leisurely pace, fanning himself with his hat. When he came to number 18 he stopped, set his tie right, passed his fingers through his hair, and walked in. He climbed slowly up to the first floor, then rang the bell energetically. A few seconds later he was overtaken by the young man in the tram.

"This is a coincidence indeed !" Gavrilescu exclaimed, seeing the young man stop by him.

The door was abruptly opened and a woman appeared on the threshold, still young but with a pale and withered face. She wore an apron and held a mustard jar in her left hand. Faced with Gavrilescu, she frowned.

"Yes, what is it ?" she asked.

"I left my briefcase," Gavrilescu timidly began. "What with talking, you know, I left it behind. I had various things to do and couldn't come sooner."

"I don't quite understand. What kind of briefcase ?"

"If she's having dinner, don't bother," Gavrilescu rapidly continued. "I know where I left it. It's by the piano."

And he tried to enter, but the woman would not budge from the threshold.

"Who are you looking for, may I ask ?"

"Mrs. Voitinovici, of course. My name is Gavrilescu, Otilia's piano teacher. I didn't have the pleasure of meeting you," he added politely.

"You're in the wrong house," the woman said. "This is number 18."

"I beg your pardon," Gavrilescu began smiling. "I've known this flat for five years or more. You may say that I'm a member of the family. I come here regularly three times a week..."

The young man watched the scene leaning against the wall.

"What did you say her name was ?" he asked.

"Mrs. Voitinovici. She's Otilia's aunt, Otilia Pandele that is..."

"She doesn't live here," the young man interrupted. "This is where we live, the Georgescu family. This lady is my father's wife. Her maiden name was Petrescu..."

"I'll thank you for being polite," the woman said, "and not come home with all sorts of characters..."

She turned her back on them and disappeared along the corridor.

"I do apologize for this scene," the young man said, trying to smile, "She's my father's third wife. She carries the weight of all the errors of former marriages : five boys and one girl."

Gavrilescu was listening quite upset, fanning himself with his hat.

"I am sorry," he began, "deeply sorry. I didn't mean to annoy her. It's the wrong time, quite true. It's dinner time. But, you see, tomorrow morning I have a lesson up in Dealu Spirii. I need that briefcase badly. Czerny II and III are in it. They're my own scores, with my personal interpretations in the margin. That's why I always carry them with me."

The young man looked at him, still smiling.

"I don't think I made myself quite clear," he intervened. "I mean to say that this is where my family lives, the Gorgescus. We've been here for four years."

"Impossible !" Gavrilescu burst out. "I was here a few hours ago, I had a lesson with Otilia, between two and three. Then I talked with Mrs. Voitinovici."

"Was it Preoteselor Street, no. 18, first floor ?" the young man inquired with an amused smile.

"Exactly so, I know the house inside out. I can tell you where the piano is. I can take you there blind-folded. It's in the drawing room, by the window."

"There is no piano in the house," the young man said. "Try another floor. Though I am positive you won't find her on the second floor either. That's where Captain Zamfir's family lives. Try the third floor. I am so sorry," he added, seeing that Gavrilescu was actually frightened, feverishly fanning himself with his hat. "I would have been glad if this Otilia lived in this house..."

Gavrilescu hesitated, looking deep into his eyes.

"Thank you," he said eventually. "I'll try the third floor, too. Though I give you my word that about a quarter past three today I was here." He firmly raised his hand and pointed to the corridor.

He began to mount the steps, breathing heavily. On the third floor he took his time mopping his face with one of his handkerchiefs, then rang the bell. He could hear tiny steps, and the door was soon opened by a small boy of five or six.

"Ah," Gavrilescu uttered, "I'm afraid it's the wrong floor. I was looking for Mrs. Voitinovici." A young woman then appeared in the doorway, smiling at him.

"Mrs. Voitinovici used to live on the first floor," she said, "but she has moved, left Bucharest for some provincial town."

"Has she been away long ?"

"Oh yes, quite a long time. It will be eight years this next autumn. She left right after Otilia's marriage."

Gavrilescu touched his forehead and began rubbing it. Then he searched the woman's eyes and gave her as gentle a smile as he could.

"I believe there's some confusion," he began. "I'm talking about Otilia Pandele, a schoolgirl in the 10th grade. The niece of Mrs. Voitinovici."

"I knew both of them well," the woman said. "When we moved in, Otilia had just got engaged to the Major, you know, that entanglement with the major, but Mrs. Voitinovici refused to consent, and quite rightly, the difference in age was so great. Otilia was a mere child, she was not yet 19. Fortunately, she met Frîncu, Frîncu the engineer. You're sure to have heard of him."

"Frîncu, the engineer ?" Gavrilescu repeated. "Frîncu did you say ?"

"Yes, he made some kind of discovery. It was in the newspapers."

"Frîncu, the inventor," Gavrilescu dreamily spoke. "Strange, very strange..."

Then he put out his hand, patted the boy's head, and made a short stiff bow :

"I'm sorry. I think I've come to the wrong floor."

Smoking and leaning against the door, the young man was waiting.

"Did you find out anything ?" he asked.

"The lady upstairs claims that she got married, but there must be some misunderstanding. Otilia's not yet 17, she's in the 10th grade. I talked to Mrs. Voitinovici, we spoke about one thing and another. She never mentioned a word abouth this."

"Strange..."

"Very strange indeed," Gavrilescu said, encouraged. "That's why, let me tell you, I don't believe any of this. But, after all, it's useless to insist. I'll come again tomorrow morning."

And having taken his leave, he began going down the steps with a firm gait.

"Gavrilescu, my good man," he uttered to himself as soon as he was in the street, "be careful, you're beginning to grow soft in the brain. You're losing your memory. You're mixing up addresses..." The tram came in sight, and he quickened his step. He sat down by the window and only then did he feel a slight breeze.

"Why, at last !" he exclaimed addressing the lady sitting in front. "It's almost practically..." but he was suddenly at a loss for a conclusion to the sentence, so he smiled a confused smile. "Yes," he went on shortly after. "I was just talking to a friend and saying that we were almost, practically, in Arabia. Colonel Lawrence, if you have heard of him..."

The lady continued to gaze out of the window.

"One more hour or two," Gavrilescu began again, "and night shall come. The dark, I mean. The cool of night and... we'll be able to breathe."

The conductor was standing in front of him and Gavrilescu began searching his pockets.

"After midnight we'll be able to breathe," he addressed the conductor. "What a long day !" he added somewhat nervously, unable to find his wallet. "Such mishaps !... Ah, here it is at last," he burst out, quickly opening his wallet.

"This one's no longer current," the conductor said returning the note." You have to change it at the bank..."

"But what's wrong with it ?" Gavrilescu asked, turning the note in his hand, quite surprised.

"It's been out of use since last year ; you may change it at the bank."

"Strange !" Gavrilescu uttered, considering the note with concentration. "It was quite good this morning. And the gypsies will take it. I had three more like this, and they took them all at the gypsy house..."

The lady turned slightly pale and rose ostentatiously, looking for a seat at the other end of the car.

"You shouldn't have mentioned the gypsies, not in front of a lady," the conductor chided him.

"Everybody does," Gavrilescu defended himself. "I travel this way three times a week, and I give you my word..."

"Yes, that's true," a passenger added. "We all mention them, but not in front of the ladies. It's a matter of decency. Particularly as they're going to have the place lighted up. Quite so, the town council has approved : they'll have the garden illuminated. Personally, I am unprejudiced, as you might say, but a gypsy house illuminated, I consider that provocative..."

"Strange," Gavrilescu said. "I haven't heard any such thing."

"It is in all the papers," another passenger added. "It's a disgrace," he spoke, raising his voice. "It's unthinkable !"

Some people turned to look at him, and Gavrilescu cowered under their accusing gaze.

"Search thoroughly, maybe you've got some more money," the conductor said. "If not, you'll have to get off at the next stop."

With a flushed face, not daring to look up, Gavrilescu proceeded to search his pockets again. Fortunately, the purse with small change was quite handy, in between the handkerchiefs. Gavrilescu counted a few coins and handed them.

"You've given me only five lei," the conductor said, showing his open palm.

"That's right, to the customs house!"

"The fare is ten lei. Don't you live in this world?" the conductor added in a stern voice.

"I live in Bucharest," Gavrilescu said, proudly looking up. "I take the tram four or five times a day. I've done it for years, and I've always paid five lei..."

The whole carriage was now eagerly listening to this conversation. A few passengers came close, and sat on seats on either side. The conductor played with the coins tingling them in the palm of his hand, then said:

"If you won't give me the rest of the fare, please get off at the next stop."

"Tram fares went up three or four years ago."

"Five years ago," the conductor specified.

"I give you my word," Gavrilescu pathetically began.

"Then get off at the first stop," the conductor cut him short.

"Better pay the difference," someone advised. "The customs house is a fairly good walking distance."

Gavrilescu looked into his purse and held out another five lei coin.

"Strange things going on in this country," he mumbled under his breath when the conductor had gone. "Decisions are made overnight, within 24 hours. More precisely, within six. I give you my word... But, after all, what's the good of insisting? It's been a terrible day. And the worst of it is that we can't do without the tram. I, at least, am obliged to use it three or four times a day. Yet a piano lesson is worth a hundred lei. A banknote such as this one. Now this one's no good any more. I must go and have it changed at the bank..."

"Give it to me," an elderly man said. "I'll change it in the office tomorrow."

The man took a banknote from his wallet and handed it to him. Gavrilescu took it reverently and studied it carefully.

"Very fine," he said. "Has it been in use for some time ?"

A few passengers smiled at each other.

"For some three years," a man said.

"Strange that I haven't seen it before. I'm rather absent-minded, I will say. An artist's temper..."

He put the note in his wallet, then looked out of the window.

"Night has fallen," he said. "At last !"

He suddenly felt tired, worn out and, with his head in the palm of his hand, he closed his eyes. He stayed thus as far as the customs house.

*

He tried the lock with his key in vain, then heavily pressed the button of the electric bell, and, having pounded on the dining room window, he came back to the front door and started pounding on it with his fists. A man in his nightgown soon appeared from the dark in the open window of the house next door, shouting hoarsely :

"What's all the racket ?... What are you up to ?"'

"Sorry," Gavrilescu said. "I can't think what's happened to my wife. She doesn't answer. Something's the matter with the key, I can't get in."

"Why should you get in ? Who are you ?"

Gavrilescu went up to the window and raised his hat :

"Although we are neighbors," he began, "I don't think I've had the pleasure of meeting you. My name is Gavrilescu and I live here with my wife Elsa..."

"Then you've got the wrong address. Mr. Stănescu lives here. And he's not at home, he's away at a resort."

"I beg your pardon," Gavrilescu spoke. "I am sorry to contradict you, but I'm afraid there's some sort of confusion. Number 101 is our home, Elsa's and mine. We've been here for four years."

"That's enough. Stop it all for goodness sake. We can't get any sleep," someone shouted.

"He claims to be living in Mr. Stănescu's house..."

"I don't just claim," Gavrilescu protested. "This is my house, and I won't have anyone... And first and foremost I want to know about Elsa, where she is, what's happened to her..."

"Ask at the police station," someone spoke from the upper floor.

Gavrilescu looked up in panic.

"What does the police station have to do with it ? Has anything happened ?" he shouted beside himself. "Do you know anything ?"

"I don't know anything, but I do want to get some sleep. And since you're going to chat all night..."

"I beg your pardon," Gavrilescu said. "I want to sleep, too. I'm dead tired... I've had a terrible day. Torrid heat, as if we were in Arabia... But I can't think what's happened to Elsa. Why doesn't she answer the door ? Maybe she was taken ill and fainted ?"

And going back to the front door of number 101, he began pounding the door with his fists again, ever more strongly.

"I told you, mister, didn't I, that he's away ? That Mr. Stănescu is at the seaside."

"Call the police," a shrill woman's voice spoke. "Call the police right away."

Gavrilescu ceased abruptly, leaning against the door and breathing with difficulty. He was suddenly feeling very tired, he sat upon one of the steps and clutched his brow in the palms of his hands. "Gavrilescu, my good man," he murmured, "be careful. Something very serious has happened, and they will not tell you what. Get a hold of yourself. Think !"

"Mrs. Trandafir !" he burst out. "I should have thought of her from the start. Mrs. Trandafir !" he shouted, getting up and making his way to the house in front. "Mrs. Trandafir !..."

Someone still standing by a window said in a quiet voice:

"Let her rest, poor woman."

"It's urgent !"

"Let her sleep, God rest her soul. She's been dead a long time."

"Impossible," Gavrilescu said. "I spoke to her this morning."

"You've probably taken her sister Ecaterina for her. Mrs. Trandafir died five years ago."

Gavrilescu was stunned, then he stuck his hands into his pockets and extracted a few handkerchiefs.

"Strange," he mumbled after a time. He slowly walked back and, climbing the three steps at number 101, he picked up his hat and put it on. He tried the door-handle once more, then climbed down and walked away uncertain. He was walking slowly, with no thoughts, unconsciously mopping his face with his handkerchief. The pub at the corner was still open, and after walking around he decided to go in.

"We only serve by the glass now," the boy said. "We're closing at two."

"At two ?" Gavrilescu wondered. "And what is the time now ?"

"It's two. Even past two..."

"It's terribly late," Gavrilescu murmured to himself.

Going up to the counter he thought he recognized the owner's face, and his heart began to beat quickly.

"You are Mr. Costică, aren't you ?" he inquired.

"That's me," the owner said giving him a long look. "I guess I've seen you before," he added after a silence.

"It looks like it..." Gavrilescu began, then got tied up, stopped speaking, and smiled an anxious smile. "I used to come here long ago," he continued. "I had some friends : Mrs. Trandafir."

"Yes, God rest her soul."

"Mrs. Gavrilescu, Elsa..."

"Ah, the trouble she's been through," the owner intervened. "What happened is a mystery to this very day. The police looked for her husband for several months, but couldn't find him alive or dead... As if he'd sunk into the earth... Poor Mrs. Elsa, she waited for him a while, then went back to her family in Germany. She sold her belongings and left. There was nothing much ; they were far from well-off. I wanted to buy the piano."

"So she's gone back to Germany," Gavrilescu said dreamily. "Has she been gone long ?"

"She left long ago. A few months after Gavrilescu vanished. It will be 12 years this autumn. It was in the papers..."

"Strange," Gavrilescu whispered, fanning himself with his hat. "Now, if I were to tell you, if I told you that only this morning, mind you that I am not exaggerating, this very morning, I sat talking to her... What is more : we had lunch together. I can even tell you what we had..."

"Maybe she's back," the owner said looking perplexed.

"No, she's not back. She never went away. There must be some misunderstanding. I am now rather tired, but in the morning I shall get the hang of it all..."

With a slight bow he went out.

*

He was walking slowly, his hat in one hand, his handkerchief in the other, stopping frequently to take a rest. It was a clear moonless night, and the cool of the gardens was pouring out on the streets. After a long time, a horsedrawn carriage stopped by him.

"Which way, sir ?" the driver asked.

"To the gypsies," Gavrilescu replied.

"Get in. It'll be forty lei," the driver said coming to a stop.

"I am sorry, but I'm short of money. A hundred lei and some small change is all I have. The hundred I need for an entrance to the gypsies !"

"It will be more than that," the driver spoke with a laugh. "A hundred lei won't take you very far."

"That's what I paid this afternoon. Good night," he said, setting out again.

But the carriage followed him at a slow pace.

"That's the nicatiana," the driver said taking a deep breath. "It's from the general's garden. That's why I like driving this way at night. Customers or no customers, I drive this way every night. I love flowers very much."

"You've got an artist's disposition," Gavrilescu said with a smile.

Then he sat down on a bench and waved him good-bye. But the driver suddenly brought the carriage to a stop nearby, in front of the bench. He got out his tobacco box and began rolling a cigarette.

"I'm fond of flowers," he said. "Horses and flowers. In my younger days I was an undertaker. Something splendid ! Six horses in black and gold trappings, and flowers, such flowes, no end to the flowers ! Why, youth now gone, everything's flown. I've grown old, a night carriage driver."

He lighted his cigarette and leisurely enjoyed a first puff.

"So it's the gypsies', is it ?" he said after a time.

"Yes, a personal matter," Gavrilescu was quick to explain. "I was there this afternoon, and there's been no end to the trouble."

"Ah, the gypsies," the driver added, with melancholy. "If it weren't for the gypsies..." he added in a lower voice. "If it weren't..."

"Quite," Gavrilescu said. "It's common talk. I mean, in the tram. As the tram rides by the garden, everybody speaks of the gypsies..."

He rose from the bench and set out again, the carriage slowly pacing after.

"Let's go this way," the driver said, pointing to a narrow lane. "It's a short cut... And we pass the church besides. The nicatiana there is in bloom. By no means as fine as the general's, but you won't be sorry, I'm sure."

"An artist's disposition," Gavrilescu spoke dreamily.

In front of the church they both stopped to inhale the perfume of flowers.

"There's possibly something else besides nicatiana," Gavrilescu said.

"Ah, there are all sorts of flowers. If there's been a burial today, a lot of flowers were left behind. Now, at daybreak, they all begin to smell good again... I used to come here a lot. It was splendid !"

"We're almost there now," he said. "Why not get in ?"

"I'm sorry, it's the money..."

"You'll give me some of that small change. Get in, won't you ?"

Gavrilescu hesitated briefly, then got in with an effort. But as soon as the carriage drove off, he fell asleep.

"It was fine," the driver began. "A well-endowed church and choice society... Why, youth..."

He looked over his shoulder and saw that the customer was asleep, so he started gently whistling.

"Here we are," he shouted, getting out, "but the gates are closed..."

He began to shake him and Gavrilescu awoke.

"The gates are closed," the driver said again. "You'll have to ring the bell..."

Gavrilescu took his hat, set his tie right, and got out. Then he began fumbling for his small-change purse.

"Don't bother," the driver said. "Save it for the next time. I'll be waiting here anyway," he added. "If any customer were to turn up at this hour of the night, it's here I would find him."

Gavrilescu waved his hat at him, then made for the gate, felt for the bell, and pressed the button. The door opened that very moment and, on entering the garden, Gavrilescu made for the brushwood. A pale light could still be seen in the window. He knocked timidly on the door. Seeing there was no answer he tried the handle and entered. The madame had fallen asleep, her head on the table.

"It's me, Gavrilescu," he said, giving her a gentle tap on the shoulder. "You've landed me in a fine mess," he went on, seeing she was coming awake and beginning to yawn.

"It's late," the Madame said, rubbing her eyes. "They've all gone."

But giving him a long look, she recognized him.

"Ah, it's you again, the musician. There's only the German girl. She never sleeps..."

Gavrilescu again felt his heart thumping and felt a slight tremor.

"The German girl, did you say ?"

"One hundred lei," the madame said.

Gavrilescu began fumbling for his wallet, but his hands shook ever more violently and, on finding it among his handkerchiefs, the wallet slipped down onto the carpet.

"I am sorry," he said, stooping to pick it up. "I'm rather tired. It's been such a terrible day..."

The madame took the bank note, got up from the stool and, on the doorstep, pointed to the big house :

"Now, mind you. Don't get lost," she said. "Walk right along the corridor counting seven doors. When you reach the seventh, you'll knock three times and say : 'It's me, the old woman sent me'."

She then stifled a yawn, tapping her lips with her hand and closed the door. Breathing heavily, Gavrilescu slowly advanced towards the building that was shining silvery under the stars. He climbed the marble steps, opened the door, and stood hesitating for a moment. A badly lit corridor was stretching before him. Gavrilescu againt felt his heart pounding as if ready to burst. He proceeded, very excited, counting aloud the doors he was passing. He soon found himself counting : thirteen, fourteen... and stopped, quite unnerved. "Gavrilescu, my good man, be careful, you've done it again. Not thirteen, not fourteen, but seven. That's what the old woman said, you're to count seven doors..."

He meant to go back and count again but after a few steps he felt drained of all strength. So stopping before the first door in sight, he gave three knocks and entered. It was a large and sparsely furnished drawing room. By the window, looking out into the garden loomed the shadow of a young woman.

"Sorry," Gavrilescu began with some difficulty. "I didn't count properly."

The shadow came away from the window, advancing towards him with a soft tread and a long-forgotten scent suddenly came back to him.

"Hildegard," he cried out, dropping his hat.

"I've been waiting such a long time," the girl said, coming up. "I've looked for you everywhere..."

'I went to the pub," Gavrilescu said in a low voice. "If I hadn't accompanied her to that beer-hall, everything would have been all right. If I had had some money on me... But as it happened, she paid the bill, Elsa I mean. And you'll agree that I was under an obligation. I felt indebted to her... And now it's late, isn't it ? Very late indeed..."

"Why should it matter ?" the girl said. "Come on, let's go."

"But I have no home, nothing at all any more. It's been a terrible day... I was talking to Mrs. Voitinovici and I forgot my briefcase, music scores and all..."

"You were always absent-minded," she replied. "Let's go..."

"But where to ?" Gavrilescu made an attempt to shout. "Somebody's moved into my house, I forget the name, but it's someone I don't know... And he isn't even at home, that we might explain it all. He's away at a resort."

"Come along with me," the girl said, taking his hand and gently drawing him out into the corridor.

"But I haven't any money, worse luck," Gavrilescu continued under his breath. "Just when the currency's changed and the tram fares are higher..."

"You're the same as you've always been," the girl said laughing. "You're afraid..."

"None of my acquaintances are here," Gavrilescu mumbled. "They're all away for the summer. As for Mrs. Voitinovici, from whom I might have borrowed, people say she's gone to live in the provinces... Ah, my hat," he cried out, and was ready to go back for it.

"Leave it," the girl said. "You won't need it now."

"You never can tell," Gavrilescu insisted, trying to extricate his own hand from the girl's. "It's a good hat, almost new."

"It that so ?" the girl asked in surprise. "Don't you understand yet ? Don't you understand something's happened to you, recently, quite recently ? Is it possible that you don't ?"

Gavrilescu looked her deep in the eyes and sighed.

"I'm rather tired," he said. "Forgive me. It's been such a terrible day... But I seem to feel better already."

The girl gently led him on. They crossed the garden and walked out without opening the gates. The driver was waiting and dozing. The girl drew him as gently as before into the carriage with her.

"I swear," Gavrilescu began in a whisper. "I give you my word that I have not a penny left..."

"Which way, Miss ?" the driver asked.

"The way to the woods, on that winding road," the girl said. "And drive slowly. There's no hurry..."

"Why, that's youth for you," said the driver, gently whistling.

She held his hand in her own, but her head was against the cushions, her eyes upon the sky. Gavrilescu was watching her, quite intently.

"Hildegard," he spoke after a while. "Something's happening to me, and I really don't know what it is. If I hadn't heard you speaking to the driver, I would say that I was dreaming..."

The girl turned to him and gave him a smile.

"We all dream," she said. "That's how it all begins. As in a dream..."

# REJUVENATION BY LIGHTNING

It was only when he heard the bell of the Metropolitan church tolling that he remembered it was the night of the Resurrection. The rain began as soon as he walked out of the station and now threatened to become torrential; it seemed suddenly abnormal. Under his umbrella he was walking fast, stooping, his eyes on the ground as he tried to keep out of the streaming water. Spontaneously he broke into a run, keeping the umbrella against his chest like a shield. But some twenty meters away he saw the red traffic light and had to stop. He waited nervously, bouncing, standing on the toes of his shoes, constantly changing places, considering in dismay the pools of water that a few steps in front of him were almost overflowing the boulevard. The red light went out and the very next moment he was blinded and shaken by the explosion of a white incandescent light. It was as if he were sucked in by some hot cyclone inexplicably bursting in the very crown of his head. "A thunderbolt quite close," he said to himself, making an effort to blink and force his eyelids open. He couldn't think why he was clinging so tightly to the handle of the umbrella. The rain was savagely lashing from all sides, yet he didn't feel anything. Then he heard the Metropolitan church bell tolling again, as well as all the other bells and, quite close, another one, fretting, alone and desperate. "Such a fright," he said to himself and began to shiver. "It's the water," he thought within a few moments, realizing that he lay flat in the puddle by the curb. "I'n shivering."

"I saw the lightning strike him," he heard the same panting voice of a scared man. "I wonder if he's still alive. I was looking that way, he was right under the traffic light. I saw him flare up from top to bottom, his umbrella, his hat, and his clothes catching fire at the same time. If it hadn't been for the rain, he would have burnt like a torch. I don't know if he's still alive," he repeated.

"And if he is what are we to do with him?"

It was a distant, tired, and seemingly bitter voice.

"Who knows what sins he may have committed to be lightning struck by the Lord on the very night of the Resurrection right behind the church... We'll see what the doctor on duty has to say," he added, after a pause.

It seemed strange not to feel anything, since, in fact, he no longer felt his body. He knew from the talk of those around, that he had been taken to the hospital. But how was he transported ? carried ? on a stretcher ? in a wheel chair ?

"I don't think there is any chance," he heard after a good while, another voice, just as distant. "Not one inch of skin unscathed. I can't realize how he goes on living. The natural thing would have been..."

Of course, everyone knows that if more than 50% of the epidermis is destroyed, you choke. But he soon realized that it was ridiculous and humiliating to reply mentally to those who were bustling around him. He would rather not hear them just as, eyes closed, he did not see them. That very moment he came to, far away as it were, and as happy as he had then been.

"So what happened afterwards ?" he asked smiling. "What other tragedy ?"

"I didn't say it was a tragedy, but in a certain way, that's what it was ; to have a passion for science, to have a single wish of dedicating your life to science."

"What science are you referring to ?" he interrupted. "Mathematics or the Chinese language ?"

"Both, and all the others that I was discovering one by one, falling in love with them as I was gradually discovering them..."

He laid his hand upon his arm as an excuse for interrupting again :

"Mathematics I understand, for if you have no vocation it's useless to go on. But what about Chinese ?"

He wondered why he had started laughing. Maybe he was amused by the way he had asked: "What about Chinese ?"

"I thought I had told you. Two years ago, in Paris, I went to a lecture given by Chavannes. I saw him after the lecture in his study : he asked me how long I had been studying Chinese and what other oriental languages I knew. It's useless to give you a summary of the whole conversation. I understood one thing : that if, within a few years, do you hear, a few years !, I should not be proficient in Sanskrit, Tibetan and Japanese, besides Chinese, I would never be a great orientalist..."

"Quite, but you ought to have answered that you only wanted to study Chinese."

"That's what I told him, but it did not convince him. Because even so I had to learn Japanese and a number of Southern Asian languages and dialects. But that was not the important thing. When I told him that I had been studying Chinese for five months, he went up to the blackboard and wrote some twenty characters, then asked me to pronounce them, one by one, and to translate the whole excerpt. I pronounced them as well as I could and translated some, but not all. He gave me a courteous smile. "Not bad," 'he said. "But if after five months... how many hours a day ?" "At least six hours," I said. "Then the Chinese language is not your subject. Very likely you haven't got the necessary visual memory. Dear Sir," he added smiling ambiguously, both affectionately and ironically, "dear Sir, in order to master the Chinese language you should have the memory of a mandarin, a photographic memory. If you haven't got it, you'll have to make an effort three or four times greater. I don't think it's worth it."

"So, basically, it's a matter of memory."

"Of a photographic memory," he gravely repeated, stressing the words.

Several times he heard the door opening and shutting, as well as other noises and a few unknown voices.

"We'll see what the professor says. If you ask me. I'll tell you honestly..."

The same thing, always the same thing ! But he liked the voice, it was certainly a young doctor, efficient, fond of his profession, generous.

"The skin was burnt a hundred per cent, nevertheless he has survived these twelve hours and, as far as we can tell, he's not in pain. Have you given him an injection ?"

"One, this morning. I thought he was moaning, but he may have moaned in his sleep."

"Do we know anything about him ? Did they find anything by him ?"

"Just the handle of the umbrella, the rest had been carbonized. Strange that it should be the handle, a wooden handle. The clothes had burnt to ashes, partly washed off by the rain, partly shaken off in the car."

He knew that this was the way it ought to have happened, yet hearing the doctor's explanations he was relieved : so the two envelopes in his pocket had also burnt to ashes. He did not realize that he hadn't closed the door properly behind him, so accidentally, he had heard : " 'The venerable one' is doting. He has told us this story three or four times already." It was true. He had been impressed by the news he had read in La Fiera Letteraria : that Papini was almost blind and no surgeon dared operate. The tragedy was like none other for an avid and insatiable reader like Papini. That was why he was constantly mentioning it. However, maybe Vaian was right : "I'm beginning to dodder..."

Then he heard the voice again :

"What tragedy happened then ? You gave up Chinese. And what else ?"

"As a matter of fact I didn't give it up. I went on learning ten to fifteen characters a day, for my own pleasure and because it helped me understand the translated texts that I was reading. As a matter of fact I was a dilettante."

"So much the better," Laura chimed in, again putting her hand on his arm. "A few intelligent and imaginative men are necessary to enjoy the discoveries of your great scholars. You did very well to give up Chinese. But then what other tragedies were you alluding to ?"

He gave her a long look. She was not the prettiest student he had known, not by far, but she was different. He couldn't tell where the attraction lay, why he was constantly looking for her, in the lecture halls he had never entered since completing his Bachelor's Degree. He was sure to find her at Titu Maiorescu's lecture. That was where he met her an hour ago. Then, as usual, while taking her home, they sat by the lake in the Cișmigiu garden.

"Which were the other tragedies ?" she repeated, calmly supporting his gaze.

"I told you that ever since I was a boy, I liked mathematics and music, but history, archaeology and philosophy as well. I would gladly have studied them all, not as a specialist, of course, but with a certain rigour, working on the actual texts, for I hate improvising and culture by hearsay."

She stopped him, boyishly throwing up her hands.

"You're the most ambitious man I've ever met! Ambitious and quite crazy! Particularly crazy!"

He knew their voices and had learnt to distinguish them. Three day nurses and two for the night.

"With a bit of luck he would die one of these days. They say that whoever dies in holy week goes straight to heaven."

"She's a kind soul, she pities me. She's kinder than all the others, for she's concerned with the salvation of my soul. What if it suddenly crossed her mind to pull the syringe needle out of the vein? I would probably survive till morning, when the resident medical student comes. If he won't notice the professor is sure to. He is the only one who is desperate and humiliated because he doesn't understand, the only one who wants to keep me alive at any cost, to find out what happened." One day he had heard him, he had given up remembering when, having touched his eyelids with infinite cautiousness he had heard him say:

"The eyeball seems intact, but whether he's been blinded or not, that we don't know. As a matter of fact we know nothing whatever."

He had heard it before. "We don't even know if he's conscious or not," the professor then said, "whether he hears and whether he understands what he hears." He was not to blame. Several times before this he had recognized his voice, perfectly understanding him. "If you understand what I say," the professor had shouted, "press my finger." But he couldn't feel that finger. He wanted to press it, but didn't know how.

This time he added: "If we could only succeed in keeping him alive five more days..."

One of the assistants had heard that in five days' time professor Gilbert Bernard, a first class specialist, was to arrive from Paris, on the way to Athens.

"Ambitions above all," Laura repeated. "You want to be, like so many others, an oriental philologist, an archaeologist, a historian, and goodness only knows what else. In other words, you mean to live an alien life, the life of other people, instead of being yourself, Dominic Matei, and cultivate your own genius exclusively."

"My own genius?" he cried timidly, in order to hide his joy. "This means that I supposedly am a genius."

"In a sense, you surely are. You're unlike anyone that I have previously known. You live and understand life in a different way than we do."

"Yet so far, at twenty six, I haven't actually done anything. Except for having passed all my exams with top marks. I haven't discovered anything, not as much as an original interpretation of the XI$^{th}$ canto in the *Purgatorio*, that I translated with a commentary."

He fancied that Laura was considering him sadly, somewhat deceived.

"Why should you have discovered anything ? Your genius should find fulfillment in the life you are leading, not in analyses, discoveries and original interpretations. Your model should be Socrates or Goethe ; but just try to imagine Goethe without his written work !"

"I don't quite understand," he said much moved.

"Do you all understand ?" the professor asked them.

"I don't quite understand, especially if you speak too fast."

He understood very well. The professor's French was impeccable ; he had certainly taken his Ph. D. in Paris. His speech was almost more accurate and elegant than that of the great specialist. Bernard was, probably, of foreign origin, but in his slow, uncertain phrases he could guess that he would not take the risk of giving an opinion — just as Vaian used to say in connection with their last headmaster's hesitation whenever an urgent and serious decision was to be taken.

"When did you realize that he was conscious ?"

"Only the day before yesterday," said the professor, "we had tried several times before, but without any satisfactory results."

"Are you sure that he pressed your finger ? Did you feel he was pressing it in answer to your question ? Or maybe that was a reflex movement, without intention, without significance ?"

"We went through the experiment several times. If you like, you could try yourself, to form an opinion."

As so many times before, he felt a finger gently slipping, with extreme precaution, under his own closed fist. Then he heard the professor's voice :

"If you understand what I say, press the finger !"

He probably gave it a good squeeze, for doctor Bernard pulled it out quickly, in surprise.

A few seconds later, having whispered "traduisez, s'il vous plaît," he pushed it in again, saying clearly, slowly, these words : "Celui qui vous parle est un médecin français. Accepteriez-vous qu'il vous pose quelques questions ?" Before the professor had finished translating, he gave the finger as tight a squeeze as before. This time he did not withdraw his finger, but asked him : "Vous comprenez le français ?" He squeezed again with lesser conviction. A few moment's hesitation and doctor Bernard asked again : "Voulez-vous qu'on vous abandonne à votre sort ?" With something like relish he kept his hand inert as if it were of plaster. "Vous préférez qu'on s'occupe de vous ?" He gave him a tight squeeze. "Voulez-vous qu'on vous donne du chloroforme ?" His hand again became limp and he kept it thus without the slightest movement while listening to the last questions. "Êtes-vous Jésus-Christ ? Voulez-vous jouer du piano ? Ce matin, avez-vous bu du champagne ?"

That night, everyone, a glass of champagne in hand, crowded around them and shouted with a sorry vulgar impudicity that surprised them both : "Don't drink any more champagne before Venice or you'll be sick !" "I'm afraid they're the ones that have had more champagne than is good forh them," Laura said when the train had left.

Then he heard the professor's voice :

"Let's have another try. Maybe he didn't quite understand your question. I'll ask him in Romanian." He went on, raising his voice : "We want to find out your age. Squeeze my finger for every ten years."

He squeezed, ever more tightly, six times then stopped without realizing why.

"Sixty ?" the professor wondered. "I would have said less."

"In this larval state," he heard Bernard's voice, "it's difficult to tell. Ask him if he's tired, if we may continue."

They continued the dialogue another half hour. They found out that he did not live in Bucharest, that he only had one distant relative, that he would rather not let him know about the accident, that he was ready for any test, however risky, to find out whether the optic nerve had been touched or not. He was lucky : they did not ask any more questions, which he, very likely, would not have taken in. Papini's eventual blindness had been a first warning. That week he had told himself that it was not the unavoidable decay of old age, that having constantly repeated Papini's story (Papini that no surgeon dare operate on), it was merely because he was preoccupied with the tragedy of one of his favourite writers ; but he soon realized that he was trying to deceive himself. One year before, Doctor Neculache had agreed that, for the time being, arteriosclerosis was incurable. He hadn't said that he himself was threatened by arteriosclerosis, but he added :

"At a certain age, you may expect anything. I, too, am losing my memory," he added, sadly smiling. "For some time now, I've ben unable to memorize the verse of younger poets that I discover and like."

"Nor can I," he put in, "I used to know practically the whole of *Paradise* by heart, and now... As for the young writers, having read them, I remember practically nothing..."

And yet... Lately, as he was lying in bed, eyes closed, he remembered with no difficulty many books recently perused, re-read mentally poems by Ungaretti, translated by Ion Barbu and Dan Botta ; they were texts he did not remember ever having learnt by heart... As for *Paradise*, during many days and nights he would fall asleep reciting his favourite passages. He was suddenly seized by incomprehensible panic, apparently springing from the very joy of the present discovery. "Stop thinking !" he ordered his brain. "Let me think of something else !..." And yet, for so long, he hadn't done anything, except recite poems and re-memorize books that he had read. "I've been a silly fool ! I was scared in vain..." However, one day after leaving home he had realized in the street that he no longer remembered where he had intended to go... "But it might have been a simple accident. Maybe I was tired, though I had no reason to be..."

"As a matter of fact, the great specialist did not shed much light," he heard the voice of one of the resident medical students.

"He was saying, however, that there have been a few other cases. That Swiss clergyman, for instance, struck by lightning and burned over almost $100^0/_0$ of his body, went on living for a number of years. He went dumb, however, just like our man here, most probably," he added in a softer voice.

"Don't speak, he may hear you," someone that he could not identify whispered.

"That's just what I want, that he should hear me. We'll see his reaction. Maybe he's not dumb, however..."

Against himself, not knowing what he was doing, he slowly unclenched his mouth. That moment he heard unusually strong crackings in both ears, as if, right and left, innumerable platforms of old ironmongery had tumbled over rocks. Although the echo of prolonged explosions deafened him quite, he went on opening his mouth. Suddenly he heard himself saying, "No," repeating the word several times. Then, after a slight pause, he added, "Not dumb." He knew he had meant to say, "I am not dumb," but did not succeed in pronouncing "am." Judging by the noises in the room, the door opening and shutting several times, he realized that these two words had caused a sensation. He kept his mouth wide open, but dare not move his tongue. Doctor Gavrilă, his favorite, the man he had initially considered to have a medical vocation, came up to his bed. He repeated the words only then realizing why they cost him such an effort : with every movement of the tongue he felt a few teeth going loose, as if ready to drop.

"That was it," Gavrilă whispered, "the teeth. Even the grinders," he added with concern. "Ring up doctoor Filip to send someone ungently- he himself would be the ideal man, they should bring everything necessary..."

He heard him again, as if from afar :

"They're loose, almost dangling. Had he taken a good gulp, he might have been choked by some grinder... Notify the professor."

He felt the pincers seizing a front tooth and pulling it out without effort. He began counting : just as gently within a few minutes, doctor Filip extracted nine teeth and five grinders.

"I don't quite understand what happened. The roots are good. It is as if they had been pushed by several wisdom teeth. But that is impossible. We shall have him X rayed..."

The professor came up to the bed, laying two fingers on his right hand.

"Try to say something, any word, any sound."

He tried, moving his tongue about with no fear, but didn't succeed in saying what he wished. Finally, quite resigned, he started pronouncing, at random, short words : pin, cuckoo, ox, man, feather, froth...

The third night he had a dream that he remembered in explicit detail. He had unexpectedly gone back to Piatra Neamț and was on his way to the high school, but the more he advanced, the greater number of people went by. He recognized about him on the street a number of his former pupils as he remembered them some 10, 20 or 25 years ago when parting with them. He grabbed one of them by the arm: "Now what's the rush, Teodorescu ?" he asked. The youngster gazed with an uncertain smile : he had not recognized him. "We're going to the school. Today is the centenary of professor Dominic Matei."

"I don't like this dream," he said to himself several times. "I don't understand why, but I don't like it." He waited for the nurse to leave, then deeply moved and extremely careful, as he had been wont these past several days, he began opening his eyelids. He had awakened one night gazing at a luminous bluish spot, ignorant that he had opened his eyes, not understanding what he was looking at. He felt his heart fluttering in panic and promptly closed his eyes. But the following night he woke up again, gazing open-eyed on the same luminous spot ; at a loss, he began mentally counting. He got as far as 72, then suddenly realized that the light was coming from a bedside lamp at the far end of the room. He succeeded in controlling his joy by considering at leisure one wall after another, the room where he lay, having been taken there on the eve of doctor Bernard's visit. Ever since he had been left alone, particularly at night, he would open his eyes, gently move his head, then his shoulders and start examining shapes and colors, the darkness and half-darkness around. Impossible to realize that such happiness had always been at hand ; just watching intently, with no hurry, the objects by his side.

"Why didn't you show us that you could open your eyes ?" he heard one of thhe resident medical students. The next moment he saw him ; he was almost as he had guessed. judging by the inflections of his voice : tall, dark, lean, beginning to go bald.

He had, therefore, suspected something, and had been on the lookout for some time.

"I couldn't say," he answered only pronouncing the words partially. "Maybe I was trying to make sure that I hadn't gone blind..."

The medical student was considering him with an absent smile.

"You are a strange man. When the professor asked how old you were, you said sixty..."

"I'm more than that..."

"Difficult to believe. You probably heard the nurses talking..."

With the humble gesture of a penitent schoolboy, he nodded. He had heard them : "How old did he say he was, sixty ? The man won't tell his age. You've just seen him yourself when we bathed him : this is a young man, in the prime of life, this fellow is not yet forty..."

"I don't want you to believe that I've been spying on you to denounce you to the director. But I have to inform the professor. It's for him to decide..."

In other circumstances he would have been cross, or afraid, but now he found that he was reciting mentally at first, then gently moving his lips, one of his favorite poems *La morte meditata,* by Ungaretti :

"Sei la donna che passa
Come una foglia
E lasci agli alberi un fuoco d'autunno..."

He remembered having first read the poem when they had been long separated, almost 25 years. Yet, as he read it. he thought of her. He did not know whether it was the love as in their early days, if he loved her as he had confessed that morning of 12 October 1904, when leaving the courthouse, and making their way to the Cişmigiu gardens. On parting, he kissed her hand, saying : "I wish you... well, you know what I mean... But I want you to know one more thing : that I will love you to the end of my days..." He wasn't certain if he still loved her, but of her he had thought when reading : "Sei la donna che passa..."

'You're now certainly in no danger whatsoever."

That was the professor's greeting the following morning, as he came up to him, smiling. The man was more impressive than he had imagined. Not too tall, chin up, the way he carried himself, straight in the back, as if on parade, leant him a martial air, intimidating to others. If his hair had not been entirely white, he would have looked severe. Even in smiling he remained grave and distant.

"You're only beginning to be an interesting case now," he added sitting on a chair facing the bed. "You probably understand why. No one has so far found a plausible explanation, either in this country or abroad. The way the lightning struck you, you ought to have been killed on the spot, or have died from suffocation in 10 or 15 minutes afterwards or, at best, have been paralyzed, become dumb or blind... Enigmas confronting us in your case grow more numerous, day by day. We don't yet know why you were unable to open your mouth for twenty-three days, having to be artificially nourished. You probably succeeded in opening it to eliminate the teeth and grinders that the gums could no longer hold. We thought of having a set of false teeth made, that you should be able to eat and, moreover, to speak normally. But for the time being we cannot do anything ; the X-rays demonstrate that a new set of teeth will shortly make its appearance."

"Impossible," he cried in amazement, distorting the word.

"That's what all the doctors and dentists say, that it's simply impossible. The X-rays, nevertheless, are as clear as possible. That's why, to make a long story short, your case becomes extremely interesting : it's no longer a case of 'the living dead', but something quite different. What exactly that is, we don't know yet..."

"I must be careful to make no mistake and give myself away. One of these days they'll want my name, address, profession. After all why should I be afraid ? I haven't done anything. No one knows anything about the white envelope, nor about the blue one." Yet, for no understandable reason, he wished to preserve his anonymity at all costs, as it had been in the beginning when they shouted : "Can you hear me or not ? If you understand what I say, squeeze my finger." Fortunately, toothless, he now spoke with difficulty. It will be child's play to pretend, to distort even those few words that he was able to pronounce. What if they should ask him to write ? Attentively, he considered his right arm and hand, as it were for the first time. The skin was smooth, with no creases, quite fresh, and beginning to recover its former color. Slowly, carefully, he felt his arm up to the elbow, then slipped two fingers along his biceps. Very strange. Almost four weeks of practically absolute immobility, also those nourishing liquids injected in his veins... "This is a young man, in the prime of life !" the nurse had said. One day before this he heard the door tentatively open, footsteps coming up to the bed, the medical student whispering : "He's asleep, don't wake him." Then an unknown hoarse voice : "It can't be the same... However, we shall have to see him beardless... But the man we are looking for is a student, hardly over twenty-two, while this one looks older, almost forty..."

Then he remembered the storm again.

"The strange thing," one of the medical students had said, "is that the rain fell only where he was walking : from the train station down to boulevard Elizabeth. It came pouring down as in mid-summer, enough to flood the boulevard, while some hundred meters away, not a drop."

"True," someone added, "we came that way back from church and the boulevard was not yet dry."

"Some people say that it was an attempt on somebody's life, since quantities of dynamite were found ; the torrential rain overtook them and they had to give up at the last moment."

"That may well be invented by the police department to justify the raids on the students."

Then they were all suddenly silent.

"I must be careful," he repeated. "They may well take me for one of the legionaries in hiding that the police are looking for. Then I will have to tell them who I am. They'll send me to Piatra Neamț in order to check. And then..." Yet, as usual, he succeeded in evading the irritating thought. He found himself mentally reciting the XI$^{th}$ canto in the *Purgatorio*, then tried to remember from the Aeneid : Agnosce veteris vestigia flammae...

"There's no coming to terms with you, Professor Dominic, you switch from book to book, from one language to another, from one science to another. Maybe that's why you divorced," he went on sadly smiling.

He had not minded. He liked Nicodim, who was a kind, honest and gentle Moldavian.

"No, Mr. Nicodim, the Japanese textbook has nothing to do with our divorce."

"But why the Japanese textbook?" Nicodim was surprised.

"I thought that was what you were referring to, the rumor in town..."

"Namely ?"

"Namely, they say that as I came back with a textbook for Japanese, Laura seeing me open my notebook and begin to study at once, would have said... Why, she would have said that I was tackling too many things and never finishing anything and that is the reason why we separated."

"That's not what I heard, no. I heard that Miss Laura had grown tired of your love affairs ; that last summer, in Bucharest, you would always be around a French girl pretending that you knew her at the Sorbonne."

"No," he said tired and shrugging his shoulders, "that was quite a different story. True that Laura suspected something, because she had heard of another former affair, but she is an intelligent woman, she knows that as to loving, she is the only one I love, that the others, well... But I must tell you that we are still very good friends."

But he did not say any more. He hadn't confessed to anyone, not even to Dadu Rareș, his best friend, who had died of tuberculosis twelve years later. Though Dadu was possibly the only one who had guessed. Maybe Laura herself had told him something, they got along very well together.

"I am listening," the professor said, his voice slightly irritable. "I'm listening and I don't understand. No progress these last few days. I think that last week you were able to say some words which now... You must cooperate. Don't be afraid of the press men. Orders are quite strict : no one shall interview you. Your case, of course, was very extraordinary, news spread abroad. There have been news, articles in various papers, mostly absurd and ridiculous. But, to continue, you must cooperate, we have to know more, several things : where you come from, who you are, your profession and the rest."

He nodded obediently and said several times : "Quite, quite !" "Things are getting hot ; I have to keep my eyes open." Luckily, the following morning, as he was feeling his gums with his tongue, he felt the stump of the first canine. With feigned innocence, he showed it to the nurse, then to the medical students, pretending to find it impossible to pronounce anything. But the teeth were rapidly coming out, one after another. By the end of the week they had all sprouted. A dentist came every morning, examined him, and took notes for the article he was working on. For a few days he suffered from gingivitis, so he couldn't have spoken clearly, even if he had wanted to. These were the most serene days, for he was feeling sheltered again, protected from every surprise. He also felt an energy and a confidence that he had not known since the war, when he had organized at Piatra Neamţ a movement of cultural Renaissance, so called by the local newspapers, which had no equal throughout Moldavia. Nicolae Iorga himself had praised it in a lecture held at the high school. Iorga had spent part of the afternoon at his house, and his surprise was manifest in discovering those several thousands volumes of oriental studies, classical philology, ancient history, archaeology.

"Why don't you write articles ?" he asked several times.

"I am working, professor, I've been striving to conclude a book..."

Then he was interrupted by Davidoglu with that inevitable joke of his :

"But ask him what sort of book, will you, professor ? *De omni re scibili !*"

It was one of their old jokes repeated as often as they saw him enter the staff room with an armful of new books received that very morning from Paris, Leipzig or Oxford.

"When will you finish it, professor Dominic ?" they would ask.

"How can I when I'm not yet half way through ?..." As a matter of fact, he knew that having spent before the war the small fortune that was left on expensive books and scholarly trips abroad, he was obliged to remain a schoolmaster in the local high school ; that he was therefore spending a good deal of time with his lessons. His interest in Latin and Italian had long been gone ; he would have liked to teach, if possible, the history of civilization or philosophy.

"To do everything that you want to, you'd have to live ten times over, and more."

He had once answered with something like :

"We know at least one thing : that for philosophy you don't need ten lives."

"Habe nun ach ! Philosophie... durchaus studiert !" the teacher of German had solemnly quoted. "You know the rest," he added.

From the loose talk of the assistants, he understood why the professor was nervous. Bernard was constantly asking for more complete and definite information. "En somme qui est ce monsieur ?" he had inquired in a letter. (But that is not certain. That is what doctor Gavrilă says, but he hasn't seen the letter either.) Of course, Bernard had long been informed that the stranger he had examined at the beginning of April had preserved his eyesight and begun to speak. He was now more interested than ever. Interested not only in the phases of his physical recovery, but in as many details as possible about his mental capacities. His knowledge of French led him to believe that he had some education. He wished to know what remained and what was lost. He had suggested a number of tests : vocabulary, syntax, verbal associations.

"But when do you think you're going to finish it, man ?"

"I still have to write the first part ; all the others, Antiquity, the Middle Ages and the Modern era, are written, almost complete. But, you know, part I : the origins, the origin of language, of society, of family, of all the other institutions... All these require years and years of study. And in our provincial libraries... I need to buy as much as I can, but now, without much money..."

In fact, as time passed, he clearly understood that he would not live to finish his one book, his life's work. He woke up one morning with an ashy taste in his mouth. He was close to sixty years old and had concluded none of the things he had begun. His 'disciples,' as he liked to call some of his very young colleagues, who, full of admiration, would meet at least one evening a week at the library, to hear him talk about the insurmountable problems to be solved ; well, these disciples went their own ways over the years, other appointments, other towns. Not a single one left whom he could entrust with the manuscripts and collected documents.

On hearing that in the local café he was referred to as the Venerable One or Papa Dominic, he realized that he was beginning to fade and lose the prestige he had won during the war when Nicolae Iorga had praised him in a lecture and would send some student from Iași to borrow books. Little by little, he found that in the staff room or at the Select café he was no longer the center of attention, that he was no longer as brilliant as before. Lately, having heard Vaian say "The Venerable One is badly doting !" he dare not tell them about the new books he was reading, about the articles in N.R.E., Criterion or La Fiera Letteraria. There followed one after another, what was meant in his private language as "the crises of consciousness."

"What are you doing in these places, Mr. Matei ?"

"I was taking a walk. A bad headache again and I was out for a walk."

"Why in your pyjamas ? It's Chistmas time. You'll catch cold !"

The next day, it was all over town. They were probably expecting him at the café to ridicule him, but he didn't go that day or the next.

"At the earliest opportunity !" he had laughingly shouted, one afternoon in front of the Select café. "At the first opportunity !"

"What's to happen on the first opportunity ?" Vaian had replied.

What was going to happen indeed ? He loked at him, frowning, trying to remember. He finally shrugged and made for home. When touching the door-knob he remembered : at the first opportunity he was to open the blue envelope. "Not here where everybody knows me, but away, in some other town. Bucharest for instance."

One morning he asked the nurse to give him a sheet of paper, an envelope, and a pencil. He wrote a few lines, licked the envelope, and addressed it to the professor. He then prepared to wait, feeling his heart beats grow faster. How long was it since he had felt such an emotion ? Possibly since the morning when he'd heard that Romania had declared a general mobilization of troops. Or, maybe earlier, 12 years earlier, when entering the drawing room where he guessed that Laura was waiting and wished to speak to him. He had then fancied that her eyes were dim with tears.

"I must tell you," she began with a forced smile. "It's much too important for both of us and I can no longer keep silent. I have to confess. I've been sensing this for some time, but it has lately become an obsession. I feel that you are no longer mine. Please, let me go on. It's not what you are thinking... I feel you don't belong to me, that you are not here by me, that you live in another world. I don't mean your research, which, whatever you may think, I take an interest in, but I feel that you're in a strange world where I cannot accompany you. For myself and for you, I think it would be wiser to separate. We're both young, we both love life... you'll understand it later."

"All right," the professor said, carefully folding the piece of paper and placing it in his notebook. "I'll be back later."

He was back an hour later. He locked the door to prevent any interruption and sat on the chair facing the bed.

"I am listening. You must not make too great an effort. The words you cannot pronounce you may write down," he added handing him a writing pad.

"You'll understand why I had to adopt this stratagem," he began quite upset. "I want to escape publicity. Here is the truth : My name is Dominic Matei ; on the 8th of January I was seventy years old, I have been teaching Latin and Italian at the 'Alexandru Ioan Cuza' high school in Piatra Neamţ, where I now reside. I live on the Episcopie street no. 18. It is my own house with a library of practically eight thousand volumes which I have left to the school in my will."

"How extraordinary," the professor exclaimed, having taken a deep breath, and considering him again, somewhat scared.

"I should think it is quite easy for you to check this. But I do beg you to do it very discreetely. The whole town knows me. If you want other evidence, I can draw the plan of the house, tell you what books are to be found in the library and give you any other details you require, but for the time being at least, they shouldn't find out what has happened. As you yourself said, it is sensational enough that I have come through safe and sound. If it becomes known that I have grown younger, there will be no peace for me. I am telling you all this because the police officers, who have already been here, will never believe that I am past seventy and, therefore, they won't believe that I am who I am. There will be investigations, and much can happen when you are under investigation. If you think my case is worth studying, I mean continuing to be worth studying here in the hospital, I would be grateful if you could find a fictitious identity for me. It will be, of course, temporary, and if in the future you shall not be satisfied with my behavior, you may reveal the truth any time."

"That's not a problem," the professor intervened. "Right now the important thing is for you to be registered. That, I hope, won't be difficult to do. Yet what age can we give you ? Without your beard you look like a man of thirty or thirty one. Shall we say thirty-two ?"

He asked once more the name of the street and number of the house and wrote them down in the notebook.

"The house, of course, is closed," the professor said after a while.

"Veta, an old woman, my life-long housekeeper occupies two small rooms close to the kitchen. She has the keys to the other rooms."

"I suppose there must be a picture album somewhere, photographs of yourself when you were young ?"

"They are all in the top drawer of the writing desk : three albums. But if the man you send talks to Veta, it will soon be all over town."

"There is no risk if we act carefully." Pensively he stuck the notebook into his pocket and was silent a few seconds, continuing to look at him.

"I'll confess that your case is most exciting," he said rising. "I don't understand anything, none of us does... The exercises you probably perform when you are alone, at night."

He shrugged, perplexed.

"I felt my legs going numb, so I left my bed and here on the carpet..."

"Did anything strike you ?"

"Yes, quite. I felt my body all over. I felt the muscles, as they used to be : tough, strong. I did not expect it. After so many weeks of practical immobility, they should have been, what shall I say ? Kind of..."

"Yes, so they should," the professor said.

He was making for the door, but stopped, turned round and sought his eyes.

"You haven't given me your address here, in Bucharest."

He felt that he was blushing, yet with an effort, he produced a smile.

"I have no address for I had just arrived. I had come by train from Piatra Neamţ. It was almost midnight. The night of the Resurrection."

The professor gave him a long, doubtful look.

"But you were going somewhere. On the pavement, by your side, there was no bag..."

"I had no bag. I had nothing on me except a blue envelope. I had come with the purpose of suicide. I thought I was doomed : arteriosclerosis. I was losing my memory..."

"You came here to commit suicide ?" the professor repeated.

"I did. I thought there was no other solutioin. The only one was the blue envelope. I had long been keeping a few milligrams of strychnine in it."

## II

He knew he was dreaming and kept rubbing his hand against the freshly shaven face, but could not wake up. Only when the car reached the end of the boulevard did he recognize the district ; he recognized it by the scent of the lime trees in bloom. We are heading for the Chaussée, he realized. He hadn't taken that way for some years past and he was excited, gazing at all of the old houses which reminded him of his student days. He was then faced with a road bordered by tall trees ; the gate opened the next moment and the car, slowly rolling on gravel stone, came to a stop in front of bluish-grey steps. "Why don't you get out ?" he heard an unknown voice asking. He looked around in surprise : there was no one. He thought that the door at the top of the steps had opened. He was therefore expected. "I ought to get out," he thought.

Waking up he was blinded by the strong light outside and looked at his watch in surprise. It was not yet six o'clock. They must have forgotten to pull the blinds. Much later he heard the door open.

"I'm bringing your clothes," the nurse said, coming up, with an armful.

It was Anetta, still quite young and most impertinent. A few days before, giving him a meaningful look, she had said: "When you get out of here, maybe you'll take me to the cinema, one night." She helped him dress, though he required no help. He guessed by her disappointed looks that the coat was not fitting, "too tight in the shoulders," she said ; the blue tie with small grey triangles did not match the striped shirt. The medical student on duty soon came in. He began closely examining him, frowning.

"You can see right away that these are not your clothes. You may become a suspect. We'll have to find something else. Doctor Gavrilă was saying that he had a few suits of the best materials ; they used to belong to one of his uncles."

"He inherited them when he died," Anetta specified. "You shouldn't wear clothes from other people's dead. From your own dead it's different : you wear them in memory of them, like a souvenir."

"It doesn't matter at all," he said smiling. "It's too late today, anyway. Maybe some other time when I come by."

"Yes," the medical student said, "but in that coat you'll be noticed and risk being followed."

"If he keeps well back in the car, maybe he won't be noticed."

Two hours later he came out of the hospital accompanied by Doctor Chirilă, a man he did not particularly like, because ever since he had found him hiding in the ward, he was constantly under the impression that the doctor spied on him. Upon seeing the car, he suddenly stopped.

"I've seen this car before," he said in a low voice. "I saw it in my dream last night. Some people would say it's a bad omen ; we may have an accident," he added.

"I'm not superstitious," Doctor Chirilă said slowly, while opening the door. "Anyhow we are expected."

As the car was making its way to the boulevard, he felt a strange peace, curiously interspersed with almost violent explosions of joy.

"We ought to open the window," he said, "for we will soon be driving under the lime trees in bloom. We are now close to the Chaussée," he spoke after a time. And later, "Wait and see the fine building, tall trees and clean gravel road and bluish-grey stone steps."

The medical student was constantly watching him, trying to maintain an embarrassed silence. The car came to a stop before the steps.

"Why don't you get out ?" a voice said.

"We're waiting for the orderly on duty," the driver answered.

Soon they heard quick footsteps on the gravel ; from behind the car a dark-haired man appeared, his face pock-marked, his hair cropped in military fashion. Chirilă opened the door.

"This is the person you have been informed was coming. Be careful not to confuse him with some other patient. From now on he's your responsibility."

"Understood. No problem. I will be on the look-out."

"Whatever he's doing indoors or in the garden," Chirilă interrupted him, "is no concern of yours. You've got to watch the gate..."

He liked the room. It was large, the windows looking out over the park and, as the professor had promised, it had a wooden table and shelves for books in the wall. He went up to the window, opened it and took a deep breath. He fancied he could smell the scent of wild roses. Nevertheless, he could not rejoice. Smiling, he passed his left hand over his cheeks, but could not help thinking that whatever had been happening to him lately did not really concern him, that something or someone else was concerned.

"Try to explain, as clearly as possible, in every detail, what you mean when you say someone else," the professor had once said. "You feel alien, in what way ? Haven't you yet accepted your new situation ? It is very important. Write down anything that crosses your mind. If you don't feel like writing, or have too much to say, use the tape recorder ; always mention the day, time and place, also mention if you dictate lying down or walking about the room."

During the last days in hospital he had filled a whole notebook. He put down all sorts of things : the books he remembered (he liked mentioning the edition, the year of publication, the year he had first read them, in order to test this miraculous recovery of his memory), poetry in every language that he had learnt, exercises in algebra, some dreams that he considered significant. But he would not reveal certain recent discoveries. He felt a certain obstruction that he could not understand, of which he had once spoken to the professor.

"It is most important for us to find out the significance of this obstruction," he had said. "Try at least to allude to it so that we can find out whether those things you don't want to say ('which I cannot say !' he had interrupted in his mind) refer to certain facts about the past, or whether it's something else, concerning your new condition, about which, let me repeat, we know precious little as yet."

He came away from the window, crossed the room a few times, pacing as he used to in his young days with arms crossed behind, then he lay down on the bed. He lay open-eyed looking at the ceiling.

"Here is your picture-album," he said one morning. "The one with your pictures in high school, at the University, in Italy... Don't you want to see it ?" he asked after a time.

"Quite candidly, no..."

"But why ?"

"I couldn't say why. I'm beginning to be quite detached from my own past. It's as if I weren't the same person..."

"Strange," the professor said. "We should find out the reason why..."

Finally, somewhat resigned, he had decided to look through it. The professor was sitting on a chair by the bed, looking at him intently, hardly concealing his curiosity.

"What are you thinking of ?" he asked suddenly after a few minutes. "What kind of recollections ? What sort of associations ?"

He hesitated, the palm of his left hand rubbing his cheek. "I know that this gesture has become a spasmodic tic with me," he had repeatedly confessed.

"I perfectly recollect the date and place where each photograph was taken. I may say I even remember the day ; it's as if I could hear the voices of people around me, the words they were saying, and I could feel the specific scent of that place and of that day. Here for instance, where I'm with Laura at the Tivoli. When I set eyes on the picture, I felt the warmth of that morning and the scent of the oleander flowers ; but I also felt a strong heavy reek of hot tar and I remembered that some ten meters from the place where we were photographed there were two cauldrons of tar."

'It's a kind of hypermnesia with side effects," the professor said.

"It's awful," he continued, "too much and useless."

"It seems useless because we don't know what to do with it, with this fantastic recovery of mmory. Anyway," he said smiling, "let me give you some good news. Within a few days, you'll receive from your own library at Piatra Neamţ, the books you put down on the first list, namely all the grammars and dictionaries you said you needed. Bernard is enthusiastic. He said I couldn't have found a betteer test. He was especially interested in your studying Chinese when young, then neglected it for some ten or twelve years, took it up again before and during the war, then, unexpectedly, gave it up for good. We are, therefore, faced with several layers of the memory. If you take the trouble of self-analysis and carefully take notes, we shall see which layer will be the first to be re-animated."

They looked at each other for some time as if each one was waiting for the other to begin.

"What do they think at Piatra concerning my disappearance ?" he asked unexpectedly. "I'm not very curious, but I should like to know as soon as possible what my chances are."

"What kind of chances ?" the professor asked.

He smiled an awkward smile. The moment he pronounced it, the expression seemed vulgar and ill-timed.

"The chance to continue the life I have recently begun, not risking integration once more in my former biography."

"I can't say anything definite at this time. Your friends at Piatra think that you are in some hospital in Moldavia, suffering from amnesia. Someone remembers having seen you on the Saturday before Easter at the station, but he doesn't know what train you caught. The man was in a hurry to get home."

"I think I know who saw me at the station," he mumbled.

"In order to get the books you required, the police staged a house search. The pretext was that, having heard of your disappearance, one of the tracked legionaries was hiding in the library".

Deep in thought, he seemed to be uncertain whether to continue.

"But evidently," he continued, "as time goes on it will be more difficult. Soon Piatra Neamţ will know what all of Bucharest does : that a man, unknown and aged, was struck by lightning and that after ten weeks, he looks perfectly fit and rejuvenated... Let's hope they won't find out the rest..."

Two weeks later, down in the garden, he met face to face with a strange beauty : a beauty that for reasons difficult to understand, she was trying to mitigate by a conscious vulgarity, awkwardly overdoing her make-up. Her present smile, provoking, yet chaste, the unknown woman reminded him of one of his latest dreams. He made a slight bow and said :

"I think we've met before."

The young woman burst out laughing. ("A pity," he thought, "her laughter is as vulgar as her make-up.")

"You're very discreet indeed," she said (she seemed to be speaking her words as on the stage). "Of course we've met and several times, too."

"Where and when ?"

The young woman frowned slightly and sought his eyes again.

"Last night, for instance, in room number six. Your room is next door, at number four," she added walking away.

The professor came that same night to return the note-book and to read the latest writings. He listened, somewhat confused, never smiling, avoiding his eyes.

"I thought you knew what it was all about and that you understood, how shall I put it ? The scientific meaning of the experiment. No test is complete if lacking the index of sexual capacity. You remember the question Bernard asked you last..."

He felt like laughing, but could only shake his head smiling.

"Don't I remember ! I thought I'd sink into the earth for shame ! Lying naked on the operating table, in front of so many doctors and foreign specialists..."

"I had warned you that it was going to be a kind of international consultation. They had all come to see you ; they couldn't believe the notice we had included in the *Presse Médicale.*"

"I didn't expect such a question, as I was still hospitaliz-ed, so I could neither confirm nor deny my possible sexual capacity."

The professor shrugged smiling. "We had found out something indirectly, of course, from the nurses."

"From the nurses, did you say ?"

"We thought it had been your initiative. In any other case, the patient and the nurse would have been sanctioned. In your case, not only did we close our eyes, but appreciated the information. The context of course is of small importance, it is the information that matters... But as to the lady in room number six," he continued after a pause, "that's a different matter. I'd better tell you now, or there may be complications later. This lady was imposed upon us by the secret police..."

"The secret police ?" he repeated somewhat scared. "But why ?"

"I won't say that I understand things very well, but I know that the secret police take much interest in your case.

Very likely they believe that we have not told them the whole truth, and they are actually right. Anyway, the secret police are very doubtful about your metamorphosis. They believe that the story making its way around town concerning the lightning on the night of the Resurrection, implying your loss of consciousness, your recovery, and rejuvenation is an invention of the iron-guardists. That this legend was in fact fabricated to conceal the identity of an important iron-guard leader and to prepare for his flight across the border."

He had been listening in surprise, and yet he was unruffled.

"My situation is, therefore, more serious than I had imagined," he said. "But as there's no other alternative for the time being..."

"A solution is sure to be found in due time," the professor cut in. "For your own full information, I must add that you are, and have been from the beginning, surveyed by the secret police. That's why you have been provided with a suit of clothes that you shouldn't wear in the street or you'd be immediately arrested. And you wouldn't dare walk in the streets in this blouse, the clinic uniform which is quite elegant. And as you grasped from the beginning, should you want a walk, you won't be able to walk through the gate... That is as much as we know. But goodness knows how many members of the establishment's personnel are informers of the secret police."

He laughed and repeatedly stroked his left cheek with the palm of his hand.

"After all, maybe it's for the best. I feel safe against surprises."

The professor gave him a long look, as if unwilling to continue. Then he suddeny decided :

"Let's now go back to a more important problem. Are you sure that in your memory all the sexual experiences seemed to be erotic dreams ?"

He sat thinking for a time.

"I'm not so sure now. Until tonight I was positive these were dreams."

"I'm asking because in the notebook that I read, you put down all kinds of dreams, yet with no manifest erotic elements."

"Maybe I should have put down the others as well, but they didn't seem significant. Anyway," he went on after a short pause, "if I have confused real experiences with erotic dreams, things are much more complicated than I ever believed."

With a childlike, ridiculous gesture, he laid his hand upon his temple, as if to show that he was concentrating.

"I am listening," the professor said after a time. "In what way could they be more complicated than they seem to be ?"

He suddenly looked up and smiled an awkward smile.

"I wonder if you grasped certain allusions in the notebook ; for some time, I don't quite know how to put it, I had a feeling of learning in my sleep, more precisely, I dreamed I was learning, for instance, opening a grammar book in my dream, going through and memorizing a few pages or consulting a book..."

"Very interesting," the professor said, "but I don't think that you put all that down clearly and accurately in the notebook I have gone through."

"I didn't quite know how to describe all this. These were serial dreams, in a way didactic ones. I was inclined to think they were a continuation of my daytime reading. I even thought I was dreaming grammar rules, vocabulary, and etymology since these were my passion. Yet I am now wondering if in some more or less somnambulate way I woke up in the night and continued my work..."

The professor gave him his full attention throughout, with a slight frown indicating that he had already observed that the patient was a prey to several simultaneous perplexities.

"As a matter of fact," he said, "you're not looking tired, you don't have the look of an intellectual who spends most of his nights reading... But if so, how come that no one noticed the light, the lamp burning late into the night in your room?" He got up and put out his hand. "What strikes me as paradoxical is the fact that this hesitation, this confusion between the dreaming and waking states, developed along parallel lines with your hypermnesia !... The things you told me about the scent of the oleanders and the reeking tar that came to you while contemplating a photograph almost forty years old..."

"But now I'm no longer sure of that either, of hypermnesia ! I'm no longer sure of anything !"

Once alone, he found he was thinking : "A good thing you said 'I'm no longer sure of anything.' That way you're always safe. You may always say 'I was dreaming' or, if convenient, you may state the contrary. But be careful ! Never tell the whole truth !"

With a turn of his head, he looked round in surprise. A few seconds later he spoke under his breath, as if addressing someone present, yet invisible by his side : "But even though I want to tell I cannot ! I don't understand why it is," he added in a much lower voice, "but there are certain things which to me are beyond telling..."

That night he fought sleeplessness for a long time. It was the first sleepless night since he had left Piatra Neamţ, and the fact irritated him. He had suffered from insomnia all his life and he thought he was rid of it. He kept thinking, as usual, of the mysterious recovery of his memory. As a matter of fact there was no question of recovery, for it was now infinitely more precise and comprehensive than it had ever been. A mandarin's memory as Chavannes said was necessary to any sinologist. He began to think it was even more than that : a most curious hypermnesia. Before the grammars and dictionaries had ever been brought from Piatra, he found himself reciting Chinese texts, simultaneously vizualizing the script and translating, while he was reciting. A few days later he had checked the writing, pronunciation and translation anxiously looking through Giles's dictionary. Not one mistake. He had scribbled a few lines in the notebook with slight regret : Bernard would be deceived ; he found it impossible to specify which layer of memory had first appeared, but he had mastered the Chinese language as never before. He could now open any book and would understand it as easily as any Latin or old Italian text.

It was a very warm night and the window looking out over the park was still open. He thought he could hear footsteps, so without turning the light on, he went up to the window. He caught sight of the watchman and knew that he had also been seen.

"Aren't you sleepy ?" he asked as softly as he could, lest he should wake his neighbors.

The man shrugged, then made for the park and was lost in the dark. "If I were to ask him tomorrow," he thought, "he would probably answer that I had been dreaming. Yet, I am certain that I wasn't dreaming this time." He went back to bed, closed his eyes, and told himself, as he used to when suffering from insomnia : "In three minutes I will be asleep ! You've got to fall asleep," he heard himself thinking, "for while asleep you learn well." Didactic dreams as he was saying the night before to the professor : "you'll have more didactic dreams. Not connected with Chinese. Something different, more important, something else..."

He liked to listen to his own thoughts, yet this time he felt a strange restlessness and whispered a threat : "If I don't fall asleep counting up to twenty, I'll go down and take a walk in the park !" But he only went as far as seven.

A few days later, never looking up from the second notebook that he had just been given, the professor asked him :

"Do you happen to remember that one night you went out by the window and walked to the end of the garden where the rose beds are ?"

He felt the blood in his cheeks and lost confidence.

"No, I don't. But I do remember that I was unable to fall asleep, so eventually I said to myself : if I don't fall asleep while counting up to twenty, I'll go down and take a walk in the park ! But I don't remember anything after that. Very likely I fell asleep immediately."

The professor considered him smiling ambiguously.

"No question of having fallen asleep immediately... Because you spent quite a while around by the rosebushes."

"Then I must be a sleepwalker !" he exclaimed. "The first instance of somnambulism in my lifetime."

The professor suddenly rose, went up to the window and stood looking out for some time. Then he came back and resumed the armchair.

"That was my own opinion, too. But things are not so simple. When the orderly on duty launched an alarm, two male servants, probably security people, ran out to inspect the street, not knowing that the guard had already found you, they discovered a car, lights out, waiting in the street just in front of the rose bed where you were. The car, of course, disappeared before they could write down its number."

He rubbed his brow several times.

"If it were not you," he began.

"I know, it sounds incredible," the professor put in, "however, there are three witnesses, common people, but trustworthy and having some experience..."

"And what did they do ? Took me in their arms and brought me back to my room ?"

"No. The guard was alone in the garden. He says that as soon as you saw him you came back. You entered your room by the window once more, as you had come out. Whether sleepwalking or not, that's of no importance. The worst is that the secret police are now certain that your escape had been prepared. The fact of being surprised on the spot where the car was waiting outside supports their opinion, that you knew about the planned escape and that you agreed. Intervention at the very top has been necessary to save you from being arrested," he added.

"Thank you," he said confused, mopping his brow.

"For the time being, the security measures have been doubled. The street is permanently patrolled at night ; a militia man in civilian clothes will be constantly on guard under your window, as he is now," he added, in a lower tone. "Another guard will be resting on a folding bed in the corridor, facing your door."

He rose and began pacing the room, absently passing the notebook from one hand to the other. Then he stopped abruptly, facing him, looking deep into his eyes.

"But you yourself, how do you account for this chain of coincidences : as you confessed you've had a spell of sleeplessness for the first time, followed by the first instance of somnambulism in your lifetime. During it you made for the rose bed, for the very spot where, behind the wall, a car, lights out, was waiting for you. A car," he added, after a few seconds, "a car that disappears as soon as the alarm is sounded. What's the explanation ?"

He shrugged, hopeless.

"I don't understand... Up to last week I found it difficult to believe that I really mixed up certain dreams with the waking state, but I had to accept certain evidences. But in this case, the instance of somnambulism, the car waiting for me..".

The professor opened the briefcase that was almost full and carefully placed the notebook among magazines and booklets.

"To use your previous saying : if I did not know you from family albums, if I had not seen pictures of you from thirty to over sixty, I should have been ready to accept the security hypothesis : that you are who they think you are."

"Why worry ?" he heard himself thinking as soon as he put out the light. "Everything is quite normal. That's how it was to happen : that you should be taken for someone else, that you should let them believe that you're no longer able to distinguish between dream and reality and other similar confusions. There could be no better camouflage. You'll see in the end that there's no danger, that you are being taken care of..." .

He ceased and after a brief pause he whispered : "Who is taking care of me ?" He waited a few seconds. He woke asking in a voice that didn't seem to be his own : "Did you think that all that's happened to you was just a matter of chance ?" "There's no question of what I do or don't believe," he put in with some irritation. "Who is taking care of me ?" He lay apprehensively expecting, for some time. Then he heard his own thought : "You'll find out later. It isn't the important thing just now. As a matter of fact you've guessed something, you've been guessing for some time, but you dare not say so. If not why don't you ever mention certain thoughts when speaking to the professor, or mention them in the notebook ? If you were ignorant that there is a something else why don't you ever allude to what you've discovered in this last fortnight. But let me go back to my question," he said trying to silence his thought. He waited a while and just as he thought he was beginning to guess the answer, he fell asleep.

"Better to talk while dreaming," he heard in his sleep. "You understand more quickly and more profoundly. You were telling the professor that you continued your diurnal studies while sleeping. Actually, you' ve long been convinced that this is not always true. You have never learned anything in your sleep, nor while awake. Very gradually you discovered that you were proficient in Chinese, just as you will later find that you know other languages that you are interested in. You dare not believe that you now remember what you once learned and forgot. Think of the Albanian grammar..." The memory of that incident was such a violent shock that he woke up and put the light on. He couldn't have believed, did not even now, a week from this discopery, believe the truth.

He knew he had never studied Albanian. Some twenty years before he had bought G. Meyer's grammar, but had only read the preface. He had never looked into it since. Yet now in opening one of the parcels he received from Piatra and seeing the book, he opened it absentmindedly, near the end, and began reading. With shock and terror he realized that he understood every word. He looked for the paragraph's translation and checked : no mistake. He got out of bed and made for the bookshelves. At all costs, he meant to check once more. It was then that he heard an unknown voice from the garden, outside the open window :

"Aren't you sleeping ?"

He went back to bed, furiously closing his eyes, contracting his eyelids, and repeating under his breath :

"I must stop thinking ! I must not think of anything..."

"That's what I've been telling you ever since the first night in hospital," he heard a voice.

He thought he was beginning to understand what had happened. A terrific concentration of electricity exploding right above him had run him through, regenerating his entire organism and fabulously amplifying his mental faculties. Yet this electric discharge made it possible for a new personality to appear, a kind of 'double', a person that speaks to him especially while he's sleeping, with whom he sometimes discusses amiably or argues. This new personality very likely took shape gradually during his convalescence, rising from the deepest layers of his subconscious. Every time he repeated this explanation he heard himself thinking : "Perfectly true ! The formula of the 'double' is correct and useful, but don't be in a hurry to impart it to the professor."

Both amused and annoyed he wondered why he should constantly insist on caution, since he had long decided never to touch on that problem. As a matter of fact he hadn't been obliged to make a decision ; he knew he could not possibly act otherwise. In their talks the professor constantly insisted on hypermnesia and on his gradually becoming detached from the past.

"We could have your manuscripts and files brought in," he had recently suggested. "In your present conditions, you could complete the work within a few months."

He raised both arms :

"No, don't !" he shouted almost in panic. 'I'm no longer interested !"

The professor considered him with surprise, a bit disappointed :

"It is, however, your life's work."

"It should be written all over again, from the first to the last page and I don't think it's worth the trouble. It will stay as it's been so far : opus imperfectum. But I was going to ask you..." he continued as if anxious to change the subject quickly, "though I'm afraid I shall sound inquisitive. What's happened to me this last week ? What was in the report of the guard and of all the others ?"

The professor rose from his armchair and walked to the window. A few seconds later he came back, pensive.

"They know how and when to vanish, but they're all on duty," he said. "Nothing sensational was reported, except that you turned on the light several times every night, on and off very quickly, within a few minutes. At least, that's what I've been told. But I'm afraid they don't tell me everything," he added in a lower voice, "I have a suspicion they have discovered something quite important, or are on their way to finding out..."

"Something about me?" he asked, controlling his emotion.

The professor hesitated a few seconds, then suddenly rose and went to the window again.

"I can't tell," he answered after a long pause. "Possibly not only about you."

On the third of August, in the morning, the professor came unexpectedly to see him.

"I wonder if we should be glad or not. You ought to know that you've become famous in the United States. An illustrated magazine has even published an interview, apocryphal of course : 'The Way I was Struck by Lightning'." The article caused a sensation and was reproduced and translated everywhere. The Press headquarters informed me that three correspondents of some important American papers arrived last night and insisted on seeing you. They were told that, for the time being, the doctors are against any kind of visit. But how long will we be able to keep the secret ? At this hour it's quite likely that the journalists have already begun their inquiries. The resident medical students and the nurses will obviously tell them everything they know and much more besides. And they will find informers right here," he added in a slightly lower voice. "As to photographs, I have no doubts : you have surely been photographed lots of times, walking in the garden, standing by the window, maybe lying in bed... But I see that you're not impressed by the news," he added giving him a long look. "You don't say anything."

"I was waiting for what is to follow."

The professor came up to him looking him deep in the eyes.

"How do you know there is more to it ?"

"So I presumed, considering your nervousness. I've never seen you quite so nervous."

The professor shrugged, smiling a bitter smile.

"You may not have noticed, but I'm quite high strung. Let's return to your case. A number of complications have appeared, especially during the fortnight when I was away."

"On my account ?" he asked.

"Neither on yours, nor on mine. You kept to your room practically all the time. I know that because I telephoned almost every day. As to myself, during these two weeks spent at Predeal, I only discussed your case with a few colleagues. I have no doubts concerning their discretion. But something else did happen," he went on, rising once more from his armchair. "First, the young lady in number six, the agent imposed on us by Security : she disappeared some ten days ago. The Security people had long suspected her of being a double agent, but they didn't know that she was a Gestapo agent."

"Strange," he whispered. "But how did they find out so soon ?"

"Because the organization she belonged to was discovered and the three agents who had been waiting for you a few nights, in a car with lights out, were arrested. The Security people had made a good guess : you were to be kidnapped and driven over the border into Germany. They were, however, mistaken about the person's identity : it was no Iron Guard leader, it was you."

"But why ?" he asked with a smile.

The professor made for the window, but turned back abruptly, considering him queerly a few moments, as if waiting for him to say something.

"Because you are such as you are, after all that's happened to you. I was never too optimistic about this," he continued, slowly walking to and fro between the door and the armchair. "I knew that some day it would come out. That's why I informed the *Presse médicale* several times. I was anxious that what was to be discovered should come straight from the source... I didn't mention everything, of course : I merely reported the stages of physical and intellectual recovery, just alluding, obscurely enough, to regeneration and rejuvenation. Nothing about hypermnesia... But everything was found out : your phenomenal memory, the fact that you recuperated all the languages you had learnt when young. So you've become the most precious human sample now living on the entire globe. All the medical schools in the world would be anxious to have you at their disposal, temporarily at least..."

"Kind of a guinea pig, or what ?" he asked with a smile.

"In certain circumstances, quite so : a guinea pig. Provided with the information given by the young lady in number six, it's easy to understand why the Gestapo wants to kidnap you at all costs."

He stood thoughtful for some time, then his face suddenly relaxed into a large smile :

"Your companion of a night, or of several !"

"I'm afraid there were several," he confessed with a blush.

"Your companion was cleverer than the security people appreciated. It was not enough for her to check your erotic potentialities, to take advantage of the parasomnambulist state you were in, pumping you for information, trying to discover your identity. She used scientific methods, too ; by means of a tiny tape recorder she registered all the conversations, in fact your long monologues, and handed them to the Security people. But she also noticed something else, that you recited poetry in many languages : when she asked a few questions in German, then in Russian, you had no difficulty in answering in these languages. Later, when you received the books, she made a list of all the grammar books and dictionaries that you used. Caution made her keep all this evidence to be used by her German employers. Very likely, some very important person in the Gestapo, after listening to the recorded tapes, decided on your abduction."

"I see," he said rubbing his brow.

The professor stopped in front of the open window looking over the park.

"Evidently," he added after a good while, "the watch is ten times as vigilant. Maybe you haven't noticed, but during the last few days the adjoining rooms have been occupied by Security agents. And you can imagine how the street is patrolled at night. Nevertheless," he added after a pause, "you'll soon have to be removed from this place."

"What a pity," he said. "I had got used to the place and liked it."

"I've been advised to begin your disguise. To begin with, you'll grow a moustache, as thick and unkempt as possible. They tell me that they'll try to alter your face, and I imagine they'll change the color and style of your hair, so that you won't look like in the photographs which have been taken during the last weeks. They'll be able to make you look ten to fifteen years older. In leaving the clinic, you'll look like a man on the other side of forty."

He stopped, exhausted, and sat in the armchair.

"Fortunately," he added later, "the instances of parasomnambulism or whatever, were not repeated. At least that's what they told me."

The day promised to be very hot. He took off his shirt and put on the lightest pyjamas that he found in the wardrobe. Then he lay down upon the bed. "Of course," he found himself thinking, "there was no somnambulism at all. You behaved as required to create the necessary confusions. But from now on you won't need this anymore."

"The Double," he whispered with a smile. "He always answers the questions that I'm about to ask. Like a true guardian angel."

"That phrase, too, is correct and useful."

"Are there any others ?" he asked.

"Quite a number. Some are anachronistic, or no longer in use, others are still quite up-to-date, particularly in such circumstances where theology and Christian practice were able to preserve immemorial mythological traditions."

"Such as ?" he asked with an amused smile.

"For instance, side by side with angels, guardian angels, extant forces, archangels, seraphs, cherubs. Beings pre-eminently intermediary."

"Intermediary between the conscious and the unconscious."

"Exactly. Yet also between nature and man, between man and divinity, reason and eros, the feminine and the masculine, darkness and light, matter and spirit..."

He was laughing and sat up. He looked carefully around a few seconds. Then murmured slowly :

"So back to my old passion : philosophy. Shall we ever succeed in logically demonstrating the reality of the external world ? To this day idealistic metaphysics seems to me the one perfectly coherent construction."

"We have strayed from our discussion," he heard again his own thought. "The problem was not the reality of the external world, but the objective reality of the 'double' or of the guardian angel, choose the term that best suits you. True ?"

"Very true. I cannot believe in the objective reality of the person I am talking with ; I consider it my 'double'."

"In a way, that is true, but it doesn't deny its objective existence, independent of the conscious whose projection it seems to be..."

"I would like to believe this, but...".

"I know. In metaphysical controversies empiric proofs are of no value. Yet, wouldn't you like to receive, right now, within one or two seconds, a few roses fresh from the garden ?"

"Roses !" he spoke with emotion, in some fear. "I have always been fond of roses..."

"Where would you like to put them ? Not in the glass, anyway..."

"No," he said. "by no means in the glass. A rose in my right hand, as I now keep it palm up, another on my knees and a third, shall we say..."

That moment he found he was holding between his fingers a very lovely crimson rose, the color of fresh blood ; while on his knees another was wavering, unstable.

'What about the third ?" he heard his thought. "Where do you want me to place the third rose ?"

"Things are far more serious than we expected." It was the professor's voice. He seemed to perceive it through a heavy curtain or coming from a long distance away. And yet he was facing him, in the armchair, the briefcase on his knees.

"Much more serious than we expected ?" he queried absentmindedly.

The professor rose, came up to him, and laid his hand on his brow.

"Aren't you feeling well ? Have you had a bad night ?"

"No, no. But the moment you came in I had the impression... well, never mind."

"I must tell you something urgent and very important. Are you all right ? Do you think you can follow me ?"

He slowly passed his hand over his brow, and with an effort produced a smile.

"I am actually very anxious to hear you."

The professor sat in the armchair again.

"I was saying that the situation is even more serious than we presumed, since we are now certain that the Gestapo will try everything — everything," he repeated stressing the word, "to lay hands on you. You'll see why immediately. There is a mysterious and ambiguous person among the intimate friends of Goebbels, a certain doctor Rudolf who has lately worked out a theory, fantastic at first sight, but comprising a number of scientific elements too. Namely, he believes that electrocution by a power of at least a million volts may produce a radical mutation of the human species. The person suffering such discharge is not killed, but entirely regenerated, just as happened in your case," he added. "Fortunately this hypothesis cannot be experimentally tested. Rudolf agrees that he cannot precisely indicate the voltage of the electric power necessary for the mutation ; he only maintains that it must surpass a million, maybe as much as two million volts... You can now judge the interest your own case presents."

"I see," he repeated absentmindedly.

"The information they've had concerning you, and they've had plenty, confirms his hypothesis. Some people in Goebbels' circle are thrilled. There have been demands through diplomatic channels, in the name of science, for the sake of humanity, and all the rest. We have been invited by several universities and scientific institutes for a series of lectures, myself, yourself, doctor Gavrilă, and whoever else we may want to join us ; briefly, they want us to lend you for a certain period of time. And since we don't jump at it, the Gestapo has a free hand."

He stopped, as if suddenly breathless. For the first time he found him tired out, aged.

"We had to hand them copies of the reports on the first weeks of hospitalization. It is the usual thing to do and we were unable to refuse. Of course we didn't communicate everything. As regards the more recent materials, including photocopies of your notebook and copies of the tape recordings, all these were dispatched to Paris. They are now being examined by Bernard and his fellow researchers. They'll be later entrusted to one of the laboratories belonging to the Rockefeller foundation, but I can see you're not listening," he said rising from the armchair. "You're tired. You'll hear the rest next time."

The rest seemed to have no end. He sometimes found it uninteresting, occasionally he thought he was hearing things that he had already discovered, though he couldn't say when or on what occasion. He was particularly amused by the inquiries concerning the lightning on the night of the Resurrection. How did they find out that the downpour was limited to a certain area, that there had been just a single bolt of lightning, striking quite unusually too, since the churchgoers, waiting on the church porch, had seen the lightning in the shape of an endless incandescent spear. Anyway, beside the specialists sent by doctor Rudolf, who collected any information concerning the shape and luminous intensity of the lightning, there came, moreover, a famous dillettante : the author of a few studies concerning etrusca disciplina. Within less than a week he succeeded in limiting the rain flooded circumference and was in the act of interpreting the symbolism of the lightning struck spot.

"These inquiries and investigations are of a mere anecdotic importance," the professor continued. 'The only serious thing is doctor Rudolf's decision to begin the electrocution tests, as soon as they complete their files by a few talks with you."

"Yet what more could I tell them ?" he asked.

"That, nobody knows. He would possibly obtain extra information by certain laboratory tests : by producing, for instance, a succession of artificial lightning flashes hoping that the intensity of the incandescence would help you to recognize the lightning flash that struck you. Possibly, they want to hear directly from you what you felt at that moment and why you state that you felt sucked up by a hot cyclone bursting from the top of your head. I cannot say. The electrocution tests are supposed to take place on politically detained persons. And this crime must be avoided at all costs."

He had grown a moustache as required, thick and unkempt.

"Face altering will take place later," he said on the night of 25 September. He had difficulty controlling his emotion.

"Chamberlain and Daladier are in Munich," he said upon entering. "Anything may happen from one day to another. Those in charge of you have changed plans," he continued later, sitting down in the armchair. "You'll be removed in the night, in utter secrecy, yet in such a way that the others might discover, actually see, the car that is going to transport you. Then, after twenty or twenty-five kilometers..."

"I think I can guess the rest," he put in, smiling. "At twenty or twenty-five kilometers an accident will be staged."

"Right. There will even be a few witnesses. The press will write about the accident like any other, in which three men died. Yet the various information departments will find out that the victims were yourself and the two agents who accompanied you on your way to an unknown destination. It shall be suggested that they intended to protect you by taking you to a highly safe place. That is, in fact, what is going to happen," he continued after a pause. "I don't know where you're to be hidden. That's where you'll be subject to the alterations that I was talking about. Within a month, at the latest, provided with a legal passport,you'll be off to Geneva ; I don't know how, I haven't been told. It was Bernard who suggested Geneva : he thinks that Paris is not the safest place just now, but he will see you as soon as possible. I will come too," he put in later. "At least I hope to."

## III

He never saw the professor again. He died at the end of October. He had had a queer feeling that this was going to happen ever since the day when, upon entering, he burst out : "Things are much more serious than we expected !" He had then seen him press his hand upon his heart and sink into the armchair groaning. Then he heard a yell, doors slammed, quick footsteps running up the stairs. It was only when the professor came up to him asking : "You're not feeling well, are you ? Have you had a bad night's sleep ?" that he was himself again. But the vision constantly haunted him. When doctor Bernard said, "I have sad news for you," he was on the point of answering. "I know, the professor died."

Doctor Bernard came to see him at least once a month. They spent practically the whole day together. Occasionally, having heard his answers to certain questions, he would draw the tape recorder nearer and ask him to repeat. Fortunately, the questions concerned memory, a change of behavior (relations to people, animals, and certain situations, as compared to his former way of behavior), his possible adjustment to paradoxical situations (did he believe himself capable of falling in love as he had done at the age he now had once more ?). These were questions he could answer without misgivings. Every time Bernard would bring a sum of money (from the Rockefeller foundation fund, he explained). He also helped him register as a student of the university, entrusting him with the task of coordinating materials with a view to a history of medical psychology.

After the invasion of France he was a long time without news, although up to December 1942 a check direct from the Rockefeller foundation continued to reach him every three months. At the beginning of 1943 he received a letter from doctor Bernard, posted in Portugal. He wrote he would soon "send him a long letter because there are a number of things to tell." But he did not get it. After the liberation of France, by talking to one of the assistants, he found out that doctor Bernard had died in a plane accident in Morroco, in February, 1943.

Every day he went to the library, taking down a lot of books and collections of old periodicals. He would carefully consult them, take notes, compile bibliographies, yet this labor was nothing but camouflage. As soon as he read the first lines, he knew what would follow ; he did not understand the process of anamnesis (as he had been prone to call it), but when faced with a text, and wishing to know its substance, he would discover that he already knew it. Some time after he began working in the library, he had a long and dramatic dream which he only fragmentarily remembered because, having woken several times, it had been interrupted. He had been particularly impressed by this detail ; as a result of the electrocution, his mental activity was somehow anticipating a condition that man was to attain after decades of thousands of years. The main feature of this new humanity would be the structure of psycho-mental life : anything that had ever been conceived or done by men, expressed orally or in writing, would be recaptured by means of a certain exercise in concentration. In fact, education would then consist of learning that method under the supervision of instructors.

"To put it shortly, I'm a 'mutant,' he reflected after waking up. I'm anticipating the existence of post-historic man. As in a science fiction novel," he added with an amused smile. Such ironic comments were meant for the 'forces' that were looking after him. "In a certain sense it's true," he heard himself thinking. "But as opposed to the characters in science fiction, you have preserved the freedom of accepting or refusing this new condition. The moment when for one reason or another, you wish to revert to the other condition, you're free to do so."

He took a deep breath. "So I'm free!" he exclaimed having carefully looked around. "I am free... and yet," but he couldn't continue thinking.

As far back as 1939 he had decided to describe in a special notebook his latest experiments. He had begun by commenting upon this fact (which seemed to confirm the humanity of post-historic man) : spontaneous knowledge, in a sense automatic, doesn't annihilate the interest for research, nor the joy of discovery. He chose an easily verifiable example : the pleasure of a poetry-loving reader in reading a poem that he knows practically by heart. He could easily recite it and yet, sometimes, he prefers to read it. Because this fresh reading is an occasion to discover new delights and meanings that he hadn't so far surmised. Similarly, this immense scholarship that he had received as a boon, all the languages and literatures he discovered he knew, none of this impaired his joy in studying them.

Some sentences when read after a few years' interval simply delighted him : "You only learn well and with pleasure what you already know." Or: "Do not compare me to an electronic computer. If correctly supplied, it may recite the Odyssey or the Aeneid like myself ; only, each time I speak the lines differently." Or : "The state of beatitude that every cultural creation may offer (mind you : I say cultural, not only artistic) is unlimited."

The memory of the mysterious epiphany of the two roses always filled him with emotion. Yet, at intervals, he liked to contest its validity as a philosophical argument. There followed long and enchanting debates : he had actually decided to write them down, especially (so he thought) for their literary value. The last time, however, the dialogue came to an end almost abruptly. That evening in 1944 he repeatedly said to himself : "After all, such parapsychological phenomena may be the effect of certain forces we have no knowledge of, but which may be controlled by the unconscious." "Very true," he heard himself thinking, "every action is determined by a force more or less known, but after such a number of experiments, you should revise your philosophic principles. You understand what I'm driving at." "I think I do," he admitted smiling.

During the war's last years he repeatedly found out that the bank deposit had nearly run out. He began curiously and impatiently expecting the solution of the crisis. At first, he received a postal money order for 1 000 francs from a person he had never heard of. His letter of thanks was returned with the statement : "Not known at the above address." Then he incidentally met a fellow researcher, a woman, in the station's restaurant. She was going to Monte Carlo for a week ; hearing this, he asked her to walk into the casino on the third day at 7 in the evening (but punctually at seven, he insisted) and on the first table, in the first roulette room, she was to deposit 100 francs on a certain number. He asked her to keep the secret. When the young woman, very excited, brought 3 600 francs, he repeated his request of secrecy.

He had been much intrigued by the last occurrence (of this he was thinking when he heard, "You understand what I'm driving at..."). He was walking past the three shop windows of the stamp store, as he usually did when returning from the library. This time, failing to realize why, he stopped and began curiously looking. Stamp collecting had never interested him and he was wondering why he should be unable to leave one of the shop windows, apparently the least attractive. His eye fell on an old unassuming album and he knew that he had to buy it. The cost was 5 francs. In reaching his place he began looking through it, careful and curious, though he didn't know what he was looking for. No doubt it had been the collection of a beginner, maybe some boy in high school. Even such an ignorant as he was could realize that the stamps were of recent make and of no interest. A sudden impulse possessed him : with a shaving blade he began to undo the paste board. Very carefully he extracted a few cellophane envelopes full of old stamps. The thing was quite plain : someone being persecuted by the régime had tried and succeeded in getting a large number of rare stamps out of Germany.

The next day he went back and asked the owner of the shop if he remembered who had sold him the collection. He could not tell: he had bought a whole lot of old albums at an auction, a number of years before. When shown the stamps extracted from the paste board cases, the merchant turned pale.

"Such rarities have not been seen for some time, either in Switzerland or in some other country."

Should he sell them now — he added — he could make at least 100,000 francs. But if he waited for an international auction he might even get 200,000 francs.

"Considering that I bought them for practically nothing from you, I think we should make it fifty-fifty. But I need a few thousand francs just now. The rest you'll place in a bank account in my name as you sell the stamps."

"Leibnitz would have been thrilled by such an occurrence!" he thought with a smile. "To have to revise your philosophic principles because, in some mysterious way..."

From 1942 on he understood that the story of the accident was no longer accepted either by the Gestapo or by other information agencies which, for various reasons, were interested in his case. Indiscretions had probably been committed in Bucharest, subsequently corroborated by certain details obtained in Paris from doctor Bernard's assistants. But though he was known to live in Geneva, they did not know either what he looked like or his name. One evening, coming out of a café, he discovered, to his surprise, that he was being followed. He succeeded in covering his traces and spent a week in a village near Lucerne. Soon after his return the incident was repeated: two men of uncertain age, wearing mackintoshes, were waiting for him in front of the library. One of the librarians was just leaving : he asked his permission to accompany him. After a time, the librarian, now certain that they were actually being followed, hailed a taxicab. A brother-in-law of the librarian worked at the office for foreigners. From this man he later found out that he had been taken for a secret agent and was given a phone number that he was to call in case of need. The fact amused him that being looked for by the Gestapo and maybe other agencies, the immediate risk was, however, due to a confusion with a mere informing agent.

During the very first year, at doctor Bernard's advice, he deposited the notebooks with personal notes in a safe, in the bank. Then he had given up the notebooks. He used a pad that he kept on his own person. Certain pages with confessions too intimate, he deposited in the safe, as soon as written.

The very night he had taken refuge near Lucerne he decided to complete the autobiographical notes :

"I am no 'clairvoyant' or occultist and I don't belong to any secret society. One of the documents deposited in the safe summarizes the life I began in 1938. The first experiments were described and analyzed in the reports of professor Roman Stănciulescu and Gilbert Bernard and mailed by the latter to a laboratory of the Rockefeller foundation. But they only consider the outer aspects of that process of mutation that started in April 1938. I have mentioned them, however, because they validate, as scientifically as possible, the other documents deposited in the safe.

I am positive that a possible reader going through the above-mentioned documents will ask the same question, that I myself have frequently asked throughout these last years : 'Why was it me ? why did this mutation have to happen to me ?' The short autobiography in folder A will make it clear that even before the threat of total amnesia, I had not succeeded in accomplishing anything worthwhile. I have always been passionately interested in many sciences and disciplines, but except for very wide reading, I did not accomplish anything. Then why should it be me ? I don't know. Possibly because I have no family. There are, of course, many other intellectuals without a family ; maybe I was chosen because when young, I desired to possess a universal science, so at the very moment when on the point of completely losing my memory, I was granted a universal science such as will only be accessible to man after many thousands of years."

"I am writing this note with the following purpose : If, in spite of all expectations, I should now disappear, I wish it to be known that there is no merit or responsibility of mine in the process of mutation that I have minutely described in the notebooks collected in folder A."

The following day he continued :

"For the reasons presented in folder B I was transported and 'camouflaged' in Switzerland, in October 1938. It may seem unbelievable that up to this day, 20 January 1943, I have not yet been identified and eventually captured. The possible reader will wonder how I could live unnoticed so many years, though I was an exceptional case: I was a 'mutant', I possessed means of knowledge as yet inaccessible to man. I asked myself the same question in 1938—1939. But I soon understood that there was no risk of self-betrayal and, therefore, of identification, for the simple reason that when in company I behaved like any other intellectual. As I was saying, in the years 1938—1939, I was afraid of giving myself away when talking to professors and colleagues at the University : I had more knowledge than any of them and I understood things that they didn't even dream to exist. But to my surprise and great relief I discovered that in other people's presence, I could not appear as I really was ; just as an adult person talking to a child knows the impossibility to communicate and, therefore, doesn't try to communicate more than facts and meanings accessible to a child's mental capacity. This continuous camouflage of the immense possibilities at my disposal did not force me to lead a 'double life' ; neither do parents or educators lead a double life in the presence of children.

My experience has, in a certain sense, an exemplary meaning. Were anyone to tell me that there are saints among us, or authentic magicians, or Boddhisatva, or any other kind of humans endowed with miraculous powers, I would believe it. By their very mode of existence such people cannot be recognized by the profane."

On the morning of 1 November 1947 he decided he would no longer write his notes in French but in an artificial language that he had passionately, almost enthusiastically, concocted within the last few months. He delighted in the extraordinary pliability of the grammar and the infinite possibilities of the vocabulary (he had succeeded in introducing into the system of purely etymological proliferation a corrective borrowed from the mathematical theory of the ensemble). He was now able to describe paradoxical states, apparently contradictory, impossible to express in the existing languages. As it was conceived and perfected, this linguistic system could only be decoded by a highly sophisticated electronic computer ; so not before 1980, he believed. This certainty allowed him to confess facts that he had so far never dared to put down in writing.

After a morning's work he went for a walk round the lake, as usual. In coming back he stopped at the Café 'Albert'. As soon as he saw him, the waiter ordered coffee and a bottle of mineral water. He brought the newspapers, but he had no time to look through them. A tall distinguished-looking man (as if descending from a Whistler picture, he thought), still young, though the old-fashioned costume made him look at least five or six years older, stopped by and asked permission to sit at his table.

"Strange that we should meet today, a day so important for you," he said. "I am the count of Saint-Germain. At least that's what they call me," he added, with a bitter smile. "But a strange encounter this, just a few days after the discovery of the Dead Sea scrolls, isn't it ? You have heard, of course."

"Only what they wrote in the papers," he said.

He gave him a long look and smiled. Then he raised his hand :

"Double, no sugar," he said. When the waiter had brought his coffee, he began : "All such meetings, among incredible persons like ourselves, have an air of pastiche. A consequence of poor pseudo-occultist literature. But we have to accept the fact : you cannot do anything against folklore of poor quality : the legends that form the delight of certain contemporaries are of sadly bad taste. I remember a talk I had with Mathila Ghyka in London, in the summer of 1940. It was shortly after the invasion of France. This remarkable scholar, writer and philosopher (let me parenthetically add that I highly appreciate not only *Le nombre d'or*, like everyone else, but also the novel of his young years *La Pluie d'étoiles*), this unparalleled Mathila Ghyka was saying that the second world war, which had just started, was actually an occult war between two secret societies, between the Templers and the Teuton knights. If a man of Mathila Ghyka's intelligence and culture could thus reason no wonder that occult traditions are looked down upon... However, I see you have nothing to say."

"I was listening. I am interested..."

"As a matter of fact there's no need for you to say much. I will only ask you to answer one question, at the end. I don't pretend to know who you are," he continued after a pause. "But we are a small group who, since 1939, have been aware of your existence. Your sudden appearance, independent of the traditions we know, leads us to believe that on the one hand you have a special mission, and on the other hand that you possess means of knowledge far above those that we possess. No need to confirm what I'm telling you," he added. "I came to meet you today because the discovery of the Dead Sea scrolls is the first sign of a well-known syndrome. Other finds shall soon follow, in the same direction..."

"Namely ?" he put in smiling.

He gave him again a long, searching look.

"I see you're testing me. Maybe you're right. But the significance of the finds is clear : the manuscripts of Qumran reveal the doctrines of the Essenians, a secret community of which nothing definite was known. Similarly, the gnostic manuscripts recently discovered in Egypt, as yet undeciphered, will reveal certain esoteric doctrines which have been ignored for almost eighteen centuries. More such finds shall soon follow revealing other traditions still secret up to now. The syndrome I was alluding to is this : the revelation of a series of secret doctrines. Which signify the approaching Apocalypse. The cycle is closing. This has been a fact known for some time, but after Hiroshima we know the way of conclusion, too."

"Very true," he mumbled absently.

"The question I wished to ask is this : Owing to the knowledge that was transmitted to you, do you know anything definite as to the organization of... the Ark ?"

"The ark ?" he asked in surprise. "Are you thinking of a duplicate of Noah's ark ?"

The other man again gave him a long, inquisitive, and yet irritated look.

'It was just a metaphor," he continued after some time. "A metaphor that has turned into a cliché, you'll find it in every so-called occultist rubbish tradition. I was referring to the handing down of tradition. I know that the essentials are never lost. But I was thinking of the many other things which, though not actually the essential, seem to be indispensable to a truly human existence : the western artistic thesaurus, for instance, music and poetry primarily, but part of classical philosophy too, plus certain scientific disciplines, as well."

"I suppose you can imagine what those few survivors of that cataclysm are likely to think about the sciences," he interrupted smiling. "Post-historic man, so I believe he is called, will probably be allergic to science for at least one or two hundred years."

"Very likely," the other continued. 'But I was thinking of mathematics. Why, that's roughly what I meant to ask you."

He sat brooding for a long time, hesitating.

"As far as I understand your question I can only say..."

"Thank you, that will do!" he burst out, unable to conceal his joy.

The count made a low bow, gave him a warm handshake and made for the door. He watched him walk away quickly, as if he was expected out there, in the street.

"I tried to catch your eye repeatedly, but you didn't see me," the owner said in a low voice. "He was formerly one of our guests. Everybody knows him : Monsieur Olivier Brisson, but some people call him doctor : doctor Olivier Brisson. He was once a school teacher, but one day he left the school and the town without telling anyone. I don't think he's quite right in his mind. He starts talking to people and calls himself the count of Saint-Germain."

He recalled this meeting, observing that, in a strange way, the scenario tended to be repeated. That year he had made friends with Linda Gray, a young woman from California, who, among other things, had what he considered a great quality, the one of being ignorant of jealousy. One evening, before he had filled a second cup of coffee, she unexpectedly said :

"I hear you were good friends with a famous French doctor..."

"He's dead," he interrupted. "He died in a plane accident in the winter of 1943."

The young woman lit a cigarette and after inhaling, she continued, avoiding his look.

"Some people think it was no accident. That the plane was shot down because... Why, I didn't quite understand, but you'll soon find out from the very man. I told him to come at nine," she added looking at her watch.

"Who's coming at nine ?" he asked smiling.

"Doctor Monroe. He's the chief or some other high-ranking person in the gerontology laboratory in New York."

He recognized him immediately. He had seen him several times in the library, then a few days before, at the café. He asked permission to be seated and once seated asked him if he had known professor Bernard.

"I knew him very well," he answered, "but I've made a promise never to discuss the story or significance of our friendship."

"I must apologize for using this stratagem," he began, putting his hand out. "I'm doctor Yves Monroe and I have examined the notes of professor Bernard in New York. As a biologist and gerontologist I'm especially interested in one thing : to stop the proliferation of new and dangerous myths : as for instance that youth and life may be prolonged by other means than those we make use of today, purely biochemical means. You know what I mean ?"

"No, I don't."

"I refer primarily to the method suggested by doctor Rudolf, electrocution by shock of one to one and a half million volts. An absurdity, nothing more."

"Fortunately, I don't think the method has ever been tested."

The doctor picked up his glass of whisky and began twirling it absently in his fingers.

"No, it has not," he spoke after a time, his eyes on the ice cubes, "but a legend is growing that doctor Bernard had knowledge of a rather similar case, a case of rejuvenation by the electricity diffused by a lightning bolt. Yet, the materials at the Rockefeller laboratory give only confused and approximate information, so that no conclusion is possible. I was told that part of the phonograms have been lost, more exactly destroyed by mistake while trying to register the contents on high fidelity records. Anyway, as far as they may be utilized, the documents collected by professor Bernard refer exclusively to the recovery and psychomental reintegration of the lightning struck patient."

He paused, carefully placing his glass on the table, without having sipped.

"I took the liberty to force myself to meet you," he continued, "hoping that you might be able to shed some light on a matter that is obscure enough. You told me you knew professor Bernard quite well. Recently, a rumour spread that the most important documents he was himself carrying in two suitcases and that the plane in which he was to cross the Atlantic was shot down precisely because of these very suitcases ; it is uncertain what they contained ; one of the rival airlines wished to make sure, to avoid any risk, as the word goes... Do you know anything definite concerning the contents of these suitcases ?"

He shrugged, much embarassed.

"I think doctor Bernard's assistants in Paris could inform you, no one else."

The doctor gave a forced smile, he didn't try to conceal his disappointment.

"Those who remember maintain that they don't know anything. The others pretend to have forgotten. I've also read professor Stănciulescu's article in the *Presse Médicale,*" he continued after a pause. "Unfortunately Stănciulescu died in the autumn of 1939. One of my colleagues, on mission in Bucharest, has recently written that all his attempts to find out more information from profesor Stănciulescu's assistants have failed."

He took up his glass of whisky again and having twirled it in his fingers, he raised it to his lips ; very carefully, very slowly, he began to sip.

"Owing to doctor Bernard's intervention you retained a Rockefeller scholarship for three or four years. What was the field of your research ?"

"Documentation for a history of medical pshychology," he answered. "I sent them in 1945, to professor Bernard's fellow workers in Paris."

"How interesting," he said, suddenly looking up from his glass and giving him a long searching look.

That night he went home in a melancholy mood ; somehow worried. He wasn't sure if Monroe had guessed hid identity. On the other hand, he wondered who Monroe thought he was : a personal friend of Bernard's ? A patient ? If, however, he had heard the recorded materials from Geneva in the years 1938—39, he must surely have recognized his voice. The next day Linda's question set his mind at rest.

"What did the doctor mean when he took me aside last night and said : 'If he ever tells you that he is over seventy don't you believe him'."

A few weeks later, in front of a newly opened café, he was hailed in Romanian : "Mr. Matei sir ! Mr. Dominic Matei !"

He looked round scared. A tall, blond, bare-headed young man was hurrying towards him, trying meanwhile to open his briefcase.

"I have learnt a little Romanian, but I'm afraid to speak it. I knew you were here in Geneva, and having so many photographs at my disposal it was easy to recognize you..."

He searched his briefcase nervously and showed him a few photos, face and profile, taken from different angles. They had been taken in the autumn of 1938 by the surgeon who had succeeded in altering his features so radically.

"In any case," he added smiling, "I also carry the family picture album in my case. Let's go in this café for a minute," he said, opening the door. "You can't imagine my excitement when I set eyes on you just now. I was afraid that hearing me shouting 'Mr. Matei' you wouldn't look round."

That's just what I was koing to do," he answered with a smile. But I admit I was curious."

They sat down at a table. Having ordered a hot drink and a bottle of beer, the stranger began contemplating him with a look of both fascination and disbelief.

"A few weeks ago, on January 8th, you had your eightieth birthday !" he mumbled. "And you don't look more than thirty or thirty-two. And you look that much because you're trying to conceal your age."

"I don't yet know with whom I have the pleasure of talking..."

"I'm sorry," he said taking a drink of beer. "I'm still very excited. As they say in gambling at the races, I backed a horse and won ! I am Ted Jones Jr., a *Time Magazine* correspondent. It all started some ten years ago when I read your interview : *Struck by Lightning*. I was highly impressed, even though I found out that it was apocryphal. But after that the war came, and few people remembered the interview."

He emptied his glass, asked him if he could go on in English and if he minded the pipe tobacco.

"Two years ago when Dr. Rudolf's famous secret archives were discovered, your case began to be talked about again; as far, of course, as it was known from the documents collected by Gilbert Bernard. Yet nothing else was known, not even whether you were still alive or not. Unfortunately, Doctor Rudolf was a notorious Nazi, as a matter of fact he committed suicide during the last week of the war, anything concerning his experiments is under suspicion."

"What kind of experiments ?" he asked.

"Electrocution of animals, especially of mammals. One million two hundred thousand volts up to two million."

"What about the results ?"

Jones made an attempt to laugh and refilled his glass with beer.

"It's a long story," he began.

In fact, he did think it was long, obscure, and inconclusive. The first inquiries into the Rudolf archives were supposed to have stated that in certain cases the victims were not killed by the electrical shock, but as the tests began a few months later, the consequences of electrocution could not be detected. In other cases, they became aware of an alteration in the genetic system. A few research workers interpreted such alterations as the prelude of a mutation, but a good many items in the archives, including the most valuable information, mysteriously disappeared. Anyway, without any information regarding the experiments on human beings, the Rudolf dossier was inconclusive. On the other hand, a great majority of American scholars rejected a priori the hypothesis of regeneration by electricity.

"You were and still remain the only argument," he exclaimed. "It was, therefore, to be expected that the few documents saved by professor Bernard should be systematically depreciated and in certain cases, destroyed."

"Do you think that is what really happened ?" he intervened.

Jones hesitated a few seconds, looking at him with a smile.

"I have good reasons to be sure. Luckily I was sent as press correspondent to Romania."

Before reaching Bucharest he had learnt Romanian, as much as he wanted, to be able to read and manage by himself in the streets and shops. He had been lucky enough to get to know and make friends with doctor Gavrilă who possessed the family picture album and all the documents collected by the professor.

"What an extraordinary article I could have written! *Rejuvenated by Lightning!* With photographs, documents, professor Roman Stănciulescu's testimony, those of doctor Gavrilă and of others in whose care you had been, plus the interview I might have taken now, as well as so many other snapshots, taken here in Geneva in February 1948 !"

He stopped, tried to light his pipe again, then gave up and looked him deep in the eyes.

"Although your English is perfect, you don't say anything."

"I was waiting for the rest."

"You're right," he continued. "The rest is just as spectacular and mysterious as your own experience. For ethical and political reasons, the article may not be published. Anything that may lead to confusion, whatever in some way seems to confirm doctor Rudolf's theory, has to be kept out of print. Especially at this moment," he added with a smile, "when substantial sums for gerontological research institutes are about to be noted. Have you nothing to say ?" he demanded abruptly.

He shrugged.

"I think that everything is happening just as it should. I'm sorry for useless work and time wasted, but the consequences of your article would have been disastrous. If people, more precisely certain people, were positive that electrocution would solve the problem of regeneration and rejuvenation, we might expect anything to happen. I think it preferable to leave it to biochemists and gerontologists. One day, sooner of later, they will reach the same result."

He smoked, watching him sip his warm lemonade.

"Anyway," Jones said after an interval, "there is you. As I was conceiving the article I didn't think of what your life might become once it was in the press !"

"In a certain sense it has already begun to become," he put in laughing. "How did you discover me so easily? I believed that doctor Gavrilă and others in Romania thought I was killed in some car accident, long ago."

"Most of them think so. Doctor Gavrilă did, too, before I informed him in utmost secrecy that you are alive and staying here in Geneva. Don't think I got the news from some person or other," he smiled enigmatically. "It was my own find in hearing that Doctor Monroe had come to Geneva to discuss certain details with a friend of doctor Bernard. My immediate guess was that this friend could only be you Evidently, neither Doctor Monroe nor the other research workers in the gerontological laboratory do not, cannot believe such a thing."

"That is good news."

"The truth will come out, however," Jones continued, not bothering to conceal his satisfaction. "It's too fascinating a story to be buried in oblivion. I'm going to write a novel," he added, cleaning his pipe. "As a matter of fact I've already started to work on it. There's no risk for you in it. The plot is laid in Mexico, before and during the war and most characters are Mexicans. I shall, of course, send you the novel if, on its issue, you're on the same friendly terms with Linda. I used to know her brother quite well, a pilot who died at Okinawa."

He stopped abruptly, as if remembering something important. He opened his briefcase.

"I mustn't forget the family picture album. I promised doctor Gavrilă to hand it over should I succeed in meeting you. Precious documents : souvenirs of... what shall I say ? Souvenirs of your first youth."

Having reached home, he wrapped the album in a blue sheet of paper, placed it in an envelope and sealed it. In the upper left hand corner he wrote : "Received on 20 February 1948, from Ted Jones Jr., *Time Magazine* correspondent at Bucharest. Album sent by Doctor Gavrilă."

"Things are getting simpler and at the same time, more complicated," he said to himself in opening the pad. He began writing in French, describing the meeting and summarizing the discussion with Jones. Then adding : "Confirms doctor Monroe's information : the systematic destruction of the 1938—39 documents, the only details concerning the process of physiological recuperation and anamnesis. The only scientific proofs of regeneration and rejuvenation by means of massive electric discharge, which means that the origin of the mutation phenomenon is no longer of interest. Why ?"

He stopped and sat thinking a few seconds. "Of course, the possible reader will gather the essential information from the autobiographic summary and other jottings as grouped in the A, B, and C folders. Yet, lacking the facts collected and annotated by professors Stănciulescu and Bernard, my confessions have lost their documentary value. What is more, my entire notes refer to the consequences of anamnesis, briefly speaking to the experiments of a mutant, anticipating the existence of post-historic man. The Stănciulescu-Bernard documents didn't include information concerning these experiments, but, to a certain extent, confirmed them as credible. I can only draw one conclusion : my confessions are not meant for a reader in the near future, the year 2000, shall we say. But then for whom are they meant ?"

"This may be a provisional answer : as a result of the nuclear wars which are to take place, many civilizations, beginning with the western one, will be destroyed. The catastrophe shall, no doubt, bring about a wave of pessimism hitherto unknown in the history of humanity, a general discouragement. Not all survivors will give way to the temptation of committing suicide, yet very few will have the necessary vitality to believe in man and hope for the possibility of a humanity superior to the species of homo sapiens. If then discovered and decoded, these confessions might be a counterweight to the universal despair and desire for extinction. By simply exemplifying the mental possibilities of a humanity to be born in the far future, such documents demonstrate the reality of post-historic man, by merely anticipating it.

"This hypothesis implies the conservation of the entire material deposited today in the safe. I cannot imagine how this safeguarding may be organized, but, on the other hand, I have no doubt that this is going to happen. Otherwise my experience would be senseless."

He introduced the written pages in an envelope, sealed it, and went to the bank. As he was locking the door, he heard the phone ring and it went on ringing as he was going downstairs.

## IV

The summer of 1955 was unusually wet and at Ticino there was a storm every day. He hardly remembered having seen a sky so black as on the afternoon of 10 August. As the first lightning flashes flared over the town, the power station interrupted the electric supply. The thunderclaps followed in succession for nearly half an hour, as if it were a single endless explosion. From his window he especially watched the thunderbolts in the west striking down upon the rocky heights, abruptly descending from the mountains. The pouring rain gradually ceased and, at about 3, the sky began to brighten. The street lights were soon lit, so that from his window he could see down to the cathedral. He waited for the rain to stop, then went down and made for the police station.

"Shortly before noon," he began in a purely informative tone, "two ladies set out, bent on climbing to the Trento. They asked me if I knew a shortcut to avoid the serpentine, I pointed out the right direction, but advised them to postpone the climb or they would be overtaken by the storm before reaching the Helival shelter. They answered that they were accustomed to storms in the mountains and that they could not change their plans, anyway. Their holidays would be over within a few days and they were due home."

The policeman listened patiently yet showed no great interest.

"I don't know them," he went on, "however, I heard the elder lady address the younger one : her name is Veronica. I think I can guess what happened. When the storm burst out they found themselves very likely on the road under the stone crag, at Vallino, where most of the thunderbolts were striking. I stood by the window and I saw them," he added, realizing that the man was considering him with interest, hardly believing him. "I suppose many rocks rolled down. I'm afraid they've been struck by lightning or buried under the stones."

He knew it would be difficult to persuade the man.

He went on after some time. "I would go in a taxi by myself to look for them, but if it happened as I think it has, the two of us, the driver and myself, will not be able to get them out from under the boulders. We will need pick axes and shovels."

In the end he was content with this solution. He would call in case of need, from a first aid post, and the police would send ambulances and everything necessary. As they came near Vallino the sky had cleared, but, in places, the stones were covering the road, so the driver slowed down.

"I don't think they had time to reach the hut. Once the storm broke out they probably sought shelter in one of the mountain caves."

"Some are very wide," the driver said.

They both saw her at the same time. She must have died of fright as the thunderbolt struck a few steps away from her. She was an old woman, with grey hair cropped short. She didn't seem to have died by the onrush of the stones, though one boulder, quite close, had caught her skirt. He fancied he heard a groan, so he began closely examining the stone wall and the rocks round about.

"Veronica !" he shouted repeatedly, slowly advancing along the stony wall.

They had both heard the groan, then a few brief yells, followed by unknown words quickly spoken as if in an incantation. When he came near the rock he understood. In rolling down, the rock had stopped right in front of the cave where Veronica was hiding, covering it almost entirely. Had he not heard the groan and the yells, he couldn't have guessed that she was buried there. You could only see the split of the cave some two meters high up. Climbing with difficulty he caught sight of her, and called her by her name, waving his hand. The girl considered him, both happy and frightened, then tried to rise to her feet. She was not hurt, but the place was too narrow, so she could only stay doubled up.

"The police will soon be here," he said in French.

Then, since the girl didn't seem to understand, he repeated the phrase in German and Italian. The girl passed her hand over her face and began to speak to him. At first he realized that she was speaking in a central Indian dialect, then he recognized whole phrases in Sanṣkrit. Bowing low over her, he whispered : "Shanti ! Shanti !" then spoke a few canonical blessing formulae. The girl smiled a happy smile, then raised the palm of her hand as if to show him something.

He stood there, clinging to the rock, listening, eventually trying to soothe and encourage her by a few familiar Sanskrit expressions, until the ambulance and police arrived. They succeeded in dislodging the rock by digging a slope under it. An hour later, the girl was able to come out by means of a chord ladder. At the sight of the policeman and the ambulance she shouted with fear, caught his hand, and came close to him.

"She's had a shock and is probably suffering from amnesia," he explained, a bit embarassed.

"But what language does she speak ?" someone in the group asked.

"Some Indian dialect I guess," he cautiously answered.

The identity papers revealed that her name was Veronica Bühler, aged 25 ; she was a school teacher and lived in Liestal, canton of Bâle-Campagne. Her companion Gertrud Frank was German, from Freiburg, employed by a publishing house. The result of the autopsy confirmed the early suppositions : death was the result of heart failure.

Since he was the only one who could communicate with Veronica, the only person in whose presence she was quiet, he spent a good deal of time at the hospital. He would bring a tape recorder that he carefully camouflaged. He recorded a few hours daily, especially what she said about herself. She stated that her name was Rupini, daughter of Nagabhata, member of the kshatria caste descended from one of the first families converted to Buddhism in Magadha. Before the age of 12, with her parents' consent, she had decided to dedicate her life to the study of Abhidharma and had been received in an *Ihikuni* community. She learnt Sanskrit grammar, logic, and mahayana metaphysics. She had memorized over 50,000 sutra, a fact which created a prestige not merely among instructors and students at the university of Nalanda, but also among a number of masters, ascetic and contemplative. At 40 she became the disciple of the famous Chandrakirti philosopher. She would spend several months a year in a cave, meditating and transcribing the works of her master. That's where she was when a storm was unleashed and she heard the thunderbolts striking the mountain overhead. Several rocks then turned loose and rushed down like a flood of stones blocking the entrance to the cave. She vainly tried to get out, then she woke up and saw him up on the rock, waving and speaking to her in an unknown language.

He was not always sure to have understood her ; even what he was sure to have understood, he largely kept to himself. He had told the doctors that the young woman thought she was living in Central India twelve centuries ago, and testified to being a Buddhist hermit. Because of the sedatives, she slept most of the time. Several medical doctors and psychologists from Zürich, Basel, and Geneva had come to examine her. As it was to be expected, the papers published articles every day, and the number of press correspondents, busy looking around and interviewing doctors, was continually growing.

Fortunately, the solution he had first thought of had a chance of being accepted. Having heard the tape with her biographical confessions, the very next day he sent a long telegram to the Oriental Institute in Rome. Then, on the third day, at the hour indicated in his telegram, he transmitted by phone certain autobiographical confessions. He had coincidentally informed one of C. G. Jung's closest collaborators. Two days later, professor Tucci came from Rome, accompanied by one of his assistants. It was the first time that Rupini was able to talk at length, in Sanskrit, about Madhyamika philosophy and, especially, about her master Chandrakirti. All the discussions were registered on tape and the assistant translated certain passages into English for the information of doctors and press people. The discussion became rather difficult when Rupini asked what exactly had happened to her, where she was, why no one understood her speech, though besides Sanskrit, she had tried a few Indian dialects.

"What do you tell her ?" he had asked the professor.

"Of course, I always begin by reminding her of maya the fabulous witch, the cosmic illusion. It isn't actually a dream, I tell her, but it shares the illusory nature of a dream, because it concerns the future, therefore, time ; for time is superlatively unreal. I don't think I managed to convince her. Fortunately, she has a passion for logic and for dialectics, and that is primarily what we discuss."

Having suggested a voyage to India, more exactly to the province Uttar Pradesh where Rupini used to meditate, Professor Tucci agreed that the Oriental Institute would sponsor this expedition. Owing to the intervention of Jung, the expenses were paid by an American foundation. When the project became public, several newspapers offered to pay the entire expense of the expedition, provided they would have the exclusive benefit of the feature reports. It was almost impossible to avoid publicity, particularly as the consent of the hospital, the Indian government, and Veronica Bühler's family were necessary, but the inquiries at Liestal proved fruitless. Veronica had settled in the town just a few years ago. Her friends and colleagues did not know anything about her family. It was found out, however, that she was born in Egypt and that her parents divorced when she was 5 years old; the father stayed on in Egypt, was re-married and had given no sign of life. The mother, with whom Veronica did not get along very well, had settled in the United States, but her address was unknown.

The hospital finally agreed to the voyage to India, on condition that the patient be accompanied by one of the doctors who had supervised her case, as well as by a nurse. It was, of course, understood that she would be sedated before leaving the hospital and would continue sleeping until almost reaching Gorakhpur.

A military plane picked them up in Bombay, taking them to Gorakhpur. Six automobiles filled with pressmen, technicians, as well as a truck from the Indian television were awaiting them. They climbed to the frontier of Nepal, to a region where, according to Rupini's directions, they were to find the cave where she used to meditate. Fortunately, besides himself, there was a pandit from Uttar Pradesh with a knowledge of Madaryamika philosophy, by her side when she woke.

At the doctor's insistent demands, all the others were hiding behind trees, some ten meters away. She angrily addressed the pandit, as if recognizing him ; she asked a few questions, but didn't wait for an ansmer. She walked fast along one of the paths, looking right before her, repeating her favourite benedictions that she had so often spoken in the clinic. After a climb of some twenty minutes, she broke into a run, panting. With arm outstretched, she was pointing to the ledge of a rock lazily propped against the mountain wall.

"That's it !" she yelled.

Then with both arms extended against the rock, she began climbing with incredible agility. Once on top she forcefully wrenched a stunted shrub, cleaned the place of moss and dry branches, discovered a split and, trembling, she placed her cheek against the stone and looked inside. She then stayed motionless.

"She's fainted !" someone shouted from below, a few seconds before he reached her.

"That's right, she's fainted !" he said, gently supporting her head.

They climbed down with difficulty, making room for the team of specialists. They carried her on a stretcher to the car. She was still in a swoon and the car was some ten kilometers away when the first charge of dynamite was heard exploding. In less than half an hour they succeeded in letting themselves in, climbing down by means of a rope ladder. By the light of an electric lamp, they saw the skeleton : it was crouching as if death had caught her in the midst of yoga meditation. Close by on the ground, there was an earthen pot, two wooden platters and a few manuscripts ; in touching them they realized that they had long turned to dust.

The nurse stopped him in front of the door.

"She's awake," she said. "But she won't open her eyes. She's afraid..."

He walked up to her and put his hand upon her forehead.

"Veronica !" he whispered.

She suddenly opened her eyes and, in recognizing him, her face lit up as he had never seen it before. Clutching at his hand, she tried to sit up.

"It's you ?" she exclaimed. "I know you ; I asked you this morning about the road. But where is Gertrud ? Where is she ?" she insisted looking deep into his eyes.

He knew, as all the other members of the group did, that to avoid publicity would be impossible. The Indian television had registered the most dramatic scenes and the millions of spectators who had heard her speak in Sanskrit and some Himalayan dialect saw her at the end of the feature stating in timid English that her name was Veronica Bühler and that she only had a good knowledge of German and French. She also declared that she had never tried to learn any Oriental language and, except for a few popularizing books, had never read anything connected with India or Indian cultures. As it was to be expected it was this very fact that attracted the Indian public and, twenty-four hours later, the world as a whole. For most Indian intellectuals, there couldn't possibly exist a clearer demonstration of the transmigration of the soul : in a former existence Veronica Bühler had been Rupini.

"But I don't believe in metempsychosis," she had whispered one night, frightened, clutching at his hand. "It was not me ! Maybe I was possessed by another spirit," she added seeking his eyes.

Because he didn't know what answer to give and hesitated, fondling her hand, Veronica bowed her head, exhausted.

"I'm afraid I will go out of my mind," she said.

They were lodged in one of the most luxurious hotels in Delhi as guests of the Indian government. In order to avoid photographers, press people, and the bold curious onlookers, the whole party were taking their meals in a dining room exclusively reserved for them and carefully guarded. They visited museums and institutions every day and met important persons. They were driven in limousines surrounded by police motor cycles, otherwise they dare not leave their floor. Not even walk along the corridors. Together with the doctor and nurse they had once tried to go down, late after midnight, hoping to get into a taxi, get away from the hotel, and take a walk in the streets, but a whole crowd was waiting at the hotel's entrance. They were forced to go back, protected by the police.

"I'm afraid I will go mad," she said once more, in stepping out of the elevator.

The following day he was able to talk to an American reporter who had vainly tried to accompany them to Gorakhpur. He promised him a long interview and other unpublished materials, for exclusive use, provided they were transported incognito, to an island in the Mediterranean, where the two of them might stay in hiding a few months.

"Waiting for the cyclone of television and printing presses to be over," he added. "Within less than a year things will be forgotten and each of us can go back to our business."

Two weeks later they were housed in a villa built after the war on a hill near La Valette. But the preparation and recording of the interview was longer than they had expected. Veronica was getting impatient.

"We talk so much and about so many things, but I don't understand one essential thing : the transmigration of the soul."

"I will explain it to you when we are alone."

She gave him an unexpected warm look.

"Will we ever be alone ?" she whispered.

One night, at Delhi, she had said :

"When I opened my eyes and saw you, as you were telling me about Gertrud, I realized that I was thinking of two different things at the same time. I was thinking that though both my parents may be alive, without Gertrud I was an orphan. And at the very same instant I was thinking that if I were five or six years older and if he asked me to marry him, I would accept..."

"I am eighty-seven years old," he said jokingly, with a smile.

That was when he first saw her laugh.

"More than I would be if I were to add Rupini's age, but as I told you, I don't believe it, I cannot believe."

"In a way, you're quite right, but, mind you, only in a certain sense. We'll discuss this problem later."

He had avoided discussing it in the interview. He had limited himself to mentioning the classical Indian conceptions, from the Upanishads to Gautama Buddha, also referring to certain contemporary interpretations particularly those of Tucci. He had succeeded in remaining anonymous : a young orientalist who had recently made friends with Veronica. He had, above all things, succeeded in preserving the same face that he had created in August : hair brushed down on his forehead, a thick blonde moustache covering his upper lip.

That evening when they were alone on the terrace, Veronica drew her lounge chair close to his.

"Now, tell me... But, before anything else, explain how you came to know..."

"I will go back a very long way," he said.

It was only one evening, at the beginning of October, that he understood. They were sitting side by side, on the sofa in the hall, watching the lights of the haven over the terrace balustrade. He thought that Veronica was giving him a strange look.

"You want to tell me something and dare not. What is it ?"

"I was thinking that seeing us always together, living in the same house, people might think we were in love."

He sought her hand and pressed it in both his hands.

"But that's how it is, Veronica. We are in love, we sleep in the same room, in the same bed."

"Is it true ?" she asked below her breath.

Then she sighed, put her head upon his shoulder and closed her eyes. A few moments later she rose abruptly and looked at him as if she didn't recognize him, she began speaking a strange language, such as he had never heard before. "So that was it," he said to himself. "That's why I had to meet her. That's the reason of all that's been happening." Gently, without hurry, lest he should frighten her, he went to the desk and fetched the tape recorder. She continued speaking, ever faster, looking at her hands, then she raised her wrist watch to her ear and listened, both surprised and happy. Her face lit up, as if she were ready to laugh. Yet unexpectedly she gave a frightened start, whimpered repeatedly and began rubbing her eyes. Sleepy, dizzy, she was making for the couch ; he saw her stagger and caught her in his arms. He carried her into the adjoining room and laid her on the bed, covering her with a shawl.

She woke after midnight.

"I had such a fright," she murmured. "I had a bad dream."

"What did you dream ?"

"I don't want to remember. I may be frightened again. I was somewhere by a large river. An unknown person, on his head a mask of dog's head, came towards me. He was holding in his hands... I don't want to remember," she repeated, putting out her arms to embrace him.

Since that night, he would not leave her by herself. He was afraid of a paramediumatic crisis coming on again, unexpectedly. Fortunately, the gardener and the two young Maltese women who looked after the house would disappear as soon as dinner was over.

"Go on, tell me some more," she would insist every evening, as soon as they were alone. "Explain it all ! I sometimes regret not remembering anything at all of what Rupini knew."

One morning, coming from the garden, she asked unexpectedly :

"Didn't you think it strange that they should wait for us by the fence ? As if they were spying on us."

"I didn't notice anything," he answered. "Where were they ?"

"They stood by the gate, as if spying on us. Two men, queerly dressed. But maybe I'm wrong," she added, her hand upon her brow.

He took hold of her arm and gently drew her to him.

"I'm afraid you've been in the sun too much," he said, helping her to lie down on the couch.

"A week has gone by," he said to himself, "so the rhythm is hebdomadal. Which means that the whole thing may last a month. But what will become of us afterwards ?

When sure that she was sound asleep he tiptoed into the study and fetched the tape recorder. For a space of time you could only hear the blackbirds and her somewhat restless breathing. Then her whole face was lit by a large smile. She spoke a few words under her breath followed by concentrated anxious silence, as if waiting for some answer that was slow in coming, or that she could no longer hear. She then began talking quietly as if she were speaking to herself, repeating certain words several times, differently intoned, yet all full of deep sadness. Seeing the first tears slowly running down her cheeks, he turned off the tape recorder and pushed it under the bed. Then very carefully he stroked her hand and began drying her tears. Much later, he carried her in his arms into the bedroom. He stayed by her until she woke up. When she set eyes on him, she grasped his hand and gave it a tender squeeze.

"I've been dreaming," she said. "It was a lovely dream, but a very sad one. It was like this : two young people were in love, but could not remain together. I don't understand why, but they were not allowed to remain together."

He had been quite right : the rhythm was hebdomadal indeed, although the paramediumatic trances (as he had decided to call them) were taking place at different hours. "Materials for the documentary history of speech," he thought. After Egyptian and Ugaritic there came a sample of, probably, proto-Elamitic and one of Sumerian. We're going ever more deeply into the past. Documents for the Ark," he added smiling. The linguists would give anything to be able to study them *now*. But how far down shall we reach ? As far as the inarticulate protospeech ? And then what ?"

About mid-December he had the strangest experience. Fortunately it was shortly before midnight, they were not yet asleep. Veronica broke into a series of guttural prehuman yells which both exasperated and humiliated him ; he was thinking that such a regression into the animality should only be tried on willing subjects, not with an unconscious subject. But a few seconds later there came groups of phonemes, clear, vocalic, of infinite variety, periodically interrupted by short labial explosions that he hadn't believed possible to be reproduced by a European. Half an hour later,

Veronica fell asleep with a sigh. "That's as far as it will go, I think," he thought, turning off the tape recorder. Then he waited. He wished to be awake when she woke up. He went to bed late, it was almost morning.

When he woke, a little before eight, Veronica was still asleep and he didn't wish to wake her. She slept on till nearly 11. Hearing that it was so late, she jumped out of bed, quite frightened.

"What has happened to me ?" she asked.

"Nothing. You were probably very tired. And maybe you had a bed dream."

"No, I had no dreams. Anyway, I don't remember anything."

They decided to spend Christmas and New Year's Eve in a famous restaurant in La Valette. Veronica had booked a table for Monsieur et Madame Gerald Verneuil. She had thought of the name and also chose the clothes for the occasion.

"I think there's no risk in our being recognized," she said. "Even though our photographs may have appeared on the front page of all the illustrated magazines."

"You can be sure they did," he put in, "and maybe they still do."

She laughed, somewhat shy, yet happy.

"I would like to see them. I mean the photos in the picture magazines. I would like to have some as a memento, but maybe it's too risky to look for them," she added.

"I'll look for them."

Although he examined a number of newsstands and book-shops, he only found one Italian picture magazine with three pictures of Veronica, all in India.

"I seem to have been younger and more beautiful then, three months ago," she said.

A few weeks later he realized that Veronica was right. She hadn't been looking quite so young lately. "It's owing to those documents for the Ark," he thought. "She's exhausted by the paramedium ecstasies."

"I feel constantly tired," she confessed one morning, "and I don't understand why. I don't do anything at all, and yet I feel tired."

At the beginning of February he succeeded in persuading her to see a doctor in La Valette. They waited, restlessly, for the results of the numerous analyses.

"The lady has no serious illness, nothing whatsoever," the doctor assured him when they were alone. "I will, however, prescribe a series of fortifying injections. It may be the nervousness that precedes the menopause with certain women."

"What is her age, do you think ?"

The doctor blushed, rubbed his hands, a little embarrassed. Then he shrugged.

"Somewhere around forty," he said after a time, avoiding his eyes.

"Yet, believe me, it was no lie when she told you that she was not yet twenty six."

The effect of the injections was slow. She was more tired every day ; often, after looking at herself in a mirror, he would find her weeping. Once, as he was making for the park, he heard steps hurrying from behind and turned round.

"Professore," the cook was whispering, quite frightened, "la Signora ha il malocchio !"

"I ought to have understood from the beginning," he thought. "We have both fulfilled our duty and now we have to part." And as he could find no convincing reason, except a mortal accident or suicide, he chose the following : "the process of rapid aging."

He only told her, however, one morning when she showed him her hair : she had turned grey over night. Leaning against the wall, her face buried in her hands, she wept. He knelt beside her.

"Veronica," he began, "it's my fault. Listen to me, don't interrupt. If I go on staying with you until autumn, you'll perish. I can't tell you more, I have no right to do it, but I assure you that you haven't actually grown old ! As soon as I'm out of your life, you'll find your youth and beauty again."

Frightened, Veronica sought his hand, took it in both of her own and began to kiss it.

"Don't leave me," she murmured.

"Listen to me ! I beg you to listen two or three more minutes. I was fated to lose whatever I loved. Yet, I prefer to lose you as young and lovely as you were and shall be again, rather than see you perish in my arms. Listen to me ! I shall leave and if in three or four months after my departure you aren't your old self of last autumn, I'll return. As soon as I get your telegram, I'll be back. I only ask this much : wait some three or four months away from me."

The following day, in a long letter, he explained why he had no right to stay with her when she had recovered her youth. And as Veronica seemed to have been persuaded into trying this experiment, they decided to quit the villa. She was going to spend the first weeks in a nuns' resthouse, he would catch a plane to Geneva.

After three months he received a telegram : "You were right. I shall love you as long as I live. Veronica." "You will be happy. Farewell." That same week he left for Ireland.

Having done away with that blond moustache and the fringe in the style of the late romantic poets, he was not afraid of being recognized. As a matter of fact, after his return from Malta, he frequented another society, mainly linguists and literary critics. Sometimes in their talks the case of Veronica Rupini cropped up. The questions he asked soon showed how little or what wrong information he had. During the summer of 1956 he agreed to collaborate on a documentary album about James Joyce. He had accepted the project because it gave him a chance to visit Dublin, one of the few towns that he wished to get to know. Afterwards, he came every year, about Christmas time or in early summer.

It was only on his fifth voyage that he met Colomban. He met him accidentally one night when entering a pub behind O'Connell street. As soon as he saw him, Colomban came up to him, grasped his hand between both his own, pressing it warmly. Then he invited him to join him at his table.

"It has been a long time to wait !" he exclaimed pathetically, almost theatrically. "This is the fifth time that I've come here especially to meet you."

A man of uncertain age, freckled, half bald, wearing coppercolored sideburns in contrast with the pale blond of his hair.

"If I were to tell you that I know you, that I know very well who you are, you won't believe me. So I won't say anything. However since I, too, am probably condemned to live to be a hundred, I want to ask you this simple question : *What shall we do with the time* ? Let me explain..."

He went on gazing and smiling ; Colomban rose abruptly.

"Or we'd better ask Stephens," he said turning to the counter.

He came back accompanied by a lean, carelessly dressed young man who gave him a timid shake of the hand, then sat down on a chair opposite him.

"You must excuse his small oddities," the young man said to him, speaking the words slowly. "He will constantly ask me pathetically to utter, maybe he believes I have a better articulation, to utter : 'What shall we do with the time ?' This would be his great discovery : that the question, 'What shall we do with the time ?' contains the supreme ambiguity of the human condition. Because, on the one hand, people, all people, want to live a long life, over a hundred if possible ; but the great majority, as soon as they are 60 or 65 and are retired, that is to say free to do what they like, get bored, discovering they have no use for the free time. On the other hand, as man advances in age, the interior time quickens its rhythm, so that those few who know what to do with their free time don't succeed in doing much. Finally, there's something else..."

Colomban stopped him, placing his hand upon his arm.

"That's enough for today. You used to say it better and more convincingly." Then, turning to him, he added : "We'll go back to the problem of time. But now I want to ask you if you have seen this article."

He handed him a page of an American magazine : "He was sometimes speaking of a new quality of life, insisting that it may and must be discovered by each one of us. The moment he woke up he discovered some great joy that he didn't know how to describe ; it was, doubtless, the joy of feeling whole and healthy, yet it was more than that : it was the joy of other people existing, of seasons of the year existing, and of each day being different from another, the joy of being able to see animals and flowers, of being able to touch the trees. In the street, without looking around, he felt ~~he was~~ part of a huge community, part of the world.

Ugly things, a vacant lot full of refuse or rusty ironware, were somehow mysteriously illuminated by some interior irridescence."

"Very interesting," he said reaching the bottom of the column. "But there must be more."

"Of course there is ; there's a whole long article. It's entitled : '*A Young Man of 70*', signed by Linda Gray."

He didn't try to hide his surprise.

"I didn't know she had begun to write," he said smiling.

"She's been writing for some time and very well too," Colomban continued, "but I wished to make sure that I properly understood : longevity becomes bearable and even interesting only if the technique of simple joys has been previously discovered."

"I wouldn't say it's a technique," he interrupted smiling.

"With due respect, I must contradict you. Do you know other examples of centenaries or quasi centenaries who experience the beatitudes described by Linda Gray, except for the Tao solitaries, or Zen masters, or certain yoga practitioners, or certain Christian monks ? In other words, practitioners of different spiritual disciplines ?"

"There are plenty of examples. Of course the majority are peasants, shepherds, fishermen, common people as the word goes. But they evidently practise a certain spiritual discipline : prayer, meditation."

He stopped abruptly, seeing an elderly man approach their table. He was completely bald and was smoking through a long amber cigarette holder.

"Useless to discuss," he said to Colomban. "In both cases the problem is the same : failing that new quality that Linda Gray mentions, longevity is a burden, maybe even a curse. And in that case what are we to do ?"

"This is Doctor Griffith," Colomban explained. "He was there with us when it happened."

He stopped and tried to catch his eye.

"Maybe we should inform him, explain what it is all about."

The doctor was sitting down and continued tensely smoking, his eyes on a faded color picture.

"Tell him," he said after a good while. "But, mind you begin with what is essential. The essential being," he specified, "not Bran's biography, but the significance of the centenary."

Colomban raised both his arms, as if to interrupt and shout for joy at the same time.

"If you say another word, doctor, I shall have to begin with the end." Then he turned and looked, he pondered a moment, then said, somewhat provokingly, "Though you have a reputation for being omniscient, I am sure you don't know a thing about Sean Bran. Even here, in Dublin, few people still remember him. He was a poet, a magician, and a revolutionary all at the same time, or rather an irredentist. He died in 1825, and thirty years later, in June 1855, his admirers, he still had a number of admirers at that time, put up a monument in his memory in a square. A poor bust on a base of sea rock. On the same day they planted an oak tree some three meters behind the statue."

"It was June 23rd 1855," doctor Griffith specified.

"Exactly. Five years ago, we, the last admirers of the poet and magician Sean Bran, organized a ceremony in the square dedicated to his name. We were hoping that on this occasion Bran would re-enter actuality. Mere illusions, for the few who still appreciate his poetry, in no way agree with his beliefs and practices in magic ; as to those politically active, those who admire his irredentist ideas..."

"You're forgetting what is essential," the doctor put in. "You've forgotten James Joyce."

"That's very important," said Stephens.

"True," Colomban agreed. "If the hopes connected with *Finnegans Wake*, had come true, Sean Bran would be a celebrity today. Because, as you know," he added, again trying to catch his eye, "anything that touches the life and work of the Great Man is subject to fame. An oral tradition, that we have not succeeded in tracing, holds that Joyce made a number of allusions to the aesthetics and especially to the magical conceptions of Bran in *Finnegans Wake*. The same tradition holds that James Joyce refused to specify more than that, refused to point out the context, or at least the pages where such allusions might be found. Some of us have been laboring for years to discover them. No result, so far.

If the tradition is authentic, the possible allusions lie concealed in the hundred and eighty-nine pages of *Finnegans Wake,* still waiting to be deciphered."

"It was only when we recognized this failure," doctor Griffith put in, "that we decided on the celebration of the centenary. Maybe our mistake was not to choose a biographic commemoration, but the centenary of a statue."

"Anyway," Colomban went on, "as soon as we got together in the square we guessed that a hopeless fiasco was in store for us. The morning had been hot..."

"It was June 23$^{rd}$," doctor Griffith specified.

"...hot," Colomban repeated, "and that early afternoon there was a bleak, gloomy sky. The few journalists who had promised to help us dared not stay. The few onlookers began to leave soon after the first rumblings of thunder and the first rain drops. When the storm broke, only the six of us who had decided to hold the commemoration were left on the spot."

The doctor left the table abruptly.

"I think it's time to walk to the square," he said, "it's not far."

"If, however, we see a taxi, we'll take it," Colomban added.

They found it before reaching the end of the street.

"So there were only the six of us," Colomban continued, "and since the rain was coming down in buckets, we sought shelter under the oak tree."

"And, of course, at a given moment," he put in smiling, "at a given moment..."

"Yes. The moment when, as a matter of fact, we least expected it ; we considered that the storm had subsided and were wondering whether in five or ten minutes we would be reading the speeches that we carried in our pockets, or would be waiting for the sky to clear, hoping that at least some of the invited guests would come back..."

"Yes," doctor Griffith cut in, "at that particular moment lightning struck the oak tree, which began to burn from top to bottom."

"But none of the six of us was touched," Stephens continued. "I only felt the terrific heat, for it had begun burning..."

"And yet it did not burn completely," Colomban went on, "for, as you see," he added, having paid the driver and got out of the taxi, "part of the trunk is still here."

They took a few steps and paused by the railing surrounding the monument. It was not illuminated but you could see it quite well in the light of the street lamps. The rock, rising aslant from the ground, was impressive, while the bust had acquired a noble, almost melancholy patina. Behind it loomed the thick mangled oak trunk. You could still see large charred patches side by side with timid green twigs.

"But how did they come to leave it like that ?" he asked quite upset. "Why didn't they pull it by the roots and plant a new one ?"

Colomban gave a short ironic laugh and nervously began to rub his sideburns.

"For the time being the Municipality is considering it. I mean the oak tree, a historic memorial. Sean Bran didn't become a popular figure, but this story, the story of the oak tree struck by lightning on the very day he would have been a hundred years old, that went around the country."

They were slowly walking around the railings. "You will now understand," Colomban went on, "why we are interested in the problem of time. They say, and I am sure it's true because my father knew several cases, they say that those who are under a tree that is struck by lightning and get away safely are doomed to live a hundred years."

"I never knew there was such a belief, but it seems logical."

The sight was impressive : the sea rock viewed from behind with that three meters tall tree trunk, stripped of its bark, carbonized, yet keeping a few live twigs, so impressive, that he asked to go back and look at it again.

"Strangest of all...," the doctor began again as they were facing the statue, "both strange and sad, is the fact that the police discovered the next day a load of dynamite under the monument's base. If it hadn't been for the rain it would have exploded during the speeches, destroyed the statue, or maimed it anyway."

He listened in awe, stopped walking, and tried to catch his eye.

"But why ?" he asked in a low voice. "Who would have wanted to destroy a historical monument ?"

Doctor Griffith and Colomban looked at each other briefly, with a meaningful smile.

"Quite a number," Stephens answered. "The irredentists in the first place, quite indignant that Bran, the revolutionary, should be vindicated and commemorated by a few poets, philosophers, and occultists."

"Secondly," Colomban continued, "the church, more exactly the ultramontanists and obscurantists who consider Sean Bran as the prototype of a satanist magician, which is absurd, because Bran was in the tradition of Renaissance magic, of the conception of Pico or of G.B. Porta."

"Useless to go into details," doctor Griffith interrupted. "It is certain that the ecclesiastical hierarchy is not inclined to accept him."

The four of them were now walking in the middle of the empty, badly lit street.

"Now," Colomban began, "getting back to the essential, to the problem facing us who are condemned to live a hundred years : what shall we do with the time ?"

"I would rather discuss this some other time," he said. "Tomorrow if you like, or the day after. Let's get together, in the late afternoon, in some garden or park."

He had agreed to meet them since he particularly wished to know Colomban's idea about his real identity. Colomban occasionally addressed him as if he were a specialist in *Finnegans Wake.* On the other hand, he had kept that fragment of the article "*A Young Man of 70*" and knew who Linda Gray was (he knew the prestige she had acquired as an author). Stephens accompanied him to his hotel. On parting, he looked round several times and said :

"Colomban is a fictitious name. And you ought to know that he deals in black magic with doctor Griffith. Ask them what happened to the other three men who were there with us, under the oak tree, when the thunder struck. Also ask them what title they are going to give the book they are writing together. Let me tell you : *Theology and Demonology of Electricity.*"

He liked the title. He wrote it down in his personal notebook, having summarized the first meeting and tried to interpret the significance of the incident of 23 June 1955. He was intrigued by the fact that the explosion which, for political reasons, was meant to destroy a statue, had been nullified by the rain and displaced by the thunder which had set the centenary oak tree on fire. The presence of dynamite was an element characteristic of the contemporary epoch. Considered in this light, the incident looked like a parody, almost like a caricature of the epiphany of lightning. The substitution of the object, the oak tree instead of the statue, remained an enigma. Yet nothing in the course of the three succesive meetings gave him any clue.

He remembered the title four years later, in the summer of 1964, at a conference on Jung's *Mysterium Conjunctionis*, when a young man joining in the discussions, mentioned the "eschatology of electricity." He began by mentioning the union of contraries into a single totality, "a psychological process which," he said, "should be interpreted in the light of Indian and Chinese philosophy. In Vedanta, as well as in Taoism, contraries, nullify each other if considered from a certain angle, good and evil become devoid of sense and, on the level of the absolute, being coincides with non-being. But that which no one dares say," the young man continued, "is the fact that within the compass of this philosophy, atomic wars if not justified, at least have to be accepted."

"However, I myself go one step further : I justify the nuclear conflagrations in the name of the eschatology of electricity !"

The tumult in the hall forced the president to withdraw his right of speaking. In a few minutes the young man left the hall. He followed and caught up with him.

"I'm sorry you were prevented from fully presenting your point of view. Personally, I am highly interested in the idea of the 'eschatology of electricity'. What exactly are you referring to ?"

The young man doubtfully considered him and shrugged.

"I'm hardly in the mood for a discussion. The cowardice of contemporary thinking drives me out of my mind. I'd rather have a glass of beer."

"Do you mind if I join you ?"

They sat on the terrace of a café. The young man didn't try to conceal his nervousness.

"I am probably the last European optimist," he began. "Like everyone else, I know what's in store for us : hydrogen, cobalt and all the rest. But unlike the rest, I'm trying to find a meaning to this imminent catastrophe and thus get to accept it, as old Hegel says. The true sense of the nuclear catastrophe can only be the mutation of the human species, the appearance of a superman. I know that the nuclear wars will destroy peoples and civilizations and will turn part of the planet into a desert, but such is the price to be paid for radically doing away with the past and forcefully bring about a mutation, namely the appearance of a species infinitely superior to the man of today. An enormous amount of electricity unleashed within a few hours or a few minutes can alone modify the psychomental structure of the unhappy homo sapiens who has so far dominated history. Considering the unlimited possibilities of pre-historic man, the reconstruction of a planetary civilization will be achieved with the utmost expedition. Just a few million individuals will survive, of course, but they will represent a few million supermen. That's why I used the expression, 'eschatology of electricity', both the end and the salvation of man will be achieved by electricity."

He stopped and drank his glass of beer without looking at him.

"But why are you so sure that the electricity unleashed by nuclear explosions will force a mutation of a superior type ? It might as well cause a regression of the species."

The young man suddenly turned his head, giving him a severe, almost angry look.

"I am not sure, but I want to believe that it will be so. Neither man's life, nor history would make any sense otherwise. We should then have to accept the idea of cosmic and historic cycles, the myth of eternal repetition... On the other hand, my hypothesis is not merely the result of despair, it is based on fact. I wonder if you have heard of a German researcher, Doctor Rudolf's, experiments ?"

"It so happens that I have, but his experiments in the electrocution of animals were not conclusive."

"So the story goes," the young man put in. "But since the Rudolf files have vanished almost entirely, it is difficult to have an opinion. Anyway, according to the information in this secret dossier, no indication of biological regression was found. On the other hand. I'm sure you've read Ted Jones's novel : *Rejuvenated by Lightning*."

"No, I haven't. I didn't even know it existed."

"If you're interested in this problem, you'll have to read it. In an afterword the author suggests that the novel is based on real facts. Only the nationality and name of the character have been changed."

"And what is the novel about ?" he asked smiling.

"Jones describes the regeneration and rejuvenation of an old man who was struck by lightning. One significant detail : the lightning struck right in the middle of the brain pan. At eighty, the person who, I repeat, is real, did not look more thant thirty. So at least one thing is sure : that, in certain cases, electricity in massive charges causes the total regeneration of the human body, therefore rejuvenescence. About the phychomental changes, the novel is unfortunately imprecise ; it only alludes to hypermnesia. But you can imagine the radical transformation brought about by the electricity unleashed by some scores or hundreds of hydrogen bombs."

In rising from the table and thanking him, the young man looked at him for the first time, with interest and almost sympathy.

Back at home, he wrote in his pocket notebook : "18 July 1964. The eschatology of electricity. I think I may add : Finale. I don't think I'll have the opportunity of noting other meetings or events of the same interest."

Yet, in spite of this, two years later, on 10 October 1966, he wrote : "Removal of materials. I'm receiving a new passport." Sometime he would have described in full detail these two episodes. Particularly the wonderful and mysterious operation of the transfer of materials. He had received, via his bank, the letter of an airway company stating that the transport cost of manuscript boxes and phonograms had already been paid to a branch in Honduras. As previously agreed a clerk at the Geneva offices was to come to his lodgings to supervise the packing of materials. He was certainly a specialist, and had been informed of the nature of the materials to be packed. Having brought from the bank two cases, almost full, they both worked until evening. Except for the notebooks with personal notes, and a few personal objects, everything was packed in cases and boxes, stamped and numbered. For a time, he was afraid that the transfer of materials might signify the imminence of the catastrophe, but a chain of consecutive dreams set his mind at rest.

Then, although brief and enigmatic, the jottings became more numerous. December, 1966 : "I shall have to write and thank him. The book is far more intelligent than I would have expected." He was referring to the novel that Jones had sent him. He wished to add : "How on earth did he guess my name and found my address ?" but gave it up. February, 1967 : "Inquiry in connection with Doctor Rudolf's archives." April : "Casually met R.A. ; he tells me in greatest secrecy that the preliminary inquiries are closed. It is now certain that in the two suitcases, Doctor Bernard had the most precious documents, phonograms, I suppose, and photographs of the professor's reports, as well as the notebooks of 1938—1939."

On 3 June 1967 he wrote : "The case Rupini-Veronica has been taken up again in India. An ever larger number of scholars are doubting the authentic quality of the registrations taken at the clinic. Decisive argument : Veronica and her companion disappeared, leaving no trace, soon after the expedition returned to Delhi ! Now that almost 12 years have gone by, so a great materialist philosopher writes, any confrontation of witnesses has become impossible." 12 October : "Linda got the Pulitzer prize for her new book : *A Biography*. Whose do you think it is ?"

Then 12 June 1968 : "Veronica. Fortunately she didn't see me." After a few lines he adds : "In the station at Montreux, with two lovely children by her side, explaining them a tourist poster. She looks her age, maybe even a little younger. The important thing is that she is happy."

On 8 January 1968 he celebrated his centenary in a luxurious restaurant at Nice, in company of a young Swedish woman, Selma Eklund, whom he admired for her intelligence and original interpretation of the medieval drama. That same month Selma was to be 28 ; he, half-jokingly, confessed being near his forties. But the evening was not a success ; she was probably not accustomed to champagne, so before dessert, he had to take her back to the hotel. He wandered long after midnight, alone, on unfrequented streets.

He wished to celebrate "his first centenary", as he liked to call it, by a rather spectacular voyage. Many years before he had been in Mexico, then in Scandinavia. He would now like to visit Java or China, but he wouldn't decide in a hurry. "I have a whole year at my disposal," he would say to himself.

One autumn night he came home earlier than usual. The quick icy rain had forced him to give up his long walk in the park. He thought of calling a woman-friend, but gave up the thought and went over to the record player. "For a cold night like this, music is the only thing... the only thing," he absently went on, taken aback to find the family picture album among the records. He took it out, frowning, and suddenly felt a shivering cold as if the windows had suddenly been thrown open. He stood a while, irresolute, the album in his hands. "What about the third rose," he heard himself thinking. "Where shall I place it ? Leave the album alone and show me where to put the rose. The third rose."

He laughed a bitter, vexed laugh. "I am, however, a free man," he said sitting in the armchair. With extreme care and emotion he opened the album. A rose freshly picked, mauve-colored, such as he had only seen once before, lay there in the middle of the page. He picked it up, happy. He had never thought that a single rose could embalm a whole room. For a long while he sat there, hesitating. He then placed it by him on the side of the armchair and gazed at the first photograph. Is was pale, discolored, misty, yet, without difficulty, he recognized his parental home at Piatra Neamţ.

## V

It began to snow a few hours before, then, after Bacău, there was a snow storm. But as the train drove into the station, it had ceased snowing and in the clear sky the first crystal stars were coming out. He recognized the station square, immaculate under the fresh snow, although newly built blocks of flats rose on every side. He thought it strange, though, that now, near Christmas, there should be so little light in the windows. He stood a long time, suitcase in hand, looking with emotion at the boulevard stretching before him. He came to just as the family he had shared the compartment with on the train was catching the last taxi, but the hotel where he had booked his room was quite close. He raised the collar of his coat and casually crossed the station-square and walked along the boulevard. It was only when he arrived that he realized his left arm was benumbed ; the suitcase was heavier than he had imagined. He produced his passport and the Tourist Office visa.

"But you speak very good Romanian," the woman at the reception desk remarked, having examined the passport.

She was grey-haired, wore frameless glasses ; he was impressed by the distinguished face and the quality of the voice.

"I am a linguist. I've concentrated on the Romance languages. I've been in Romania before. I've even been to Piatra Neamț," he said smiling. "My student days... by the way, is the café 'Select' still there ?"

"Of course it is. A memorial : Calistrat Hogaș used to go there, you must have heard of him."

"Of course I have".

"He frequented it between 1869 to 1886, as long as he taught here as a school teacher. They put up a memorial plaque too. You're in number 19, third floor. You may use the elevator."

"I think I will first go to the 'Select'. It's not far. I'll be back in an hour or an hour and a half."

He thought the lady was giving him a surprised look over her glasses.

"Beware of catching cold," she said. "The streets are covered with snow and there'll be more snow soon."

"One hour, one and a half at the most," he repeated smiling.

After some ten minutes, he realized that the lady at the desk had been right ; some streets were actually filled with snow and walking was difficult, but around about the entrance of the café the snow had been shoveled off, so he quickened his pace. In front of the entrance he paused to catch his breath and still his heart beats. Walking in, he recognized the smell of beer, of freshly ground coffee, and the smoke of cheap cigarettes. He made his way to the back room where they used to meet. The room was practically empty ; only at one table three men were finishing their mugs of beer. "That's why they only turned on one bulb hanging from the ceiling : they're economizing on electricity." He sat on the couch next to the wall, a vacant look on his face. Expecting the waiter to come, he hadn't made up his mind whether to ask for a glass of beer or a bottle of mineral water and coffee. The three men soon rose noisily, ready to leave.

"Once more we haven't come to any conclusion," one of them said as he wrapped a grey woollen shawl round his neck.

"Nothing to worry about," said the second.

"Nothing to worry about !" the last one repeated laughing and giving them both a meaningful look. "You know what I mean, don't you ?"

Left by himself, he was debating whether it was worth waiting, when he fancied that someone was timidly approaching, hesitating, curiously considering him. It was only when he stopped in front of him that he recognized him : it was Vaian.

"Is it you, Mr. Dominic, sir ?" he uttered taking a step forward ; he took his hand, pressed it between both his own. "Thank God you're back ! You're quite recovered." Then he looked over his shoulder and shouted : "Doctor ! Come here quick, Mr. Dominic is back !"

He kept his hand between his own, shaking it. Within a few seconds the whole group rushed in, Doctor Neculache first, Nicodim, a bottle of Cotnar wine in his left hand and a glass half full in his right hand. They were all looking at him both with joy and fear, jostling one another to see him better, repeating, shouting his name. He was so moved, almost afraid that he would soon feel tears running down his face, yet with an effort he managed a laugh.

"So," he said, "the story begins all over again. I'm dreaming and when I wake it will be as if I were only then beginning actually to dream... Like in that story of Ciuang-Tse, the story with the butterfly..."

"Ciuang-Tse ?" Vaian repeated under his breath. "The story of Ciuang-Tse's butterfly ?"

"I've told it to you so many times," he put in suddenly, in very high spirits.

He then heard a voice at the far end :

"Send someone to inform Veta !" But he shouted :

"Leave Veta alone ! I believe you, Veta or no Veta. I perfectly realize that I'm dreaming and that in one or two minutes I'll wake up..."

"Don't get excited Mr. Dominic, sir," the doctor intervened, coming up and laying his hand upon his shoulder. "You've been through a lot. Don't get excited."

He burst out laughing again.

"I know," he began in a quiet voice, as if anxious not to vex them, "I know that all these things, our meeting here and all that is to follow, everything could have actually happened in December 1938."

"But that is just what is happening, Mr. Dominic, sir," Vaian put in, "since it is 20 December, 1938."

He looked at Vaian ironically, yet with something like pity.

"I dare not tell you what year this is for us, other humans, who live outside this dream. If I were to make an effort I would wake up."

"You're awake, Mr. Dominic, sir," the doctor spoke, "but you're tired... As a matter of fact you look very tired," he added.

"Well now," he suddenly burst out, impatiently, "you'd better know that in between 20 December 1938 and tonight many things have happened. The second world war, for instance. Have you heard of Hiroshima ? Of Buchenwald ?"

"The second world war ?" someone asked at the far end of the room. "It's coming alright, quite soon, very soon."

"Much has happened since you vanished and gave no sign of life," Nicodim began. "There have been house searches. They've taken books out of your library."

"I know, I know," he stopped him, raising his arm. "I told them what books to look for and to bring them to me. But that was a long, long time ago."

He began to be irritated by not being able to wake, although he knew he was dreaming and wanted to wake up.

"We've been looking for you everywhere," he heard a well-known voice. "The doctor looked for you in the hospitals..."

"We heard that you were in Bucharest," Neculache said, "and that they took you for somebody else."

"That's how it happened," he said, "that's exactly what happened. I was taken for someone else because I was rejuvenated." He hesitated a moment, then went on triumphant and yet enigmatic : "I can now tell you the truth. After the lightning struck me right on the top of my head, I grew younger. I looked twenty-five to thirty years old and I haven't changed since. For the last thirty years I've looked the same age."

He could see them looking at one another, and shrugged quite impatiently, then tried to laugh.

"I know you can hardly believe it. Yet if I were to tell you all of the things that happened because of the same lightning, the number of oriental languages I learnt, that is, I didn't even have to learn them, because I suddenly found out I knew them. I'm telling you this now because I'm dreaming and no one shall ever know these things."

"You're not dreaming, Mr. Dominic, sir," Nicodim gently spoke. "You're here with us, with your friends, you're in the café. That's how we imagined it was going to be when Mr. Dominic recovered, when he recovered from his amnesia and returned, the first place he would stop would be at the 'Select', you just wait and see !"

He burst out laughing again, and looked at them with sudden intensity, as if afraid of waking up at that very moment and losing track of them.

"If I weren't dreaming you surely would know about Hiroshima, about the hydrogen bombs, about Armstrong, the astronaut who landed on the moon last summer in July."

They were all silent, afraid to look at each other.

"So that was it," the doctor said after a short, while, "you were mistaken for someone else."

He wished to answer, but was beginning to feel worn out. He passed his hand over his face several times.

"As in that story with the Chinese philosopher, you know the one, for I often told it ?"

"Which Chinese philosopher, Mr. Dominic, sir ?" Vaian asked.

"I've just told you his name," he answered nervously. "I can't remember the name now. That story with the butterfly... Anyway, it's too long to repeat once more..."

He felt a strange weariness throughout his body and for a moment he was afraid of fainting. "Yet maybe that would be be better," he said to himself, "if I faint I'll instantly wake up."

"We've ordered a taxi to take you home, Mr. Matei," someone said. 'Veta has built a fire in the stove."

"I don't need a taxi," he uttered as he was getting up. "I'll walk. When the question crops up, I'll know how to answer !"

"What question, Mr. Matei ?" Nicodim asked. He wished to say : "The question that worries us all !" but he suddenly felt all his teeth wobbling. Humiliated, furious, he clenched his jaws. Then took a few steps towards the door. To his surprise the others drew back to let him go by. He wanted to turn around once more, to salute them all by raising his arm, but every movement exhausted him. Tottering, breathing heavily through his nose because his mouth was clenched shut, he walked out into the street. The cold air revived him. "I'm going to wake up," he thought. When he thought no one was looking, he put the palm of his hand against his mouth and spat out his teeth, two or three at a time. He vaguely remembered, as you do a dream half-fotgotten, that the same thing had sometime happened to him before : he hadn't been able to speak for a time because all his teeth were wobbling. "So it's the same problem !" he thought serenely, quite pacified.

That night the hotel porter vainly waited for the return of the guest in number 19. When it began to snow he rang up the 'Select' café. They told him that a stranger had come early that evening, going straight into the back room. But after a short time, possibly because the room was empty and badly lit, he had left without a word, covering his mouth with his right hand. The next morning on Episcopie Street, in front of the house at number 18, a very old man, a stranger, was found frozen to death. He wore an elegant suit and a rich fur coat. Both suit and coat were so loose that there was no doubt they didn't belong to him. As a matter of fact in the coat pocket there was a wallet with foreign currency, and a Swiss passport to the name of Martin Audricourt, born in Honduras, on 18 November 1939.

## NOTE ON THE PRONUNCIATION OF ROMANIAN WORDS

The purpose of this note is to give English-speaking readers some indication as to the correct pronunciation of Romanian words.

Romanian ortography is almost entirely phonetical, a letter representing one and the same sound, in all positions, with a few exceptions.

Here are the letters of the Romanian alphabet and their pronunciation :

a — as *a* in *half,* but shorter. E. g. Arnica, Sanda.

ă — as *er,* in *father.* E. g. Dunăre, Gavrilă.

b — as *b* in *ball.* E. g. Bălănoaia

c — before consonants, before a, ă, î, o, u, and at the end of words, as *k* in *sky.* E. g. Christina, Moscu
— before e, i, as *ch* in *cherry.* E. g. Paşchievici

d — as *d* in *dwell.* E. g. Dominic

e — as *e* in *pen.* E. g. Egor, Veta

f — as *f* in *far.* E. g. Frîncu

g — before consonants, before a, ă, î, o, u, and at the end of words, as *g* in *got.* E. g. Gavrilescu

h — as *h* in *behind.* E. g. Hogaş
— in the groups *che, chi, ghe, ghi* it is mute, having the role of showing that *c* and *g* preserve their original sound

i — as *ee* in *see.* E. g. Simina

î — similar to *o* in *wisdom* or to *e* in *morsel.* E. g. Dîmboviţa, Înviere

j — as *s* in *measure.* E. g. Prajan

k — as *k* in *kilo.* E. g. Kogălniceanu

l — as *l* in *like.* E. g. Laura

m — as *m* in *mother.* E. g. Matei

n — as *n* in *neither.* E. g. Nazarie

o — as *o* in *short.* E.g. Otilia

p — as *p* in *special.* E. g. Piatra

r — similar to the rolled *r* of Scotland. E. g. România, Radu

NOTE

s — as *s* in *soil*. E. g. Smaranda

ş — as *sh* in *fish*. E. g. Braşov, Bucureşti

t — as *t* in *stay*. E. g. Trandafir

ţ — as *ts* in *cats*. E. g. Neamţ

u — as *oo* in *look*. E. g. Georgescu

v — as *v* in *voice*. E. g. Voitinovici

x — as *x* in *excellent*. E. g. Alexandru

z — as *z* in *zone*. E. g. Zerlendi

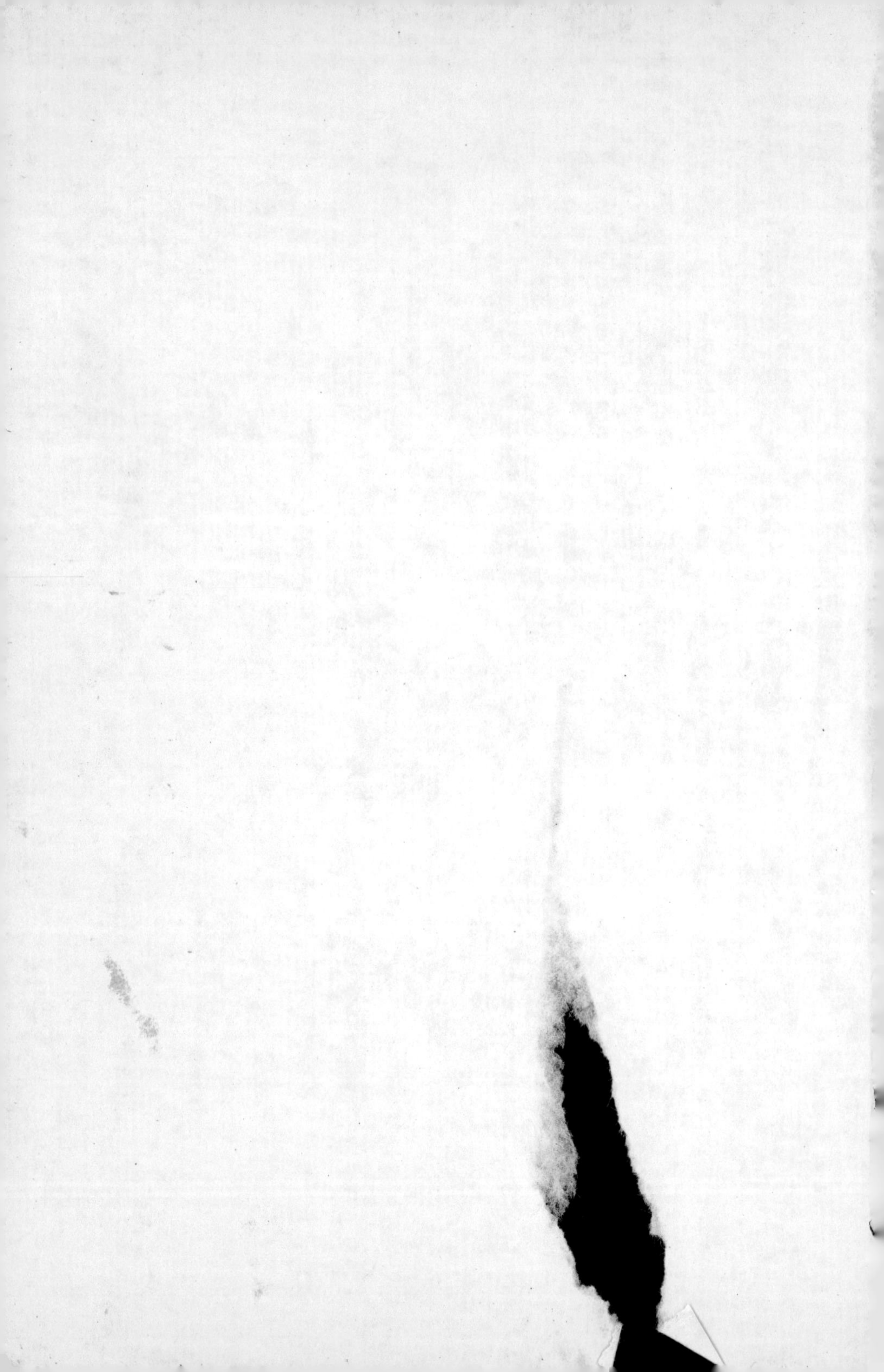